Sign up for our newsletter to hear
about new and upcoming releases.

www.ylva-publishing.com

OTHER BOOKS BY CHEYENNE BLUE

Switcheroo
I Do
Not for a Moment
For the Long Run
The Number 94 Project
All at Sea
A Heart This Big
Code of Conduct
Party Wall

Girl Meets Girl Series:
Never-Tied Nora
Not-So-Straight Sue
Fenced-In Felix
The Girl Meets Girl Collection (box set)

Cheyenne Blue

A HEART FULL OF HOPE

ACKNOWLEDGEMENTS AND DEDICATION

It's that time again, when I wave the pom-poms and cheer all the people who helped make this book what it is. While I'm lucky and have some people who weigh in on all of my books, others are new, or unique to each book.

My wonderful betas and typohounds are suckers for punishment and keep coming back for more: Sophie Lennox, Jan Gwin, and Marg once again did a fabulous job. Tough love and positivity—it's a great combination.

For this book, I was joined by fellow author, Elle Armstrong, who not only beta-read the manuscript but also did sterling duty as a sensitivity reader. Thanks, Elle. To better understand Hazel's character, I also spent many hours watching Footless Jo on YouTube. Jo gives great insight into the everyday life of someone with a below-knee amputation, and I recommend her channel if you, too, want to learn more.

Astrid and the crew at Ylva Publishing were as efficient and organised as ever, and get a standing ovation from me every time. This time around, Sarah Smeaton was my editor, and she did a fantastic and thorough job. Her comments and suggestions were spot on, and anyone who appreciates Tim Tams gets a thumbs up from me.

The fantastic hive mind of my pride-festival stall mates, S.R. Silcox, Liz Rain, and Neen Cohen, gets a special mention. Thank you for brainstorming titles with me, and for the laughs and support along the way. Good mates are golden, and you're the best.

My partner, D, doesn't get enough mentions in the acknowledgements. So, here you go, D—thanks for drinking all the Bundy rum so I don't have to.

Most of all, huge thanks go to YOU, the reader. You amazing people who buy, borrow, listen, and read my books. Thank you for picking this book up and reading on. A writer is still a writer even if no one reads, but having great readers such as you is the happiest of things.

Keep on reading!
Cheyenne Blue
Queensland, Australia

CHAPTER 1
HOME DELIVERY

Hazel stopped her vehicle outside George's house. Whenever George was on the schedule for delivery, he was always the last stop. As usual, she'd moved his groceries from the Good 'n Fresh delivery truck to her own ute. Her excuse was that then she'd go straight home. The reality was that she enjoyed George's company. And someone had to look out for him.

She hefted the shopping and walked along the cracked concrete path, pushing through the overgrown jasmine bushes. Maybe she could suggest trimming them.

Her left thigh twinged as she set down the bags. Long days on her feet could do that, and today had been longer than usual. It was time for another massage.

The front door swung open before the chimes of the "Waltzing Matilda" doorbell managed to get to the part about camping by a billabong.

George's stooped and wire-thin body rested on his stick. His lined face, under the shock of grey hair, broke into a grin. "You're late."

"And you're rude." Hazel returned his smile and picked up the bags again as George swung the door wider. "You know very well why I'm late. If you want your groceries an hour earlier, you only have to ask. But then I'll have to leave them on the doorstep as I do for everyone else."

George's scruffy little terrier danced around her ankles, sharp teeth bared, obviously thinking about a bite. "Don't, Chip," she warned him. "You know what happened the last time you attacked my ankle."

"I'd rather see you than get my groceries on time. And Chip won't bite you. He knows there are dog treats in those bags." George led the way upstairs to the kitchen. "Kettle boiled a few minutes ago. I'll give it another blast."

Hazel unpacked the two bags of groceries, arranging cans in the half-empty pantry.

With gnarled fingers, George placed teabags in two mugs, then opened the packet of biscuits and set four on a thick, white china plate.

The door of the pantry had swollen, and when she tugged it closed, the handle came off in her hand. Hazel staggered backward, her left leg unable to cope with the sharp movement.

"Steady on, cobber." George put out a hand and grasped her arm as Hazel regained her balance. "I've been meaning to fix that handle. Been loose for a while."

"I'll reattach it for you after we've had our tea." And there was the other reason she always took her own truck to George's house: because her toolbox was on the back, and there was always something small needing attention.

George carried the mugs out to the back deck where there was a view over the farmland that surrounded Dry Creek.

Hazel followed with the plate of Tim Tams and sat in one of the shabby canvas chairs. She picked up her mug and blew on it. "So tell me what's new in your world."

"Since I saw you a week ago?" George side-eyed her. "Seems I should ask you that question. You young 'uns have a more exciting life than senior citizens."

"I don't know about that. Last time, you'd won a bottle of Bundy rum and fifty bucks in the pub raffle, planted green beans, and trespassed over the fields with Chip."

"It's a pleasant walk. Better than the streets. Chip likes it too. There are things for him to roll in."

"At least you gave him a bath."

"So, what's new with you? Any young man or woman in your life yet?"

"You know there isn't. Live for the moment, that's me, and if that moment doesn't include a Hayley Raso or Carlos Alcaraz clone, that's fine by me."

"You need to start looking. You're nearly thirty. Your best breeding days are behind you."

"George!" Hazel set down her tea. "I can't believe you're so sexist! As if a woman's life is only fulfilled if she has kids. And twenty-five is a long way from thirty. I thought we'd got past—" Too late, she saw the twinkle in his eyes and the slow grin spreading across his face.

"Gotcha."

"You're wicked," she grumbled. "You know how to push my buttons. It's lucky I like you."

The smile softened on George's face, and he reached out to squeeze her arm. "I'm the lucky one, Hazel. You brighten my week."

"Bring you Tim Tams and fix your cupboards, you mean?"

"That too," he agreed.

Hazel relaxed into the chair. Really, it was very comfortable for an old canvas thing. She sipped her too-strong tea and let her gaze sweep around the surrounding fields where brown cattle picked over the drying grass, and the dry creek that gave the town its name meandered a course through. Now, at the end of winter, it lived up to its name, but summer rains could send it raging. The late-afternoon low sun outlined the hills on the far side of the fields, the magpies were whistling their "where are you" calls to their mates, and the rumble of traffic on the main road had increased to a dull roar.

Hazel sighed. This view never got old, and neither did living in Dry Creek.

"Going to senior citizen night at the RSL later," George said. "Half-price steaks this week."

"When's the courtesy bus picking you up?"

"Six. Do you think I look all right? Mavis might be there, and I'm still trying to make an impression."

"Interesting shirt. The blue suits you. Not sure about the orange squiggles. You get it in the op shop?"

George smoothed the front of it. "Yah. I like it. It doesn't need ironing."

"Good enough reason to buy it. Mavis won't miss you in that."

"That's the idea." He drained his mug and set it down.

Hazel did the same and stood. "Let me see if I can reattach that handle." She went out to her ute and pulled out some hand tools, and the smaller case that held bolts, screws, and washers.

The handle was an easy fix. She tugged it, and the door creaked open. "Next time, I'll plane the bottom of the door to stop it sticking so much."

George watched as she packed up her toolbox. "How much do I owe you?"

He asked every time, and every time her answer was the same. "A cup of tea and a chat."

He pulled a twenty from the drawer by the stove and held it out. "Take this."

"No, George. That was ten minutes' work."

"Thanks, love." He tucked the cash back in the drawer.

Hazel washed her hands at the kitchen sink. The tap was dripping. She tried turning it tighter, but it made no difference. "Are you home tomorrow morning? I'll be passing, so I can drop in and fix this for you. It won't take long. Some plumber's tape and a new washer should do it."

"Not going anywhere," George said.

"Then I'll see you tomorrow." She kissed his grizzly cheek and waggled her fingers at Chip.

He lifted his upper lip and gave her a half-hearted growl.

"Love you, too, Chip."

It was only a few minutes' drive home. Her mum and dad were in the kitchen. She kissed her dad, Simon, on top of his bald head and hugged her mum, Maxie, around the waist as she stood at the stove reading a book as she stirred something. Her dad put down his iPad. "Look what the cat dragged in. You look dishevelled, Hazel. Everything all right?"

"Yeah. Long day at work, and then I had to fix George's cupboard. Petunia's rubbing a bit, too. Have I got time for a shower before dinner?"

"Of course." Her mum stirred faster. "I've got to get this lemon butter done first. It's taking longer than usual."

Hazel went into her bedroom and began her shower preparation. Stool in the cubicle, two towels on the rail beside the walk-in shower, body wash, and shampoo within reach, clean clothes on the closed toilet lid. She turned on the shower, then sat on the bench alongside the shower to remove Petunia—her below-knee prosthetic leg. She propped Petunia and the liner where she could reach them afterward, and stood, gripping the safety rails as she balanced on her one leg before swivelling to rest her nubbin on the shower stool and take a swift and careful shower. In the past, she'd slipped on the wet, soapy tiles, and she was in no hurry to repeat that.

When done, she manoeuvred back to the bench in the bathroom using the safety handles. Dry and dressed, she sat to inspect her nubbin. It was slightly swollen, red up to the knee where the cup had rubbed. Petunia would get the evening off.

Instead, she put on shorts, and reached for her knee crutch against the wall. Once strapped in, she heaved a sigh of relief and scooted back to the kitchen.

"Need a hand with anything?" she asked her mum.

Maxie wiped the jars of lemon butter with a cloth. Her library book lay on the counter. "No, all good. Dinner's in the oven. You've got another few minutes."

"I'll set the table." Hazel grabbed cutlery from the drawer and plates from the cupboard. "What sauces do you want?"

"Spicy," her mum said. "It's baked chicken and rice."

Hazel scooped three different hot sauces from the fridge and set them on the table, then she went over to the sink and started putting away the dishes from the drying rack. "Can I take a jar of that lemon butter to George tomorrow?"

"Of course," her mum said.

Her dad tapped his iPad with a finger. "How did your quote go today?"

Hazel gave a little wiggle, and the knee crutch jiggled on the wooden floor. "Great! Mary wants me to do the work. It's not much—just some shelving in the garage—but she'll need more work in the future."

"Well done." Her dad pulled her into a sideways hug. "You're building your business, slowly but surely."

"I'd love for it to grow faster, but I still need to work at Good 'n Fresh. One day though…"

"You'll get there." Her mum finished wiping the jars and opened the oven, flapping away the steam that rose. "Dinner's ready."

Hazel manoeuvred her knee crutch to her chair, unstrapped it, then lowered herself on one leg to sit.

Her mum set the food on the table. "I was going to make curry, but I got stuck in my book."

"And are we surprised?" Her dad sent his wife a fond look.

"It's a Miss Fisher murder mystery," her mum said. "I had to find out how it ended."

"And we'll eat chicken and rice without complaint." Her dad uttered a theatrical sigh and squeezed Maxie's hand. "Nothing wrong with that. It's as good as a five-star restaurant."

Hazel stared at her plate to hide her smile. That was her dad's response every time her mum lost track of the time—but it was true, everything she cooked was great, and who wouldn't rather read than cook? Her mum had perfected the art of doing both simultaneously.

Hazel's fingers clenched the fork. Now if only she could perfect the art of building her fledgling business and earning enough to keep her afloat—well, that would be worth celebrating.

CHAPTER 2
BREAKING AND ENTERING

Hazel backed her truck into George's driveway. The blinds were still down in the two-storey house, but Chip was barking inside. She yanked her toolbox off the back of the ute and went up to the front door. Chip let loose a volley of barks when the "Waltzing Matilda" door chime sounded, but there was no other sound. George had to be on the back balcony.

She waited a couple of minutes, then rang the bell again. Still nothing other than intermittent thumps on the door, which had to be Chip hurling himself against it. Hazel sucked her lower lip. This was unusual. She hesitated, then pressed her ear to the door. Chip whined and scratched the timber.

"Shh, Chippie. I'm trying to listen."

Chip whined once more, then was quiet. She banged on the door. "George? Are you there?" When she pressed her ear to the door again, a faint "Help" sounded through the wood.

Hazel's heart turned to ice. *What's happened?* Scenarios of medical emergencies ran through her head—or maybe the toilet door had stuck again and trapped him. "I hear you, George. I'm coming." She walked as fast as she could around the house. None of the downstairs windows were open and the garage door was locked.

An upstairs window yawned open, but even if she had a ladder, there was no way she could safely climb it and scramble through the window. Her prosthetic leg was good, but not action-woman ready. She circled around the house again. She could call the police, but they'd likely break down the door. If she couldn't enter in the next three minutes, she'd call them.

One of the sliding garage windows gave a few centimetres when she tugged it. She yanked harder, worry for George making her fingers slip. The window slid some, then jammed again. By jiggling and tugging, she got it open enough that she could slip through. She grabbed the trestle from her ute and placed it under the window. Hoping it wouldn't tip, she pulled herself up until she could straddle the sill, and then lowered herself to the floor.

"George?" she called. "I'm inside. Where are you?"

"Bathroom." His voice, fainter than usual, drifted down the stairs.

She hurried up the internal stairs, panic hammering in her head. Chip danced at the top, too distracted to even growl at her.

The bathroom door was half open, and there on the floor… Hazel's heart froze at the sight of George lying on the tiles.

"Oh my god!" She pushed the door open further.

George was slumped at an awkward angle, half covered by a towel. Cool air drifted in from the open window, and his skin had a grey tinge.

"I slipped getting out the shower. Pretty sure I've busted something." His lips were blue. "Hip probably. I'm a goner, Hazel."

"You're not. I'm here now, and I'm calling an ambulance. You'll be okay." Hazel swallowed the anxiety in her throat and squeezed his hand. Then she hurried to his bedroom, dragged the quilt from the bed, and grabbed the pillow. Back in the bathroom, she covered him with the quilt and lifted his head to position it on the pillow. Then she pressed triple zero.

The operator's calmness helped steady her skittering heartbeat.

"An ambulance is on its way. Can you open the front door for the crew? You've done the right thing getting the quilt. Try not to move him, but if there are more blankets, put them over him, as long as it doesn't hurt his hip."

Another blanket. Where did he keep them? The only one she could think of was Chip's dog blanket, and that was more dog hair than anything.

"Hall cupboard," George said, apparently reading her mind.

Of course.

Chip was barking again, so she grabbed his collar and dragged him to the bedroom and shut him inside. She went downstairs and opened the front door, propping it with one of George's boots. Then she snagged a second quilt from the cupboard.

"Can I have some water?" George asked. His voice held a quiver she'd never heard before.

"I'm sorry, but no. If the paramedics say it's okay, you can, but not before then. What else can I do for you?"

"I suppose a double brandy's out of the question?"

"You suppose right." He had to be in a lot of pain. Should she give him a painkiller? But the ambulance would be here soon. One advantage of a small town—they didn't have far to come. "How long have you been here?"

"Last night." George's breath came in shallow pants. "Knew I should have got one of those alarm thingamajigs you wear around your neck."

"The ones for old people?" Hazel tried to smile. "That's what you always said."

"Mebbe eighty-four is old, after all." He fell silent again.

Please hurry. Hazel shot him what she hoped was a reassuring smile and wished hard for the ambulance. Would they use sirens? Maybe not.

And then "Waltzing Matilda," chimed, and a male voice called, "Ambulance. We're coming up."

"We're in the bathroom," Hazel replied.

The small room was suddenly crammed with two men wearing navy paramedic uniforms. One crouched by George and started assessing him, attaching monitors and inserting an intravenous line to inject something. The other asked questions.

Hazel squeezed past, back to the hall. Her hands shook and her knees trembled. Would George be all right? The paramedics were cheery and reassuring, but she had the feeling they'd be like that even if the patient was drawing their final breath.

"Almost certainly a fractured neck of femur," one said. "We're taking you to the hospital, George. Will your granddaughter be coming with you?"

They meant her, Hazel realised. "I'm just a friend. George, do you want me to call anyone?"

"My brother, Bill. He's in Melbourne. The number's in the drawer under the phone."

She nodded. "I'll come with you if you'd like."

"Will I be home this evening to feed my dog?" he asked the paramedic.

"'Fraid not, George. We'll have to keep you in for a bit."

"I'll be right, Hazel. Will you look after Chip for me?"

"I'll feed him," Hazel said. "Or take him home with me."

"Chip will like that," George said. His eyes were closing. Whatever was in the injection had to be making him drowsy. "Spare key is under the garden gnome at the back."

"I'll find it. Don't worry. I'll make sure everything's okay here."

Hazel stood aside as the ambos stabilised the hip and transferred George onto a stretcher and then to a wheeled trolley by the front door. With the oxygen mask on, George's face was losing the grey tinge, but his forehead wrinkled, as if he was in pain. "I'll call the hospital later. See how you are."

He gave her a weak thumbs up, and then the paramedics rolled the trolley to the waiting ambulance.

Hazel found the key under a creepy-looking gnome in the overgrown garden bed and went back into the house.

She let Chip out of the bedroom. He growled and backed until his butt was against the wall. Despite his grumpy demeanour, her heart went out to him. She kneeled carefully and held out her hand. "It's okay, Chippie. I know you're scared. I am too. We both have to hope your daddy is okay."

His growling intensified and his ears flattened on his head.

"You're going to come home with me, okay? I can't leave you alone." She kept talking nonsense until Chip edged forward.

His nose touched her hand, and he sighed.

"I'll find your leash, and you get to live with us until your daddy's home. You'll like it. I think you'll be spoiled rotten."

Chip gave an almost human-like sniff and sat at her feet. She fondled his ears. "That's it. You know me, and sometimes you even like me. Hold on to that thought, Chippie, you're going to need it."

She sat for a couple more minutes, then levered herself to her feet. She needed to call George's brother.

CHAPTER 3
THE ZOMBIE APOCALYPSE

Imogen went around behind her assistant's desk to stand at her shoulder. The flurry of fingers on the keyboard and the sudden appearance of an Excel spreadsheet told her Serenity had been playing her zombie apocalypse game again. She watched as Serenity entered some figures, seemingly at random, and delete them a moment later. "What level did you reach?"

"Thirty-two. Oh!" The back of Serenity's neck flamed red.

Imogen turned away. "Please check your e-mail. I sent you a To-Do list for today nearly twenty minutes ago." She stalked back to her office.

She tapped her fingers on the oak desk as she waited for Serenity's acknowledgement that she'd received the e-mail. On the other side of the glass wall, her assistant bit her lip, pulled her chair closer to the monitor and started typing.

Imogen switched her attention back to the quarterly budget—her least favourite task. She frowned. Once again, no figures had arrived from Tim, manager of the Enoggera store. She dashed off a quick e-mail with a curt request he have them to her by close of business.

A tinny version of a hip hop track sounded. Imogen compressed her lips as Serenity abandoned work and snatched up the phone. If she'd had her way, Serenity would have been history six months ago, and she'd have a capable assistant. HR's answer was to send Serenity on a productivity course, the only benefit of which Imogen could see was teaching Serenity to alt-tab to hide her zombie game.

Imogen got up and closed her office door. Maybe, once the budget was done, she'd sit down with Serenity and come up with some suggestions for further learning. With a stab of guilt, she remembered having that conversation with Serenity some months ago—but there had never been time to follow through.

Her desk phone rang, and she snatched it up on the second ring. A Melbourne number. Maybe it was Head Office. "Imogen Alexander."

"Imogen, it's Father." The crisp baritone rolled down the line. A voice to project into a packed courtroom, or to enthral an auditorium of students enough that they put down their phones and listened. "How are you?"

"Fine, thanks. And you and Mother?" She modulated her tone to the same even delivery that he preferred.

"We're both in rude health. Hoping to get away for a break somewhere warmer now that the semester is over."

She made a non-committal noise. Maybe they were coming to visit—although her parents' visits were fleeting: a few days when they would stay in a five-star hotel rather than in her townhouse, and they would dine out together every night. Once the pleasantries were done, and enquiries made as to her career (on the rise), her relationship status (still gay, still single), and her finances (considering the purchase of an investment property), the conversation would meander over her parents' careers (both professors at Melbourne University) and amusing stories about their students. Really, it was all very civilised and all very predictable and pleasant.

"You're welcome to come and stay with me—"

"We've actually booked to go to the Maldives," her father said. "We're supposed to be leaving tomorrow."

"But—" Imogen frowned. Maybe one of them had a work commitment they couldn't get out of.

"I had a call from a friend of George's," her father said. "He's in the Dry Creek hospital. Seems he fell and fractured his hip."

"Oh no." Imogen gripped the phone harder with suddenly icy fingers. Was this a soft lead in to worse news? "Is…is he going to be okay?"

"The surgery was successful, but with elderly people, the rehabilitation and recovery is most important. He'll be ready for discharge in three days."

She let out a slow, careful breath. George was okay—and that was the main thing. How long had it been since she'd seen her uncle? She couldn't remember. More than a year—maybe even two. But it was a flight or a seven-hour drive to Dry Creek from Brisbane, and she seldom had the time. "I'll try to get up to see him this weekend. He should be home by then."

"That's not why I'm calling," her father said. "The hospital won't discharge him unless there's someone to stay with him. He'll qualify for home nursing, but someone needs to get that set up for him. You know what a stubborn old fool George is—he's apparently still swearing that he doesn't need help, and he just wants to go home. Of course he can't. He'll still be mainly bedridden."

Imogen licked her dry lips. "I'll take Friday off and go for a couple of nights. I can collect him from the hospital and stay with him that weekend."

"He'll like that." Her father sighed. "You always were his favourite family member."

"Save the flattery; it's not like there's much choice. You, Mother, me. That's it."

"Still, it's true. Can you arrange for home care? You'll need to do that as soon as possible."

"Surely the hospital social work team would be better able to do that?"

"Maybe years ago. Now, there's barely a social worker, let alone a team. The hospital asked us to do it. Ada would arrange it, but our flight leaves at seven tomorrow morning. Better they have someone local to contact—at least you're in Queensland."

"Don't worry, Father, I'll manage it."

"You're a great girl."

The praise warmed her. Thirty-four years old, a regional manager of a nationwide chain of convenience stories, her own million-dollar townhouse, and still her daddy's approval was something she craved. "Maybe George is *my* favourite relative," she teased.

Her father laughed. "That could be true."

Imogen caught sight of Serenity through the glass wall of her office. She was still talking on her mobile. Her lips thinned. "I have to go, Father. But I'll sort out some care for George and go see him this weekend. I hope you and Mother have a pleasant holiday."

"Thank you." Now that their trip was assured, her father's voice hummed with satisfaction.

She ended the call and considered her diary for the rest of the week. She could free up Friday—if she put in extra hours today and tomorrow.

Serenity laughed and ended her call. If she had a competent assistant, it would be a breeze—she could offload some of her tasks. She tapped her pen on the desk as she thought. Maybe this was the time to put some of that responsibility on Serenity. Maybe she'd just been waiting for a chance and would rise to the occasion.

Imogen started an e-mail to her assistant and typed a list of things to do before the end of the day. Five items. That shouldn't be too much for her, although she'd never attempted two of them before. Still, she was a personal assistant; she needed to act like one.

Opening her browser, Imogen started hunting for aged-care providers in Dry Creek. There were two in town, and more in Rockhampton, the larger town thirty minutes away.

Through the glass, Serenity snapped upright in her seat and reached for her mouse. Good. She must have received the e-mail.

A moment later, there was a knock on her door.

"Come in."

Serenity sidled into the room, her ever-present mobile clutched in one hand. "Uh, Imogen, can I talk to you a moment?"

Imogen dragged her eyes from the screen. "Sure. Have a seat."

Serenity sat on the edge of the chair to one side of the desk. Her short skirt rode up, revealing plump, pale thighs, and a flash of lacey underwear. Imogen averted her gaze. At some point, they needed to have a chat about appropriate professional wear.

"The list you sent. I've never called the lawyers. They always ask for you when they call."

"There's no reason you can't talk to them." Imogen sent her a cool smile. "Familiarise yourself with the WorkCover claim and ask the paralegal for an update."

"Um, okay." Serenity squirmed in her seat. "But wouldn't it be better if you did that?"

Imogen steepled her fingers. "Serenity, it's time to give you more challenging tasks. Maybe then you won't be so unoccupied that you have time for computer games."

Serenity's mouth dropped open and she fidgeted in her seat. "Uh, sorry. But I've never been taught about legal stuff. I don't want to mess up."

Really. Imogen suppressed a sigh. "Fine. I'll call the lawyers. Are you okay with the rest of those tasks?"

Serenity's pink cheeks matched the blouse straining across her bosom. "I guess."

Abruptly, a vestige of sympathy stirred. Serenity couldn't be over twenty, and this was her first job. "Okay, I'll call Tim as well. But there's a trade-off. Normally, I wouldn't ask you to do this, as it's a personal matter rather than a work one, but it's urgent." She turned her screen so Serenity could see. "Can you call the aged care providers who service Dry Creek and obtain their rates for twenty-four-hour nursing care for…say five days, and then the hourly rate for in-home care thereafter. Find out how quickly they can begin. Note it all down and send it to me by Thursday lunchtime. Can you do that?"

Serenity nodded. "Yes. That's more what I'm good at."

"Great." Imogen summoned a smile. "Please attend to the other things on the list first before doing this. Next week, you and I will sit down and come up with some sort of personal development plan for you. One you have input in, rather than HR."

"Yes, Imogen. Thank you, Imogen." Serenity stood, her head bobbing like a nodding dog on the parcel shelf of an old Holden. She hurried out of the office, sat and picked up her desk phone.

Hopefully, this time, Serenity would produce some results.

Imogen ended Thursday's Zoom meeting with a sigh of relief. Persuading Foodsters to give Whistlestop a better deal on their products had been a tough sell, but she'd finally got them to agree to a small percentage reduction by reminding them that Whistlestop was opening more convenience stores around Brisbane. Imogen rose from her desk and picked up her bone-china cup and saucer then went out to the office kitchen to make a cup of tea. As she spooned the loose-leaf Earl Grey into an infuser and waited for the kettle to boil, she mentally ran over her remaining tasks. It all seemed under control—even Serenity had completed her allocated work.

Except Serenity hadn't got back to her about care for George. Tea in hand, she headed back to her office and stopped at Serenity's desk. With an internal sigh, she noted the girl's quick Alt-Tab and the nonsense spreadsheet appeared once more. "How did you go with the aged care providers? I haven't seen your summary yet. Please send it over as soon as possible."

Serenity fidgeted with the mouse. "I, er, haven't finished it."

Imogen tightened her lips. "And why not?"

Serenity blanched at the icy tone. "I spoke with one in Dry Creek. Two of the ones in Rockhampton said they didn't travel that far. Another didn't answer. And the other three said they'd get back to me and haven't."

The girl was hopeless. Incompetent and lazy. "Did you follow up with the ones who said they'd get back to you?"

"Uh, no. I figured if they hadn't called back, they had nothing to say."

"Or they were answering the queries of people who *did* call back. The squeaky wheel gets the grease, Serenity. That's as true in business as it is in life." Imogen turned away. "Send me what you have immediately." She stalked into her office, closed the door, and counted to ten. Next week, whether HR liked it or not, she and Serenity were going to have a serious chat.

She took a sip of tea, letting the fragrant brew calm her.

Serenity was typing frantically. No doubt she was only now preparing the e-mail about care providers. Imogen would give her until she finished her tea.

As she took the last sip, her e-mail pinged. Imogen settled her glasses more firmly on her nose and opened the message. It was as Serenity had said: the only details were from one provider—Coreena Care—who could assist. There was no mention of urgent or emergency care. And the hourly cost made her eyes water. Imogen tapped out a quick reply to Serenity, asking her to follow up with the remaining providers and send her an e-mail ASAP in summary.

It was gone four, and her flight to Rockhampton left at eight the next morning. With a sigh, Imogen turned back to her computer.

CHAPTER 4
THE BAKED BEAN THIEF

"Your daddy's coming home today." Hazel extended a hand to Chip, who growled in response. "C'mon, Chippie. Isn't it time you stopped with the grumpiness? You know any second now, you'll be begging for a treat."

Chip wagged his tail and levered his chubby body into a begging pose, front paws under his snout.

"See? What did I tell you?" Hazel reached further and scratched Chip behind his ears.

He glared at her but didn't growl.

"Good boy. We'll go for a walk in the reserve, you and me, before we go to George's house."

Chip woofed once at the "W" word.

Hazel walked into the kitchen where her parents were eating breakfast. She pulled down a bowl and filled it with cornflakes, adding sliced banana and milk, then sat at the table.

"Going over to George's?" her mum asked. "There's a plate of last night's roast lamb in the fridge for him. All he'll have to do is microwave it." She frowned. "Assuming there's someone to stay with him tonight."

"Thanks," Hazel said. "When I visited him yesterday, he said his niece, Imogen, is flying up from Brisbane for the weekend."

"I didn't know he had a niece," her dad said. "Have you met her?"

"No. Apparently, she doesn't come up often. I'll go around to George's place after work and put some things in the fridge for him. I can take the dinner then."

"I'll do a second plate for the niece," her mum said. "Save her having to cook when she arrives."

"That's kind." Hazel pulled out an elastic and fastened her wild hair, so it didn't fall into her breakfast.

She finished her cereal and put the bowl in the dishwasher. "Gotta go. I'll be back around two. Are you okay with Chip?"

"Of course," her dad said. "Chip's no problem." He pushed back from the table and patted his lap.

Chip rested his front paws on her dad's leg and let himself be lifted up. He turned around once and settled in, looking smugly at Hazel as if to say, "See? I don't growl at *everyone*."

"Dog whisperer." Hazel kissed her dad on top of his head and went to work.

It was 2:30 pm when she pulled her truck into George's driveway. The house was as she'd left it yesterday when she'd collected more food for Chip. The blinds were still down, and there was no sign of anyone. George couldn't be home yet, and either Imogen was yet to arrive, or she'd already gone to collect him.

Hazel adjusted her leggings, settling them more firmly over the sleeve that mimicked the shape of her calf and fitted over her prosthetic leg. When covered by clothing, it was hard to notice.

Chip, who'd been curled up on the passenger seat, worn out by his walk, stood and put his front paws on the sill. His ears went up and excited little whines sounded.

"You're home, Chippie," Hazel said.

She set the groceries at the door while she fumbled for the key. The door swung open, and Chip barrelled in and up the stairs. Hazel followed more slowly. Chip's stout shape careened down the hall and into all the rooms with open doors, before he returned to Hazel's side, his tail dragging.

"He'll be home soon." Hazel bent to scratch his ears and was rewarded with a growl.

She carried the groceries into the kitchen and set them on the counter. As she crouched to put the milk in the fridge, a noise made her freeze. It sounded like footfalls. For a moment, her heart thundered a panicky beat, then reason broke through. Old houses creaked all the time. It was nothing. But then another slow footfall sounded, and Chip started an ominous, rumbling growl.

Hazel rose to her feet. If someone were in the house, being in a crouching position wasn't good for anyone. For someone with a prosthetic leg, it was even stupider. She spun around to face the door and gasped.

A woman stood there, ash-blonde hair shining under the kitchen light, and her cheekbones were the sort of sharpness Hazel envied. Any other time, she would have admired the toned arms, but right now, she couldn't look away from the raised hand holding a table lamp aloft.

She thrust her hands out in front of her, as if to ward off a blow, and glanced at the woman's face. The cobalt-blue frame of her glasses enhanced piercing blue eyes. Her skin was pale, as if she seldom saw the sun, and her body was lean to the edge of underweight.

Hazel sidled away from the fridge. "If you're hungry, help yourself to food. But my dad will be home soon, so you'll need to be gone by then, or he'll call the police." She lifted her chin and stared the woman in the eye.

"Food?" The woman huffed a brittle laugh. "It looks to me as if you're taking food from the fridge. And this is not your father's house. You need to leave now, or *I'll* call the police."

Reason crashed into Hazel's brain. *Wait.* While the woman was thin, it wasn't the look of someone who didn't get enough food. Also, she was wearing jeans that Hazel would bet had a designer label on the rear. A thin gold chain hung in the scoop neck of her T-shirt. She lowered her hands. "I think there's been a mistake."

"I think you're right," the woman said. She didn't lower the lamp. "Care to explain what you're doing in this house?"

"This is George Alexander's house. George is in hospital with a broken hip. I'm his friend, Hazel Lee. I brought groceries for George, so he has food when he comes home later today. And I'm guessing you're George's niece, Imogen."

The table lamp lowered slightly. "I've never heard of you. And that doesn't explain why you were taking things from his fridge."

"I was putting them in!" Hazel said in frustration. She waved at the bag on the counter. "If I was stealing from George, I wouldn't bother with cans of baked beans and packets of sliced ham."

The lamp lowered further. "Why didn't you ring the bell?"

"George gave me a key. And there was no car outside, no sign that anyone was home. The blinds are down."

"I was working on my laptop. I prefer dim lighting. My car's in the garage."

Chip stalked closer and then, with a growl like rumbling thunder, made a dive for Imogen's ankle.

Hazel suppressed a snort of amusement. For once, Chip had got his attack mode right.

Imogen jerked and moved away before Chip could fasten on. "Please get your dog under control."

"Chip, come here." Hopefully, he would listen to her for once.

Astonishingly, he did and sat at her feet. The hairs on the back of his neck stood on end, and he emitted a constant stream of low snarls.

"The dog's a menace. You shouldn't have brought him." The woman set down the lamp and folded her arms.

"He's not my dog. He's George's. I'm surprised you didn't know that."

"I don't come up all that often."

"Or speak on the phone, either. Chip has been George's dog ever since he got him from the shelter nearly two years ago."

"Should have left him there," Imogen muttered.

"Chip or George?"

The woman's lips twitched into a small smile. "Maybe we should start this conversation afresh. Obviously, you are George's friend." She held out a hand. "I'm Imogen Alexander. My father and George are brothers."

"Bill?" Hazel shook the proffered hand. It was cool and dry, despite the warm day. "I called him to let him know George was in hospital."

Imogen withdrew her hand. "That's him. He contacted me, and I came as soon as I could." She glanced at a gold watch on her wrist. "As wholesome as this chat is, I need to call the aged-care services again before picking George up from the hospital."

"Are you arranging nursing care?" Hazel moved back to the bag on the counter and continued unpacking the groceries. "The best provider in Dry Creek, with the most caring staff, and good accountability, is Us Together."

"I'll call again." Imogen nodded stiffly. "But if I can't speak with someone there, I'll have to go with Coreena Care. It's the only one who has responded, so far."

"Coreena Care has a reputation for unreliability," Hazel said. "It doesn't pay too well, and staff sometimes don't turn up."

"Hardly good business practice," Imogen said. "How can it keep going?"

"There's only two aged-care service providers in town. Good luck getting anyone to come from Rockhampton."

"I'll take that on advisement. Now, if you're done with the groceries, I won't hold you up any longer."

Dismissed. Hazel gave a mental shrug. Well, she wouldn't stay where she wasn't wanted. And the prickly niece wasn't her cup of tea either.

"My mum provided two roast lamb dinners for you and George, so you don't need to worry about food tonight. They're in the fridge. Do you want me to show you where Chip's food is?"

Imogen's eyes slid to the little dog. Chip shifted closer to Hazel and rested against her prosthetic leg, uttering a constant rumble of growls.

"He's not very friendly, is he?"

"He takes a while to warm up to people." No need to mention Chip still growled at her.

"I don't suppose you'd keep him another couple of days?"

"I could—if George wants it. But George has asked about Chip each time I visited the hospital—and Chip has been pining for him. Chip's staying here, unless George says otherwise."

Imogen inclined her head. "If that's the case, then I guess I'm stuck with him."

Hazel placed a carton of prune juice in the fridge and shut the door. "I'm off now." Her left thigh cramped as she stood, and her prosthetic leg dragged momentarily. She straightened, shot Imogen a cool glance. "I'll see you tomorrow. I'll come to see George."

She forced herself to walk without a limp as she went downstairs and out to her ute. Once in the driver's seat, she reversed out of the driveway and headed for home.

So that was George's niece. Prickly, cold, and untrusting were the words that came to mind to describe her. *And gorgeous.* But she wouldn't go there. Better to focus on Imogen's more unlikeable qualities so she could forget her delicate collarbones and lightly muscled arms. Hazel's own arms were built like a bricklayer's, as her dad liked to say. A side effect of crutches, and moving herself with her arms more than the average person.

She glanced in the rear-view mirror and caught sight of Chip's basket, blanket, and bag of food still in the back of the ute. *Dammit.* Imogen had rattled her enough that she'd forgotten to leave them. She'd have to return. Another glance in the mirror, and she made an illegal U-turn and returned to George's house. She didn't particularly want to see Imogen again, who was no doubt on the phone, anyway. She parked in the street and made a couple of trips with Chip's worldly goods, leaving them on the porch, where Imogen couldn't fail to see them.

CHAPTER 5
CHIP'S REVENGE

Imogen eyed Chip warily. The little dog stared right back at her, as if deciding whether she was someone he should chase from the house. She stayed still as Chip came closer to sniff her shoes. Then, with a human-sounding snort, he scampered downstairs to stand by the front door.

Did that mean he wanted to go out? Well, he'd have to wait until after her phone call. She had no idea if the yard was fully fenced, and she couldn't wait around for him to do his business.

Chip barked once and scratched at the door.

Imogen turned on her heel and went back to the guest room, which she was using as an office. She sat at the desk and found the number for Us Together. Chances were, Hazel knew the best provider, seeing as how she was local. Or maybe she worked there, or a friend did. Imogen gave a mental shrug. Whatever the reason, it was a place to start.

Hazel seemed very young. Maybe only twenty or so—a similar age to Serenity. Although maybe her wild mane of hair—all twists and corkscrew curls—made her seem that way. Still, she knew her way around George's house, and how to deal with his grumpy dog. Why would a young girl want to befriend an old codger like her uncle? Surely she had better things to do.

Not my problem.

She picked up her phone and pressed the number for Us Together.

Twenty minutes later, Imogen ended the call with a sigh. While Us Together had been professional and courteous, the manager had said the wait time was around one month—even if she paid directly. It seemed there simply weren't the staff.

She should have got Hazel's number, if only to ask for more details on other providers. An image of Hazel leaped into her head. Her ridiculous hair so huge compared to her tiny frame. Even so, Imogen had stood a head taller than her.

Hazel was a casual dresser: a T-shirt and leggings covering her curvy breasts and hips, although she was otherwise slender. A tattoo encircled one wrist. Some small lettering that Imogen hadn't been able to read.

Imogen glanced at her watch. She'd have to leave to collect George in twenty minutes, so it looked as if Coreena Care was her only option if she was to return to Brisbane on Sunday evening. If they couldn't assist, she had no idea what she'd do.

She picked up her phone again and made the call.

───❀•❀───

Imogen parked the hire car in George's driveway and looked across at him. "Here we are."

"Thanks, Immie." George fumbled for the seatbelt.

"Wait until I get your crutches." She jumped out and grabbed the crutches from the boot, then rested them against the car door so she could help George to his feet.

He hissed through his teeth.

"Sorry. Did I hurt you?" Worry twined through her chest. It had to hurt, despite George saying he was okay.

"No, love, I'm fine." His sudden pallor told a different story. "Happy to be back. Can't wait to see Chip."

"I'm sure he'll be glad to see you. I don't think he likes me very much."

"He'll come around, eventually. He's grumpy with all new people."

Imogen matched George's shuffle to the front door and opened it.

Chip barrelled out, barking. He saw George and his bark morphed into excited little whines. His rear end twerked at high speed, and he raced toward George.

"Stop, Chip." Imogen used her displeased-boss voice. If Chip leaped at George, he could be back in the hospital with a second broken hip.

Amazingly, Chip screeched to a halt, and approached George at a slower pace. He sniffed his legs from shoes to knees and whined again.

"Let's go inside," Imogen said. "Do you want to go to bed or sit in the living room?"

"The living room," George said. "I've had enough of lying in bed like a corpse." He managed the stairs at a slow pace.

She helped him to the armchair. "Cup of tea?"

"You're a love. And mebbe one of them pain tablets from the hospital."

Imogen went to the kitchen. A puddle of liquid glistened in the middle of the floor. She frowned. What could be leaking? As she came closer, she smelled it—Chip was the leaky part. She'd forgotten to let him out. She turned on the kettle and found some paper towel to wipe up the mess. Then she made the tea and brought it in along with George's tablets and a packet of biscuits.

"This is the life," George said. He sat in his chair, Chip snuggled by his side. "I put Chip outside when I go out. He gets nervous by himself and there's been a couple of accidents."

Imogen looked at Chip, who lifted his upper lip in a small snarl, for all the world as if he were daring her to dob him in.

"Not this time." She sipped her tea, suppressing a grimace at the taste—she'd have to get some Earl Grey.

"You bought my favourite bikkies!" George said. "I like the caramel ones best."

"That wasn't me. Your friend Hazel dropped off some groceries, including these."

"She's a lovely lassie. So very kind. She drops in to see me a couple of times each week."

"She said she'd come around tomorrow." Imogen set the tea aside. There was no way she could drink the stuff.

"That's good. Did you have a nice chat with her?"

"She didn't stay long."

"Don't scare her away, Immie. She's a good friend."

Imogen suppressed a sigh. She needed to have a chat with him about that terrible nickname. It had been cute when she'd been four, but now she was thirty-four, it didn't sit well at all. But now wasn't the time. "She seemed like a kind person."

"She is. Does all sorts of little things for me. Brings my groceries, fixes things that break, walks Chip sometimes, and drives me places, too."

"That's good of her." Too good. What was Hazel expecting to get out of this?

"She helped me with all the Internet stuff for my pension."

A red alert blared in Imogen's head. Was Hazel worming her way into George's confidence to defraud him? Scams and elder abuse were all over the news. "You need to be careful with that, George. People can take advantage of you if they gain your private information."

He glared at her. "Are you accusing Hazel of something?"

"I'm not." *Not yet, anyway.* "I'm just saying to guard your personal information."

His bushy eyebrows lowered. "Hazel is a good, honest girl, and I trust her. She helped me sort out a problem."

"How did she do that? You don't have a computer?"

"She brought hers around."

Oh, this was so not good. George's identity was probably now stored on Hazel's laptop. She'd have to have a talk with her. "You must know her very well to trust her with that."

"Mebbe three years. And I know what you're thinking, but it's not like that. Hazel didn't look while I put in my information. I told her to enter it, but she wouldn't."

Now was not the time to push harder on this. Imogen managed a smile. "I'm arranging some home nursing for you. Around the clock at first. After that, someone can come in for a few hours in the day to help you with housework."

"I don't want a stranger in my house. I'll get friends to look in on me. My mates from the pub. Hazel. Mavis from the RSL." He reached out a wrinkled hand. "You're a good girl, Immie, love, but I'll be fine. Mebbe you could get me one of those alert things you wear around your neck. Hazel said she'll come if I need her. And Frank is going to drop around."

"I think you need a nurse. At least at first."

"Last I checked, you weren't a nurse either," he shot back. "And you're here now, to help me to the dunny and put me in the shower. What's the difference between you and Frank?"

"I've read all the information the hospital provided. I know what to do." He had a point, though. Business skills didn't translate easily into caring for obstinate old men.

"Okay then. But if I don't like the carer, I'll tell them not to come back."

"Fair enough. Someone's coming Sunday early evening and will stay with you overnight. I have to work on Monday, George. I wish I could stay longer."

"I wish you could, too." He patted her hand. "But I'm happy you came for as long as you could."

Guilt twisted her stomach into a knot. She should have come more often. George had been there for her in the past—including when she'd been nine and her parents spent a summer in Europe without her. George had invited her up without a second's hesitation when she'd told him she hadn't wanted to go to her gran's. That summer in Dry Creek still shone golden in her memory: fishing in the creek, panning for gold in the fossicking area, learning to ride a horse, and trips with George—to the beach, and weekend camping. He'd even sat patiently at the back of a gymnastics class for the three weeks it had taken her to realise she would never be an Olympic gymnast.

"I'll come back soon," she said. "And maybe, when your hip is better, you can come down and see me in Brisbane."

"What would I do in a big city?"

"Whatever you want! It's not too late to pick up some bad habits: drinking, gambling, sex clubs…"

He laughed. "You think I don't know what they are? Maybe I'll tell you my secret formula to win at the races."

"Lose more like."

"If you come back to see me, mebbe Hazel could show you around a bit. It would be nice if you had a friend up here."

"This isn't kindergarten," Imogen said. "I don't need you to hold my hand, take me into the classroom and ask another child to be my friend."

"I just thought you and Hazel might enjoy a night out."

"We have nothing in common. I must be fifteen years older than her. She probably goes clubbing."

A vision of Hazel dancing exuberantly under pulsing lights, her wild hair a halo around her head, flashed into Imogen's mind.

"She's more a homebody. Lives a quiet life."

"Then why should we go out?"

"As friends," George said. His wide-eyed innocence didn't fool her at all.

"What else?" She shot him an irritated glance. "She's still too young."

"She's twenty-five. Nine years isn't much of a difference."

"She looks younger. The way she dresses…that hair." Imogen rose and took her mug out to the kitchen. "Just drop it, please, George. I'm sure Hazel's lovely, and it's good that you like her, but for both of our sakes, please don't push her on me."

George shrugged. "Thought if you had a friend here, you might come more often."

The guilt squirmed again in her stomach. "Enough of the emotional blackmail, please."

"You're right. Sorry. Can you pass me another Tim Tam?"

She passed him the packet. Perhaps he had a point, although not the one he thought. If she got to know Hazel, maybe she could figure out if she was all she seemed.

Imogen shifted her back against the headboard of the bed in George's spare room. The bed was softer than her own, but still comfortable. Her laptop rested on her knees, and her best friend Jess's face filled the screen.

"It's like I've gone back twenty-five years," Imogen said. "I swear George's house hasn't changed since the summer I spent here. Same timber kitchen, same shower cubicle with the pink shower pan. Same patterned tiles on the veranda, although now they're retro and rather appealing."

"Not everyone feels the need to redecorate every couple of years," Jess said. She pushed her thick, black hair over her shoulders. "Not that your townhouse isn't gorgeous—as it was when you had all-white decor, and before that when it was pale blue and grey."

"And not everyone feels the need to clothes shop every weekend." Imogen grinned at her friend.

Jess smoothed the sleeve of her wine-coloured jacket. "What can I say? I like designer clothes as much as you like paint charts. If you have to visit George more often, maybe you can bring his home into the twenty-first century."

"If he lets me. He seems to like it exactly the way it is."

"Don't decide to move there permanently. I doubt he'd enjoy your piano moving in, too."

"I'm not that bad." Imogen frowned in pretend affront.

"The house must take a lot of upkeep. Or is it all crumbling into the ground?"

"It's old and shabby, but most things are in working order. He has a friend who does maintenance for him and doesn't charge."

"That's good. Maybe there's a Men's Shed in Dry Creek. Many of the homeless men we help go there."

"This is a young woman who helps him. I've met her. She's pleasant, but I can't help wondering if she's after something. Why would a twenty-five-year-old spend a few hours each week with George?"

Jess snorted and her light-brown face went out of focus as she moved closer to the screen. "Imo, not everyone has an ulterior motive. Not everyone is looking for something for nothing. There are people in this shitty, fucked-up world who just are kind and want to make things better for others. Maybe this woman is like that."

Imogen tutted. "George says that's exactly what Hazel is like. But I worry that she's… I don't know. After money. Or a mention in his will. Or a free place to stay. She doesn't look as if she has much."

"So ask her," Jess said. "You're not one to prevaricate."

"Maybe I will. She's coming here tomorrow."

"Do that," Jess said. Her gaze slid away, then back. "Sorry, a work e-mail. From the header, we may have received the extra state government funding we applied for."

"Read it," Imogen said. "I'll wait."

Jess went quiet, her eyes scanning the screen. Then a grin split her face. "We got the money to expand the homeless shelter in the city! Let no one say Jess Tran can't get things done. Also, let no one say the current government is shit. They're not. Not totally, anyway."

"Congratulations. That's huge."

Jess fanned herself with a hand. "I thought we'd missed out. I'm sorry, Imo, but I've got to go—I have to let people know. And yes, before you say it, even on a Friday evening." She kissed the tips of her fingers and pressed them to the screen.

Imogen mirrored the gesture. "I'll be back on Monday. Come around—we'll get dinner delivered and drink something good."

"You got it." Jess wiggled her fingers, and the link closed.

Imogen shut the laptop. The old-fashioned alarm clock beside the bed said it was just gone 7:00 pm. George, she knew, was impatiently waiting for his dinner. For a second she wondered what to cook, then she remembered the roast lamb dinners Hazel had mentioned. Perfect. She got off the bed and went to do battle with the elderly microwave.

CHAPTER 6
AS PLEASANT AS A PAP SMEAR

Hazel stood on George's front porch and listened to Chip barking in counterpoint to the "Waltzing Matilda" door chime. After a minute, the front door opened and Imogen, dressed in navy shorts and a sky-blue T-shirt, stood there. Her short hair was mussed as if she'd repeatedly run her fingers through it.

Nice. Hazel took in her casual attire and concentrated on her face rather than on the long length of thigh. Imogen stared into her eyes, making her stomach flutter.

Hazel glanced down, and when she looked up, Imogen was staring at Petunia. It was a warm day, and Hazel, too, was wearing shorts, and Petunia, her usual serviceable prosthesis, was unadorned. The neoprene that covered the cup and reached halfway up her thigh as well as the stainless-steel post that comprised most of her artificial leg were on display. Imogen's stare slid away then, up to Hazel's face.

Hazel looked into her clear blue eyes behind the large-framed glasses, holding her gaze until Imogen flushed and glanced away.

So, she was uncomfortable around an amputee. Hazel gave a mental shrug. Imogen wouldn't be the first person to react like that, and she was used to it now. It seldom bothered her.

"I'm sorry," Imogen said in a low voice. "I didn't mean to stare. I was just caught by surprise. I didn't realise…" She kept her eyes on Hazel's face.

There was none of the avid curiosity or revulsion Hazel sometimes saw. Imogen flushed pink, but she didn't break eye contact. Not the worst reaction she'd ever had.

"Don't worry. I'm fine with people looking—most of the time, anyway." She proffered a large container. "My mum—Maxie—baked a cake for you and George."

"Thanks. That's really kind of her." Imogen took the cake and stepped aside. "George is eager to see you."

"Let me just get a couple of things from the truck." With a nod, Hazel returned to grab her toolbox and the raised toilet seat she'd bought.

When she returned to the house, Imogen was in the kitchen, and the kettle was rumbling to the boil.

"In here, lovey."

She walked toward George's voice, then bent and kissed his cheek. "It's good to see you home."

"It's good to be home, and all the better for seeing you. Seems I owe you even more."

"You owe me nothing. Chip, though, he owes me a month of no growling."

On cue, Chip lifted his upper lip in a half-hearted snarl.

"See? He likes you better already. Besides, he now has Immie to grump at."

Imogen came into the living area with a tray holding three mugs and a plate with slices of Maxie's cake.

"Immie? Oh!" Hazel suppressed a smile. Calling Imogen "Immie" was like calling a panther "Fluffy".

Imogen shot Hazel a quick look through narrowed eyes. "Chip does grump. George…I'd really prefer you to call me Imogen. Immie was fine when I was small and cute."

"I can do that," George said. "Sorry, Immie—Imogen."

"Don't do it on my behalf. Immie suits you so well." Hazel beamed an amused smile at her. She wore the name Imogen like a power suit. It made Hazel think of business meetings, expensive gin on ice, and people with a level of cool she would never possess. It was a superior sounding name, much like the woman who wore it.

"Hazel is like family, she won't mind." George waved her to the couch. "Tell me all the news."

"Since I saw you the day before yesterday?" At George's nod, she continued. "I completed the job I told you about. Garage shelving. The customer is happy—she wants me to paint her spare bedroom."

"Your business is taking off now. You'll be too busy to see me." George eyed the slices of cake.

"Three jobs in total?" Hazel accepted the mug of tea from Imogen. "I won't be giving up my actual work any time soon. Enough of me. Tell me how you are."

"Been better," George said. "But I've been worse, too. Got a hip that's worth more than your truck."

"So a cheap hip, then. Hope it doesn't rust like my truck."

"I'll get my money back if it does. Going good so far. I'm walking, sort of. It's still a bit sore. I'm glad I have Immie—Imogen—here to help me."

"That's good." She flashed Imogen a glance. She looked uncomfortable at George's praise. As well she might. In the three years Hazel had known George, this was the first time Imogen had made the journey north to see him.

Imogen cleared her throat and proffered the plate of cake to George. "This looks delicious."

"It's Mum's current favourite cake," Hazel said. "She got the recipe from the free magazine at Good 'n Fresh."

Imogen's brow wrinkled. "Is that the only supermarket in town?"

"There's one of the national chains, and there's a cheap European supermarket recently opened, but Good 'n Fresh is the one I use. Their deliveries are the most reliable." George winked at Hazel.

"Of course." She caught Imogen's bafflement out of the corner of her eye. Obviously, George hadn't mentioned where she worked. She stifled a smile. Time to change the subject. "The cake is lemon and yogurt. It's gluten free but not dairy free—we didn't know if there's anything you don't eat, Imogen."

"This is fine. It looks delicious." She nibbled a corner and set the cake down again on her plate.

Maybe she was careful with her diet, or had a naturally super-charged metabolism, but she didn't look as if cake was a regular choice. Hazel took a big bite. It was as good as ever—and it should be—this was the third time her mum had made it this week. One for the family, one for the library morning tea, and now one for George and Imogen.

George broke off a corner. "This is the best thing I've eaten all week. Hospital food is dull as ditchwater."

"Remember what they told you on discharge: to go easy on food. You're not too mobile at the moment and you don't want to add extra weight while you're healing." Imogen softened her words with a small smile.

Damn. Hazel closed her eyes momentarily. Imogen was right, of course. She should have suggested her mum make something healthier. Next time, that's what she'd bring.

"Can't a man enjoy a piece of cake in his own home?" George grumbled.

"Imogen's right," Hazel said. "I'm sorry. I should have thought of that. Once you're up and about more, I promise I'll bring cake again. We want you to get better as quickly as possible." She caught Imogen's nod. The approval sent a shaft of warmth through her. Really, it shouldn't matter what Imogen thought, but if she was going to be more involved with George now, it would be better if they got on.

She sipped her tea. "I've got you a present, George. Don't get too excited—it's practical, not pretty, but I hope it will make your life a lot easier in the next few weeks—it's a raised toilet seat; recommended after hip replacement."

George looked more pleased than most people would at the idea of a toilet seat for a present. "You're a darling, Hazel."

"I'll install it for you in a minute."

"Should we get a plumber?" Imogen asked.

"No need. It will only take me a few minutes," Hazel replied. *Really?* Imogen thought they needed a skilled tradesperson for that simple job? She swallowed the last of her tea and rose. "I'll do it now."

She carted her toolbox into the toilet and installed the seat. That should make things a lot more comfortable for George.

With the toolbox clutched in front of her, she backed out of the narrow toilet. A yelp, a snarl, and a waft of air near her bare right ankle told her she'd nearly flattened Chip, and he'd attempted to sink his teeth into her in revenge. Poor Chip. He'd had a miserable few days without George, despite how spoiled he'd been by her parents.

"Sorry, Chippie. It's not your fault you're so low to the ground." She bent to pat his head, not put off by his bared teeth. She had his number now: he was all bluster—until someone nearly stepped on him. Then he meant business.

She returned to the living room. Imogen had a laptop on her knees and was scowling at the screen.

"How long are you staying?" Hazel asked.

Imogen glanced up through her blue-framed glasses. "I'm flying back tomorrow. But I'll try to come back again soon." A slight smile. "Sooner than last time."

"Do, Immie, love," George said. "It would be lovely to see you again. Isn't that right, Hazel?"

"Of course." Lovely and fun, just like a visit to the gynaecologist. Imogen made her uncomfortable, like her gynae's attempts at humour. There would never be anything remotely funny about a pap smear. She encircled her left wrist with her right hand, pressing against the tattooed words that ran around her wrist. "Did you arrange nursing care?"

Imogen closed the laptop with a snap. "There's someone coming from Coreena Care. Initially it will be twenty-four-hour care, but hopefully in a few days, George will be more mobile."

"I'm mobile now." George's eyebrows lowered toward his nose.

"You're doing amazingly well," Imogen said. "I'm doing this for me, so I don't worry about you."

Coreena Care. Hazel breathed deeply. There had to be something good about them—but she couldn't think what. Still, at least there was someone coming. "Did the hospital give you one of those personal alarms?"

George harrumphed. "Guess I am old enough to need one. No, they didn't."

"We can get you set up with one." Imogen tapped one long, slender finger on the laptop case. "It's on my list of things to do."

Hazel kept her expression blank. "What else is on the list? Maybe there's something I can help with."

"Thank you, but you've done enough to help already. The professionals can take it from here."

That sounded much like a dismissal. She flicked a glance at Imogen, who had reopened her laptop and was typing fast, a wrinkle marring the smooth skin of her forehead.

"Well, I'll come around and see you after work on Monday," she said to George. "Call me if there's anything you want me to bring."

"I will do, lovey." George accepted the proffered kiss. "I'll look forward to it."

"Bye, Imogen. It was nice to see you." Maybe "interesting" was a more apt word than "nice". "I'm sure we'll meet again."

Imogen set the laptop aside and stood. "Thanks, Hazel. I'll see you out."

Hazel carried her toolbox down to the truck and heaved it onto the tray. She strapped it down, then turned to face Imogen.

Imogen held out her hand. "Thank you for your care of George. He's lucky you arrived when you did after he fell."

Hazel shook the proffered hand. It was cool, despite the warm day. She stifled a giggle. Maybe Imogen was like a lizard and needed some sun to warm her up. "No problem. If you want, I'll give you my number in case there's anything I can help with." *In case Coreena Care proves as unreliable as everyone says.*

"Thank you, but that shouldn't be necessary. The care arrangement's in place." Imogen gave a professional smile, as if she were escorting an interviewee from the premises.

"Okey-dokey." Hazel stuck her hands in her shorts pocket and shrugged. "George has my number anyway. *He* often calls."

Imogen's eyes narrowed. *Good.* She'd obviously noted the intended rebuke.

With a flutter of her fingers, and a wide, fake smile, Hazel lowered herself into the driver's seat and started the engine, pulling away before she could do anything stupid like tell Imogen to loosen up.

The carer had arrived—finally. Despite Imogen asking them to arrive fifteen minutes early so she could be sure George was happy, the carer was five minutes late.

Imogen's gaze drifted from the solid torso and thick arms down to legs that seemed larger than her waist. He looked like an Olympic weightlifter. He also looked about sixteen.

"Aaron?"

"Yeah, that's me." He gave a shy bob of his head and stared at his feet.

"Come and meet George."

Aaron followed her into the lounge where George was watching TV.

"So you're going to keep me in line, then?" George said. "Do you have a car? If we leave in the next half hour, we'll catch happy hour at the pub."

"Uh, sure," Aaron said.

"No way." Imogen folded her arms. "George is joking. Isn't that right, George?"

"If you say so. But I don't see why not."

"You need to get stronger on your feet first." She beckoned to Aaron. "If you come with me, I'll run through what you need to do."

He lumbered behind her as she made her way to the bedroom. "George needs a shower. You'll have to help him wash and have the towels ready and so on. He'll lie down after that, so you'll help him into bed. Then you can prepare his dinner. There are the ingredients for a simple pasta in the kitchen, and a bag of salad."

Aaron shuffled his feet. "Uh, okay."

"Now, are you a nurse? His dressing is due to be removed." She tilted her head and regarded him. He didn't look old enough, but Coreena Care had assured her a qualified nurse would do the early care.

"Uh, no. I'm just a carer." His gaze flickered around the room, taking in the commode, the frame over the bed, and the bell on the nightstand. "They said nothing about any of this."

Imogen faced the window and took a deep breath. "What did they tell you?"

"That I just sit with him and get him stuff from the fridge when he asks. Pick up things he drops. That sort of thing. They said nothing about cooking and showering."

"Is that what you do in your other jobs?" She glanced at her watch. If she was to get to the airport, return her rental car, and make the flight, she had to leave in five minutes.

"Yeah. But I've only done one other job for them." His bulky shoulders moved up and down in a shrug. "It's just sort of babysitting."

"Don't let George hear that," she snapped. "Look, I don't have any other option at this point, but I specifically booked a nurse. I'll contact Coreena Care tomorrow morning." She sighed in exasperation. "You'll have to do the best you can. I hope you can at least cook."

"I can microwave."

"How old are you?" Her simmering annoyance had reached the point of overriding tact.

"Twenty. I'm just a college student earning money. I wasn't told anything about this."

It wasn't Aaron's fault, but someone at Coreena Care was going to get their ears singed on Monday.

"There's a list on the kitchen counter with George's routine. Please follow it. My mobile number is on it if you have any problems, but I'm on the eight o'clock flight to Brisbane, so you won't be able to reach me then.

Aaron nodded, and together they went back out to George.

"I have to go." She bent and kissed his cheek. "You'll be okay?"

"Me and Aaron will be fine," George said. "Safe trip, Immie, love. Call me to let me know you've arrived home safely."

"I will." She gave his shoulder a last squeeze and headed out of the door.

Once in the rental car, she tipped her head back against the rest. At least Aaron seemed quiet and kind. She lifted her head, started the car, and set the navigation app for the airport. She cursed herself for not getting Hazel's number. But the girl had been so irritatingly upbeat, so chirpy, so carefree she'd just wanted her gone. For a second, she wondered what she worked as. Maybe she was a childcare assistant—that would suit her upbeat personality.

An image of Hazel gripping the tattoo on her wrist flashed into her mind. The lettering was a curly cursive that wasn't easy to make out. Probably some popular slogan.

Imogen shrugged; it wasn't her concern how Hazel adorned her body. But a worm of shame stirred as she remembered Hazel's half-smile when she'd caught Imogen staring at her prosthetic leg. As if she was resigned to being stared at. As if she realised that people would gawk, and she'd long decided it was their problem, not hers.

As it should be.

But her own reaction hadn't been good. She'd just been so surprised to see the prosthesis and feelings had rippled through her: surprise, shock, guilt for her previous assumptions about Hazel, and then pity. Did Hazel want her pity? Somehow, she doubted it. She shook her shoulders and forced her thoughts back to George.

Once she'd caught up with whatever mess Serenity had left her in the office, she'd see about another long weekend in Dry Creek. She was overdue for holidays, too, and while Dry Creek wasn't a destination resort like the luxury hotel she sometimes stayed at in Noosa Heads, it was a pleasant town. It might be quite fun to explore once more.

But there was no way she'd take up George's suggestion of getting to know Hazel better. They were simply too different, their outlooks on life polar opposites, the age gap too great.

No, Hazel was best left alone.

CHAPTER 7
LIGHT READING

"I managed everything on your list except arranging the call with Lucien Drake from the Darling Downs region," Serenity said. "Your manager told me to book lunch for you and Lucien instead, and suggested Sky Windows."

Damn. Imogen released a slow breath. Another dull lunch making stilted conversation with someone she had nothing in common with. Why Whistlestop put such emphasis on face-to-face meetings, she didn't know. Phone calls or Zoom meetings were a much more efficient use of time.

"Sky Windows is booked out," Serenity continued. "I didn't know where else to try, but Jaya in HR suggested a sushi restaurant on Southbank. Apparently, a lot of corporate lunches happen there, according to the expense receipts. I didn't book it though. I wanted to check with you first."

Imogen swallowed the surprise at Serenity's initiative. "Well done. But sushi won't work for Lucien—he's a very plain eater. Please try the steakhouse in the Rialto building. Let me know how you go."

Serenity's smile wobbled a bit, and she twitched the frilled cuff of her pink shirt into place. "No worries." She turned to leave.

Imogen returned to the daily list of Serenity's tasks.

1. Call Ron Lessing's assistant at Central Dairies and follow up on the requested quote.

2. Complete and send my expense report to HR for August. I've attached my credit card statement.

The rest of the list was straightforward, and in a few minutes, Imogen sent the e-mail. Outside her office, Serenity straightened in her chair and reached for the mouse. *Good.*

Once the urgent tasks were out of the way, Imogen picked up her own mobile and pressed George's number.

He answered on the fourth ring.

"Hello, favourite uncle. How are you today?"

"Not bad, Immie, love. Be better when I can move more."

"Did Aaron give you your tablets with breakfast?"

"He did. Nice young man. We had a pleasant evening. I taught him to play cribbage."

"Who won?"

"I won the first two. He won the next."

She pulled a pad toward her. "What did you have for dinner? And did he help you in the shower?"

"Pasta and cheese. A bit ordinary, but he made a nice salad. And he helped me shower. That was good. I was getting a bit whiffy."

At least George got on with Aaron. "Who's there for the day shift?"

"A lovely lady called Pippa. She's making me a cup of tea right now."

"Is she a nurse? A nurse needs to assess your wound."

"I dunno. She didn't say. But Chip likes her."

Imogen rolled her eyes. "Of course that is the most important thing."

"She gives him treats," George continued. "He lets her rub his tummy!" His voice held awe at Chip's change of personality.

"I'll call Coreena Care and find out if she can do your dressing," Imogen said. That would be easier and more productive than asking to speak with Chip's new best friend. "What else is happening today?"

"Not much. Hazel said she'd drop around after work. Her mum's coming too. She's going to bring me some new library books."

"Nice of her."

"Maxie works there, so it's easy. She knows what I like to read."

Which was more than she did. Thrillers maybe? Tales of war? Spy stories? She snorted. She was stereotyping in the worst way. "Which is what?"

"Biographies, books about cricket. General fiction—I like that Jodi Picoult."

Well, she hadn't expected that. "She's got a new one out." She'd heard two of the assistants discussing it in the lunchroom.

"Maxie said she put it aside for me. Large print edition."

"Good for Maxie." An e-mail notification flashed on her screen. "I have to go, George. I'll call you when I know who's looking after you tonight. Bye." She ended the call, checked her e-mail, then picked up her desk phone to call Coreena Care.

She had to listen to ten minutes of elevator music on hold before the coordinator, Sally, picked up. Imogen asked if Pippa could remove George's dressing.

There was the sound of a clicking keyboard, then Sally said, "Pippa is very experienced—she has a Certificate III in Aged Care. George has"—more keyboard sounds—"George is recovering from surgery on his hip. Pippa is more than competent for that."

"Surely a nurse is needed to assess the wound?"

"Not necessarily," Sally said in a brisk voice. "If Pippa is in any way concerned, she can call our twenty-four-hour nurse hotline."

She tapped her pen on the pad. "Who are you sending tonight?"

"Aaron is going back."

"I'd be happier if you could send a nurse—I was told this wouldn't be a problem."

"I'm sorry, but we don't have anyone available. Now, do you want Aaron to attend?"

"Yes, please." What else could she do?

Hazel set down the bags of groceries and rang George's doorbell.

"Does he know how irritating that bloody bell is?" her mum asked as "Waltzing Matilda" chimed out. "Could you accidentally break it and replace it with a normal chime?"

"He loves it," Hazel replied. "So no. I won't touch it."

The door swung open and a hulking shape filled it. Hazel's eyes traced the bulky body. He had to be one hundred and fifty kilograms of solid muscle.

"Hi," he said. "I'm Aaron, and you must be Hazel and Maxie. Come in."

Hazel called a hello to George and carried the bags through to the kitchen, leaving Maxie to talk to him.

Aaron followed her out. "The old boy hasn't stopped talking about you."

Chip barked.

"And Chip hasn't stopped growling. Does that dog like anyone apart from George?"

"Not many people." She picked out the eggs and lettuce from the bag and opened the fridge, placing them in.

Without saying anything, Aaron started handing her groceries to put away.

"Thanks."

"Just another thing that works better with two."

He was quite sweet. And he had to be kind, working as a carer. "How long have you been a carer?"

"To be honest, this is my second-ever job. I worked as a security guard before this. I mean, look at me." He swept a hand over his body.

"I can see you would be intimidating."

He shrugged. "Yeah, but I didn't like dealing with drunk people. You can cop a lot of abuse that way. I much prefer this." He handed her a bag of carrots and a couple of zucchini. "I don't even drink."

"I hope you don't mind being around people who do. George likes a small port after dinner."

Aaron waited while she shelved the veggies, then handed her a block of cheddar and a litre of milk. "Our coach forbids us to drink. I don't mind what other people do."

She shot him a glance. His golden skin shone with healthy living. "Do you always do what you're told?"

"I'm trying for a sports scholarship in America, so I follow his advice."

"I hope you get it." Hazel crouched in front of the fridge again. Aaron had to be a few years younger than her and he had a plan for his life that went beyond "have fun, be kind, and live every day the best you can". Her plan seemed pathetic compared to his. She should take tips from him.

For a second, she thought of Imogen. It had been obvious what Imogen had thought of her: an annoyingly cheerful kid without a grain of ambition, still sponging off her parents. She pushed that from her head: what did it matter what Imogen thought?

"I'd better see what Mum and George are up to." She gave Aaron a quick smile and went back to the living room where her mum was perched on the arm of George's chair.

"…this book's about a cellist who's an assassin." Maxie thrust a copy of *Requiem for Immortals* at him.

"That sounds good." George perused the back. "Sounds up your alley, too, Hazel. Being the women loving women sort and all." He set the book on the table next to him along with the Jodi Picoult.

Beside her, Aaron deflated, and Hazel stifled a smile. Maybe she'd mention that she was bisexual—he'd been pleasant and seemed very kind. Or maybe not. He was also very young.

"And you didn't ask for this, but I saw it on the shelf and thought of you. Well, of Chip," her mum said. She handed him a copy of *How to Socialise Your Dog*.

George pursed his lips. "Chippie don't need no socialising."

"He does," Maxie and Hazel said together.

Aaron nodded as well.

"He's quite off-putting if you don't know him," Hazel said. "Remember how he nipped at Imogen's ankles the other day? If he did that to the wrong person, it might not end well."

"For them or for Chip?" George fired back.

"Both," her mum said. She put the book on George's pile. "I'll leave it here. Maybe you'll run out of other things to read."

Hopefully, for all of George's visitors, that would happen.

Chapter 8
Uncommon Care

Imogen's mobile rang on Tuesday evening as she juggled bags and the front door key. By the time she'd got in the house, and set down her laptop, handbag, and a bag of takeaway, the phone had stopped ringing. She picked it up to check who had called. As she did, it rang again. She pressed the answer button. "Hi, George, how's things?"

"I dunno, Immie. This is bloody terrible, being laid up like this. I've dropped my stick and I can't reach it, and I'm not game to walk to the kitchen to get my sandwich without it."

She glanced at her watch. "Surely Aaron is there by now?"

"He told me he couldn't do tonight. Said someone else would come, but no one has. Pippa left at five."

Frustration surged in Imogen's blood. What could she do for George when she was a seven-hour drive away? And why had no one come?

"Do you have your neighbour's number? Maybe they could come around and help you for a few minutes."

"I don't have that," George said. "Never needed it."

"What about Frank?" She ground her back teeth together in frustration.

"It's the Joker Draw at the pub. He never misses it."

"Maybe he would, just this once. Are you in your chair or in bed?"

"The chair. Mebbe I could make it to the kitchen. Pippa put a sandwich in the fridge. I'm so hungry I could eat the crotch out of a low-flying duck."

She stifled a snort of laughter at the colourful expression. "Please don't move, George. If you fall again, you could really hurt yourself." The name of the obvious person to call hovered in her mind. But Hazel had integrated herself so fully into George's life already. With a guilty start, she remembered she'd never talked with Hazel about the inappropriateness of assisting George with his personal information. Nothing she could do about that right now. "What about Hazel? Maybe she or Maxie would come around."

"I'm sure Hazel would," George said. "But she does enough for me. I don't want to scare her away by asking her all the time."

"This is urgent. You can't stay in your chair all night. Promise you'll call Hazel. I'm going to get onto Coreena Care now."

George agreed, and Imogen ended the call.

Coreena Care's number went to voicemail, but it gave an after-hours number. That, too, rang off unanswered.

Imogen slammed the phone down on the counter. What sort of care organisation didn't answer the emergency number? A bloody useless one, that's what.

She was contemplating dinner, when her mobile rang. She answered.

"Good evening, this is Lucinda from Coreena Care in Dry Creek. I have a missed call from this number."

"Yes. This is Imogen Alexander. I've just had a call from my uncle, George Alexander. He's very disturbed that his evening carer hasn't arrived, and he's alone in the house. He's dropped his stick, and he's not able to pick it up or walk safely without it. Why is there no carer?"

"One moment." Lucinda sounded nervous—as well she might. "Aaron Newell is George's night carer—"

"And he informed my uncle yesterday that he wasn't coming today, but that someone else would be there."

"Uh… I need to check what's happened. Can I call you back?"

"As long as it's within the next five minutes. My uncle isn't able to get food, go to the toilet, or to bed."

"Five minutes." The call ended.

She went over to the window and stared out at the city lights. What a mess.

Her phone rang again, and she snatched it up.

"Imogen, it's Lucinda again. I'm very sorry, but there's been a mix-up. The night that Aaron couldn't work was entered into our system as tomorrow night."

Cold fury sat in a ball in Imogen's throat. That was the most basic of errors, one that even Serenity wouldn't make. She sucked in a deep breath, then another when the anger was unabated. "So how quickly can you get someone around there?" Icy. Polite. It wouldn't help anyone to let rip at the hapless Lucinda.

"Uh, I'm sorry, but we have no one available tonight. Pippa will be there tomorrow morning, and Aaron will be there tomorrow night."

"So you're leaving my uncle alone in a chair, unable to move safely? Unable to get to the toilet, unable to get food? If he falls again, it could be catastrophic. That isn't good enough."

"I called Pippa, but she's unable to come any earlier."

"You must have other people on your books for exactly this scenario."

"There's a nationwide shortage of aged care staff," Lucinda said in a trembling voice. "It's difficult to get suitable—"

"Then pay them more," Imogen snapped. "That's basic supply and demand. Can you go?"

"—I have three small children. I can't leave them."

"Get a babysitter." She thrust a shaking hand through her hair. The inappropriateness of her demand sat heavy in her chest, but what the hell else was she to do?

"I can't. I'm sorry." Lucinda's voice gained strength. "As the mistake was ours, I will go around in an hour to make sure George has food and help him to the toilet and to bed. My kids will have to come with me though."

She pressed shaking fingers to her forehead. "Let me make a call. I'll see if someone can go around, so you don't have to drag your kids out. But, Lucinda, please know that I'm very upset about this. It's unacceptable that a basic administrative error put my uncle at risk."

"I understand. I apologise."

"I'll let you know if I need you to check on George." She ended the call.

Her mobile rang immediately. "Hazel's coming around," George said. "She's on her way."

A shaft of relief went through Imogen and her grip on the phone eased. "Thank goodness."

"Thanks for trying, Immie." George sounded a lot chirpier now he knew the cavalry—in the shape of Hazel—was coming.

Now wasn't the time to remind him she hated the name. "Please thank her for me."

"Will do."

Her stomach rumbled and she eyed the takeaway sitting on the kitchen bench. She'd had her usual fruit and yogurt for breakfast and had skipped lunch. The char kway teow from her favourite Malaysian restaurant was calling her name. But it would have to wait.

She made a quick call to Lucinda to let her know she wasn't needed. Lucinda was effusive in her apologies and said it wouldn't happen again. Imogen pressed her lips together. *Too damn right it wouldn't.* She'd just put the phone down and opened the bag of takeaway when her phone rang again.

"Hazel's here," George said. "She's in the kitchen making me dinner. Some sort of ricey thing, I think. Better than the sandwich Pippa left."

"That's good. Can I talk to her for a minute?"

"Hazel! Hazel!" George yelled.

Had he never heard of holding the phone away before he did that?

"What is it, George? Are you okay?" Hazel's worried voice sounded.

"I'm peachy. Immie wants to talk to you."

"Okay. Let me just turn down the stove." Receding footsteps came over the line, then returned. "Hi, Imogen."

"Hello, Hazel. Thank you so much for going around. I'm sorry, this doubtless messed up your evening."

"It did. I had to wind up the illegal strip poker gambling ring early. It was very difficult getting everyone to put their clothes back on." Laughter threaded Hazel's voice. "No, seriously, Imogen, that's fine. I was home in front of the TV."

"Well, thank you all the same. I really appreciate it—and I know George does, too."

"No worries. When is the replacement carer coming? I can stay until they arrive."

Imogen hesitated. "Unfortunately, they don't have an alternative. I hope George will be fine until Pippa arrives in the morning."

"I'll stay. If you don't mind me using the spare room."

Relief warred with an instinctive refusal. Hazel did enough. Hazel did too much. And Imogen was still concerned about George's dependence on her and what it might mean. "You don't need—"

"I do." Hazel's voice held an obstinate firmness, very different from her usual light, breezy tone. "It's what friends do. And seriously, Imogen, someone needs to be here. It can't be you, unless someone's invented the teleport and forgotten to tell me, and there's no one else. Hang on… I'll put the phone on speaker. George, are you okay with me staying over tonight?"

"Depends. If you burn the dinner, mebbe I'll reconsider."

"Shit. Why didn't you tell me?" The phone was set down with a thump.

"It's me again," George said. "Dinner isn't burning, but it might be a bit crusty. Hazel's gone to sort it out."

"Are you okay with her staying? I'll pay her the Coreena Care rate."

"Perfectly good with me. We can play cribbage. Not sure I want her helping me in the shower though. Not right for a young girl."

"You can shower when Pippa comes." She had to smile. Most women of Hazel's age had seen it all, and some. Hazel was probably no exception.

The sound of uneven footsteps returned. "Dinner's fine. I've stirred it. Have you convinced Imogen to let me stay?"

"I have." George sounded smug. "She's going to pay you the money Aaron would have got."

"No. I don't charge friends. Not for this. Can I talk to Imogen please, George?" A rustle as the phone was handed over, then Hazel's voice came louder. "I won't take money, Imogen. I'm not a carer—just a friend."

"I would have paid Aaron, who apparently is not a qualified carer either." Imogen pinched the bridge of her nose where a headache threatened. "Please accept—"

"No. And if you insist, I will go home."

Her stomach rumbled again, and for a second she was lightheaded with hunger. "Okay. You win. I won't pay you this time—but if Coreena Care lets us down again, and you offer to step in, then I reserve my right to reconsider and insist."

"Are you sure you're not a lawyer?" Amusement threaded Hazel's voice. "Because right now, you sound like one."

"No, just a businesswoman. One used to paying for services." She licked her lips. That hadn't come out right, but those noodles were singing her name. "Thank you, Hazel. That's very kind of you. Please use the spare bed—I changed the sheets before I left."

"Thanks, Imogen. Or if I'm sleeping in your bed, do I get to call you Immie?"

She growled in the back of her throat like Chip. "Don't push it."

Hazel's laughter echoed from the phone before Imogen ended the call. For a second, a visual of Hazel in the bed she'd slept in flashed through her head. That tousled mass of hair, even wilder, and spread over the pillow in the morning. An oversized T-shirt, maybe, slipping off one shoulder. She pushed the images away.

Imogen put the noodles in the microwave and poured herself a small glass of wine. What would have happened if Hazel hadn't stepped in? George was mentally sharp, but it was obvious he was physically frail.

She sipped the wine, absently staring out of the window. Her residential street was quiet; a solitary car slowed for the speed bump, then pulled into a driveway opposite. Who lived there? She didn't know.

What if this happened again—another let down from Coreena Care? There was every chance it would happen. Lucinda was right; the aged care system in Australia was stretched to the limit. George would qualify for a government assistance package, but there was a long wait for the services to start. She couldn't keep asking Hazel to step in.

The wine was gone, yet she didn't remember finishing it. Imogen went back to the fridge for a second glass—something she seldom did.

She took her wine and returned to the window. The Brisbane skyline was visible over the rooftops of houses. Her city. She'd always been a city girl, trading Melbourne where she'd grown up for Brisbane where she'd gone to university, and where she'd remained.

But now, it seemed, that would have to change.

She would go to Dry Creek for a few weeks until George was better able to look after himself. He would doubtless tell her there was no need, that he and Chip would be fine by themselves. But if anything happened to the ornery old bugger, she would never forgive herself. George had been good to her as a kid. It was now time for her to repay the favour.

The second glass of wine disappeared as she thought. She swallowed hard. She'd have to get permission to work from Dry Creek full time. Serenity would have to step up. And there might be some necessary travel.

It wasn't what she wanted to do, but it was the right thing. She clicked her tongue as she thought. It was terrible timing. With the rumour of her boss, the state manager for Queensland, potentially announcing his retirement soon, she was in a position to make a strong play for his post—difficult if she wasn't in Brisbane.

She poured an unheard of third glass of wine.

But she might not be in Dry Creek for too long. George would get stronger, and he'd reach the top of the waiting list for Us Together. If it were three weeks, or a month, well, she could do that. The fine sauvignon blanc was crisp and cold in her mouth. Her goal could still be on track, even if she spent a month in Dry Creek with George.

National manager of Whistlestop convenience stores by forty. She could still do it. The state manager position was a stepping stone, and she was sure she could make that happen.

The noodles she hadn't been able to wait to eat now held no appeal. She went over to the microwave and pulled them out anyway, drowning them in hot chilli sauce.

It would take a few days of organisation, but she could be in Dry Creek in less than a week.

CHAPTER 9
NUTRITIONAL GUIDANCE

Imogen looked around George's spare bedroom. The large room held a queen-size bed, bedside table, and older-style built-in wardrobes. They'd probably been the height of luxury in 1954 when the house had been built. The room would be fine for the few weeks she'd be there.

She went to the smaller, third bedroom. The door creaked open to reveal empty boxes, excess cookware, a garden hose cosied up to a chair with a broken leg, and a sack of dry dog food. No wonder the door was always closed. If given the chance, Chip would no doubt gorge himself until he exploded. The room was at the front of the house. Good. She'd be able to see the driveway and any callers while she worked. She just needed a desk, an office chair, and a side table for her files. All doable.

She went back to the kitchen. George was shuffling from the pantry to the kettle, a jar of instant coffee in his hand.

"Remember to use your stick," she chided him.

He glared at her. "You think I'm a frail old geezer? And me in my prime. Frank and I are thinking of going bowling next week."

"Via the pub, no doubt."

"Course. Equal time at both places. And don't lecture me about mixing pain meds with alcohol. One light beer won't kill me."

"I wasn't going to," she lied.

"Want a coffee? Hazel brought some of Maxie's Anzac biscuits."

"I'll have an Earl Grey, thanks."

His fingers shook as he found the teabag and then spooned coffee into his mug, some of it falling on the counter. Had he always been this unsteady, or was it since his fall? She had no idea. Hazel would know. The thought sat uneasily in her mind. Hazel, it seemed, was the guru of all things George.

While George rummaged in the cupboard for the Anzacs, she picked up the drinks and took them out to the back veranda. The morning sunlight hung low, lighting the cows grazing in the paddock at the end of the garden. A flight of pale-headed rosellas twittered loudly on their fly-past. It seemed a million miles away from her sleek, modern townhouse.

"Would you mind if I use the third bedroom as an office?" she asked. "I'll organise the furniture I need."

"You do whatever you need to be comfortable, Immie. That was Christine's sewing room. I haven't used it since she died."

"Can I move some of the stuff downstairs?"

"Yup. Downstairs is empty. Thought one day, I could do it up for me and Chip. Save me dealing with the stairs."

"We could get you a stairlift."

"No, I like the idea of being downstairs. I don't need all this space up here. Hazel says I could easily rent it."

Hazel again. Was her motivation cheap rent from George?

"Wish Hazel would move in," George said, "but she likes living with her parents."

So not Hazel's plan then, unless she was craftier than Imogen was giving her credit for.

"I'll sort it out this afternoon. Do I need to get groceries?"

"Nah." George dunked his Anzac and took a large bite. "Hazel will drop them off."

She fought the urge to roll her eyes. She was getting sick of hearing that name. "She does a lot for you."

"She does. Lovely girl. And now you're here for longer, she can show you around a bit."

"Maybe. I've got a lot to do first." And surely, Dry Creek hadn't changed that much that she needed a tour guide. Three pubs, the sports club, the RSL, tennis courts, soccer club, the goldfields where you could pan for gold, the Fitzroy River that flooded in the wet season, and a small shopping centre. That seemed to be it. Still, now she had her car here, she could explore a bit. Maybe take George out too.

Her phone rang, and she fished it from her pocket and glanced at the screen. "I've got to take this."

"You go," George said. "I'll be here, watching the birds."

She stepped back into the house. "Hello, Serenity. Is everything okay?" Imogen pictured her assistant sitting on the edge of her chair, winding a section of her hair around her finger.

"Yes." Serenity didn't sound as if it was.

"Do you have questions about today's tasks?"

"Uh, no. That's all fine. But…did you say Richard could use your office?" Serenity said in a rush. "Because he is, and he thinks using your desk means he can get me to do things for him."

She frowned. "No, I didn't. Did he say why he's using it?" It was probably something simple, such as a cabling problem in his office. But Richard had his own assistant—the very capable Vera. He should have no reason to load Serenity with work.

"No. He just went in and then asked me to sort his end-of-month invoices and send them to accounts."

"I'll call HR and see if there's something from them," Imogen said. "Do my work first, and then, if you have time left over, see if you can help Richard. Call Vera if you have questions."

"Okay. Thanks, Imogen." Serenity's voice ticked up at the end.

"Keep at it, Serenity. Richard may not be as polite about the zombie apocalypse as I am."

"Okay."

She ended the call and started browsing desks and chairs online.

Imogen pushed her limp hair back from her forehead. Her new office faced west, and the sun beamed onto the glass heating up the room to an uncomfortable level. She'd have to see if George had a spare fan she could use. But at least now the room was empty of clutter and dog food, dusted and vacuumed, and ready for the furniture which was being delivered tomorrow.

The slam of a car door made her glance out of the window.

Hazel stood by her truck, lifting a couple of supermarket bags from the back.

Imogen met her at the front door. "Hi. Want me to carry one of them up?"

"Thanks, but I'm fine. If you could get the kitchen door, though, that would be good." She walked up the stairs.

Imogen followed. It was impossible not to notice the neoprene sleeve over Hazel's stump and the metal prosthesis that showed beneath the leg of her shorts. Was it uncomfortable on a hot day like this? "It's good of you to bring George's shopping," Imogen said. "But I'll be here for a few weeks now, so I can either order online or else shop myself."

"Up to you." Hazel flashed a smile, and her wild mop of hair swung around her shoulders as she set the groceries on the bench. "But it's no trouble. I always deliver them last on my run so I can visit George." She started unloading the groceries, as if she was in her own kitchen.

"You work for Good 'n Fresh?" Imogen focussed on Hazel's branded polo shirt.

"Yes, part-time as a delivery driver."

That explained the groceries. Imogene noted the chocolate biscuits, TV dinners, and bags of chips. She frowned. A quick tour of George's pantry this morning had seen the lack of healthy food, but she'd put it down to the carers wanting to make life easy. Now she was here, that would change. "Does George normally eat like that?"

"Like what?" Hazel turned, a bag of pasta in her hand. "Like high carbs and snacks? Yes, mostly. But there are vegetables—they're in the other bag."

"He'd be better with a lower calorie diet now he's less active." She picked up the bag of salt-and-vinegar chips. "These add nothing to his diet."

"Except pleasure." Hazel flashed her a smile and pulled out two more bags of the same, putting them in the cupboard. "George is underweight, and according to his GP, apart from his bad hip, he's healthy. No need to deny him these small pleasures."

"He'll stay healthier in the long term if he has more fresh foods and less of those." She nodded toward the pile of frozen dinners on the counter.

"That's true. But until you arrived, he lived alone. And while Mum gives him occasional home-cooked dinners, and he enjoys the weekly senior's special at the RSL, this is what he eats. By choice. He's not a cook—never has been."

"It's not too late for him to learn. I could teach him simple things that are better than"—she picked up the nearest dinner—"fried chicken with mashed potato and gravy. I'll do the ordering this week."

"That dinner also has peas." Hazel put the stack of dinners in the freezer and turned to face Imogen, her butt resting against the counter.

Imogen concentrated on her face rather than her small, curvy body outlined by the tight polo shirt.

"I simply bring George's groceries. So what he orders is what's delivered. I'm not the food police."

"I'm cooking now, so I'm sure George and I will come to a compromise. After all, he likes your mum's cooking."

"Yes, but his tastes are plain. My mum once sent over a casserole with herbs and red wine in it. George didn't like it. And he doesn't like Brussels sprouts, cauliflower, firm-cooked carrots, fresh corn—"

"I get the idea. He's obviously set in his ways. Let me see if I can coax him into healthier eating."

Hazel sucked her lower lip, and Imogen's gaze snapped to the movement. She hadn't noticed Hazel's lips before—indeed, why would she?—but her lower lip was full and plump, and now that she thought about it, usually smiling.

"Good luck with that," Hazel said.

So, she didn't appreciate her interference. Imogen gave a mental shrug. Tough luck. She was George's carer, at least for the next few weeks, and that should be plenty of time to effect small changes that would benefit him in the long run. She'd make a list of dinner suggestions this evening and talk to George about it.

"I suppose you've got a list." Hazel regarded her steadily, head tipped on one side. "George isn't something to be ticked off. He's not on a performance plan, or whatever you do at work. He's someone trying to live his best life the way he wants."

She drew herself up, squaring her shoulders. "I'm doing the best for my uncle." The frosty tone was the one she'd perfected on Serenity over the past few months. But while Serenity would shrink in her seat, and refuse to meet Imogen's eye, Hazel kept her stare on Imogen's face, a faint smile twitching her lips.

"See that you do. He's someone special." She turned away. "I'll just say a quick hello, and then I have to get home. Mum's made macaroni cheese. Not a vegetable in sight. It will be delicious."

Imogen was left in the kitchen, a melting frozen dinner in her hand, with the feeling she'd been bested.

Chapter 10
Flat Pack

Two days later, Hazel stood on George's doorstep. "Waltzing Matilda" chimed out, and Chip barked along. But although Imogen's sleek car was in the driveway, no one answered the door. She rang again and waited. Maybe they were out, gone in the courtesy bus to the pub. She snorted; she could no more see Imogen in the bar of the local than she could see herself in Imogen's no doubt luxurious and high-powered office in Brisbane.

She was about to head away, when the tip-tap of someone coming fast down the stairs sounded, and the door was flung open.

"Hi, come in. Sorry, I was in the middle of something." Imogen stood there, wearing a pair of dark jeans and a loose top, her blonde hair ruffled. The top draped low in the front, revealing delicate collarbones and creamy skin on her chest, but the jeans were tight enough that they clung to her hips, upper thighs, and flat stomach.

Hazel looked away for a second. *Nice.* She followed Imogen up the stairs and stood for a moment watching her pert bottom disappear into the room she used as an office.

"Don't stand there staring," George said. "You'll go blind."

"I think that's something altogether different."

"Mebbe. Mebbe not, the way you were fixed on Immie's bottom." He winked at her.

"That's borderline inappropriate, but I'll let you off this time. And I know you're totally appropriate most of the time."

"I am," George said. "You taught me political correctness."

"I didn't need to teach you to be kind though." She bent to kiss his wrinkled cheek. "You already had that nailed."

He harrumphed, and a faint pink flush stained his cheek. "You being polite? I don't know which way to look."

She sat in the chair opposite. "How's things with you?"

"Good, mostly. Chip's grumpy, but I'm not."

"Chip's always grumpy. What in particular has set him off this time?"

He blew out his cheeks. "Immie won't let him sleep in my room anymore. Says he has to sleep downstairs."

"Why's that?" *Really?* Imogen's control-freakiness seemed to have grown every time she came.

"Because he jumps onto the bed, and it's not his fault, but he doesn't know where not to jump. Landed on my hip once. But if he's shut out of the room, he scratches at the door and whines all night. So downstairs it is."

Much as she'd like to sympathise with George, she had to admit Imogen was right. "Poor Chip. Maybe I'll take him for a walk this afternoon. Would he like that?"

"He'd love it. He hasn't been out for a while."

A crash sounded from the other end of the house. "Dammit!"

Hazel cocked her head. "Imogen's work not going too well?"

"She's finding she's not as competent as she thought in some things. Like assembling her fancy-pants desk that was delivered yesterday. So far, it's taken her two hours to put the chair together, and three for the desk—and it's not done. Last time I asked, IKEA is incompetent, doesn't supply instructions, and didn't provide enough screws and brackets. She got one side on, but it was upside down." He chortled.

She grinned. "Don't act so pleased. It's difficult assembling stuff like that if you don't know what you're doing."

"And she doesn't. IKEA isn't to blame; she is."

Hazel looked toward the crash. A steady stream of expletives came from the room that Imogen had claimed for her office. "Should I offer to help, or will I make things worse?"

"It will be worse at the start, but better in the end. You'll get it done. It will be Christmas before she does."

Hazel stood. A tingle spread from her stomach. Maybe this would be a chance to prove she wasn't the ditzy weirdo Imogen obviously thought she was. She could probably assemble the desk with her eyes closed. "I'll offer. If she turns me down, we'll have a cuppa and a Tim Tam."

"No Tim Tams." George's mouth turned down at the corners. "I ate them all, and Immie says I shouldn't buy more."

"There are ways around that. But first, let me see if I get bawled out the room."

She went down the hall to where the office door stood ajar. The swearing had stopped, but a low and angry muttering had taken its place. Imogen kneeled in the centre of the room. An empty IKEA box rested against the wall, and piles of screws, washers, bolts, and brackets were scattered around. Imogen was attempting to screw one side of the desk to the top. The side wobbled wildly as she looked up.

"You need a hand?" Hazel asked.

"I'm doing okay, but thanks."

Suppressing a smile, Hazel went across and grabbed the side of the desk, holding it steady in position. Imogen flashed her a glance and resumed tightening the long screw that was sticking out at an angle.

"Have you thought of drilling the holes first?" Hazel asked. "You're less likely to split the timber that way."

"I don't have a drill."

"I have one in my truck. Let me grab it."

With a grunt, Imogen made another turn on the screw, and swore as the point poked through the timber of the desktop.

"Let's prop this against the wall, then I'll get it. It will make removing that screw easier, too."

Together, they dragged the desk closer to the wall.

"I'll be back in a moment." Hazel clattered downstairs and grabbed her toolbox from the truck.

When she returned, Imogen was studying the instructions. The paper was crumpled, as if it had seen much use.

"May I?" Hazel held her hand out.

"Be my guest." Imogen stood. "I need water. Want some?"

"That would be great, thanks."

She waited until Imogen had stalked out of the room before she set to work. It was easy enough to remove the misplaced screw with the power drill. She could fill and sand the hole later. Her lips twitched. Imogen had been trying to attach the side back to front. Quickly, she reversed it, and using the wall to brace it, she marked where the screws were to go.

Imogen returned with the water.

"Can you support the side like this?" Hazel asked.

Imogen opened her mouth as if to disagree, but then with a curt nod, she grabbed the side and held it steady as Hazel attached it.

Forty minutes later, the desk was assembled. Hazel wiped a hand over the polished surface. "Nice desk. Very extravagant, seeing as you're not going to be here that long."

"I'm sure George can use it when I'm gone."

"Sure. He can play the stock market and tinker with his foreign investments."

If Imogen's eyebrows went any higher, they'd merge with her hairline. "Is that what he told you?"

"No. I'm joking. If George does that, I don't know about it."

Imogen's mouth opened, and she gripped the desk with both hands. "Actually, I wanted to talk with you about that."

"I know nothing about foreign investment except apparently now is not the time to buy US dollars." There was no reason she could see for Imogen to talk about George's finances…unless she was trying to learn how much he had. She frowned; Imogen didn't look as if she needed money. Her car, her clothes, the snippets she'd learned about her job in Brisbane made it seem she was far wealthier than George.

"George told me you helped him sort out his pension."

"He doesn't have a computer, so I used mine to set him up with an online account."

"So you're now privy to his identifying information?"

"No. I showed him what he needed to do and left him to it. He let me know when he was done."

Imogen's fingers tapped a one-two-three pattern on the desktop. "But it's likely his information is now stored on your laptop."

"I clear my cache after every session. What are you getting at, Imogen?" It sounded almost like an accusation. A curl of irritation lodged in her chest.

Imogen tapped her teeth with a finger. "You do a lot for George. He appreciates that, and considers you a friend…"

"Of course he does. We've been friends for a few years now."

"George doesn't have that many friends. And for an elderly man alone, having someone to run his errands and fix small items is a bonus."

Hazel folded her arms across her chest. "Spit it out."

"What's in it for you?"

For a moment she froze in disbelief at what she thought Imogen had said. "What did you say?" She jammed her hands on her hips.

"I asked, what's in it for you?" Imogen matched her posture.

She shook her head. "George's company. He's a *friend*. We've both been saying this. I could ask you the same thing. What's in it for you that you're appearing here all of a sudden? George never mentioned you until he was hurt, and you haven't visited. You're implying I'm after George's money? Maybe I should throw that question right back at you."

"I have all the money I need. Can you say the same?"

The anger increased from a simmer to the boil. "I'm content with what I've got. With my life, my friends. You don't know me, and you certainly don't know how I live. Money is not everything."

Imogen blinked, as if taken aback by the fierceness of her response.

Good. Maybe she'll think about what she just said, and how bloody rude she was. Hazel increased her glare.

"I didn't mean to insult you."

"Didn't you? Because there's no other way I could have taken your question. What did you expect me to answer? Oh, yeah, Imogen, I'm only cosying up to George because I want his house." She drew a deep breath. "It's doubly insulting when I've just spent an hour putting your desk together. Maybe I should send you a bill as, according to you, I can't have done it purely to be kind." She reached for her drill and crouched by the desk. "I'll dismantle this again, seeing as how you don't appreciate a friendly gesture." She set the drill bit to the screw head.

"There's no need for that."

"Oh, but I think there is." She shot her a furious glance and revved the drill. "What the hell is it with you? You've appeared here in George's life—and yes, he's delighted that you're here—but why now? When you haven't shown your elegant face for so long?"

"It's the right thing to do for family."

"It's also the right thing to visit relatives, at least occasionally."

"There were reasons…"

Hazel took a deep breath. She was being judgemental as hell. She licked her lips. "Your reasons aren't my business. I'm sorry. I shouldn't have presumed to dictate your life."

A brief nod. "Apology accepted."

Hazel waited. Now would be the time for Imogen, too, to apologise, but her lips pressed tight and she turned away.

Fine. She gave a mental shrug. She packed up her tools, and carried them back to the truck, then returned to George.

"Shall I make you a sandwich for lunch?" she asked him.

"Only if you stay and have one with me."

"That would be nice."

She went to the kitchen and pulled out the ingredients for a ham sandwich. Plenty of mayo, no mustard, as George liked. Her hand stilled as she buttered the bread. Sharing lunch with Imogen would be like eating with a cactus—but it was churlish not to include her. She went back to the office.

The end of a power lead waved through the cable port on the desk.

"Can you grab that?" Imogen's voice came from under the desk.

So she apparently had her uses. Hazel grasped the cable, waiting until Imogen had climbed to her feet before asking, "Would you like a sandwich?"

"Thank you, but no. I don't usually eat lunch."

No wonder she was borderline skinny. *Not my problem.* "No worries."

George came out to the kitchen as she was setting plates on the table. "That looks lovely." He sat and lifted the top slice of bread. "Ham *and* cheese."

She sat too. "Of course. What good is a sandwich without cheese?"

He took a bite. "Imogen doesn't agree. She's got me on this low-fat diet. Not even real milk in my tea. It's white-coloured water."

"She's taking care of you."

"She's got me organised. In an hour, she'll be out to make sure I'm doing my exercises. Every day, at ten and two."

"What exactly does she do that she can work from this far away?"

"She's some sort of manager for Whistlestop convenience stores. She's doing well."

That explained a few things. She was obviously used to organising people at work. "I'd hate to be her assistant."

"Her actual assistant doesn't seem too keen, either. I keep hearing Immie on the phone, giving the poor girl directions like she's ordering her to invade New Zealand."

She could imagine Imogen doing that, all clipped instructions and not a please or thank you among them. Imogen needed to loosen up and enjoy life. Hazel shook her head to dislodge the thought of Imogen's piercing blue eyes. She finished the last of her sandwich. "How about we sit in the sun and have a game of cribbage?"

George's eyes lit up. "I'd love that. If you've got time?"

"Depends how long you take to beat me. I'm working at three, but I have until then. You get the board and cards, I'll clear up the lunch stuff." After all, she didn't want Imogen to have anything else to complain about.

CHAPTER 11
INAPPROPRIATE

Imogen walked out of the Telstra store with a new broadband modem under her arm. At least having reliable Internet would be one less headache. Serenity would doubtless agree—the last couple of days had been stressful for them both as Imogen had barked instructions over the phone and her assistant had tried to follow them.

She looked at her list. The only remaining item was returning George's library books and picking up his reservations. If she hurried, she might have time to grab a takeaway coffee—if anywhere in Dry Creek could make a decent espresso. She eyed the major supermarket as she hurried past. Why George insisted on getting his groceries from the small, local supermarket was beyond her, when the nationwide chain had so much better selection.

She put the modem in her car, picked up George's books and went across to the library. She dropped the books in the chute and walked inside. A chalkboard proclaimed *Borrow a Person Day*. A person? What, did you take them home to do your laundry and clean the cupboard under the sink? She went across to the noticeboard. It seemed *Borrow a Person* was a twenty-minute "Ask Me Anything" session. The board gave details of today's people: Sadia, a Muslim woman who wore full burka, and Hazel, a bisexual amputee. Oh! That was unexpected. She glanced around. She doubted there was another amputee called Hazel in Dry Creek. Which meant that George's friend Hazel was bisexual.

Surprise shafted through her and butterflies tickled in her chest. *Hazel is bisexual.* She smashed the butterflies. That changed nothing.

The woman in the burka was sitting in a lounge chair talking to a man with a shaved head and tattoos. There was no sign of Hazel. She found George's name on the reservations shelf, collected his books and took them to the desk where she proffered his library card.

"George's card," the librarian said. "You must be Imogen. Nice to meet you. I'm Hazel's mum, Maxie."

Her mind snapped to attention. The woman in front of her had the same crinkly curls as Hazel, but Maxie's hair was cut much shorter. She had the same brown eyes and a ready smile.

"Yes, I'm Imogen. Thank you for the meal you sent us, and the cake. That was kind of you."

"You're welcome." Maxie turned the books and ran them over the scanner. "These books are obviously for George. He and Hazel are both big readers. Hazel persuaded George to read a romance, and he persuaded her to read a cricket biography—not with great success on either side. If you'd like, I can sign you up as a temporary member while you're here."

"Thanks, but I don't really have time to read for fun."

Maxie tilted her head. "Don't let Hazel hear you say that. She's here today, if you want to see her. She loves doing the *Borrow a Person* days. Changing prejudices one person at a time."

"I saw the sign and wondered if it was her."

"You must have known about her."

"The amputee part, yes. We don't know each other well enough to have known about the other."

"That's why these days are so good." Maxie slid George's books across the counter. "No filter necessary. You'd be surprised at some of the questions she's been asked. But people are mostly respectful. 'Can we have a hopping race?' is the question she gets most from kids." She tilted her head. "She's free at the moment. Want to borrow her for a session?"

"I really have to get back—" Her throat burned at the memory of the last time she'd seen Hazel. The accusations she'd made.

"I can put you through as a temporary visitor…and it's done." She handed Imogen a slip of paper. "She's in the end room. Go on down."

"Maxie, thank you, but I need to—"

"No need to thank me. And George will be fine." Maxie looked over Imogen's shoulder and addressed the person behind her. "Come past. I'll get those books checked out for you."

A teenager sidled past Imogen and put their books on the counter.

Dismissed, she moved to one side. What was the point of talking to Hazel? She saw her often enough as it was, and Hazel wouldn't want to talk to her after last time.

Although, she had to admit she was curious about some things—about being an amputee, not about her bisexuality. Imogen clicked her tongue impatiently. That was not her interest or concern.

She meandered through the stacks, telling herself she wasn't going in the direction Maxie had pointed, but somehow she ended up at the small rooms at the rear of the library.

Hazel sat on a chair beside a small table. The other chair was vacant. She was browsing her phone, with one ankle—the prosthetic one—crossed on the other knee.

Imogen cleared her throat. If Hazel looked annoyed to see her, she'd just smile and keep walking past with a small wave and complete the circuit back to the front door. The apology she hadn't made last time was a ball of guilt in her chest. Should she apologise? Was it too late? She hovered with unaccustomed indecision.

"Hi." Hazel looked up from her phone. "Are you collecting George's books?" No smile, just a neutral expression, one, she realised with a pang, she hadn't seen on Hazel much.

Oh yes, she needed to say something…not an apology exactly, she still held some doubt about Hazel's motives, but an explanation.

She held up the cloth bag of books. "Yes. His new borrowings."

"Then you must have met my mum at the front desk. I can't chat, Imogen; she just texted to say I've been 'borrowed' for twenty minutes."

"Uh, yes. You have." She put the slip Maxie had given her on the table. "I'd say she talked me into borrowing you, but really, she didn't give me any choice. If you're not comfortable with this, I'll just leave."

Hazel put down her phone. "I'm fine. But if Mum pressured you, then please don't feel you have to stay."

Imogen sank into the chair opposite and gripped the bag of books in front of her chest. "I'm glad I've seen you. I want to explain about last time."

"When you accused me of befriending George for financial gain?"

She cringed at the coolness in Hazel's voice. "Yes, that. You have to understand, I don't know you well. People scam the computer illiterate all the time. I was just looking out for my uncle."

Hazel considered her in silence for a few seconds. "I understand that. But you'd met me several times. I've helped you out a few times, and George often. Yet you still assumed the worst. You're also implying you don't trust George with his own decisions."

She licked her lips. "I'm sorry if I offended you—"

"You did." Hazel folded her arms. "But I'm going to assume we both want the best for George. Maybe you could at least try to think the same."

Hazel's set posture radiated hurt. Was it an act? It didn't seem like one. It seemed…genuine. She looked away, to the poster behind Hazel's head advertising story time for preschoolers. "I'll give you the benefit of the doubt. But I have to look out for George. With everyone, not just you."

Hazel's lips twitched. "I can't argue with that, as I'll be watching you, too. Just because you're family doesn't mean you have his best interests at heart."

"Fair enough." She gripped the book bag, preparing to rise.

"You're going?" Again that tilt of the head, so like Maxie's, and a tiny smile. "You've borrowed me for twenty minutes, if you want to do this."

Would it help them get over their mutual distrust? She hesitated long enough that Hazel said, "Only if you want to, of course."

The challenge in Hazel's voice decided her. "I'd like to. But I'm not sure of boundaries in this context."

"There aren't any formal ones. If I'm uncomfortable with a question, I tell you and don't answer. It doesn't happen often."

Imogen crossed her arms over the bag of books. "So I just ask you what I want to know?"

Hazel flicked her hair over her shoulder. "That's the idea. Fire away."

Imogen clicked her tongue as she thought. Nerves twisted in her stomach. Despite Hazel saying it was fine, it felt oddly intimate to quiz someone like this. For a moment, she thought about treating it as a job interview where she was the interviewer, but she thought any HR department would take issue with the questions in her head.

"Does it hurt?" She pointed to Hazel's prosthetic leg. That should be an easy enough question to start with.

"Yes. Not all the time. Not too often now. I remember pain when it was amputated, and phantom pain for a few months after. That's when your body still feels pain in the limb that's missing. But that faded with time. At the end of a long day, though, if I've been active, my nubbin—that's what I call my stump—can swell and make the prosthesis rub. If I'm tired, I favour the leg and my other hip hurts. And sometimes I get bruises from the prosthesis rubbing and that can be incredibly painful and I can't walk more than a few steps."

A few steps? That was all? She thought of everything that made up a normal day. Simple things, like walking to the kitchen for a cup of tea.

Hazel must have seen her expression. "Don't feel bad. Many people assume you get a new leg and that's the end of it. Normal life resumes. But it doesn't. It takes time to adapt, and it's never what most people consider 'normal'."

Right. Hazel wore a resigned half-smile, as if she knew Imogen was flipping through the range of potential responses for the most appropriate: sympathy, horror, shock, comforting, bracing. She glanced away rather than get it wrong. "Do you wear your prosthesis all the time?"

"No. I take it off to shower, to sleep, and to swim. When I'm at home, in the company of people I know well, I take it off for comfort and use a knee crutch to scoot around. Or I hop for short distances. I'm a champion hopper—but that's not a good thing to do—you can stress your other leg too much."

"How do you drive?"

"I have an automatic car. Really, Imogen, these are primary school questions. I expected better from you." Her eyes crinkled as she smiled.

"It seems invasive to ask more. I wouldn't dream of asking you anything like this in any other setting." She fidgeted with a book that lay on the table.

Hazel leaned forward and placed her hands over Imogen's, stopping the fidget. "I've had people asking if I feel ugly, if I've got a partner, how much compensation I got, if I live in a nursing home. If these sessions help even one person understand disability better, then that's a good thing. I had one man ask if he could masturbate over my nubbin. Nothing you could say could equal that. And before you ask, I told him that fetishising me was highly inappropriate, and the library loan was over. He apologised and left. I've seen him since in the supermarket—he hides behind the dairy cabinet to avoid me."

Hazel's fingers were warm and the touch almost too personal for what was, surely, a comforting gesture. Imogen resisted the urge to pull her hand away. She swallowed hard. "Okay, then. How did you lose your leg?" *Lose* seemed such an inadequate word, as if Hazel had mislaid it one day along with her house keys. But it also seemed gentler than asking why her leg had been amputated.

Hazel removed her hands and sat back.

Warmth lingered on Imogen's skin from her touch. No. She was imagining things.

"That's still an obvious question. I had meningococcal meningitis when I was eight. My parents took me to the emergency department, but the doctor said it was stomach flu and sent me home. The delay meant that when I got so sick that they took me back to hospital, the bacteria in my bloodstream had affected blood vessels in my foot and lower leg. They had to amputate to save my life. At first, they thought I might lose my right hand as well, but that recovered."

Imogen fell silent. Imagine a kid with no leg. Reaching down to touch its absence. Suddenly unable to run, to jump, swim, do a million and one active things a kid does.

"Did you have many friends as a kid?"

Hazel tilted her head in the same gesture Maxie had made a few minutes earlier. "Yes. Some dropped me when I was out of school for so long. Others when I couldn't keep up with them in some things. Kids can be cruel like that, whether or not they mean it. But my core group of friends stuck by me—invited me to parties, picked me for their team at netball, that sort of thing. I went to school here, and they're all still my friends, although most of them have moved elsewhere. The city mostly, where it all happens. As you obviously know."

"Do you date?" That question had come from nowhere, sprung fully formed from her mouth. She closed her mouth with a snap, wishing she could take it back.

"Yes, sometimes. Right now, I'm not dating anyone."

The question hovered: *mostly men or mostly women?* Imogen clenched her jaw so the question wouldn't leak through her teeth. It was inappropriate and invasive, even given this setting. Bisexuality didn't involve filling quotas like supermarket shelves. One man and ninety-nine women was still bisexual, if the person identified that way.

"Is it harder to meet someone because you're an amputee?"

"Meet someone, no. Have them not put off by their perception of my disability—sometimes. It's probably close to the amount of people who can't handle my bisexuality, or those who think I'm incapable of holding a proper job." She shrugged. "It's their loss, not mine."

Imogen clenched her fingers so tightly on the bag of books on her lap that her knuckles went white. She, too, had made assumptions about Hazel, although not the ones Hazel was talking about. An uncomfortable feeling made her shuffle her feet, and the urge to escape Hazel's all-too-knowing gaze nearly choked her. She pushed back her chair, preparing to stand. "Thank you for the chat. It was unexpected, but I appreciate your honest answers." The stilted words sounded like something she'd say at the end of a job interview to a candidate she had no intention of hiring.

From the twitch of Hazel's lips, she'd clearly noticed her discomfort. "You're welcome. You don't need to rush off—there's still ten minutes left." She pinned Imogen with a direct gaze. "No questions about bisexuality? I'm sure you're not going to ask if I'm up for a threesome with you and your boyfriend. I've had that question, too."

"That's the last thing I'd ask," she spat.

As Hazel's eyes shuttered, she realised how it had to have sounded. As if Hazel was the last person on earth she'd be interested in.

"Sorry, that came out wrong." She leaned forward. "I meant that I don't have a boyfriend, am not polyamorous, and that such a question would have objectified you in an unacceptable way."

Hazel's expression relaxed. "Thank you for clarifying. For a moment, I thought you found me so loathsome that I wasn't even a suitable sex object." She gestured to her prosthesis. "For all that I'm used to Petunia being a part of my life, thoughtless comments still knock my confidence."

"I'm sorry. That was wrong of me, and this is just one reason this is a terrible idea." The uncomfortable feeling grew.

"I know I'm being irrational. Most women don't want to be treated as a sex object, and here am I with hurt feelings because you didn't mean it that way."

For a second, their eyes met. Hazel's lips quirked, and then she snorted before a full belly-laugh rolled out of her.

Imogen stared as she continued to chuckle, and then the absurdity of it caught her as well. Her lips twitched, and then she laughed, too, her amusement blending with Hazel's.

"We're in the library," Hazel said between giggles. "Stop laughing."

For some reason that made her laugh harder. Imogen gripped the table and took a deep breath. This was inappropriate and undignified behaviour, and not anything she'd do in Brisbane. Heaven forbid if anyone from Whistlestop saw her. She took a deep breath and pushed down the laughter. "Thank you for the chat." She stood, clutching George's bag of books. "But I have to get back to George. And I'm expecting a work call."

That lip twitch again. "Right. Well, I'm sure I'll see you soon, Imogen."

As she headed for the exit, she was sure she could feel Hazel's eyes on her back. And she was sure she was smiling.

CHAPTER 12
RAGE AGAINST THE MACHINE

Hazel entered the break room at Good 'n Fresh ten minutes before the start of her shift. She made herself a cup of tea, grabbed one of the free muesli bars, and sat at the table to check her socials.

She'd just opened Instagram, when someone slid into the chair opposite.

"Hi, Nat." She put her phone down and grinned at her friend. "How's life as the Face of Good 'n Fresh?"

"I wish I'd never won that bloody competition." Nat pursed her lips, her Scottish accent pronounced. "My face is on the back of the bus that goes down my street, and every single customer mentions it as I scan their groceries, and half of them tell me to smile. Why did they pick me to be the Face of Good 'n Fresh?"

"Good teeth," Hazel said. "And probably no one else entered. I know I didn't."

"Still, I got a two-hundred-dollar shopping voucher." Nat leaned across the table. "But that's not what I came to tell you. Did you hear?"

"Hear what?"

Nat glanced around and lowered her voice. "There's a rumour they'll be laying off some staff. Business is down now that Aldi opened—we can't compete on prices. Lucy and Rowan have applied there, and Bec is saying she might retire. No one's been laid off yet, but Troy and Aditi are now casual employees."

"I hadn't heard that," Hazel murmured.

"There's no gossip hotline to the delivery truck."

"Maybe Troy and Aditi going casual will be enough." She fiddled with her phone. She knew business was down. Her delivery rounds were shorter, and people were buying less.

"I hope so." Nat bit her lip. "Djalu's only casual at the abattoir. We rely on my wages."

"You've been here for years. You have seniority. They probably couldn't afford to pay you out! Besides, they can't lay off the Face of Good 'n Fresh."

"They could. And I bet they would, if it came to it."

"I'm only part time. Maybe they'll make me casual. I hope not." The thirty hours she worked was enough to live on—just—and gave her time to grow her handywoman business. Not that she'd been doing much of that lately, what with helping George. She glanced at the clock above the door. "I need to go. Don't want to give them any reason to fire me."

"Go." Nat stood. "My break's over anyway. Back to the trenches."

Hazel watched her leave, worry sitting heavy in her chest. Good 'n Fresh already had competition from the national supermarket that had a store in Dry Creek. Although Good 'n Fresh was pitched as a local supermarket, and many people still preferred that to the larger corporate stores, there was no way it could compete with the new cheap store. She stood and went off to load her truck for the late afternoon deliveries.

"Richard's still using your office. And I've been told I have to assist him first, and you afterward."

Imogen frowned at Serenity's words. "That's not what I was told."

"Vera's gone on indefinite leave. And"—her voice lowered—"I heard the Queensland manager has resigned although there's been no announcement, and that Richard is likely to get the job."

A chill seeped into Imogen's chest. She hadn't expected the announcement for at least a couple more weeks, and she'd thought her efforts at positioning herself as the frontrunner for the position were working. Until, that was, she'd had to come to Dry Creek.

National manager of Whistlestop by age forty. That was the goal she'd set herself, and Queensland manager was an essential part of the process. She'd dismissed Richard as a serious contender. His too-long lunches and unwillingness to take on extra work or adopt new technology should have taken him out of contention. But now, it seemed, he was the frontrunner.

"Assume nothing," she snapped. "The position isn't even vacant yet, and there will be more contenders than Richard."

"Richard asked if I'd like to be his assistant when he gets the job," Serenity said in a rush. "Vera's not coming back. But no one's supposed to know that. I'd get more money."

"Richard is in no position to make you an offer like that." The chill gave way to red-hot anger. "For starters, there's been no formal announcement of Wayne's resignation. Secondly, there are others in Whistlestop as qualified—or better—than Richard, who would probably want to be considered. And thirdly, Whistlestop would probably advertise the position to ensure the best candidate got the job. Any of those scenarios may mean the selected candidate already came with an assistant." *And why would anyone pick Serenity anyway?*

"So, what do I do? Richard's given me a whole heap of typing, and he's going to send me on an Excel course so I can work on the budgets."

Imogen swallowed hard. She should have prioritised Serenity's development plan instead of micromanaging her to avoid the worst mistakes. An Excel course was a good idea. But, a tiny voice argued that trust had to be earned and Serenity had never stepped up. She'd never shown the remotest interest in bettering herself. The zombie game was probably still her most used program. But now Serenity was excited that she might get a better position. Or, more likely, she was simply looking forward to the extra money.

Still. There was no denying she should have invested more time and confidence in her assistant. "Do Richard's work first, seeing as HR said that." She ended the call and drummed her fingers on her new desk as she collected her thoughts. Then she picked up her mobile again to call HR.

"Company policy is that remote workers don't have a dedicated assistant," Carlita in HR said briskly. "They utilise the overflow staff. You'll see that mentioned in your remote working agreement."

"Which is temporary," Imogen said. "One month to six weeks was the agreement. It doesn't make sense to assign Serenity to Richard—he has his own assistant."

"Vera is on indefinite leave. It makes perfect sense to reallocate the resources we have. If you want to use the overflow staff, you can access them through the portal. Turnaround time is usually two to three business days."

"That's unacceptably long. I have deadlines and scheduled tasks that I need an assistant to complete before then."

"I'm sorry." Carlita didn't sound it. "But that's always been the procedure for those who choose remote working. When you're back in the office three or more days a week, you can request a dedicated assistant again."

Imogen gripped her phone hard. This was not a battle to fight right now. "I've heard that Wayne Johnson is on the verge of resigning as Queensland Manager. Can I ask when the position will be opened up? I'm extremely interested in being put forward."

"I believe internal candidates are already being considered," Carlita said smoothly.

"Am I on that list?"

"I can't tell you. The selection process is confidential, of course. But if you are, you'll be contacted in due course."

"Who is involved in the decision-making process?" If she had a name, she could contact them, ensure her name was in the mix.

"I'm sorry, but I can't give out that information. Now, is there anything else I can assist with?"

"No. Thank you for your time." Imogen ended the call. This wasn't good at all. If she was under consideration, she surely would have heard something by now. A tip off from Wayne at the very least. He was her supervisor; he would surely know something. She contemplated calling him and congratulating him on his decision to retire.

After all, if someone as low in the food chain as Serenity had heard, it would be obvious that she would have, too. She mentally shuffled through her tasks to come up with a legitimate reason to call him, then pressed his number.

"Imogen, hello." Wayne's gruff tones came down the line. "What's happening? Must be important for you to call."

He was right. She preferred to work steadily, problem solving her work as she went without outside interference. Unlike Richard, who was constantly in and out of Wayne's office. Realisation made her stomach tense. Maybe that was the issue: she wasn't seen as much of a team player.

"I'm working on the Foodsters contract, specifically the clause about shelf placement. I think we can do better for them, but I want to run it past you first."

"You do? Isn't this something you've handled yourself in the past?"

"Not for as major a supplier as Foodsters. We've guaranteed them end placements during—"

"Imogen, I trust you to do this—you don't need my input. Is there anything else you want? I'm sure you've heard I'm finally retiring—everyone else in the company has, it seems—so there are a lot of ends to tie up and decisions to be made."

"I had heard. Congratulations, Wayne. I wish you many good times ahead. Marybeth will be happy to have you around more often."

"Thanks. Of course you'll be on the invite list to my retirement dinner."

"Any word on your replacement?" She moistened her dry lips.

"Corporate is working through possibilities at the moment."

"Are you able to put forward recommendations? Because I am very keen to be under consideration. I've been working—"

"You?" Surprise shot over the phone line like a bullet to her chest. "But, Imogen, you've only been with the company a few years—"

"Nearly nine."

"—and you're one of our most reliable regional managers."

"All the more reason you should consider me for the position of state manager."

"A new state manager will need the best team under him."

"Or her."

A beat. "Or her," he agreed. "Imogen, I'll be blunt. You're intelligent, efficient, capable, and hard-working. You're one of the best performers on the regional team. But you don't have the social skills we're looking for here. A state manager needs charisma; people skills. Leadership skills, if you will. I don't think those are your strengths. Leaders need to delegate sensitively, soothe ruffled feathers, all the while getting the best from people—our employees and our customers and suppliers."

Her chest pulled tight, and it was suddenly hard to breathe. "Whistlestop sends people on management courses. You've never put me forward. I assumed that meant you were happy with my performance in that area."

"I'm sorry, Imogen, but the short list is already under consideration, and we have the likely person in our sights." His voice softened. "I look forward to seeing you soon, at least at my retirement dinner, when my successor will be announced."

"Thank you. I'll look forward to that, too." What else could she say. She rested the phone on the desk and put her hands over her face. Shame and anger twined in her chest. How could she not have known Wayne thought that of her? He'd never said. Or had he? A memory surfaced, when Serenity had become her assistant, of him telling her that while Serenity wasn't the most experienced PA in the firm, with guidance and the chance to find her level, HR was confident she would shine. And had she given Serenity that chance? No. Instead, she'd given her lists of tasks, micromanaged her to the extreme, and allowed her no autonomy.

But state manager wasn't about coaxing performance out of substandard employees. Surely, it was about guiding the team as a whole in a profitable direction, ensuring Queensland was a growth state for Whistlestop. That had been her focus for the stores she oversaw, not holding subordinates' hands.

Was it too late for her? Wayne's words had indicated that it was. And, reading between the lines, there was every chance that Richard would be the new Queensland state manager. He had those people skills down to an art. Those long lunches...maybe they were client focussed after all. And he'd obviously seen something she'd overlooked in Serenity.

The door banged open and George entered, a mug of tea in his hand. "Thought you might like this. It's that girly one you like." He set the mug on her desk.

The Earl Grey teabag floated in dark and inky liquid. Way too strong. She smiled her thanks. "Are you having one too?" At his nod, she said, "I'll come out and sit with you for a few minutes."

His face brightened. "That would be lovely, Immie."

At least something was going right.

CHAPTER 13
HOT DATE WITH REBEL WILSON

Hazel's old truck predated Bluetooth by several years, so when her phone rang, she had to pull over to answer the call.

"Whatcha doing tonight?" George asked.

"The usual. Hot date with Rebel Wilson. French champagne, she'll hand feed me grapes and chocolate truffles, and we'll discuss the stars, the universe, and the glorious eternity of our love."

"Rebel's married," George said. "That's the only reason I know you made it up. Well, you do have a hot date tonight. Frank and I are going to the RSL for roast night. I'm hoping it's pork—I'll have my teeth in so I can chomp on the crackling. So Immie has the night off. I've booked the two of you a table at Marilyn's at seven and dinner is paid for. About time that niece of mine went somewhere nice."

Oh no. Nerves threaded their way around her body. There was no way she wanted to face Imogen over a linen tablecloth and silver cutlery in Dry Creek's fanciest restaurant. The one the whole town went to for date nights. They would have nothing to talk about, and she'd spend the evening staring at Imogen's coolly disinterested face. "I don't think she'll want to go with me. You should go with her."

"Immie won't want to come with me and Frank. Now, I'll tell her to pick you up before seven. Your old truck probably has glue guns and things all over the passenger seat."

It did, but that wasn't the point. "George, I really don't think—"

"Please, Hazel? Will you do it for me? Immie has been so good to me, and I'd like to do something nice for her. She can't eat by herself at Marilyn's."

She could, and she'd probably prefer to, but Hazel knew when she was beaten. "Okay. But I'm doing it as a favour to you. Not for any other reason." Certainly not because it would make a change to sit across from a beautiful woman and eat a delicious meal.

"Thank you, love." George ended the call, leaving Hazel staring at her phone. It was nearly five. If she was going to Marilyn's for dinner, she'd need time to get ready. It wasn't the sort of place you sauntered into wearing jeans and a T-shirt.

"I appreciate the thought, George, but I'm not missing Brisbane at all. You don't need to buy me dinner. I'll have a quiet evening here with Chip, while you and Frank are out." Imogen pushed her glasses up her nose and rested her hands on the keyboard, hoping George would take the hint and leave.

"I know you don't, Immie, love. See, Hazel has done so much for me, and she doesn't ask for anything in return. I wanted to treat her to dinner as a thank you."

"I'm sure she'd rather go with you than me."

"I want her to feel appreciated. She so seldom dates, and it would give her a boost to be seen with such an elegant woman as you."

"This is not a date! Hazel and I are not interested in each other." She pushed aside the thought of Hazel's compact and curvy body and the sweet slope of her neck that was revealed when she pushed aside that mass of hair.

"Not a date," George agreed. "You're doing this as a favour to an old man. Hazel won't take anything from me. Please, love?"

She closed her eyes in resignation. "Okay. Just because you asked so nicely."

"Thank you. I told Hazel you'd pick her up just before seven. Make sure you wear something nice. Marilyn's is a fancy place."

Imogen perused the scanty wardrobe she'd brought with her. Business suits and casual wear with very little in between. She wasn't sure what "wear something nice" meant in Dry Creek. She pulled out a sleeveless linen dress in a soft shade of blue. Maybe this. If she left off the jacket that turned it into business wear, and accessorised with some chunky jewellery, it would work. She snorted. She was probably fussing over nothing. Hazel would doubtless wear jeans.

Just before seven, she drew the Tesla to a silent stop outside the address George had given her. The two-storey weatherboard house was old, but well maintained, with a cared for and luxuriant garden. She was wondering whether to knock on the door or hoot the horn, when the front door opened and Hazel stepped out.

Imogen caught her breath. Hazel wore some sort of silky dark pants that hid her prosthesis. The pants clung to her upper thighs before flaring softly around her lower legs. A short-sleeve top, shot through with gold thread, clung to her breasts, and her hair was swept back revealing her neck and the curve of her shoulders. Imogen caressed that smooth, pale swoop with her gaze. The clothes made her look older—less the teenager and more the twenty-five-year-old woman she was.

Hazel slid into the passenger seat of the Tesla. "Hi." Her voice held a breathless quality to it, as if she'd hurried, instead of gliding down the steps and into the car. "Thanks for picking me up."

"It made sense. After all, we're going to the same place, thanks to George."

"Thanks to George," Hazel echoed. "Do you need directions?"

Imogen tapped the GPS. "Under control." The Tesla glided away, and, in a few minutes, they stopped outside Marilyn's.

The restaurant was on the ground floor of an ornate Victorian house. Wrought-iron lacework decorated the balcony, and soft music floated out across the manicured garden.

"Do you come here often?" Imogen asked as the host led them to their table.

"My parents brought me here for my twenty-first birthday." Hazel's lips quirked up. "Most of my dates are more casual. I'm more of a beer and pizza girl. Not that this isn't lovely. I'm sure you're used to places like this."

"Somewhat. Entertaining is a necessary part of my job." She pushed aside the thought that it was the part she was apparently not very good at.

"I'm not entirely sure what you do," Hazel said after they were seated and the waiter had brought menus and a wine list. "George just said you're something big at Whistlestop."

"George exaggerates. I'm a regional manager. There isn't a store in Dry Creek, though. I think the closest is Rockhampton."

"I know them. Your job must be full on; it's good of you to make time for George."

She lifted a shoulder in a shrug. "He's family. My parents are always busy with their lives. George hasn't got anyone else."

"He has friends." The sharp edge in Hazel's voice hinted at her hurt. "Me, Frank, Mavis, my parents. Others too."

"Of course. I didn't mean to imply otherwise. But it's usually family that comes charging in at times like this."

Hazel opened her mouth as if to argue the point, but instead picked up the menu. "The seafood is good here. The chef's brother is a delivery driver for the fisheries up the coast. He makes sure Marilyn's gets the best."

"I'll keep that in mind." Imogen perused the menu. It was surprisingly varied for a small town, and seafood was well represented. Prawns, scallops, fish of the day. She looked for the salad options. Crayfish salad. Maybe she'd have that, although… The market price of crayfish was astronomical, so she revised her choice. George was paying; it would be unfair to make him pay for the most expensive item on the menu.

Opposite, Hazel set down the menu. "I'll have the sweet potato soup and then lemon chicken."

Two of the cheapest options. Her estimation of Hazel ticked up a notch. If she was out for what she could get from George, she'd probably have chosen crayfish.

"I'll start with the Caesar salad, then the grilled flathead." It was the cheapest seafood option on the menu.

"Do you want to pick the wine?" Hazel asked. "George was insistent we get a bottle."

She flicked through the small but good wine list and picked a modestly priced sauvignon blanc. They gave their orders to the attentive waiter.

"So." Hazel broke the awkward silence. "Tell me about your life in Brisbane. What do you do in your spare time?" She tilted her head and regarded Imogen with her light-brown eyes. "I'm guessing you go to the gym, run most mornings, attend galleries and concerts. Eat out in places that make Marilyn's seem like McDonald's?"

She laughed. "Hardly. You're right about the gym, though—I do a spin class three times a week, but to be honest, I'm busy with work most of the time." *And look where that's got me. Overlooked and ignored.* She pushed down the bitter thought.

"Weekends? You surely don't work all the time."

"Then I catch up with friends for coffee or lunch. Or we go for walks."

"That sounds very…pleasant." The twitch on Hazel's lips suggested she thought it was anything but.

The waiter returned with their wine and poured a small amount for Imogen to taste. She nodded her approval and waited while he poured them both a glass. "I'm taking piano lessons."

"Oh? Hazel's eyes glowed with interest. "Is this something you've always done?"

"No, I started a few months ago. I bought a piano last month. I wasn't progressing fast without one."

"Bach? Chopin? The classical stuff?"

Imogen allowed herself a secret smile. "No, jazz piano. My aim is to get good enough to play ragtime. Scott Joplin, that sort of thing."

The low lighting picked out golden highlights in Hazel's curls and made those intriguing eyes shine. "I didn't expect that. You seem too self-possessed for that sort of music."

A tickle of pride made Imogen smile. Let no one think Imogen Alexander was predictable. "I aim to surprise. But it's music I enjoy. I can't say the same for Chopin. Doesn't he write mainly funeral dirges? If they're not, they sound like it."

"There's a jazz band that plays at the Beachside Tavern on Sunday afternoons," Hazel said. "They're probably not city standard, but they're enthusiastic. Good sax."

Imogen froze. Did Hazel just say, "Good sex"?

"And a trumpet player."

Right. Not sex then. Imogen shook her head as if to clear her ears. It wasn't like her to mishear something like that. Maybe it was because Hazel seemed so natural, free, and unfettered.

"They do mainly classical jazz, if that's your thing," Hazel continued. "We could go one day, if you'd like. None of my friends really like jazz, so I don't go often."

It seemed a spontaneous gesture. And it would be good to get out a bit more. "Sure, if we can find someone to stay with George."

"Mavis from the RSL would do it as long as the biscuit tin is stocked with chocolate ones."

"I think George already has them on the shopping list." No matter how often she crossed them off, every week, those damn Tim Tams made a reappearance. They were more invasive than Serenity's zombie game.

"He does." Hazel fiddled with her cutlery. Her wine remained untouched. "There are a few things that are standing orders: Tim Tams, block cheddar, baked beans, potatoes, and a family bar of rum and raisin chocolate. I get them automatically for him; he tells me what else he wants. He's added things since you've been here: salad, brown bread, and canned tuna."

"I meant to take over his shopping order," Imogen said. "Thanks for reminding me. I need to encourage him to eat leafy green things—at least occasionally."

"Good luck with that. I tried repeatedly, then gave up. George likes what George likes. And at eighty-four, I figure it's up to him."

"There's no need for you to shop for him. Maybe you could show me where you've been putting the receipts, though, so I can use them as a starting point for my orders." And so that she could see exactly what Hazel was buying. Was she sneaking her own groceries in on George's order? The more she got to know Hazel, the less likely it seemed, but there was still a flicker of doubt. A large flicker, if she were honest.

"I put them on the kitchen counter with his change," Hazel said. "I don't know what he does with them. Throws them out, probably."

The waiter returned with their starters, and Imogen smiled her thanks. She took a tentative bite of her Caesar salad. Her eyebrows raised. The salad was crisp, the croutons fresh, the Parmesan freshly shaved. Shreds of anchovies dotted the plate, and rather than the greasy fried egg she'd expected, there was a soft poached egg. To top it off, the dressing was light, tangy and obviously house made rather than from a bottle.

Opposite her, Hazel's eyes widened as she spooned her soup. "This is delicious."

"Mine, too." She pierced the top of the egg and watched as the yolk oozed sweetly over the salad.

The conversation halted, until, with a sigh, Hazel laid her spoon next to her empty bowl.

Imogen pushed away the rest of her salad.

"I thought you liked it," Hazel commented.

"I do. But I'm not a big eater, and if I finish this, I won't want the main course."

Hazel blinked but remained silent. Thankfully. There were enough people already questioning her food choices—including George, who pressed biscuits on her as if it was his life's work.

"I'm happy it's the weekend. I'm having a massage tomorrow. That's the excitement of my week," Hazel said, as the waiter cleared their plates.

A flash of Hazel lying on a massage table covered only by a towel spun in front of Imogen's eyes. She pictured strong hands kneading muscles, or maybe it was more the relaxation type of massage.

"I treat myself once a fortnight or so. It helps with swelling and circulation."

"Even now?"

"Even now. Having my leg cut off wasn't the end of my problems. Still"—she picked up her wine glass and spun it slowly between her fingers—"that's not very exciting. What might be, though, is I have a date next week."

"Oh?" Something dark beat its wings in Imogen's chest. *Interesting.* What did she care if Hazel dated? It was nothing to do with her. She concentrated on the cursive writing tattoo on Hazel's wrist instead. She still couldn't read it. "Where did you meet them?"

"I haven't yet." Hazel sucked her lower lip. "I'm quite nervous, to be honest. I work with Nat, and it's her friend's brother." She shrugged. "I've seen a photo. He looks okay, but you never know. We're meeting at the local soccer club to watch the game, and then grab a burger. Low key."

"I hope it goes well."

"We'll see. I've learned not to get my hopes up. What about you? Any hot dates on the horizon?"

"No. I haven't had time, to be honest, and, well, I'm up here now. Not exactly sapphic central."

"You'd be surprised. I can introduce you to someone if you want."

"Thanks, but no." She suppressed a shudder. Somehow, she thought anyone Hazel thought suitable was likely not her type.

"There's a librarian where Mum works. Nell. She's Irish, lives here now. Right firecracker."

"You date her then, if she's that great."

"I did. Twice. We're now friends. Would you like me to—"

"No. Thank you." She glanced around. Stilted conversation about dates was not her thing.

"Then as you don't want to date, I'm a most suitable person to hang out with. No pressure, but I can show you around. There's a great swimming beach close by, or bush walks if you like that. We've got a spot opening up on our pub trivia team if you're still around in a few weeks." Hazel's voice tilted up at the end in question. She was as upbeat and bouncy as a caffeinated kangaroo.

"Thanks, but I'll need to get back to Brisbane at some point soon. Remind them who I am." *Right.* Even though it seemed they'd all but forgotten about her already. Even Serenity was defecting.

"I thought I'd see if George wants to come to the beach tomorrow. It's Goldilocks weather: not too hot, not too cold. Not too windy, certainly not raining. Sunny with light cloud." She sounded like the Bureau of Meteorology.

"He'd like that, I think. Particularly if you take his grumpy dog, too."

"George won't go without him. I'd invite you along as well, but my truck only has two seats. Unless you want to drive?"

That tip-tilted question in Hazel's voice again. She opened her mouth to refuse—she could have an uninterrupted working day, despite it being Saturday—but the words stalled in her throat. "That could be pleasant. I haven't been to the beach in a long time. And if you're talking about Breakwater Bay, then I remember how beautiful it is. I'm happy to drive."

"We have a not-date then." Hazel shimmied her shoulders. Was she genuinely excited at the outing, or was it all fake enthusiasm?

"A definite not-date." Imogen raised her glass for Hazel to clink with hers.

Hazel's eyes sparkled and her ridiculous hair bounced on her shoulders as she leaned forward. "There's the Beachside Tavern for lunch, too."

The waiter arrived with their main courses and set them down.

Hazel eyed her chicken. "That's if I can eat anything at all tomorrow after this huge meal." She waited until Imogen had picked up her cutlery, then ate a piece of chicken. "This is delicious. I think we owe George a day out after this."

Her shimmery top was as eye-catching as the highlights in her hair. Imogen took another sip of wine to ease her dry mouth. In the low lighting—wall lights flickering a candle-like glow—Hazel seemed ethereal. Her crazy hair was a shimmering mass of golden-brown, highlighting her pale skin and the swoop of her top past her collarbones.

A pang of longing to wind one of those long corkscrew curls around her finger overtook her. Her hand shook, and she placed her glass down. Since when had Hazel been someone she would have found attractive? Her glance skittered down to Hazel's lips, curving sweetly over her wine glass.

Since a few minutes ago, was the answer.

And that was a complication Imogen didn't need.

The Tesla drew to a halt outside Hazel's home. The flickering light of the TV showed through the living room window.

Hazel glanced across at Imogen, who sat with both hands on the steering wheel, looking straight ahead.

Hazel hesitated. "Thanks for dropping me home."

Imogen turned her head to stare at her. "It's on the way. Thank you for a pleasant evening."

"No worries. I'm sure George will be pleased we went out. I think he's concerned you work too hard."

One manicured eyebrow lifted. "And he wanted to thank you for your help."

Hazel raised a shoulder. "Sounds like he wanted to do something for both of us." She glanced at the living room light again. Should she offer what was on her mind? Would Imogen think it too date-like? Or worse, would she consider it an invitation for something else? "Would you like a coffee? Mum made oatmeal cookies this morning. She'd be happy to see you again." That should make it clear there was no ulterior motive.

Which is almost a pity. Her gaze dropped to Imogen's lips, and she wrenched her eyes away. It was a good thing she had the blind date next week—it might take her mind off Imogen, and their not-date tomorrow. With George as chaperone.

Imogen's fingers tapped a pattern on the steering wheel. "Thanks, but I better get back in case George is home."

"Of course. I'll see you tomorrow for our beach trip."

Imogen leaned across, and Hazel's heart stuttered. Was Imogen going to kiss her goodnight? She froze in her seat. What would her kiss be like? How would she respond? But then Imogen reached for her bag on the floor behind the centre console. She pulled out her phone. "I should take your number." She activated the phone and arched an eyebrow expectantly.

Oh. Amusement shimmered in Hazel's chest. What had she been thinking? She was obviously the last person Imogen would want to kiss. She reeled off her number.

Imogen's fingers flashed over the keypad, and Hazel's phone pinged. "Now you have my number. Is ten a good time to pick you up tomorrow?"

"Uh, sure. That's fine." She reached for the door handle. "Thanks, Imogen. I'll see you then."

She exited the car, and turned to watch it glide away, before letting herself into the house. A not-date tomorrow. For a moment, her mind spun into what-if territory. What if it *was* a date, just the two of them—sand, sun, salty skin, and kisses?

She snorted. She could hardly blame the two glasses of wine she'd drunk with dinner for her out-of-control thoughts. And while Imogen was definitely gorgeous in a stand-offish sort of way, she was so far out of Hazel's league she might as well be in the stratosphere. No, she would be friendly and no more tomorrow, and channel her hopes into the blind date later in the week.

CHAPTER 14
WIND, HAIR, AND GLASSES

Imogen sat with George on a bench overlooking Breakwater Bay. The tide was out, and the wet sand gleamed in the sunlight.

Hazel returned from the store behind them, three ice cream cones in her hands. "I love the Italian ice cream shop here. It, alone, makes the trip worthwhile. Here"—she handed one to each of them—"lemon sorbet for Imogen, and choc-mint for George."

"Thanks, love." George took his cone. "What's yours?"

"Mango and coconut." Hazel licked a circle around the top of her cone where the ice cream was threatening to drip.

Imogen froze. Hazel's tongue, licking oh-so-delicately around the cone was doing strange things to her belly. A twitching, fluttering feeling twirled around her insides. She looked away, toward the ocean.

"Good ice cream, love." George gave a piece of his cone to Chip, who sat on the bench next to him.

"It is." Imogen quickly took a bite. The cold instantly hit her head, but she ignored it and took a second nibble. It was better than drawing Hazel's attention to her flustered state.

"Why don't you both take a walk on the beach?" George said. "I'll be fine here in the shade."

"I'm fine," Imogen said quickly. "You go on, Hazel."

"It's no fun on your own." George's bushy eyebrows raised.

"That's okay." Hazel's lips turned down. "It's hard for me to walk on sand. One leg sinks more than the other. Besides, you know how sand gets *everywhere*. Everywhere means something different when you've got a prosthesis. My sandcastle days are over, unfortunately."

"Were you good at that as a kid?" Imogen took another bite of her sorbet.

"The best! I won all the competitions. Turrets, moats, windows, drawbridges, arches, multi levels. The secret is to find the right sand: not too dry so it crumbles, not too wet so it slumps. Rougher sand is best."

"Maybe that's where you got your handyperson skills from," Imogen said.

"Maybe." Hazel shot her a grin.

"So, we're all going to sit in a row like a senior citizen's bus trip?" George thumped his stick on the ground. "Not much fun for you girls."

Girls. Imogen suppressed her eyeroll and patted George on the knee. "I like sitting here with you."

"Don't patronise me." George scowled. "What harm can I get to here? Don't you sit with me all the time at home? You and Hazel go for a walk. Up to the lighthouse, mebbe. Go anywhere that isn't here. I'll be fine for half an hour or so. It's lovely to be out."

Hazel stood. "Okay, I can take a hint. To the lighthouse I go. Would you like to come, Imogen? The view is worth the climb. Sometimes you can see dolphins and turtles."

"Sure." Imogen dropped the remainder of her cone into the bin and stood, too, dusting off the front of her navy pleated shorts. "Anything for you, George."

She glanced over her shoulder as she strode off with Hazel. George had switched benches and was already talking to an older woman with a small dog.

Imogen suppressed a smile. Chip's bristling posture meant he was doubtless already growling. "Did George get rid of us so he could talk to the woman with the dog?"

Hazel, too, stole a look. "Probably. We must be cramping his style."

George would talk to anyone—Imogen had been embarrassed as a kid when he'd strike up a conversation with the person at the next petrol pump, debate pasta brands in the supermarket, or adamantly state to the bank teller that AFL footy was for sissies who wouldn't play rugby. "He could simply have said," Imogen muttered. "No need to send us off on a hike."

"Don't feel obliged. If you'd rather have some alone time, don't worry about me." Hazel increased her pace. Her metal prosthesis flashed in the sun as she powered up the hill.

Imogen walked faster to keep up with her. "I didn't mean that. I'm happy for your company. As George keeps telling me, I don't have many friends. Here, that is. I don't have many friends *here*."

Hazel glanced across with a quizzical expression. "You have lots of friends in Brisbane? I had you pegged as the loner workaholic."

She jammed her hands in the pockets of her shorts and cursed the flush that crept up her neck. "You're not so far off, although I catch up with my best mate Jess most weeks."

There was a momentary silence from Hazel. The unspoken "and?" hung in the air.

"And colleagues from work. Social tennis." Except there hadn't been time for that for a few weeks. She huffed a breath. Make that months.

Hazel nodded. "Your work must be pretty full on, if that's all you have time for."

All? Imogen compressed her lips. That embellished list was more than she would normally do, even if work wasn't the all-encompassing thing it was. Although, would it be now? The golden promotion had slipped away. Not surprisingly, there had been nothing from HR, nothing more from Wayne, except a request for quarterly figures. Nothing about her performance, her prospects, her request to be added to the consideration list.

And if Richard became her new boss, she was sure Whistlestop would fall further into being a jolly boys' club. It already hovered on the edge of that. And if that happened, her chances of ever becoming state manager would be hacked down like George's weeds by Hazel's whipper-snipper.

Hazel was still waiting for her answer. "It has been, yes. But this time in Dry Creek is making me reconsider a few things. Work related things." Where had that come from? She'd barely acknowledged it to herself, and now she'd blurted it out to the most unsuitable person she knew—Hazel, with her complete lack of business knowledge. Hazel who had no reason to know about Imogen's problems. "Er, the lighthouse isn't far now. I wonder if there'll be dolphins?"

Hazel's lips twitched. "It's okay. I won't ask about your work. But if you ever do want to talk, I'm happy to listen."

Static buzzed in her head. *That's a hard no, Hazel.* "I went whale watching on the Sunshine Coast once. We only saw one whale, but there were many dolphins riding the bow wave of the boat. It was magical."

"Right." A small smile. "I often see them up here. Let's hope we get lucky."

They reached the headland and stood at the lookout, scanning the ocean.

"There!" Hazel pointed past the rocks at the bottom of the cliff. "Three dolphins."

The dolphins' graceful arched backs curved out of the water in a synchronised movement. Imogen sighed. It was a special thing to see—animals in the wild. She looked across at Hazel who was watching them. Her lips were parted and her wild hair was whipped into a frenzy by the breeze. Hazel grasped it with one hand and held it bunched on her nape.

Imogen forced her gaze back to the ocean and was rewarded by the dolphins surfing an incoming wave. She turned to point them out to Hazel, when the breeze snapped a tangled mass of curly hair in her face.

"Sorry." Hazel grabbed at her hair again, but the wind kept pulling it free. "I swear I'm going to shave my head."

"Don't you dare." She removed a bunch of hair from across her cheek. "It suits you."

"You like it even now, when it's harassing you?" Hazel tried to step further away but stopped. "My hair's caught on something. Maybe your glasses."

Imogen felt around the hinge of the frame. "It has." She tried to free it, but Hazel's hair was as strong as wire. She removed her glasses and turned her back to the wind, forcing Hazel to turn too. They stood close together, and their fingers reached simultaneously for the glasses.

"Sorry," they said at the same time, and then, "You do it."

Imogen laughed. "Let me try." She tried untangling the brown strands, but they were wound tighter than cotton on a spool.

"Just tug it," Hazel said. "It doesn't matter if it breaks. I have plenty more where those came from."

It took some untangling, and then Hazel grew impatient and yanked at her hair. She separated hair and glasses, leaving several long strands wound around the hinge of Imogen's glasses.

Hazel's mouth turned down. "I'm sorry. I shouldn't have stood so close. You'll probably need to cut them off."

When Imogen replaced her glasses, the hairs tickled the side of her face. She shivered. It seemed somehow intimate, as if Hazel's hair had brushed her skin in another way. She took a deep breath. "Maybe we should get back to George."

"We should."

Together, they turned and walked down the path, slower this time.

George was where they had left him, but his new friend and her dog had left. Chip sat on George's lap, king of all he surveyed.

"Did you have a good walk?" George looked from one to the other.

"We saw dolphins!" Hazel mimed them leaping through the waves.

"That's nice. Not many dolphins in Brisbane, are there, Immie?"

"Not in the Brisbane River, no. But there are in Moreton Bay." Not that she'd seen them. Not that she went down to the coast that often.

"Are we going to the pub for lunch?" George looked from one to the other. "I was talking to a lady while you were walking. She says they catch the fish locally. Been a while since I had good fish and chips."

Imogen looked out over the bay. In her quest for healthy eating, she wouldn't cook chips for George. Oh, she was sure he dived into a plateful whenever he went to the RSL with Frank, but there was no need for her to encourage him.

"Oh, neither have I!" Hazel said. "I hope the fish is whiting. With lots of chips and aioli." She had to have caught the frown on Imogen's face, as she added, "And a big salad."

George struggled to his feet. "Shall we go?"

They found an outside table where Chip could sit at George's feet. Imogen placed the order at the bar. Three fish of the day: two battered, one steamed, two with chips and salad, one with just salad.

Hazel returned with their drinks: one beer, and two soda, lime, and bitters.

"Nice to see you taking a day off, Immie," George said. "You work too hard."

She forced a smile. He was right, but until she figured out where her career was going, she had no option. Nearly nine years with one company, not wasted, but not appreciated either. She sipped her drink, wincing at the amount of lime cordial in the soda. Still, George was right. This day off reminded her of everything she'd missed out on. Sunshine, a day at the beach, a relaxed lunch. Scratch relaxed lunch. Any lunch was unusual these days.

Maybe it was time to consider a change.

CHAPTER 15
MALE AND STALE

Hazel sipped her beer and watched the on-pitch action. Soccer wasn't really her thing, but Angus's excitement was fun to observe. Right now, he was on his feet, screaming for his team. The striker got the ball and banged it past the opposing goalie. Angus leaped to his feet with a fist pump, then abruptly groaned and sat again.

"What's wrong?" Hazel asked. "It was a goal, wasn't it?"

"Offside." Angus swallowed a mouthful of beer. "Dammit."

Hazel remained quiet. She knew enough about soccer to know she'd never understand the offside rule, no matter how many times she watched the scene in *Bend it Like Beckham* with the French mustard, the teriyaki sauce, and the sea salt. She squirmed on the hard bench and focussed on the game.

Angus's team lost two-one at full time. He turned to Hazel. "Shall we get out of here?"

"Sure." They'd hardly exchanged a word in the last couple of hours, what with his focus on the game. Maybe now, they could get to know each other better. "How about the burger place by the river?"

He didn't answer, but instead led the way to his car.

Hazel hesitated. "My truck's here. I can follow you."

"Seems silly to take two cars," Angus said. "I'll drop you back when you're ready."

She shrugged. He was Nat's friend's brother. Nat wouldn't have sent her off with a psychopath.

A couple of minutes later, they passed the turnoff for the river. Hazel tapped his arm. "It was that way. Still, I think you can take the next left."

"I thought we'd go to my place."

Uh, no. "I prefer the river. The burger place should be quiet, easier to talk."

Angus changed gear, then glanced across at her with a big grin. "Who said anything about talking?"

She froze in her seat, alarm bells clanging. "That's what people do on a date. They talk, get to know each other. Find out if they want to see more of each other."

Angus gripped the steering wheel. "Uh, Hazel, you seem very nice, and everything, but I'm not looking to date anyone."

Right. Things were becoming as clear as glass. And she needed to talk with Nat about her friend. "What were you expecting from today then?" She kept her voice even. "Someone to sit next to at the game?"

The tips of his ears flushed red, and in that instant she felt almost sorry for him. It didn't take a genius to figure out what he was expecting. How quickly could she remove Petunia to thump him?

"Uh, I thought you wanted…that is, I was told you were after…" He scratched the back of his neck and his flush deepened.

"You think because I'm an amputee, I must be desperate for sex?"

"That's what… Uh, no. You're prettier than I expected."

She took slow, deep breaths. Should she eviscerate him now or give him one final chance?

"Why invite me to the game if all you wanted was a hook-up?"

"Uh, because women want—"

The simmering impatience snapped. "What women want is not to be generalised or taken for granted. We're not sitting around waiting for a man to notice us. Yes, women often hook up. But I don't like your assumption that's what I wanted. Communication is sexy. Consent is sexier. Why did you assume that's what I was after?"

Angus pulled the car over to the curb. "I should shut up now. I'm sorry, Hazel. This is a misunderstanding. You seem like a nice person.

If you'd like, we can go for that burger. Or I'll drive you back to your ute."

His hangdog expression tamped her anger somewhat, but she didn't want to hear what other offensive generalisations he may be about to come out with if he said more. "Please take me back to my car." She pressed her lips and her legs together and stared out through the windscreen.

"Of course." He flicked a glance at his mirror and pulled out from the curb to do a U-turn.

The screech of brakes sounded loud, and Hazel closed her eyes, waiting for the crash.

❖•❖

"I would be present at the assessment," Imogen said into her phone. "But my uncle lives alone, hence the request for some home help."

She stared out of the window as she listened to the Council's response. Hazel's truck pulled up, and she got out, before going around to the rear and lowering the tailgate with a clang. Then she pulled out some planks and clattered a lawnmower down to the verge.

Imogen forced her attention back to the phone call. "Assuming the assessment identifies a need for home help, how long before the package starts?" She tapped her pen on the pad as she listened to the non-committal explanation about wait times and prioritising care needs.

Hazel yanked the cord and, with a roar, the mower fired up. She pulled some earmuffs from the truck and trundled the mower to the edge of the lawn.

"George needs assistance with housework, mainly. He can't bend easily, so cleaning the shower, skirtings, and floors is difficult. He also needs grab handles installed in the shower for safety."

Hazel pushed the mower past Imogen's window, and the roar of the engine blotted out the Council's reply. "I'm sorry, would you mind repeating that?" She got up and slammed the window shut with more force than was necessary.

"I said, if needed, we can coordinate with tradespeople to do that," was the response. "If approved, the cost is covered by the package."

The mower ground to a halt with a screech of blades on rock. Hazel backed up and restarted. The noise reverberated through the window like a 747 coming in to land.

"I'm sorry, I'll have to call you back when it's quieter."

"I understand," the coordinator said. "Tradies always come at the worst times, don't they?"

"You're right about that." Imogen clenched her jaw so hard her teeth hurt.

Call ended, she stomped through the house and threw open the front door.

Hazel was marching back and forth, pushing the lawnmower and it wasn't until Imogen went and stood directly in front of her that she stopped the mower and removed her earmuffs.

"Can you please stop that racket! I was on a call and couldn't hear a thing."

"Hello, Imogen. How's your day going?" Hazel shot Imogen a narrow-eyed glare which set Imogen's nerves even more on edge.

"Can you do this another time? I would really prefer if you could call ahead to make sure it's convenient."

Hazel raised an eyebrow. "It's convenient for me. George is fine for me to come whenever it suits."

Sweat beaded her upper chest, shining in the vee of the red-and-black Good 'n Fresh branded polo shirt. Her legs, too, were distracting. Both of them. Why did she feel the need to wear such short shorts? It showed off one muscled and curvy leg from the hem of the shorts to her ankle, and the other from the shorts down to where her leg was covered by the sleeve at the top of her prosthesis. Her thighs had a golden tan from all the time she spent outside. Imogen focussed on them, mentally comparing them to her own pale limbs.

"It's customary to look at someone's face when you're talking to them," Hazel snapped.

Heat spread up Imogen's neck. "I'm sorry." She switched her gaze to Hazel's face.

"Thank you." The anger softened in Hazel's face. "I'm sorry for making noise, but I'm not a tradie you book. I'm a friend cutting George's grass, and I have to fit it in around my other commitments.

So I've come straight from an early shift, and I want to get this done so I can go home."

"You're not the only one with commitments. I was trying to set up home help for George for when I return to Brisbane. I had to end the call."

"I'm sorry." Hazel didn't look it. "I can cut the rear lawn first, but in twenty minutes, I'll be back here."

"Maybe I should just add lawn care to the home package." Imogen ran a hand through her hair.

"You could," Hazel agreed. "And George will pay fifty bucks per hour from his package. That fifty could be used for other things." Her lips twisted. "If George doesn't want my help, then I'll use the time for myself. Get a massage. Go for a walk. But if *you* don't want me here because it inconveniences you…well, I don't think that's your call to make. Last I checked, this was George's house."

"If you could just be considerate to my work—"

"Be considerate? That's ripe. Today is not a good day, Imogen. Today is a fucking shit of a day, when I would rather stay in bed, put the covers over my head and scream. Today is a day when I took a stronger analgesic than normal just so I could walk without too much pain. Today, I only dragged myself out of bed because my friend George needed me, and if I didn't do his grass today, it would be another week.

"You may not realise this, Imogen, but my life is a struggle every day. With pain, with things taking longer than they do for an able-bodied person. I struggle to accept help. I struggle with well-meaning people who try to help, even when I tell them I'm fine. And yeah, I sometimes even struggle with the unfairness that I don't have a leg, and that life will always be harder for me than for someone like you. And today is a hard day." She turned her hand to stare at the tattooed writing on her wrist. "See this? It says, *I can do more.* It's my mantra. But right now, I can't do more. I can barely get by."

Imogen stared at the cursive writing. To think she'd assumed the tattoo was something shallow, some pop culture saying. She closed her eyes briefly. It seemed she'd underestimated Hazel—again.

Hazel heaved a shuddering breath. "So, I'm sorry, but you being slightly inconvenienced by lawnmower noise doesn't even rate a mention." She pulled the earmuffs from around her neck and hung them on the bar of the mower. "Tell you what. I'll go and have a cup of tea with my friend, and you can make your call in peace. Then, when you're done, you can mow the grass."

With a final tight-lipped glare, Hazel pushed past her, but not before Imogen had seen the brackets of pain on her face and the sheen of tears in her eyes.

Shit. Imogen stared at Hazel's retreating back. Her head was up, her back straight, but now, as Imogen looked closely, there was a tiny hesitation each time Hazel shifted her weight onto the prosthesis.

She'd messed up big time with Hazel. Because she presented in such a positive, cheerful way, Imogen had assumed that was how she was. That her amputation really didn't bother her. That she had no pain. That life for Hazel was…not easy, but that it was how she wanted it to be.

What else did Hazel struggle with that she wasn't talking about?

Hazel, who could probably access disability assistance for herself if she wanted, was helping George instead.

She inspected the lawnmower. A cord to pull start. What looked like a grip handle to get it moving. Well, she could do this.

Squaring her shoulders, she started the mower and settled the earmuffs into place.

Chapter 16
Instant Karma

"I shouted at her, George." Hazel wiped her eyes with the back of her hand. "There was no need."

Below them, the roar of the mower continued. So far, Imogen had run the self-propelled mower into the edge of the raised bed and overshot onto the gravel pathway. The cut was patchy but the front lawn and most of the back lawn was done.

"There was every need, love." George rested both hands on his walking stick. "Immie's got a good heart, but she's a bit unthinking at times. Impatient. She needs to be reminded that not everyone has it as good as her."

"I could have been nicer about it."

"Mebbe. But mebbe your problem is you're too nice, too accommodating. Even to me. Put yourself first sometimes, Hazel love. You didn't have to do my grass today. You could have told me it was a bad day. I would have understood."

He would, too. George had seen her bad days before. When he'd been more mobile, he'd come around to her home and bullied her into going for a walk with him. Or to play cribbage if the pain was stopping her walking.

"You try too hard to be the same as everyone else. When will you accept that you are different, whether you want to be or not? It's not weakness to ask for help, love. Look at me. I ask you all the time." He sucked his teeth. "Mebbe I should stop."

"No! Don't stop. You help me, too, George. You help me focus on someone other than myself. If not for you, and my parents, and the library *Borrow a Person*, I'd probably be a ball of self-pity huddled in the corner."

"Never that." George reached out a wrinkled hand and took hers. "Now, if Immie's stopped murdering my lawn and breaking your mower, let's see if she wants a cuppa, too. She's doing her best, you know. She didn't have to upend her life for me—but she has. You and her…mebbe you've got more in common than you know."

Hazel looked down to where Imogen had stopped the mower and was trying to get the grass catcher off. "I don't think so. She's intelligent, successful, gorgeous looking…" What part of her mind had that sprung from? She hadn't meant to say it.

George's eyes twinkled. "So you have noticed, eh? Was beginning to think you were blind as well as missing a leg."

"George!" She thumped his arm. "You don't need to pass that on to Imogen. But she's everything I'm not. I'm an aimless supermarket worker with a small business that I can't get off the ground no matter how I try. I'm still living at home in the small town I've lived in all my life. If you look up 'failure' in the dictionary, it says 'Hazel Lee'."

"Rubbish. Don't define yourself like that. Now, why don't you call down to that niece of mine and offer her a cuppa?"

Hazel nodded.

Instead of calling, she went downstairs and out to the lawn.

Imogen looked up as she approached. Sweat darkened her T-shirt, and a pink flush stained her cheeks under her dishevelled hair. "How does this catcher come off?"

"There's a release button on the other side," Hazel said. "Leave it. Come and have a cuppa with me and George."

Imogen set her jaw. "I'll finish this first."

"The grass will still be there afterward." She hesitated. "I'm sorry for snapping at you. No matter how bad my day, I shouldn't have taken it out on you. I had a bad night last night, too."

A smile flickered over Imogen's face. "And I should have been more considerate of you. A lot more. I'm sorry, Hazel. I've been berating myself since you went off." She hesitated. "Was yesterday your date? I hope that wasn't the bad part."

"It didn't help." Hazel pushed her hands through her hair.

"Oh?"

Hazel huffed a breath. "Apparently, he thought I'd not worry about the getting-to-know-you part and would be happy to go straight back to his place. He wasn't wanting to date, just to hook up."

"And that's not what you want?"

"Not with him." The remembered annoyance made her cheeks flush. "When he was bumbling around trying to explain without making it worse, he said, 'I was told…' and then shut up. And I can't help but wonder *what* he was told and by whom, or if he just assumed I was desperate for sex because I only have one leg."

"That makes no sense."

"It wouldn't be the first time someone's assumed that." She sighed. "He was very apologetic."

"It sounds like a horror date."

"Horror not-date. But then, when I'd turned him down, he said he'd take me back to my car. He was so flustered he didn't look properly before doing a U-turn and pulled out straight in front of a police car. The cops nearly T-boned us."

"Really?" Imogen's lips twitched. "What happened?"

"He got done for driving without due care and attention, and making an illegal U-turn. They searched his car—found nothing—but he also got booked for driving an unroadworthy vehicle. He has to replace two tyres and the windscreen. I don't know how many demerit points that will be, but from his expression, it's a lot."

"That sounds like expensive instant karma to me."

"I felt a little sorry for him," Hazel said. "Not sorry enough to accept his invitation for coffee another time, though." She switched her gaze back to the mower. "Leave that for now. Come and have a cuppa with George. He's been lecturing me about all sorts of things—if you're there, he'll probably stop."

There was a smudge of dirt on Imogen's sharp cheekbone, and lawn clippings in her hair.

Very cute. Hazel blinked. Imogen, cute? She shoved her hands in the pockets of her shorts. She had to stop thinking that.

"Sure," Imogen said. "And we can have some Tim Tams from the packet George thinks I don't know about."

She laughed. "I'll tell him to find a better hiding place."

"Emma?" Imogen smiled at the middle-aged woman on the doorstep. "Thank you for coming."

"No problem," Emma said. "It's good to help the poor old dears."

"George isn't exactly an old dear," Imogen said. "He just needs some help with the heavier housework. He's not as agile as he was."

"That's why I'm here." Emma slipped off her outdoor shoes, replacing them with soft ones.

Paws pattered on the wooden boards, and Chip barrelled around the corner, teeth bared in a snarl, heading straight for Emma's ankles.

"Chip! Stop that! Sit!" Imogen stepped in front of Chip and pointed a finger at him.

Chip took no notice, simply swerved past her and continued his glowering dance around Emma.

"Oh no!" Emma backed up until the wall stopped her. "Please, can you get rid of that dog?"

"I wish I could," Imogen muttered. She made a grab for Chip's collar and missed. "He doesn't bite. Well, not often."

"Oh…" Emma's eyes grew rounder. "Please, take him away."

At her second attempt, Imogen managed to grasp Chip's collar and she dragged him down the hall and shut him in her office. She returned to where Emma waited. "Sorry about that. He's secured now. I'll make sure he's shut away before you come next time."

"Please do." Emma dusted the front of her dark pants. "It's in the information leaflet: all animals are to be secured before we arrive."

"Of course," Imogen said. That was something she should have thought of. "Come and meet George."

George was puttering in the kitchen.

"Nice to meet you, you poor old duck," Emma said. "I'm here to make your golden years a little easier."

Really? Imogen kept her face blank with an effort.

George's eyebrows lowered to his nose. "My best years are ahead of me. But if you can clean my shower, I'd be right grateful."

"That's what I do. Now, how about a cuppa before we start so we can get to know each other a bit?"

Two hours later, Emma left with promises of returning in a week's time. She'd been efficient, cleaning the shower, the skirtings, and doing all the vacuuming and mopping—everywhere except the office.

The office! Shit. She'd forgotten about Chip. Imogen hurried down the hall and opened the door.

Chip was sitting on her office chair in a cloud of dog hair. A glistening puddle decorated the wooden floor under her desk. Imogen sighed. Chip was a vindictive horror—he'd been outside for a pee just before Emma had arrived. But there was no point telling him off.

She found some wipes and cleaned up his mess.

No doubt satisfied he'd made his point, Chip trotted out and found his master.

Imogen went out to George. "Emma did a good job."

"Humph. But she talks too much. And I don't like being called an old duck, either. Not polite."

"I'll mention it to the agency. But you've got a sparkling shower, and all the dog hair's gone."

"There wasn't much anyway. You keep things good and clean, Immie."

"But I can't stay here forever, George. In fact"—she dragged in a deep breath—"now that you've got Emma to do the heavy things, and you're okay by yourself, it's time for me to go back to Brisbane. Go back to the office." And try to salvage her position in the company, if that was even possible.

"I suppose you must, but I wish you could stay longer."

"I wish I could too." With a start, she realised that was true. Although that was probably to avoid the situation in the office. If it were possible to work from here yet keep her career on track, well, she would. But now she had to salvage what she could from Whistlestop and then make some serious decisions about her career.

"I'll have Hazel, still," George said.

Hazel. "Yes, Hazel. But is it fair to rely on her so much? She struggles, you know, with her leg."

"I know that. And I don't ask her to do anything. She does what she wants."

"She's a giver. The sort of person who will always do more than expected." When had she realised that? When had she stopped mistrusting Hazel's motives?

"I know. Glad you're seeing that too. She's never asked me for anything more than a cup of tea and a biscuit. Not many like her in the world."

There weren't.

"How do you feel if I go back on the weekend? Emma will come next week. And you have your personal alarm."

"Not sure I like that Emma, but you go back, Immie."

"I'll visit again." And she would. It wouldn't be years between visits.

George sighed. "I love that you came for as long as you did. My own brother didn't come."

No surprise there. Her parents were busy and self-absorbed in their own work and careers. As she had been, Imogen realised with a start. And as she would have to be going forward.

CHAPTER 17
RETURN TO THE SALT MINES

IMOGEN STRODE INTO WHISTLESTOP'S HEAD office the following Monday morning and hoisted her laptop bag further onto her shoulder. She nodded to the receptionist and walked the corridors to her office. It was shortly before eight, so many of the offices were empty, or contained small groups of people catching up after the weekend.

Imogen rounded the corner to her office. The lights were dim, the office equipment in sleep mode, and, as expected, Serenity's desk was deserted. A pink cardigan hung over the back of her chair, and the desk held a litter of Disney figurines.

Imogen's lips tightened. It seemed Serenity had gained no professionalism in her absence.

She flicked on the light in her office. A high-end laptop sat on the desk next to a stack of paperwork, and a suit jacket and tie hung on a stand in the corner. Her rather basic executive chair had been switched for a leather and chrome model. Imogen glanced at the papers on the desk. As she thought; Richard had yet to vacate her office.

She pushed his laptop to one side and put hers down in its place. She'd make coffee and go see HR.

"Hi, Imogen. It's good to see you back." Carlita moved a stack of files from the chair opposite her desk so Imogen could sit. "Want a coffee?"

"Thank you, but I've just had one." No need to mention she'd had two while waiting for Carlita to arrive.

"I just need you to sign your new working arrangement—it's the same as before, that is, you're once again working full time from the office. Is that correct?"

Imogen smoothed down her skirt. "That's right. I just went past my office, but it seems Richard is yet to vacate it."

Carlita's gaze shifted to one side. "There's no need for Richard to move again. We've given you a new office—it's further around on the east side of the building, next to the marketing department."

"I would prefer my old office back."

"Richard's assistant, Serenity, sits outside that office. It's easier to move you rather than two people."

So Serenity was to remain with Richard then. That was okay. Maybe she'd have someone more efficient assigned to her.

"Who's my new assistant?"

"With the short notice of your return to the office, we've no one available at present. We'll place a recruitment ad. You can, of course, have input into that process and we'll make it a priority. In the meantime, you'll need to continue to use the overflow staff."

"That isn't working too well." Imogen kept her gaze on Carlita's face. "Surely there's someone I can use at least part of the time. Even Serenity—she knows much of my work."

"I'll put in the request to Richard. If he's agreeable, we'll have Serenity allocate some hours to you each week. Now"—Carlita stood and rounded her desk—"let me show you your new office."

Her new office had barely enough room for a second chair on the other side of the desk, and there was no outside window.

Carlita shuffled her feet. "I realise it's not what your position merits. As soon as a larger office opens up, we'll move you."

"What about Richard's old office?" She turned a slow circle. The overhead light flickered, and the noise coming from the open-plan marketing department echoed in the space.

"That's been given to the new office manager."

"I see." She didn't, but she would be professional about this.

"I'll ensure that the recruitment ad for your assistant runs this week, and I'll send maintenance around to attend to that light." Now that the awkward things were done, Carlita managed a smile. "I'll let you settle in."

"Thanks, Carlita." She offered a nod in return.

Once Carlita had gone, Imogen returned to Richard's office to collect her laptop. Luckily, Richard hadn't yet arrived, but Serenity was at her desk.

"Hi, Imogen. Nice to see you back." Serenity gave an awkward sort of half wave.

"It's good to be here. How's things with you?"

"Fine." Serenity arranged her glow pens in a neat line. "Richard's good to work for."

"HR is going to check if you can spare a few hours to cover some of my tasks. It would be just until they recruit a new assistant. I hope you're agreeable to that."

"Uh, I guess. If Richard says it's okay. He keeps me pretty busy."

Imogen swung the laptop bag onto her shoulder. "Well, it's good to see you. I'll be in touch about covering my work."

Back in her new office, she arranged her desk to her satisfaction, then made a trip to the stationary cupboard for supplies.

With an irritated glance at the noisy marketing department outside her door, she got to work. Wayne thought she wasn't enough of a team player, and that her management style was lacking. Well, starting from now, that was going to change. She sent a meeting request to Wayne to catch up now she was back in the office. And she scheduled a visit to the Enoggera store with a suggestion that they have a team lunch.

And if Whistlestop still didn't recognise her skills and abilities?

Well, she would come up with an alternative plan.

CHAPTER 18
A WAY THROUGH THE MAZE

Hazel juggled four bags of shopping as she trudged up the cracked concrete pathway to one of Good 'n Fresh's customers. There was no one home, so she left the shopping in the carport.

Her phone rang as she got back into the delivery truck. She glanced at the screen. "Hi, Imogen. How's the big smoke?"

"Big. Not too smoky." Imogen's husky voice came down the line. "Have you got a moment to talk?"

"I'm at work," Hazel said. "But I have a few minutes."

"I'll make this quick. I need to ask you a favour."

There was a pause on the line, and Hazel imagined Imogen in a dark business suit sitting at a massive desk. There would be a single silver-coloured pen on a pristine pad. Nothing like the cheap biros that littered Hazel's home workspace.

"George is having a full assessment for the age care package next week, but I can't come up for it. While I could attend by phone, I think it would be good if someone was there in person. I was wondering if you—"

"Of course I can. When is it?"

"Next Wednesday at 10:00 am."

Hazel checked the calendar on her phone. "I can do that." She entered it in.

"Thank you," Imogen said with a sigh. "I appreciate that. And, Hazel, please send me an invoice for your time."

A spurt of irritation rose in her chest. "I've said before: George is a friend, and I don't charge friends for things like this."

"But this isn't—"

"Imogen. This is non-negotiable."

A pause. "I'm sorry. I don't mean to insult you. In my world, this would be a business transaction."

"Not in mine." The irritation withered. Imogen was trying.

"Maybe if there are any minor modifications to the house needed, that's something you could do as part of your business?" Her voice was tentative, as if she were expecting to be shot down on this as well. "After all, someone has to do it and be paid. Why not you?"

Hazel pondered. "Let's see what they come up with first, but that's a good idea."

"You're welcome. I'll forward the details of next week's assessment. Thank you, Hazel." Another hesitation. "How is George doing?"

She hadn't called him? Hazel pushed down the niggle that said it would have been easy to do. People had lives of their own. They did the best they could. "Fine, mostly. He's still not happy with Emma. She cleans just fine, but he gets annoyed she's so condescending, calling him a poor old thing, and telling him to be careful with sharp knives."

"What do you think?"

"She is a bit controlling, but I think she works mostly with people who are less independent than George and maybe need reminders."

"I'll take that under advisement. Maybe there's someone else who can come instead."

The sound of a person laughing came over the phone. "Someone's happy in your office," Hazel said.

"Too happy. It's difficult to concentrate at times. I have the door shut." Imogen sighed.

"You and your high-powered job," Hazel teased. "In the meantime, I'm still running around Dry Creek in scruffy shorts and a T-shirt, mowing lawns and delivering groceries."

"Sometimes, I think you have the better option." Another burst of laughter came over the line, accompanied by clapping.

"It's the marketing department's morning tea. Which is followed by the marketing department's lunch, the marketing department's afternoon tea, and the marketing department's after-work drinks. At least the last one takes place outside the office. Mostly."

"It sounds like a fun place to work. Do you go along to the drinks?"

"No. I'm still working when they leave. And I'm not part of their department, so they don't invite me."

Oh. Hazel pursed her lips. Surely, that shouldn't stop them inviting a colleague who shared their office space. It didn't sound very inclusive. Maybe Imogen's sometimes prickly demeanour had dissuaded them. Or maybe—

"I wouldn't go anyway," Imogen snapped. "So you can stop feeling sorry for me."

"I wasn't," she lied. *Not much, anyway.* "I need to go, Imogen, or I'll be running behind. I'll let you know how the assessment goes. Maybe I'll call you one evening, and we can have after-work drinks together. Me on my veranda, you in your apartment or townhouse, or wherever you live. We can compare views." Now what had made her say that?

She could picture Imogen's surprised expression in the hesitation that followed. Then Imogen said, "That's a good idea. Let's make it after George's assessment."

Warmth trickled through her. A chat with Imogen about George, sure, but maybe it could be a chat with a friend, too.

Imogen, a friend? Well, maybe.

"Wine and Korean food." Jess held up a bottle and a takeaway bag. "Because no one's heard from you for days and I'm channelling my mother and worrying if you're eating right and brushing your teeth."

Imogen held the door wider. "I'm doing both, thank you." She bared her teeth like Chip. "Whiter than white, see?"

Jess poked her in the waist. "And thinner than thin. Are you eating, Imo? Because it doesn't look like it." She brushed past her and set the wine and food on the counter. "Seriously, is everything okay?"

"Yes. No." She was tempted to blow off Jess's concern, but if she couldn't talk to her best friend, who could she talk to? Her parents weren't an option. They would be bracing and tell her to harden up. As if she wasn't rigid enough already. There was obviously no one she could confide in at Whistlestop. Hazel? She pushed it to one side. Hazel wasn't confidante material.

But Jess was.

"You pour us a glass while I change, and then we'll talk."

When she returned in a soft T-shirt and drawstring shorts, Jess had the wine poured and a bag of corn chips open on the counter.

"Spill." Jess sat on the couch and drew her legs up under her. "What has my friend strung tighter than Coco Gauff's tennis racquet?"

Imogen picked up her wine and sat next to Jess. "Work. What else? And to a lesser extent, George." She turned the wineglass in her hand, wondering where to start. "I returned to the office this week."

"That's good, right?" Jess leaned forward and rested a hand on Imogen's knee. "You're interacting with people again, not just George. You can swoop in and remind them of your awesomeness, which is harder to do on a Zoom call."

"That was the idea. But Richard has taken over my office and my assistant, and I've got a smaller office next to the marketing department. The rest of my team are at the other end of the building."

Jess frowned. "Go on."

"They're recruiting a new assistant for me. I've approved the ad, and hopefully I'll get someone efficient this time. But I'm trying to put myself out there more. Wayne said"—she swallowed hard as the words stuck in her throat—"my lack of people skills are the reason I wasn't considered for the promotion. Apparently I don't interact enough."

Jess bit her lip. "And did he offer any solution? A management course?"

"No. He said I'm appreciated for the work I do, but I don't have the leadership skills to go further. So I'm trying to address it myself. I'm arranging face-to-face meetings instead of Zoom. I'm stopping by colleagues' offices to chat. But it's harder when they're at the other end of the building from me." She didn't mention the surprise on people's faces when she dropped in to see them. Yet that was what Richard and others did all the time.

"You've been there, what, nine years?"

"Pretty much. And I'm now questioning if it's the right place for me." There. She'd said it out loud for the first time. The churning in her stomach that had stolen her appetite all week intensified.

"Do you want to fit in with Whistlestop's culture, or do you want somewhere that will fit in with you? Because from what I know of you, my friend, your leadership skills are fine."

"I don't know. I'm starting to think I need to put myself out there more. I always thought keeping my head down, doing the work, getting the results, was all I needed to advance." Her lips twisted. "It's not. Richard has worse results than me. He just schmoozes more. And he's likely to get the promotion."

"What you see as schmoozing, management sees as building connections, encouraging people to produce their best." Jess squeezed Imogen's knee. "I'm not saying that's the right way—I wish my team would use Zoom more often instead of long working lunches—but it's obviously the Whistlestop way."

"I've never been a people manager. I'm not sure I want to be."

Jess was silent for a minute. "Imogen, this is coming from a place of love. You know that, right?"

She nodded.

"There are jobs out there that will appreciate your ethics—employers who will be delighted at how much work you churn through, and won't care how you do it. So, if that's how you want to keep working, I'm sure you'll find a better fit for yourself somewhere other than Whistlestop. From what you've said, they don't appreciate you—and there's a lot you do brilliantly. But, equally, maybe it's time to consider a softer approach in some ways. I know you and love you, my friend, but sometimes you can be too blunt. A little too direct. And not everyone appreciates it. I mean, I do. But not *everyone*."

"It's how I am."

"Right there. That's the bluntness and inflexibility I'm talking about. Maybe that's what Whistlestop sees, too."

"So you think I should start buying flowers for the assistant I don't have yet? Paint my office pastel pink? Start asking my team to tell me what they're feeling, and replying that I sense a problem with their budget figures?" Imogen sat back and folded her arms. "That's not me, Jess."

"Now you're being ridiculous, and you know it." Jess tried a smile. "Lavender is a better colour for you than pink."

Imogen blinked back the hot tears that threatened. Even Jess was suggesting she try things differently. But wasn't that what she was doing already—albeit in a smaller way?

She rose and went to get the bottle of wine and topped up their glasses. "Is that how you manage?"

"Not entirely. Part of being a successful people manager is figuring out tailored approaches to individual people. Some respond to the carrot, others to the stick. But all respond better if they can see you're at least trying to understand and get to know them."

"This isn't Counselling 101. Workers—"

"People. Not workers. People with lives outside of work: families, friends, pets, interests. Work doesn't necessarily define us."

"People, then. I'm not sure they want me chatting about their partners, and how naughty Pixie shat on the rug."

"Some won't. Some will. I'm not saying you need to turn yourself inside out, Imogen. Just that management is different these days. It can be softer without losing authority. Australia is, generally speaking, a very casual work environment. We don't call our bosses Mr or Ms Smith. We call them Rob or Trish. We might not be friends, but we're friendly. I call my gynaecologist, accountant, and bank manager by their first names. Aussies don't Sir and Ma'am anyone."

Imogen sat back on the couch again. Her head spun with Jess's words. Was she right? The pang of criticism—however gentle, however well-meaning—still stung. Was that what the likes of Serenity felt when Imogen corrected her? Maybe.

Probably.

No wonder Serenity had never performed her best for Imogen. By all accounts, she was doing fine with Richard.

"This is a lot to take in."

"I know, and I'm sorry to lay it on you. But you asked. I'm not saying I'm right either, but it's something to think about."

Her glass was empty. When had that happened? "We might need another bottle of wine."

"We might," Jess said. "Good thing I took an Uber over here."

Imogen rose and went to her wine rack, selecting a bottle of pinot noir. She couldn't remember the last time she'd opened a second bottle of wine in an evening.

"The thing is, I'm almost certainly going to have to stay with George again." She twisted the cap and refilled their glasses. "His care assessment is tomorrow, but I've been told he'll have to wait for a vacancy to open up in the schedule—and it could be weeks. He's barely okay by himself—he's still very frail and I worry about him."

"It takes a long time to recover from a fractured hip," Jess said.

"He's got friends that go around to help—that was fine when I thought it would only be for a week or two, but we can't keep imposing on them. I should go again, at least for a couple of weeks."

"Friends? Including Hazel?"

"Yes, Hazel. She's very caring. I misjudged her at first—you were right, Jess, she doesn't seem to have any ulterior motive. Not that I can see, anyway."

"Are you getting on with her better?"

"Mm. She's enjoyable company."

"So not the ditzy young thing you first thought then?"

An image of Hazel's laughing face and wild hair rose in her mind. And her compact body and muscled limbs. A swell of warmth perfused her body. Hazel was many things, and Imogen was appreciating them more. And she now knew the upbeat perkiness that had so irritated her was Hazel's way of dealing with the world, of dealing with her disability.

"No, she's tough. She has to be." If Hazel was her subordinate, how would she have managed her? Would she have made allowances for her disability—not that she thought Hazel would have ever asked her to. Sure, she'd have made any HR-specified modifications, but would she have understood that it took Hazel longer to do some things? That her mental health needed care as well? That while she was insistent she could do most everything, some days were harder than others, and other days were bloody impossible?

With a curl of shame, she realised she would have been as impatient with Hazel as she was with Serenity.

"I'm worried that another two weeks in Dry Creek will negate anything I've achieved being back in the office." Which wasn't much, if she were honest.

Jess bit her lip. "Maybe it is time to look around."

"I am, already. But until things are settled with George, it's hard. Not many places allow remote working, at least at first. Not in my field, anyway."

"Is there anyone else who can visit George instead of you? What about your parents?"

"It's term time. And mother told me they're off to build houses in Cambodia in the next break. I honestly don't know how useful they'll be. They call the handyman if they want the nails banged down on their deck."

Jess rolled her eyes. "Right. The idea of volunteering is better than the actual experience. We have a few volunteers like that. Can you redirect them to visiting George instead?"

"I tried. Their flights are booked."

Jess's lips twitched. "We seem to have backed ourselves into a corner. Let's eat."

Her stomach was churning so much she doubted she'd manage much. It had been the same since she'd returned to Brisbane. No wonder Jess thought she was skinny. She focussed on her friend. "And you can tell me what's new in your life. What's new in the world of non-profit?"

"How about I tell you about my dating life?" Jess smiled. "In the interests of expanding past work chat."

"I didn't know you had a dating life. Neither of us do."

"Well, my friend, I've been practicing what I've just preached to you. And dating I must do. So far, it's not going well. But I will persevere."

And that, Imogen thought, was what she needed to do, too. Keep winding her way through the maze, negotiating the twists and turns and obstacles until, hopefully, she was spat out the far side in one piece.

CHAPTER 19
GETTING OLD

"Grab handles in the shower and toilet, certainly," Annie, the social worker, said. "Installing a small ramp instead of the two steps down to the balcony. And George's smoke detectors aren't compliant. All of that we can address."

"That's okay," George said. "Mebbe Hazel can do that for me."

"Once your package is approved, you can pick your own contractor. So, if Hazel is registered with us, she can do the work."

"I've got the forms. I just need to complete them." And increase her public liability insurance and obtain WorkCover. Which cost money she didn't have.

"George, I'm concerned about you managing these stairs to the front door," Annie said. "It's not safe using your stick. Would you consider a stairlift?"

"Ride up and down in a chair like an old person?" George snapped.

"It's not about age; it's about making it safe and easy for you to keep living in your home." Annie offered him a smile.

"I'm not leaving." George banged his stick on the ground. "Chip and I will live out our days here."

"And that's what we're trying to ensure."

Hazel cast a worried glance at George. His hand shook on the stick.

"The stairlift would be good, George. You could get out into the garden more often."

"What's downstairs?" Annie asked.

"Garage, a second toilet and shower, and the fourth bedroom," Hazel answered.

"I thought mebbe when I was old, I could move down there," George said. "Rent out the top floor. Be nice to have more income."

Hazel exchanged a glance with Annie.

"Let's have a look," Annie said.

It took George a few minutes to negotiate the stairs. Hazel bit her lip. He *had* got slower, and she hadn't really noticed. And she was now the one who walked Chip and took him outside. Chip had had a few accidents, too, when George hadn't been able to take him out.

Annie looked around the downstairs. "You've got a decent space here. Good-sized bedroom, French door to the outside. You could even have a small patio to sit out there. And the plumbing is here for the bathroom already. It should be easy enough to put in a small kitchenette."

"Is that work the package would pay for?" Hazel asked.

"Not all of it—especially as George would then rent out the upstairs. But some of it, sure. Would you consider the stairlift in the meantime, George?"

"Suppose Chip might like it."

Annie's lips twitched. "Sure he would. Anyway, I think we're done here. George, I'll write up my recommendations, and we'll see how quickly we can get you started on the package."

When Annie had gone, Hazel helped George back up the stairs. "Cuppa before I go? I'm delivering groceries this afternoon."

"That would be nice."

Hazel made the tea and retrieved George's hidden pack of Tim Tams and took them out to the balcony. "That space downstairs will make a great granny flat."

"I was going to ask if you'd do it for me." George slurped his tea. "Paid. I won't let you do it otherwise. There's nothing you can't handle. And if this Annie gets some of it paid for me, that would be good."

A frisson of pleasure rippled through Hazel. A project like this? Start to finish? Why, that would give her business a real boost. Get her name out there for bigger projects. "I'd love to do it. And I'll give you a good price."

"Was always going to do this when I got old." He pursed his lips. "Guess I'm old."

"I gave my friend shit for suggesting Angus for your date." Nat plopped down opposite Hazel in the break room. "She said her brother's not normally such a dickhead."

"He wasn't a total dickhead," Hazel said. "Just unthinking, pigeonholing, sexist, and ableist."

"That equals dickhead to me. But if you want to give him another shot, he's apparently keen to see you again."

Hazel shook her head. "No way. I've sworn off dating for a while. There's no one I want to date, and definitely not Angus." An image of Imogen flashed through her mind, short blonde hair, those razor cheekbones, and intent expression. *No way.* She didn't want to date Imogen. She focussed on Nat. "I haven't seen you around lately."

Nat's mouth turned down. "They cut one of my shifts. I'm hoping they don't cut more. It's quiet in the store. Rowan says Aldi is really busy. They're hiring. I don't want to go there, but if I lose any more shifts, I'll have to consider it."

"My hours are unchanged," Hazel said. "But there's less for me to do. Which is sort of good. I don't have to hustle as much to get the deliveries done."

"Three supermarkets in a town this size is a lot."

Worry flickered again. They wouldn't close, surely? But if Nat was losing shifts…

"Did you see you're nominated for employee of the month?" Nat inclined her head to the noticeboard. "It's between you and Sven in the deli. That fifty-buck voucher could be yours!"

"Sven will get it."

"Don't be too sure. This is what, your third nomination? You know what they say about three times."

"Always the bridesmaid, that's me." Hazel ripped open a bag of chips. "Want some?"

Nat took a handful. "If you could change anything about your job right now, what would it be? I'd win the lottery so I didn't have to work at all, but I don't suppose that counts."

"Not much," Hazel said. "Although, I'd like for my small business to get bigger so I don't need to worry so much about getting shifts here."

Her fingers tingled with anticipation. Maybe, thanks to George, that might just be about to happen.

CHAPTER 20
COMPLICATED DECISIONS

Imogen sat at her dining table, absently picking at a plate of chicken and rice. The Brisbane city lights sprawled in front of her, but she barely glanced at the view. Her laptop took all her attention.

The executive position alert she'd set up had delivered two potentials. One was a sideways move into a regional manager position with a national shoe store chain. Brisbane based, but with frequent travel to Far North Queensland. The salary range was below her current one, but if the position offered her growth, she'd suck that up.

The second though… As she read the advert again, her phone rang, and she spared it an irritated glance. The screen said Hazel. She picked up.

"Chip bit me today," Hazel said. "It didn't end well."

"Oh no." Imogen grimaced at the phone. "Are you okay?"

"I'm fine. I'm not calling to say I'm suing George, if that's what's got you worried. George says Chip should sue me."

"I don't think Chip has legal capacity. So, what happened?"

"For context, Chip has already bitten me twice since he came to live with George. The first time on the right ankle, the second time on the left." Hazel paused, as if waiting for a response.

Oh! Her left ankle. Of course. "So he bit you once, and Petunia the second time?"

"That's it."

Imogen settled back on her couch; the phone pressed to her ear. She could imagine Hazel's grin.

"And he's never bitten me again until today. Poor Chip. The memory of that second bite must have faded, as he bit me on the left calf. Or where my left calf would be, if I had one. I was wearing my sleeve and leggings, so it wasn't as obvious though."

"Is he all right? Although I don't think I should worry about Chip; he worries about no one except himself."

"He broke a tooth." Hazel sighed. "He was whimpering, and George was frantic with worry. We took him to the vet. Chip had the tooth removed this afternoon under anaesthetic and he's staying overnight. We'll pick him up tomorrow."

"Can George afford that?"

"He says he can. And he'd do anything for that damn dog. But George is upset, so I'm staying with him tonight. I thought you might like to know."

"Thank you. That's very good of you," Imogen murmured. The glowing laptop screen seemed to draw her in. That position, the second position. It would solve a few things, not just her growing annoyance with Whistlestop.

"So, what are you up to?" Hazel's upbeat tone lifted higher. "Drinking champagne at a gallery opening? Cruising the Brisbane River? Eating something that isn't from a can?"

"Answer D: none of the above," Imogen said. "I have cold chicken and rice, and I'm at home browsing the Internet."

"Chicken and rice is much better if you microwave it," Hazel said. "And add lemon and chilli sauce."

"It was warm when I started eating."

"Oh, I'm sorry. I didn't mean to interrupt your dinner. I'll leave—"

"No, it's not you. It was already cold before you called." Imogen picked up her fork and moved the rice around on her plate.

"What's so interesting on the Internet?" Hazel asked. "Click bait? Sam Kerr's back flip?"

Imogen clicked her tongue. She wasn't ready to tell anyone except Jess her thoughts about job seeking. "Just browsing the aged care website," she said instead.

"Oh! That reminds me. George's assessment was yesterday." A pause. "Do you want that drink now? You in Brisbane, me in Dry Creek? Two friends having a drink together, but seven hundred kilometres apart?"

Imogen laughed. "We could do that. Just let me pour a glass of wine."

She returned a minute later with a glass of pinot noir. "What are you drinking?"

"A wheat beer. It's pretty good. Not as fancy as your wine, though."

"You overestimate my city life," Imogen said. "It's the end of a bottle I started with a friend a few days ago. So, how did the assessment go?"

"It went fairly well," Hazel said. "The social worker said he'd qualify for a package. But she flagged that George struggles with stairs."

Imogen shuffled on her chair. She'd noticed that but hadn't offered any solutions. A worm of guilt made her stomach ache. She should have said something.

Hazel related their thoughts about the stairlift and George moving downstairs.

"That sounds potentially good," Imogen said. "As long as there was a quiet tenant upstairs. I can't see George being happy with a noisy family."

"He wants me to do the work," Hazel said in a rush. "It would be arranged through the aged care provider—as long as they agree. I know you don't think much of my skills, Imogen, but this is something I can do. I'd get qualified plumbers and electricians where needed, but the bulk of the work is within my capabilities."

"Why are you telling me this?"

"Because I thought you might object. And if you're going to talk George out of using me, then I'd rather know now. So I don't get my hopes up. A project like this would be a dream for me." A sigh. "I don't want to be a delivery driver forever."

As for talking George out of it, Imogen didn't think that was possible…but could Hazel handle the work? A major renovation was a long way from reattaching doorknobs and mowing lawns. Hazel had talked about this, though, when they'd been out for dinner. How people didn't believe in her capabilities. Wasn't that what she was doing right now?

"Imogen, I would never rip off George. Anyone, actually, but especially not George. I want you to know that I intend to go for this project. I hope you'll be happy with that, but if you're not…well, unless George changes his mind and wants someone else to do it, I'm going to put myself forward for the work. Even if you don't agree."

She was being ridiculous. Her doubts about Hazel's ulterior motives were unfounded. George was right, Jess was right, she was wrong. The more she saw of Hazel, the more she realised she was simply a genuine person trying to help a friend. "I have no problem with that. It's a good idea. And what George wants, George gets, right?"

"Right." Hazel's huge sigh came down the phone line. "It makes it easier if you're happy with the idea. I didn't want to make things difficult."

"It's a good idea, Hazel." Would Hazel want to move in upstairs when it was done? Maybe not. She'd never mentioned it. "Do you know when you can start?"

"Not yet. Maybe not for a while. George has to get his aged care package approved, and get to the top of the wait list first. How quickly that happens depends on the assessment. But, to be honest, I have very little handyperson work happening. People struggle with my ability to do it. Ha! I'm the one who is supposed to be struggling. Well, me and Chip right now."

"I hope he comes home as his usual grumpy self."

"I'm sure he will. I better let you get back to your cold dinner," Hazel said. "Thanks for sharing a drink and listening to me. It's a relief, to be honest, that you're not horrified at the idea of me working on George's house."

"It's a great idea," Imogen said firmly.

"I hope I can repay your trust."

Imogen's stomach muscles clenched. She hadn't shown Hazel much belief in her abilities until now, and that was all on her. "Maybe we can go out for coffee or something when I'm next in Dry Creek. Catch up." The words had risen, almost by themselves. The twitch of anticipation as she waited for Hazel's reply surprised her. She and

Hazel had so little in common. And an age gap. A career gap. A financial gap. Just a *gap* gap. Yet here she was, hoping Hazel would agree.

"That would be nice. I'll look forward to it. Bye, Imogen."

She ended the call and picked up her plate to put it in the microwave. Hazel's call had left her smiling. Feeling warm inside. Was it because now she knew there was someone trustworthy keeping an eye on her uncle? Partly. But not all. Hazel was just an interesting person.

Her laptop screen glowed brightly, reminding her of the second job advert. The microwave pinged, and she retrieved her dinner, taking it back to the table.

Area manager with Good 'n Fresh, a small chain of supermarkets. Not a major competitor in the game, but one that positioned themselves as the locals' store with great customer service. That made sense—it was where George insisted on shopping, and where Hazel worked.

The position allowed for remote work if the applicant was prepared to travel, but head office was in Rockhampton. Imogen stared at the advert until the words blurred in front of her. Rockhampton was thirty minutes from Dry Creek. She could live with George and work locally. The question was: did she want to do this? Moving to a regional town might be a good short-term move, but would it set her back in the long-term, if—when—she wanted to return to the city? Area manager was only a small step up from her current position.

The advert had been listed for a week. If she was going to apply, she should do it now.

She could always decline if she were offered the job.

CHAPTER 21
A SIDEWAYS SLIDE

Hazel scooted around the kitchen on her knee crutch, making dinner.

Her mum closed the book she was reading with a bang. "I'm glad I gave that author a go. Very different style. Not an easy read."

"The harder things can give us the most rewards. Isn't that right, Hazel?" asked her dad, glancing up from his phone.

"I guess. But sometimes, I'd just like life to be full of the easier stuff."

"Really?" Her dad set his phone down on the table. "Then why do you keep taking the difficult options? Like picking Chip up from the vet rather than having him delivered like a parcel?"

"Dad!" She thumped his arm. "That was so not an option."

"Like taking the late delivery shifts at Good 'n Fresh when your nubbin is swollen, rather than the early ones?"

"The late shifts pay better. Next question."

"Like not using a dating app to meet people. This isn't 1970 anymore. Your chances of sitting next to an interesting stranger in a coffee shop are Buckley's and none."

"No one says Buckley's and none anymore. Are you sure it's not still 1970?"

"I met your dad in a coffee shop," her mum said. "So it's not impossible."

"That was in 1989," her dad said. "My point in relation to Hazel still stands. Maybe we should arrange a marriage for her."

"Dad!" She double-thumped his arm. "Since when have you been so old-fashioned?"

"Never." Her dad smoothed his Rip Curl T-shirt. "The latest fashion, see?"

"From 1970, maybe. And maybe I'll sign up for a dating app when I've finished George's project. And"—she gave a little wiggle on the knee crutch—"he told me today he's been approved for a level two package. That means the downstairs reno can go ahead!"

"That's great news." Her dad stood and engulfed her in a hug. "This could be the start of something big for you."

"I hope so. Big enough that I can get noticed by others. Even if it means I'm still picking the hard road."

"You'll make enough money to replace that clunky old truck of yours," her dad said.

"Find work that satisfies your soul," her mum added.

"All of the above. But first, I have to get this project happening."

Imogen collected her luggage from the console and followed the trickle of passengers through Rockhampton Airport to the car rental counter. She was soon driving along the main road toward Dry Creek.

She'd texted George when the plane had landed to ask if she should pick up takeaway. Her phone pinged and the car audio read George's text in a staccato voice. "As long as it's not curry."

That limited it somewhat, so she pulled in on the edge of Rockhampton and picked up Chinese takeaway. Twenty-five minutes later, she reversed into George's driveway.

Taking her bag and the food, she fumbled for the key, and let herself into the house. Chip pranced at the top of the stairs, his sharp little teeth wafting the air around her calves.

"Remember what happened last time you bit someone," she warned him.

"Five hundred dollars, he cost me," George grumbled from his armchair. "Nearly gave him back to the shelter and got a different dog. Would have been cheaper."

"You wouldn't do that," Imogen said. *Unfortunately.* She bent to kiss his grizzled cheek.

"I wouldn't," George agreed. "Me and Chippie are pals. Did you get sweet and sour pork? He likes that."

"Of course. But there's only enough for the humans."

George hobbled into the kitchen and found plates and cutlery. "There's a bottle of wine here. Shall we open it to celebrate your visit?"

"Sure." She glanced at the label. It was a tooth-achingly sweet moscato, but it would do.

When they were sitting at the table, plates piled with sweet and sour pork, chicken chow mein, and mixed vegetables, George said, "So what brings you here this time, Immie, love? Not that I'm not happy to see you, but it's only been a few weeks since you went back to Brisbane."

Imogen picked out a piece of broccoli and ate it while she thought how best to answer. *"To see if I would be happy living here,"* would be a truthful answer, along with, *"To look at Rockhampton as a potential workplace."* But if the job didn't pan out, she'd have got George's hopes up for nothing.

"I had a gap in my diary, so I took advantage of it." No need to tell George she'd spent an hour making that gap—a task so much harder without an assistant.

"And you could have gone to Noosa or Sydney or somewhere exciting," George said. "I'm very happy you came here. Your bed's made up with clean sheets. Hazel did it for me once we knew you were coming."

"That's nice of her."

"She said the two of you are going out for coffee."

"Yes, I hope we can find the time."

George pointed a finger. "Make the time! I'm also going to take you both out for dinner at the pub. If we go tomorrow night, it's free dessert for the over fifties."

"That would be you," Imogen said. "Or we could go another night and skip dessert."

"What's the point of that? But maybe we will, and you and Hazel can go for dessert at the new late-night wine bar in town. Apparently, they do cake. And they're open past nine at night!"

"Imagine that." Imogen stifled a smile.

"Why do I feel we're being pushed together?" Hazel took a sip of wine and set her glass back on the table. "It's eight o'clock. George never goes to bed before ten—there's no way he's tired. He took the pub courtesy bus home the minute he finished his meal."

"He's trying to matchmake." Imogen swallowed a mouthful of her red wine. "We're his pet project."

"His last project was trying to train Chip. That didn't end well. He must think he'll have better luck with us." A blush stained Hazel's neck.

"When you live here and I live in Brisbane? Not so easy."

"That's assuming we're romantically interested in each other in the first place." The pink had now spread to Hazel's cheeks. "Uh, I mean you're gorgeous, and kind, but—"

Imogen put her hand over Hazel's, stilling her twitching fingers. The heat from her hand rivalled the blush in her cheeks "Don't worry. I know what you mean. We're chalk and cheese. But we're probably the only two women who date women that George knows."

"You're right. I know he'd love it if you were here more often, though, so there's that. I hope you don't feel pressured."

"I don't." But the job with Good 'n Fresh was still a possibility as far as she was concerned. She'd driven around Rockhampton that afternoon, imagining herself working there. Good 'n Fresh's head office was in a modern building overlooking the river. It didn't have the upmarket feel that Whistlestop's office building had, with its marble foyer and uniformed security, but it wasn't a backyard shed, either.

She glanced around the cosy space. "This place has great atmosphere. I love the armchairs and pre-loved old furniture." *Pleasant company, too.*

"Glad you think so." Hazel tucked some unruly curls behind her ear, where they promptly sprang free again. "Honestly, this must be dull for you."

"It's not." And it wasn't. The small wine bar was surprisingly intimate, more like a city laneway bar, with its dark-panelled wood and quirky decor. The soft jazz playing was a bonus, too. If she moved here, would George make room for her piano? Maybe, there'd be more time to play it, too. She'd barely opened the lid in the last couple of weeks.

Hazel propped her chin on her hand. "Well, so far, this not-date is a lot better than my last date." Her eyes sparkled in the candlelight.

Suddenly, Imogen couldn't look away. The way Hazel's lips curved up was captivating. As if she was thinking pleasant thoughts. Amused by something. "The last date being Angus? Or has there been another highlight in your dating world?"

"Angus. Nothing since then. Nat heard he got his car back on the road, but he won't be driving it for a few months. Seems he'd previously lost a few points for speeding, so this swag of points tipped him into disqualification."

"Should I feel sorry for him?"

"I do a bit, to be honest. That was quite a wallop of karma. What about you? Been on any exciting dates lately?"

"Honestly, no. I don't date much."

"Tell me about the last person you dated. It can't be a worse experience than Angus." There was that grin again, and Imogen found herself smiling in response.

"I don't have any exciting stories."

"Doesn't have to be exciting. I'm just curious as to who you'd date."

"Lorelie. A lawyer I met at social tennis. We went out for a couple of months."

"Pretty name. Was she gorgeous? Actually, scrap that question. I'm sure anyone you date would be gorgeous and poised and polished, with designer clothes." She gestured to herself. "The opposite of me, actually."

"You're gorgeous. Don't put yourself down." The words tumbled out before she could censor herself. Instantly, she wished she could retract them.

Hazel blinked. "Well, I didn't expect that. But thank you. I don't think I've ever been called 'gorgeous' before. Always 'cute', or 'perky', or 'friendly', as if I were a puppy."

The urge to take back the words evaporated in the face of Hazel's obvious surprise. "You're very attractive." She squashed the times she'd used 'cute' to describe Hazel in her head.

"I guess being small and somewhat curvy brings on the puppy comparisons. If I was willowy and tall like you, it would be different. I bet you don't get called cute."

"Never."

"Elegant, polished, professional, strikingly beautiful." Hazel looked down at her wine. "Seeing as we're finding adjectives to describe each other... You're breathtaking, Imogen. And I say that in a non-threatening way. At least, that's how I mean it. You're safe from my advances."

What if I don't want to be safe? The thought flashed into her head. But she wasn't interested in Hazel, was she? She'd only just got past the distrust and irritation to find the intriguing woman behind the... perkiness. There really was no other word. She smothered a smile.

"You're thinking cute and perky, aren't you? I can tell by your smile."

Imogen looked down at the table and wished for something to do with her hands. "Maybe." She looked up to see Hazel watching her. Their gazes collided and the cute pink flush spread up Hazel's cheeks again, before she looked away.

"Sorry," Hazel said. "Sometimes, I can't stop looking. I could at least make it less obvious."

A frisson of pleasure tickled in her stomach. So Hazel found her attractive. *Breathtaking*, she'd said. How long had it been since someone had been so openly admiring? She couldn't remember—maybe it hadn't ever happened. She placed her hand over Hazel's once more. "I don't mind. To be honest, I like it."

Hazel turned her hand over so their fingers interlaced. "Compliments are good, if they're genuinely meant. And I meant them, Imogen. You're gorgeous, but more important than that, you're a decent person. An interesting one."

She looked at Hazel, really looked at her. Past the crazy hair, past her young-presenting facade. "You are too."

Their gazes continued to lock.

Imogen's heart rate sped up until it was pounding heavily in her chest. Something hot unfurled in her belly. She couldn't look away from Hazel's parted lips curved in her trademark slight smile.

Would Hazel's lips curve as sweetly into a kiss? The need to know pounded in her head. If they weren't in a wine bar, sitting on opposite sides of a table, she'd draw Hazel into her arms, pull her against her body, wind her hands into that mass of hair and kiss her. Kiss her as a prelude to more, or just to see how it felt?

Her breath wheezed in her chest. That was a crazy idea, but one that had taken up residence in her head and now wouldn't be dislodged. She withdrew her hand. Her palm tingled where it had touched Hazel's skin. She reached for her bag. "Would you…would you like another glass of wine?"

Hazel's eyes were wide and dark. She blinked. "Yes, thank you. That would be good."

Imogen found her wallet and went to the bar. She perused the surprisingly varied wine list, even though she knew what she wanted. But it gave her time to steady her breathing and centre herself, and by the time she returned to the table, her reaction was under control.

"Thanks." Hazel accepted the glass of wine.

For a minute, they were both silent, staring down into their glasses as if the secrets of the universe lurked within. Imogen looked up and across at Hazel at the exact time that she did the same. Their gazes locked, and in that instant she couldn't breathe. Hazel's gaze could have sparked a bushfire.

Then Hazel looked away and took a gulp of wine. "Great wine. A better one, I think, than the cheap one I usually get."

"Hazel!" A dark-haired woman with a Scottish accent swooped down and wrapped her arms around Hazel's neck from behind. "I thought it was you."

"Hi, Nat." Hazel accepted a kiss to the cheek. "Are you here with Djalu?"

"Yeah, date night. His parents have the kids." Nat peeked sideways at Imogen. "Are you going to introduce me to your date?"

"We're…friends," Hazel said. "This is George's niece, Imogen."

Nat extended a hand. "I've heard about you. It's good of you to visit so often. Not many people would."

"It's what families do," Imogen said. *And I'm making up for all the times I didn't come.* But she wouldn't tell Nat that.

"Not all families," Nat said. "But don't get me started." She looked from one to the other. "I get the feeling I'm interrupting. I'll leave you to it. See you soon, Hazel." She disappeared as quickly as she'd arrived.

"Uh oh," Hazel said. "Nat thinks we're on a date. Otherwise, she'd have stayed and asked you a million inquisitive questions. She loves meeting new people. I'm going to get the third degree when I next see her."

"But you said we're friends."

"I did. But Nat can read the room. She picked up on this…tension between us."

"Tension?" She knew, of course.

She blew a breath. "Imogen, I've said you're beautiful and a good person. And you're holding my hand like you never want to let go. Whether we like it or not, there's something sparking between us. We don't have to see where it goes, but we should at least acknowledge it."

"You're saying George is right to matchmake?"

Hazel finished her wine in two big swallows. She stood and held out a hand. "Come on."

"Where?" Her own wine was already finished. When had she done that? She didn't remember.

"I've made you uncomfortable, and I didn't mean to. People tell me I'm too direct, but I've learned the hard way it's better to be upfront about things. Like telling people I'm an amputee. Like telling them I don't have much money. And yeah, that I find them attractive if I do. Why prevaricate? But now, you're uneasy, wondering where I'm going with this." She flashed her a grin. "Nowhere, Imogen. I'm not pressuring you for anything. So right now, we're going home."

Her directness was like a glass of ice-cold water on an empty stomach. "I'm sorry, I didn't realise I was so easy to read. I like you, Hazel, and yes, on one level, I'm attracted to you. Who wouldn't be?" She shrugged. "But you're right; we're very different, you and me, and—"

"It's not logical or wise to take this further. So, I'm being mature and sensible and saying let's go home." Hazel wiggled her fingers. "Now take my hand, and let's get out of here."

There was an uncomfortable feeling in her chest, as if she'd slid sideways out of her skin. People in her world didn't behave like Hazel, nor did they take control like this. She was the leader here, the one who should control their interactions. She was the older, more experienced person, the one who should have made the decision to go ahead or drop back. Not Hazel. But right now, with her world off kilter, it was the way it was.

With a short nod, she picked up her bag and, ignoring Hazel's outstretched hand, she stalked out of the wine bar and over to her car.

CHAPTER 22
RECONNAISSANCE

A COUPLE OF DAYS LATER, IMOGEN entered Good 'n Fresh and picked up a basket at the door. There was nothing she needed; Hazel still delivered George's groceries. But she wanted to get a feel for the store ahead of her interview with them in a week's time. She still wasn't sure how she felt about that.

She looked around. The fruit and veg area had a brightly signed local produce section where piles of spiky pineapples cosied up to red and yellow paw paws. Imogen selected a pineapple, picked up a bag of passionfruit, and a couple of mangoes. She moved on, ambling up and down the aisles. Not a great product selection, and some shelves were empty of stock. The flooring was worn in places, and the signage was old-fashioned. She picked up a couple of random items and put them in her basket.

She stopped in the dairy aisle and stared unseeingly at the yogurts. Was this rather shabby look purely due to the competition in town, or was management holding the store back? The look was of a store struggling to turn a profit.

Whatever the reason, did she want to get involved with a failing brand?

Imogen picked a couple of yogurts and a block of cheddar, then headed to the checkout. The woman ringing up the customer ahead of her at warp speed looked familiar. Imogen frowned; she couldn't place her. But then the dark hair, pale skin, and friendly smile reminded her. It was Hazel's friend Nat.

She glanced unobtrusively around to see if she could move to a different checkout, but Nat finished with the customer ahead of her and caught Imogen's eye. Nat exchanged a few pleasantries with her customer, ending with a warm laugh that left the older man smiling.

"Hi, Imogen," Nat said. "How was your date the other night? Oops—" She pressed her fingers to her mouth. "Hazel's already chewed me out about that. Your not-date, I mean."

Really? The fact that Hazel had been so quick to correct her friend stung—which was strange. Hazel had been the one complimenting Imogen, talking about the tension between them. But then she'd turned around and refuted that to her friend. Except…she was right: it hadn't been a date and Hazel had backed off when she'd thought Imogen was uncomfortable.

"Do you want this pineapple separate? It'll pierce the bag if not—it's a spiky one." Nat's hands kept scanning and bagging. "If you're here to see Hazel, she's not working today."

"I'm not. I didn't think she'd be in the store, anyway."

Nat paused and rested her hands on the weigh scale. "That's right—she's always out in the delivery truck. The oldies love her as she never minds taking their groceries right into the kitchen. That's how she met George."

That sounded exactly the sort of thing Hazel would do.

"She's part-time," Nat continued. "I think she might be rostered tomorrow."

"That's okay. I'll catch her another time. Thanks." She pulled out her wallet and concentrated on selecting the right card.

"That will be nineteen dollars and forty-three cents, thank you. Would you like to sign up for our loyalty card? You get five per cent off your biggest shop each month, plus access to exclusive deals. Although George is a platinum member, so that covers both of you."

Nat was good, her promo speech done with a smile, and recognition of George's customer loyalty. "No, but thank you for asking." She tapped her credit card on the reader and picked up the bag and the pineapple.

"I'm sure I'll see you around," Nat said with a smile. She turned to the next customer. "Hello, Meryl, did you find what you needed today?"

Back at the house, Imogen placed the fruit on the counter, and the yogurt and cheese in the fridge. Good 'n Fresh was in that difficult grey zone between major chain supermarket, expensive convenience store, and local specialty store. How much input would the area manager have to make changes? If she'd be stuck having to follow along with outdated practices, she might as well stay with Whistlestop and start shoving her way to the top with more assertiveness rather than waiting for her efficiency and hard work to be recognised.

Although… She looked at George, asleep in his recliner. The job with Good 'n Fresh wasn't only about a career move. Her heart swelled with love for her uncle. George and Christine had never had kids—and only now did she realise she'd never asked why. George had been a widower for longer than Christine had been alive, and of course, Imogen had never met her.

But for all George was a childless widower, he'd made Imogen's life magic that summer in Dry Creek when she'd been nine. She hadn't wanted to return to Melbourne, and memories of that summer were a major reason she'd moved to Brisbane. For the sun, certainly, away from Melbourne's grey days, but also to be closer to George.

And now she was considering moving to Dry Creek—not for a job she wasn't even sure she wanted, but for George.

George snorted and jerked awake. His puzzled expression eased as he saw her. "Immie, love, you're back. Shall I put the kettle on?"

"That's a good idea." She pulled a packet out of the bag of shopping. "I bought some Tim Tams."

It was all very well doing the demolishing part. It was the putting-back-together that had her worried. Hazel scrunched her eyes and stared at the stud wall in the downstairs area of George's house. Whichever way she looked at it, the timbers were rotten. Damp and crumbling. Water was getting in somewhere—and she wasn't sure if she could handle it.

Her nubbin ached, and she absentmindedly rubbed around the top of the prosthesis below her knee. What had she been thinking to believe she could do George's renovation? It was a job for a master builder with years of experience, not for her, winging it with only a tiny shed full of tools, and little knowledge. YouTube videos had got her so far, but the hollowness in her stomach told her she and YouTube might have reached the end of the line.

She swallowed away the sinking feeling, the worry that she'd given George a thumping great bill he might not be able to afford.

No.

She wouldn't do that. George trusted her and had given her a chance to do a bigger project. She just had to woman-up and find a solution to what was, hopefully, a small problem.

She poked at the damp timber with a finger and winced as her finger went a centimetre into the rotten wood. *Okay, so not a small problem.*

First, find the water leak. Then assess the amount of damage, and what needed replacing. Then replace it. *Easy, right?*

She rolled her eyes. *Right.*

She went outside and her gaze tracked the patches on George's lawn. A line of green grass along the water main, brown and sparse everywhere else. How come she'd never noticed that before? Hopefully, the leak would be on the Council's side of the meter and their responsibility.

Hazel went back inside. The wall would need to dry before she could do much more to it. No worries. There were a million other things she could do in the meantime: plan out the kitchenette, put in the waterproofing on the shower, work on the new patio, arrange an electrician to install recessed lighting and a ceiling fan, and an air conditioning tech to service the extremely old unit.

The doubts of earlier evaporated like water in the sun. She *could* do this. She just had to believe in herself, drag her positive attitude out from wherever it was currently hiding, and get to work.

She gripped the tattoo on her wrist. *I can do more.*

CHAPTER 23
UNDER THE SINK

"Coffee," Imogen announced. She pushed open the door to the ground floor with her hip. Dust hung in the air, and she coughed.

"Just a moment," Hazel's muffled voice replied.

Imogen edged further into the room and set the tray of coffee, Earl Grey, and biscuits down on a battered old table Hazel was using as a workbench. She pushed aside the assortment of plumbing parts, screws, and tile samples to make more room.

The sight of Hazel's rear, clad in dusty jeans, sticking out from under the sink greeted her. As Imogen watched, Hazel shuffled out and clambered to her feet.

Imogen took a step forward, the words, *Can I help you?* dying on her lips as Hazel straightened and walked toward her.

"Sorry about that. Had to get the water turned off before I dismantled the pipe. What brings you to my dusty world?"

"Coffee." Imogen gestured to the tray. "We said we'd go out for coffee while I'm here, but I have to head back tonight. So I thought we could have one here at least."

"We could. Or upstairs in the clean comfort of George's living room."

"Mavis is there fussing over George. I thought I'd leave them to it."

"Wherever we are, coffee is welcome. Thanks, Immie, love." Her sparkling eyes gave away the tease.

"Not fair. I don't know what nicknames you have."

"Honestly? I don't have any. It's just Hazel. And yes, I've heard all the jokes about being named after a nut."

"It's a lovely name." It suited her: straightforward, pretty, and natural.

Hazel blinked. "Well, thank you. Yours suits you. Cool and classy. Well, half classy right now."

Imogen looked down at her pale-blue blouse, ironed to a perfect finish. "Only half classy? This blouse is new."

"It's not the blouse I'm talking about." A thread of amusement filtered through Hazel's voice. She pointed below Imogen's waist.

Her lips twitched. "You mean not every best-dressed businesswoman is wearing cotton shorts?"

"Wrinkled, stained cotton shorts," Hazel said. "Did you drop your breakfast on them this morning?"

Heat crawled up Imogen's neck. "That was Chip. He knocked me as I was eating yogurt. I've just come off a Zoom meeting. They only see me from the waist up. I wasn't going to change into a smart skirt."

"As long as you didn't have to get up and grab something."

"At least I had more than undies on," Imogen shot back. "I swear you prefer the scruffy vibe to my perfect businesswoman look." The heat increased. That had sounded as if she assumed Hazel liked how she looked. *If in doubt, double down.* She raised her chin and gave Hazel a cool stare.

"I do actually. It's more the real you, than the polished version." She nudged Imogen's arm. "Would you poo-pick Chip's nuggets from the back garden in a business suit?"

"You have a point." It was hard not to smile at Hazel's enthusiasm—or the mental image of herself tottering around the back garden in high heels picking up dog poo.

"Thanks for the coffee. I needed the energy boost." Hazel slumped into a camp chair. "Pull up a chair and tell me something that isn't about plumbing."

"Trust me, I will never tell you anything about plumbing."

Hazel's eyes crinkled at the corners as she smiled. It seemed everything she did was genuine, without false politeness. Just an unscripted response. Imogen's gaze wandered down Hazel's yellow T-shirt. It hung loose over her jeans. Her pale skin showed through a rip in one side, halfway up to the arm. Hazel shifted in the chair and for a second, Imogen had a flash of white cotton bra.

"Caught you looking." Hazel grimaced. "I love this T-shirt, but now it's barely decent. I hope I've got a shirt in the truck to get me home without being arrested."

"I can lend you something." Imogen averted her eyes. Her fingers itched to reach over and stroke up that soft-looking skin. To trail around the lower edge of Hazel's bra. *What am I thinking? That isn't a good idea.* She exhaled slowly through her mouth, trying to calm her suddenly racing heart.

"I'll take you up on that." Hazel flapped the front of her T-shirt. "This is now a rag."

It had been hard to look away before, but now it was impossible. Hazel's movement exposed a few centimetres of toned belly. Of course, Hazel would be fit. She'd have to be, not only to make it easier on her body, but because of her work.

Work. For a moment, Imogen considered asking her about Good 'n Fresh but she discarded that thought almost immediately. If she were to pursue the area manager position, she didn't want to make it awkward for either of them. Chances were, she'd never meet Hazel in a work sense. An office-based manager and a part-time delivery driver were unlikely to interact.

Hazel took a couple of big gulps of coffee and set down the mug. "Seeing as you're partly in old clothes, would you have a minute to help me with something?"

"Sure, if I can." Imogen forced her mind away from Hazel's stomach and the possibility of workplace relations and concentrated on her words.

"I'm trying to disconnect the old plumbing pipes from the existing sink, and I need someone to stop the top pipe twisting. You just have to use the wrench to hold it steady while I unscrew the bottom. You'll need to find an old T-shirt or something, though. That fine blouse would be ruined."

"I can do that." Imogen stood. Anything that stopped her eyeing up Hazel like she was a particularly fine glass of wine. "I'll be back." She went upstairs, returning in her poo-picking T-shirt of the morning.

"Much better." Hazel ran her gaze up and down Imogen's body. She crouched and turned onto her back before wiggling her way under the bathroom sink. "Grab that wrench and hold the pipe steady."

Imogen sat and put the wrench around the pipe. Her knee brushed Hazel's thigh. The warmth of her leg heated even though the jeans. She pulled her knee back.

Hazel grunted as she turned the joiner. "Can you stop it turning? It'll snap if you can't."

She tightened her grip, but the pipe still kept turning.

"Lie on your back and wiggle under the sink so you're closer to it," Hazel said. "You should be able to get a better grip then."

Imogen looked around. There barely seemed to be room for one person under the tiny vanity, let alone two. She did as Hazel had suggested. Her shoulder brushed Hazel's arm, and their breath was loud in the small space. So oddly intimate. She repositioned the wrench around the pipe and squeezed as hard as she could.

Hazel's legs flailed as she sought to brace herself, then she wedged one leg against the cabinet door. The other—the prosthetic leg—pressed against Imogen's calf.

She gasped as the metal rod pressed into her flesh. No, not just a metal rod; it was part of Hazel, part of her body. She shifted, trying to free her calf from the pressure.

"Keep still," Hazel grunted. "I think it's turning." Her shoulder dug into Imogen's, and her muscles corded with effort.

Imogen dropped her gaze from Hazel's tanned arms working to release the pipe.

Big mistake. Now the rip in Hazel's T-shirt was directly in her line of sight. And Hazel had an honest-to God sixpack under her slight padding. Imogen clenched her hand on the wrench so she wouldn't reach down and slip her fingers into the tear of the material.

With a final yank, the pipe loosened.

"Hooray!" Hazel groped for the bowl she'd left on the floor by the vanity. "If you don't want to get covered in stagnant water when I remove the U-bend, now is a good time to leave."

Leave. She should back out of the vanity, stand, dust herself off, and saunter back upstairs, leaving Hazel with the mess and inevitable cleanup. She should. But she couldn't.

Mere centimetres separated her face from Hazel's. Close enough to see the slight unevenness of her cheek, smell her body wash—something minty. A curl of her wayward hair tickled Imogen's cheek.

Hazel blinked, and a wash of pink crept into her cheeks. Her gaze flickered away from Imogen's and darted around the cramped cabinet before returning to study Imogen's face. Close up, her light-brown eyes appeared darker in the shadows under the vanity.

Imogen set down the wrench. Her heart pounded with a nerve-wracking intensity, as if it might break out of her chest and fly free. Her fingers shook as she reached to touch Hazel's cheek. "You have dirt on your face."

Hazel gave a slight smile. "More than on my face, I'm sure." Her voice lowered. "So do you." She reached and brushed at something on Imogen's forehead. "Cobwebs. No spiders though."

"Lucky." The urge to move closer was overwhelming, to give into the pulse of desire that even now was making her fingers shake.

"Hazel…" A last look into those compelling eyes, seeking for a sign that Hazel, too, wanted this.

Again, that slight, tremulous smile, and with a small sigh, Imogen cupped her hand around the back of Hazel's head, pushing into the mass of hair, and drew her closer.

Hazel's head banged on the pipe. Imogen's shoulder jammed against the U bend. With a shaky laugh, she reset their position, and this time, their faces came together with nothing between them.

She shouldn't do this.

She wanted to do this.

With a swift intake of breath, Imogen closed the gap and pressed her lips to Hazel's. For a few heartbeats, she simply rested there, Hazel's lips slack and soft under her own, the slight puff of Hazel's breath tickling her lips.

Then Hazel freed her hand and wrapped it around Imogen's upper arm. She squeezed, her grip firm. "If you're going to kiss me, at least do it like you mean it."

The words vibrated on Imogen's lips, and blood thundered in her head. She tightened her grip on Hazel's hair and her lips pressed harder against Hazel's, moving firmly over her mouth, urging her lips apart.

With a gasp, Hazel complied, and the pulse in Imogen's head ratcheted up to a driving, pounding beat. Their noses bumped, awkward in the confined space. Their lips meshed, melded, drew apart, and joined together again in a sweeter, softer kiss, that grew in intensity.

When Imogen opened her eyes, she found Hazel leaning into the kiss, a small wrinkle between her eyebrows, as if she couldn't believe what was happening.

She wasn't the only one.

With an indrawn breath and a spinning head, she moved closer. The sweetness of Hazel's breath puffed against her mouth right before Hazel's tongue flicked out to touch Imogen's lips.

And then Hazel withdrew, and her hand rested on Imogen's shoulder.

Imogen's lips tingled, and she touched her tongue to them, as if she could again feel Hazel's lips. Was Hazel going to say this was a mistake? Should she apologise first?

"That was unexpected. Nice though." Hazel tilted her head, wincing as it banged on the wall of the vanity. "Better than nice, actually."

Her breath left her body in a slow exhale of relief. "I'm glad you think so."

"And you don't?"

She loosened her grip on Hazel's curls. "If you seriously think that, then we have a communication problem. I can't say I've ever kissed anyone underneath a sink before."

"It's hardly high on the list of romantic places," Hazel agreed. "Maybe it's even a world first."

"Possibly." Her hip dug into the base of the cabinet, and she wasn't sure she could move her shoulders. "Maybe we should try this again, somewhere more comfortable."

"Is that what you want?" Hazel's gaze searched her face. "Or maybe we should chalk it up in the new experience column and move on."

She opened her mouth to say she wanted more, then hesitated. The upcoming interview with Good 'n Fresh pulsed in her mind. If she got the job—if she took the job—it would put her higher in the food-chain than Hazel.

Hazel watched her silently and her expressive face folded in on itself to a blank mask. "It's okay. The experience column it is. I'm sure you've never kissed an amputee before."

Ouch. Imogen wiggled out from under the sink and stood, dusting off her T-shirt. She waited until Hazel, too, stood, then said, "That was unfair and unnecessary. Also incorrect. I kissed *you*, Hazel, not just a person with a prosthetic leg."

Hazel blinked, and opened her mouth, then closed it again. She looked away, biting her lip. "You're right. I'm sorry. It's just…" Her hands made random patterns in the air. "I guess I'm a bit more sensitive than I realised after the date with Angus."

A short nod. "I understand. I'm hesitating for other reasons. I live in Brisbane." *For now*. "I'm older than you. I have a lot on my plate. I really can't handle any more distractions at the moment."

Hazel winced. "Ouch. Okay, that's my place. I better go and stand in it. It's the one marked 'meaningless distraction' and it's over there in the corner behind the water heater, where it's easy to ignore." She bent to pick up the abandoned wrench. "Thanks for helping me with the pipe. And for the coffee. Now if you don't want to get close to stagnant water, now is the time to leave."

The dismissal was clear, even as it stung. She opened her mouth to say…to say what? How had they gone from kisses and banter to a steely chill in the space of a couple of minutes?

Still. It was probably for the best. She picked up the tea tray and headed for the door. In the doorway, she turned around. Hazel was crouched by the sink, her attention focussed on plumbing.

She'd just kissed Hazel. Imogen shook her head. She still wasn't sure how it had happened. But that kiss—pleasurable as it had been—could not happen again.

Definitely.

CHAPTER 24
WALLPAPER WITH ROSES

Imogen straightened her jacket, making sure the neckline of her blouse was smooth, and that her hair was neat. A final check of her make-up in her compact, and she was ready. With a deep breath, she clicked on the video link with Good 'n Fresh.

The head of HR, Tamika Carpenter, greeted her with a nod and a smile. "Imogen, thank you for making time to chat again today."

"Thank you," Imogen said. Her professional smile stretched across her face. "I'm very happy to be called back for a second interview."

"I'll cut to the chase," Tamika said. "We were extremely happy with your first interview, and you're our first choice for the area manager position. We believe you have exactly the skill set and personality to drive Good 'n Fresh as we embark on this period of growth."

Wow. Imogen struggled to keep her professional smile, but the corners of her mouth twitched up even higher. This was extremely promising, more than she'd dared hope. The previous interview in front of a panel had ended with a polite notification that they would contact her if she was selected for a second interview.

"Thank you," she murmured. "I appreciate this opportunity to demonstrate how I am best suited for the position."

Tamika glanced down at some notes on her desk and clasped her hands. "We're already convinced. You've done your research on us, and we like your eagerness to position Good 'n Fresh in the specialty store market, as well as retaining the local customers that we rely on. We'd like to make you an offer."

Imogen inclined her head, even as her heart pounded a fast drumbeat. An offer! This was unexpected. "I'm listening."

"I'll e-mail you through the full details, but the gist is that you work full time from our Rockhampton office. You'll be responsible for the redirection of Good 'n Fresh on the central coast. If this is successful, we envisage rolling out the new approach across Queensland." Tamika paused. "Should that eventuate, we'll need a state manager. You, of course, would be in an excellent position to apply. The area manager salary is…" She glanced at her notes, then named a salary that was slightly more than her current salary at Whistlestop. "Given you're currently Brisbane based, we offer a relocation package as well."

For a moment, she thought of what had brought her to this point. Losing out on the promotion with Whistlestop. Wayne's conviction she wasn't *management material.* Even losing her office with a window, and the promised new assistant who had still failed to materialise. Serenity was happy as a clam working for Richard and had politely refused Imogen's request that she consider returning to work for her.

Not leadership material, my arse. She straightened her shoulders. "Thank you, Tamika. I'll review your offer when it arrives and let you know."

"That would be great. Please get back to me directly if there's anything you're not completely happy with. We'd appreciate your answer within three business days, if possible."

"I'm sure I'll manage that."

After some further courtesies, Tamika ended the video link.

Imogen leaned back in her chair and blew out her breath. With a start, she realised she was already thinking about the move. Whistlestop was no longer for her; it hadn't been since they'd failed to consider her for the state manager role. No, it was time to move on.

But before she could accept the position, she had to talk to George.

Hazel slumped into the chair and looked around the ground floor of George's house. There was still so much to do. She rubbed her left thigh, wishing she could remove Petunia and give her nubbin a break. In addition to her delivery shifts with Good 'n Fresh, the extra time on her feet doing George's work was taking its toll and her nubbin was swollen most evenings. It was only three in the afternoon, but already the prothesis's cup was digging into her flesh.

"Hazel, I've made tea." George's voice wafted down the stairwell. "Come and get it before I give your Tim Tams to Chip."

"Coming," she called. With a last look around, she went up the stairs and out onto the balcony where George had the tea. "You know dogs can't eat chocolate. I'll get him some proper doggo treats."

She extended a hand to Chip who sniffed it then backed off with a small growl. "Knock it off, Chip. I know you don't mean it."

Chip wagged his tail and allowed her to rub his ears for a few seconds before he trotted off to sit with George.

Hazel relaxed into a chair with a sigh of relief, shifting so that her nubbin was more comfortable.

"Got news for you," George said when they were settled with their tea and were both eating their second chocolate biscuit.

"Chip's going to start dog agility classes?"

"He's too old for that. Like me."

"Mavis finally agreed to go out with you?"

"Still working on that. She sees me as a friend."

"What then?" Hazel asked.

"Immie's coming back to Dry Creek." George cracked a grin and almost vibrated in the old canvas chair.

"Oh? How long for?" Hazel clasped her hands on the mug of tea to stop them shaking. In the three weeks since she'd seen Imogen, she hadn't heard from her directly. Although why should she? One kiss that they'd both agreed not to take further didn't make for any sort of instant friendship.

"She's moving here!" George crowed with delight. "Forever! Well, mebbe not forever, but she's got a job in Rockhampton. She didn't say where, but it's a good job. A step up from where she works in Brisbane."

"Really?" A buzz started in Hazel's stomach. Imogen. Here? Or at least nearby. Did that change anything between them? Maybe not.

After all, proximity was low on the scale of reasons to get closer to Imogen. Or not. Maybe, if she were closer, things would change.

"Yes, really. Not for a month. She has to give notice at her old job…although she's hoping for an early release. Now ask me where she's going to live."

"Where's Imogen going to live, George?" Hazel repeated obediently, although from his expression, she could make a good guess.

"Here! She's going to live with me. She'll need a better bathroom, though, so I thought mebbe when you've got the downstairs bathroom done, you could do something about the one up here."

"I can do that," Hazel said. A pleased tremor ran through her. More work. Maybe, soon, if word about her work spread, she could give up being a delivery driver. But not yet. Not until she was getting regular work from customers who weren't George. And talking of…

"I have to go. I'm doing the evening delivery run. Want anything? I can bring it around tomorrow, if you do."

"No, I'm right." He patted her hand. "I voted for you in that Employee of the Month thing again. I do every month."

"You do. But the face-to-face staff always win. They're the ones the customers remember."

"Mebbe. We'll see."

He said that every month.

"Immie's coming back, which is nice for me *and* you." He shot her a meaningful look. "Be good if you could spend time with her. Introduce her around a bit. Seeing as how she's coming to live here and all."

"I'm not the social butterfly you think I am. I'm sure Imogen would rather find her own friends."

"Who said anything about friends?" George snorted. "I may have a dodgy hip, but my eyes work perfectly. I saw how she looked after that night you went to Marilyn's. And I saw her come up the stairs covered in dust, and pink as a carnation last time she was here. Said she'd been helping you."

"George…" She folded her arms. "If you're matchmaking—again—you can stop right there. We both know what you're trying to do, and you're not helping."

"You're not helping yourselves. When was the last time you went out on a date?"

"A few weeks ago, actually. I don't tell you everything. You're worse than my parents."

"Can't have been a good date," George shot back, "or you'd have told me." He slurped his tea. "Thought it would be nice if we tidied up Immie's bedroom. Make it more pretty, like."

At least he'd changed the subject. "Sure, we can do that. Or does that 'we' actually mean me?"

"I thought you could do the work and I could direct you. Do you think she'd like wallpaper? Mebbe with roses on it?"

"I'm not sure Imogen's a roses kind of woman," Hazel said. "And wallpaper? Paint is better in a tropical climate."

"You're right," George said with a sigh. "I just want to make it nice for her."

She patted his hand. "You do. She's coming here to live with you—if she didn't want that, she'd get a place in Rockhampton. And now, I really do have to go." She pecked him on the cheek and headed for the door.

Her left leg twinged as she descended the stairs and the socket of her prosthesis dug into her skin again. Maybe it was time to see the prosthetist again for a revision.

CHAPTER 25
INSTANT REPLAY

When it came time, it was surprisingly easy to walk away from Whistlestop. She did the rounds of her team to say farewell, and while it was tempting to tell Richard and a few others exactly what she thought of them, Imogen knew that burning bridges was never a good idea.

She stopped by to see Serenity and gave her a box of chocolates, telling herself it wasn't a guilt gift, but really, there was no other way of looking at it. She made a promise to herself not to treat her new assistant at Good 'n Fresh in the same high-handed way.

Her final stop was to see Wayne.

"All the best, Imogen." He shook her hand and then drew her into an awkward one-armed hug. "Who'd have thought you'd be beating me out the door!"

She gave him a brief smile. "My new position is an upward step. It had become obvious that sort of progression wouldn't be available to me here."

Wayne's cheeks flushed. "You've made a good move, and I wish you well. You're still welcome to attend my retirement dinner in a couple of weeks. I'm sure everyone would love to see you."

"Thank you, but I won't be back in Brisbane then. Good luck, Wayne. I expect a monthly update on your golf handicap."

"That won't change for a while. Marybeth has a list of all the jobs she wants done around the house. And she's cancelled the lawn-care service. I'm not sure how much golf time I'll have."

"I'm sure you'll find some. Thank you, Wayne. It's been a pleasure working with you these years."

Clutching the huge bouquet she'd been given, and the envelope containing the card and gift voucher, she exited the office, nodding and smiling as if she were a politician on election day.

Once in her car, she exhaled gustily. So, that was the end of that. Her nine years at Whistlestop wrapped up in a bouquet of tropical flowers and a Myer gift card. She glanced back at the building, at the tinted windows, the Whistlestop signage over the foyer, at the landscaped entrance, and waited for the pang of regret.

It didn't come.

She was done. She was now the area manager at Good 'n Fresh, tasked with bringing the chain back to profit and into the twenty-first century, with a state manager position on the horizon.

She wouldn't blow it.

"This is kind of you." Imogen glanced around the Returned & Services League club. It was the same bland decor that characterised sporting clubs and RSLs all around Australia. Blue patterned carpet, functional tables and chairs, and a menu that held all the popular dishes. Imogen knew without looking there'd be three types of steak, chicken parmigiana, beer-battered fish, and salt and pepper calamari. All served with chips and a token salad.

"What would you like?" George asked. "Steak is good here. And it's my treat."

Hazel rose. "Then I'll get the drinks."

There was only one salad on the menu. Imogen set the menu aside. Decision made. They stood in line to order their meals, then returned to their table.

Hazel raised her glass. "Here's to Imogen. Congratulations on the new job."

They clinked glasses. "Thanks. I'm looking forward to starting on Monday."

"What is it you do exactly?" Hazel asked. "I'm sure it's something high-powered in a business suit."

"I'll be the area manager for a retail chain. But importantly, I'm tasked with bringing them more up to date. They're somewhat old-fashioned." She shut her mouth with a snap. She'd just been about to mention the name. There was no need to make Hazel uncomfortable at this stage. "I intend to make the most of this weekend. I'm sure I'll be very busy for a while. You mentioned a jazz band before." She directed the words at Hazel. "Would they be playing this Sunday?"

"No. They only play the third Sunday of the month," Hazel said. "I guess you'll have to miss jazz for a while, unless you've got your piano tucked into the boot of your car."

"I wish," Imogen said. "There's not really room for it at your place, George, even if we could get it up the stairs. It's in storage, along with the rest of my furniture."

"You could put it in the living room," George said. "We could hoist it up over the balcony."

Imogen shuddered. "I don't think so. Maybe I'll take up the flute or something portable instead."

"As long as it's not the mouth organ." Hazel grinned. "Can you sing? They have karaoke here at eight." She pointed to a poster on the wall.

"Not well. I wouldn't want to empty the room."

"Hazel does it sometimes," George said. "She sings 'I Will Survive' or other disco stuff. Dances too."

Hazel shook back her hair. "Gotta out drag queen the drag queens—not that there's many of them in the RSL. It's usually George's mates singing 'My Way'." She looked at Imogen. "Will you have a go?"

"No, I don't think so." What if someone from her new job heard her singing off-key? Zero respect then. "But you go for it. I'll applaud."

"Thanks. It will be nice if someone does."

A server brought over their meals. George rubbed his hands. "Nothing better than a good steak. Is that all you're having, Immie?"

Imogen looked down at her salad. It looked fresh and appetising with plump chunks of chicken among the rice noodles and greenery. "This is huge. I probably won't finish it." She levelled him a stern look. "No need to tell me to eat more."

"I wasn't going to." He paused. "But since you've mentioned it, it's not a bad idea."

Once dinner had been eaten, second drinks ordered and finished, George looked at his watch. "I'm beat. If I go now, I can get the courtesy bus home. You two stay here, though, and enjoy the karaoke."

Imogen gave an internal eyeroll. George was so unsubtle. His RSL nights usually went a lot later than this—he'd stay and play the pokies or prop himself in the bar and bend the ear of whomever would listen. No, he was matchmaking again. Pushing her together with Hazel just because he could. Never mind that they had nothing in common, nothing that made them compatible on any level.

She sucked in a quick breath. Except that wasn't true. A kiss under a cramped and dusty sink had changed all of that. She flicked a glance at Hazel.

"George," Hazel said in an exasperated voice, "please stop throwing us together. Imogen is lovely, and we're becoming friends, but that's all." Pinkness stained her cheeks. Maybe she, too, was remembering the kiss.

"Who said anything about matchmaking?" George said. "I'm tired, that's all. And I forgot to let Chip out."

"I let Chip out," Imogen said. "And back in again, not that he deserves it. So that excuse is shot down. Stay and enjoy the karaoke."

Hazel's gaze skittered about the table and then she stared fixedly at the stage where staff were setting up the karaoke. Awkward, much. Imogen didn't want to sit and make stilted conversation. No, she'd rather wind her hand into Hazel's hair and encourage her closer and then kiss her again with both of them standing, and not a cobweb in sight.

Where had that thought come from?

George heaved himself to his feet. "All the same. I'm beat. See you both tomorrow. I'll be in bed when you return."

Hazel stood as well. "Would you like me to walk with you to the courtesy bus?" She placed a hand under his elbow as he lent on his stick.

George patted her hand. "I'm fine, but thanks for offering."

Imogen watched as he hobbled away.

Hazel, too, was watching, a wrinkle between her brows. "He's getting stiffer, and I hope he can manage the stairs after two beers. Maybe I should have gone with him."

"I don't think he'd have let you," Imogen murmured. She switched her gaze to Hazel. "But I'm very glad you're getting on so well with the downstairs apartment conversion. He may need it sooner than he thinks."

"I've priced stairlifts. There's a company in Rockhampton who can install one within the next two weeks. Maybe it's something to consider? He'll need the lift so he can come upstairs to visit you."

"Am I muscling in on your turf? Were you assuming you'd move in upstairs?"

Hazel fixed her gaze on Imogen. "Still mistrusting my motives?" Her voice was cool.

"No. I'm sure you'd offer George fair rent."

"I'm very happy living with my parents—even if that makes me a twenty-five-year-old loser. But it suits all of us. I did wonder if I'd offer to rent the upstairs when it came to it, purely so George had someone close by if he needed anything." A shoulder lifted. "But I'm happy to turn that responsibility over to you."

Imogen reached across the table and took Hazel's hand. "I misjudged you, Hazel. I worried you were trying to take advantage of George, but now I know you really do care for him."

Hazel's lips twitched. "Thank you. I think. I'm not used to being judged for that. Other things, sure, but no one's ever questioned my motives before."

"I'm sorry." Imogen ran her thumb over the back of Hazel's hand. "I hope we can be friends." Was that what she wanted? Friends seemed cold, bloodless. Their kiss had been anything but. She bit her lip, wishing she could recall those words.

"Friends," Hazel repeated. "Of the kissing sort? Or of the meet-for-coffee sort?"

Imogen swallowed. How should she answer that? In the past weeks, Hazel had wormed her way into Imogen's thoughts in a way anyone seldom did. Now she saw Hazel's perkiness was a fierce determination to make the best of everything that came her way. Her upbeat personality was a joyful expression that only someone who'd experienced crushing lows could understand.

She closed her eyes as a longing to be the kissing sort of friends consumed her.

But there was more than that. From next week, she'd be a lot higher up the Good 'n Fresh ladder than Hazel. Not her direct boss, but a superior who might have to make decisions that impacted her. She'd have to find out what, if any, their interactions would be.

"Can we leave it open?" she asked. "Take it as it comes? I like you, Hazel. I like kissing you. But it's going to be a hard few weeks for me, getting to grips with a new job, settling into life in Dry Creek." For a moment, she considered telling Hazel about her new job. That would go a long way to explaining her hesitation to commit. The thought died as soon as it was born; more likely she'd only add another layer of complication to something that didn't need it.

"I can do that." Hazel turned her hand over so she could grip Imogen's, and squeezed.

An urgent longing to lean across the table and kiss Hazel, to stand, take her in her arms, take her home, consumed her. She opened her mouth to say she'd changed her mind.

"Karaoke sign-ups are open." A compere tapped the mic and indicated a whiteboard to his left. "I see a few familiar faces here, so don't delay."

"Are you going to sign up?" Imogen asked. Her heartrate steadied, the distraction welcome.

"Thought I would. Are you?"

"No. I meant it when I said I'm really not a singer."

"That means nothing here. Wait and see." She bounced out of her chair and headed for the board, writing her name on the short list.

Hazel hadn't been wrong about the quality of the singing. A shaky version of "Blue Moon" followed an off-key rendition of Natalie Imbruglia's "Torn". Thankfully, after that, an enthusiastic version of "Y.M.C.A." complete with dance moves from four tradies still wearing their high-vis and work boots brought the most applause.

"Those blokes install solar panels," Hazel said. "They were working on a roof a couple of doors down from my parents' place. Tom Petty's 'Free Falling' came on the radio. They turned it up and sang along, all the while pretending to fall off the roof."

Imogen laughed. "They're the best so far."

"They're the highlight most weeks. Better than me, although you get to judge that now."

Her name was called, and she went up to the stage.

An infectious disco beat from the '70s started and Hazel launched into Dan Hartman's "Instant Replay", complete with shimmying, twirls, and a lot of shaking back of her hair. Hazel's obvious enjoyment in her performance and infectious grin combined with the catchy tune had everyone clapping along. She received nearly as much applause as the tradies.

She returned to her seat and set down two vouchers for a free drink. "Want another? Two vouchers today; they must have liked it."

"I'm driving," Imogen said. A pang of regret shafted her stomach. It would have been fun to sit here and drink more wine, to laugh with Hazel and keep a polite smile for the more awful singers while cheering the good ones. A stout, older lady was singing Midnight Oil's "Beds are Burning" and making an excellent job of it.

"That's CeCe," Hazel said with a nod of her head. "She was a cabaret singer when she was younger, and she learns a different song each time. She even does punk rock." She looked at some kids making their way to the front. "But if you want to go, now's a good time."

Imogen nodded, and stood, waiting as Hazel adjusted something on her prosthesis and stood as well.

Outside, the street was quiet, even though it was barely nine. Shops on either side of the RSL were dark, and the only person outside was a staff member having a smoke break.

"It's usually like this," Hazel said. "Small towns. You could run naked down the main street at midnight without anyone seeing you."

Imogen laughed. Her fingers found Hazel's, and she squeezed. "I like it, to be honest. The city is exciting, but most nights I stayed home." Hazel's fingers were warm in hers. She linked them firmly together. Hand holding was allowed. That was in the friend zone—she often held hands with Jess.

"You surprise me, Imogen Alexander. Moving here. Liking it. Guess you weren't the only one to make assumptions."

Hazel's hair, unrestrained after her karaoke performance lifted in the breeze, tickling Imogen's cheek. She brushed it away with her free hand, but more took its place.

"Sorry. I seem to have lost my hairband." Hazel tried to smooth it down, one-handed. "It's a losing battle."

Imogen headed toward her car. Hazel's hair was soft, smelled of something botanical, and brushed Imogen's face in a distracting way.

"Don't worry." She gave up the attempts to brush it away, and let its soft waves tickle her cheek.

They reached the car. "Thanks for the lift," Hazel said. "I'd offer to walk home, but to be honest, my leg is a bit sore today. Achey. The dancing didn't help, of course, but it was fun."

"Do you ever take Petunia off when you're out?"

"It depends. If I feel safe, if I'm with friends I'm comfortable with, then maybe. But if I think I might need to move quickly, then no. Or if I'm with people I don't know well."

"Do you take it off at George's?"

"Sometimes. Not often. I'm usually doing things for George—small tasks, putting groceries away and so on, so it's easier to leave it on."

"I don't mind if you want to take it off. If you're comfortable with that." Imogen got into the driver's seat to give Hazel time to consider.

Hazel, too, slid into the car. "Thanks. For the offer, that is. I'll be home in a few minutes, so it's okay. But I'll remember what you said." She rubbed her thigh above Petunia.

Imogen put the Tesla in drive and pulled away. In only a few minutes, she pulled up outside Hazel's house. She put the car in park but left the engine running.

"Thanks," Hazel said. She rested her head back on the seat. "I could sleep here. Soft, comfy, luxurious leather." She straightened and rubbed her leg once more. "But I'd better get inside before my knee stiffens up."

"Do you need help?" Was it the right thing to offer?

"No, I'm fine, but thanks for asking. I'll ice my nubbin and sleep in a compression sock. It's nothing new."

Imogen's gaze dropped to where Hazel was kneading her left thigh. She sounded so matter-of-fact about her limb loss, but after, what, maybe seventeen years without it, why wouldn't she be? If she was in Hazel's position, she didn't think she would manage half as well.

"I was so angry after my amputation. I cried a lot. Wouldn't get out of bed most days, even when the doctors told me I could. Flung myself in dramatic fashion around my bedroom declaring my life was over. Teenage drama come early."

"I think you had good reason for the drama." She took a breath. "How did you know what I was thinking?"

"Honestly? Because you were staring at my leg, and your eyes went soft. Sad. Contemplative. Then you closed your eyes briefly and your hands shook. You're very empathetic, Imogen, even though you put on this cool facade. Look at all you're doing for George. I don't believe for a second your new job is the step up you're claiming."

Imogen gripped the steering wheel. When did Hazel get to be so perceptive? "You should be a psychologist, not a handyperson."

Hazel huffed a laugh. "I don't think so. I just got good at reading people when I was sick. I soon figured out those who thought I'd get better, those who thought I'd die. And I learned to deflect the sympathy because I didn't need it. I just wanted to stay angry at first. It's easy enough to read people if you simply observe them." She cocked her head. "You manage people. I'm sure you've learned to do the same—knowing which employee will work the hardest, take on the challenging tasks, and who will slide out of almost anything if they think they can get away with it."

Serenity's pale face slid through Imogen's mind. She'd failed Serenity, and by extension, she'd failed herself. "You're wrong. My skills are practical ones, not people management."

"I'm sure you keep your chilly shell at work. You don't have to be friends with your subordinates, but you do have to be approachable."

A spurt of irritation made her hands clench on the steering wheel. That was one step too far. Hazel knew nothing about her management style, her workload, or how to run a business. Nothing. She was a delivery driver and a handyperson. That didn't qualify her to pass comment on Imogen's business practice. "Thank you, Dr Freud. I'll keep your advice in mind." Her voice would have frozen lava.

Hazel blinked. "I'm sorry. I've obviously overstepped. My bad—I thought we were talking more personally." She fumbled for the door handle. "Goodnight, Imogen. Thank you for the ride home. I'm sure I'll see you at George's soon."

They stared at each other across the darkened car.

"Well, goodnight then." Hazel opened the door and got out without a backward glance.

Imogen watched her upright back and determined effort to walk without a limp. What else could she have done? She couldn't let Hazel criticise her management style. It would be highly unprofessional if it got out in Good 'n Fresh that Imogen was taking advice from a delivery driver.

No. She'd had no choice but to shut that down.

CHAPTER 26
MOVING TO ROCKHAMPTON

So far, Imogen's impressions of Good 'n Fresh were positive. Tamika had shown her around the office, introducing her to everyone from Grayson Fowler, the CEO, down to Kai, the sixteen-year-old high-school kid on work experience. She'd already received invites to lunch with the marketing department (all two of them), and to a baby shower for one of the admin assistants.

Sure, Head Office had the outdated look of a family business, but everyone had been perfectly professional, perfectly polite, and seemed to have a genuine warmth about them that had been missing at Whistlestop.

Tamika threw open a door to reveal a large corner office. "This is yours." An old-fashioned wooden desk dominated the room, but the executive chair seemed new. A sleek silver laptop and curved external monitor rested on the desk. "If you want any other equipment, you can put in the order." Tamika turned to the woman who stood in the doorway. "This is Ruth, your PA. You'll find her invaluable as you settle in. She's been here several years, and she knows the business back to front."

Ruth smiled and came forward, hand extended. Her smooth grey hair winged back from her unlined face, and she wore a skirt and white blouse, with low-heeled pumps. "Pleased to meet you, Imogen. My office is next to yours."

"You, too," Imogen said as she shook Ruth's hand. Her first impression of Ruth was positive. She was maybe forty, with the warm, unforced smile she'd come to expect from the staff here, and a confident, professional demeanour.

"We've scheduled you to have your one-to-one with Grayson straight after lunch," Tamika said, "but after that, I suggest sitting down with Ruth so she can go through our systems and software with you."

"Sounds good." Imogen nodded to Ruth.

"Come and find me when you're ready," Ruth said. "The PAs around Queensland usually have a video team meeting between three and four, but I can skip it if that's your only available time."

Wow. So different from Serenity and her diffident attitude. She couldn't imagine Ruth playing the zombie apocalypse.

"I'll fit in with you," Imogen said, and received a smile in response.

"And now," Tamika said, "Come with me to HR and we'll get you set up with a pass card and parking permit."

———⋘•⋙———

"I won't fudge the issue, we're bleeding money." Grayson ran a hand over his thinning hair. "We have a good buffer, and over the years, the group has invested wisely in property, so there's no immediate worry, but obviously, this can't go on. We've discussed closing some of our least profitable stores, and we've already reduced the hours of some staff, but we don't want that to continue."

He eyed Imogen curiously. "I'm told you've driven the budgets for Whistlestop these last few years, and implemented changes that have kept the chain very profitable."

"That's right," Imogen said. "Sometimes, hard decisions have to be made, but if we can identify a new way forward, then Good 'n Fresh should continue long into the future."

"So, you're the person to make the tough decisions." He nodded. "Good. We've tended toward the soft approach until now. Family business and all that. We need someone clear-eyed and not afraid to take on the hard stuff, while still doing the best we can for our staff."

He leaned forward. "Let me show you where we're at and see where we can go from here."

Hazel hummed as she applied grout to the tiles in the new bathroom. George had given her free rein with the decor, his only request being "not pink". Hazel had no argument with that.

The open shower had easy access—even for a wheelchair if needed—and the spacious bathroom included a washer and dryer.

The stairlift was being installed the next day. George was already talking about whizzing up and down like Superman.

Hazel huffed out a breath. If she could get the grout finished before George—

"Hazel! Tea's ready."

Too late. "I'll be a few minutes. Can't let the grout harden."

"Come up when you're ready."

It was almost ten minutes later when Hazel mounted the stairs. "It's looking good down there. You should come take a look. After all, you have to live there."

"It will be lovely." George patted her hand. "Now, would you like to stay for dinner tonight? Immie's promised to be home by seven."

No way. Hazel pasted on a smile. "Mum's making egg and lentil curry."

"That doesn't sound good. Do you need an excuse to avoid it?"

"It's better than it sounds." It wasn't, but it was better than sharing dinner with Imogen, whom she hadn't seen since the frosty end to their karaoke evening.

George's face fell into folds of disappointment. "Another time."

"Sure."

A key scraped in the door, and Hazel's stomach plummeted. It wasn't seven already, surely?

"Hi, George. And Hazel." Imogen, wearing a silver-grey shirt and cobalt-blue skirt that matched her glasses came into the lounge. She kicked her shoes off and lined them up neatly by the door. "My final meeting was postponed, so I'm home early. I thought you might like to get fish and chips, George, and take them to the park." She offered Hazel a tight smile. "You, too, Hazel, of course."

"That's a lovely idea, Immie, love, but can we do it tomorrow, after my stairlift is installed?"

"Of course. I'll see if I can get away at a similar time."

Hazel's stomach plummeted. In two minutes, her good mood of earlier had evaporated. Imogen obviously didn't want to have anything to do with her. She'd let her mouth run away with her all too much after karaoke—and in the process had cut short anything that might have happened between her and Imogen. She looked away, blinking fiercely. Not that she had wanted anything to happen. *Ha! Right. I can't even fool myself.*

But as well as the churning disappointment from Imogen's reaction, there was something else here. Something more important. George, not wanting to walk down the stairs to inspect his new living quarters. George turning down fish and chips in the park, preferring to wait for his stairlift. George asking her to walk Chip, saying Chip would like to go a little faster than he could. So not so. Chip was a slug on the leash, often plonking his butt down at the corner and refusing to move. She frowned. George hadn't been the most mobile since his hip surgery, but he'd been improving. Walking more. Until…

"George, did something happen the night we went to the RSL? When you came home early?" She went and crouched in front of him and took his hands. "Did you do something to your hip?"

Across the room, Imogen's eyes snapped to alertness, and she leaned forward.

"Why do you ask?" George's chin jutted forward like a prizefighter. "I'm fine. As I always am."

"It's just that you haven't wanted to look downstairs all week. And you haven't left the house. Is your hip all right?" Her nubbin throbbed, and she stood again.

George's glance shifted to where Chip slept in his basket. "Reckon I'm fine. Jus' need a little more time. It was only a little fall."

"A fall?" Imogen jerked up. "George, you should have said. You should have gone to the doctor, get checked out, x-rayed—"

"That's why I didn't tell you. Knew you'd fuss. I'm *fine*. Just a little sore."

"Is it your hip?" Hazel asked.

"My knee. It's coming good."

"Thank goodness for that," Imogen murmured.

"Can I have a look at your knee?" Hazel asked. "I may not be a nurse, but I know something about stuffed knees." Her smile trembled on her face. Was George hiding something serious?

"It's nothing. Just a little bruised."

"All the same, it's stopping you going anywhere." Imogen came over and sat on the footstool by George's feet. She touched his knee. "This one?"

He glowered at her but didn't stop her as she raised his pants leg. The knee was purple and yellow, but there didn't appear to be much swelling. "Can you put your weight on it?"

"Yes. It's just going up and down stairs that's difficult."

"How did you fall?" Hazel met Imogen's eyes. The injury didn't look too bad to her. It was why George had fallen in the first place that was the real worry.

"Tripped over the bottom stair. Must have twisted my knee as I fell. Lucky I didn't land on my bad hip."

"This time," Imogen said briskly. "It could have been a lot worse, George. Why didn't you mention it?"

George thumped his stick on the floor. "Will you both stop fussing like a pair of old chooks? I'm fine. It's just a bruise."

"You might have broken your hip again. Or the other hip," Imogen said.

Hazel looked from one to the other. Right now, with their set faces and mutinous expressions, it was obvious they were related. For a few moments, Imogen's and George's gazes remained locked.

Then with a sigh, George looked away. His hand shook as he rested it on his good knee. "Fine. I didn't tell you as I thought you'd think I was too much trouble. Too hard to look after. I thought you'd put me in a nursing home. I don't want that. I want to stay here with Chip. Hazel's making me a lovely place downstairs that I can manage, so if you don't want to stay here now, you can go and live in Rockhampton. Chip and I will be fine."

Tears pricked at the back of Hazel's eyes. *Oh George*. How could he think that—unless he knew what Imogen would want to do. After all, the news was full of stories of uncaring kids who shoved their elderly relatives into aged care homes when they became too much trouble. Or simply wanted their assets for themselves. Imogen wouldn't do that—would she? Hazel's breath hitched. What would Imogen say?

Imogen's mouth formed a soundless O, and her shoulders slumped. Then she shook herself. "George Alexander, do you really think I came all the way up here just to dump you in a nursing home? If I wanted to do that, I could have arranged it from Brisbane. I came here as I thought it would work for *both* of us. I have a new job; you have someone around to help you with things that are harder. Mainly, though, it's so you can keep living where you love."

Chip, maybe alerted by his master's distress, pattered over. His lips lifted in a half-hearted growl.

"And Chip," Imogen amended. "So that you and Chip can stay here."

Hazel exhaled carefully, long and slow.

"I want to be here. I like living with you. Do you not think I could have found my own place if that was what I wanted?"

"Bill may have pressured you," George said. "I know he pushed you into coming here in the first place."

"He suggested it," Imogen said. "But it was my decision." She put her hands over George's, stopping their shake. "I love you, George. Where else would I want to be?"

Hazel's heart melted at Imogen's words. She'd long wondered why Imogen was moving up—surely the job wasn't that good. It seemed it was good old-fashioned love. She bent her head to hide her moist eyes.

"You're a good girl, Immie, love."

She crept toward the door. There was no need to disturb them, and she was so hungry that her mum's egg and lentil curry was starting to sound appealing.

"And Hazel's a great friend." George's voice reached her, and she paused. "Doing all this work for me so quickly." He held out a hand.

Hazel went across and took it. Her eyes locked with Imogen's and her breath caught. Imogen's blue eyes stared back at her, soft, almost tender. What did it matter if she and Imogen rubbed off each other like a match over sandpaper? "Imogen's right, George. You're the important one."

Imogen's soft smile as she locked gazes with Hazel warmed her chest like a trickle of flame. A flash of memory of how Imogen's lips had felt on her own. The heat from her body. The flame in her chest moved lower, down to between her thighs.

She shook her head. What she was thinking of was a dream. It was best they had stopped the kissing. If she kept telling herself that, surely she would come to believe it.

No. Hazel would stay away. Friends and no more.

CHAPTER 27
CRACKS IN THE MACHINE

Imogen rubbed the base of her skull where a tension headache threatened. In the weeks that she'd been at Good 'n Fresh, she'd been pleasantly surprised at how well her plans to bring it into the modern age had been received, and she'd been asked to put together a formal presentation for consideration.

Now, she stood in the boardroom presenting her ideas to position the chain in the speciality food market—gourmet products, local meat and vegetables, and small producers the national chains overlooked. So far, so good. She'd shown them profits from other independent stores that had followed a similar path, and they were encouraging.

"We'll be keeping the customer service," Imogen said. "The friendly staff and camaraderie at your stores is a huge asset. But when the changeover for each store happens, you'll temporarily have excess staff and a smaller floor area. We can work on each store in three parts, upgrading a section at a time so that downtime is minimised, but I estimate you can reduce your cashiers, fillers, and deli staff by one quarter."

"Anywhere else?" Grayson asked.

Imogen hesitated. She'd hoped to avoid this, had hoped the more major cuts to other staff would render it unnecessary. But she couldn't not say it. Good 'n Fresh now had her loyalty, and that had to come above anything else. Anyone else. "The logs show many of the delivery drivers have significant downtime during a shift. I suggest reducing the available delivery hours during the changeover—maybe to three days per week: three hours in the mornings and the evenings. That will allow you to reduce your delivery staff by half. Given there's only two to three delivery drivers per store, it's a small saving though."

"Fair enough," Grayson said. "Okay, Imogen. You have the go ahead to drive all of this. We've identified Dry Creek for the pilot store. It's close enough for you to be on site during teething problems, and it's a smaller store. Less disruption and downtime than starting with any of the Rockhampton stores."

She nodded even as a wedge of unease drove into her chest. Dry Creek. Where she lived. And the Dry Creek store. Where Hazel worked. Her hands shook, and she clasped them tightly together.

"I suggest you arrange an all-staff meeting on site," Grayson said. "Give them the heads-up as to what's happening. They already have an inkling—there have been staffing cuts at that store already. Take Tamika with you—she'll draw up a list of possible redundancies—that way she can answer the inevitable questions about redundancy payments and so on."

Would Hazel be on that list?

Imogen pressed her lips together. Almost certainly yes. What if she were to mention the possibility to Hazel in confidence? Tell her enough that she could draw her own conclusions and be prepared? But even as she nodded at Grayson and said she'd liaise with Tamika to arrange the meeting, she knew she couldn't tell Hazel. It would be a huge breach of confidentiality—and what if Hazel told Nat, and Nat told someone else? No, she couldn't do that.

She hoped Hazel would understand.

Nat slid into the seat opposite. "Have you heard?"

"Heard what?" Hazel put down her phone. "I haven't had the call up for the Matildas yet, if that's what you mean. They'll have to make do with Sam Kerr for a while longer."

"Funny girl." Nat didn't laugh. "There's a compulsory all-staff meeting tomorrow at seven, before we open." The wrinkle between her eyes grew more pronounced. "Talk is they might close the store."

"Who says that?"

"Zak. His girlfriend is mates with someone who works in Head Office."

Hazel chewed her lip. "Could be wrong."

"Given the people who've already had hours cut, it could be right. And why else call an all-staff meeting? They don't even do that for employee of the month. Congratulations on that, by the way. About time you got it."

"Thanks. My one to your three."

"What can I say?" Nat's usual wide grin was more subdued than usual. "I deserve it."

"True. I don't care about my photo on the wall in the corridor of fame, but the fifty buck voucher is nice."

"It won't last long if you're out of a job."

"I hope it won't come to that. I'll be Barbie-Bright-Side until I hear otherwise."

"I hope you're right. Djalu and I still need my job." Nat levered herself to her feet. "See you tomorrow." She rushed out, leaving Hazel to sit at the table and worry.

Acid reflux burned Imogen's throat, and her stomach was tied in knots. Tamika had led her down a long corridor lined with photos of the employee of the month. There were dozens of them. Hundreds, even. And then, at the end, right near the door to the lunchroom was a photo of Hazel. It was a head and shoulders shot, like all of them, but Hazel's hair seemed more exuberant, her smile wider, her whole image seemed almost to vibrate with life.

Ridiculous for what was just a photo.

Tamika pushed open the door, and Imogen followed her inside. The room was packed. Staff crammed together on the couches, sat on the counters, or leaned against the walls.

Imogen pasted on a professional smile and avoided meeting anyone's eyes as she followed Tamika to stand at the front of the room.

All eyes swung in her direction.

Hazel would be here somewhere. Imogen suppressed a shiver. She could feel Hazel's shock at seeing her and the icy glare on her face already.

The list of potential redundancies was in a red folder tucked into Tamika's briefcase. She'd scanned through it, heart in her mouth looking for Hazel's name. She'd seen Nat's name first. When she'd found Hazel's, a chill of foreboding had stolen through her chest. How would Hazel manage without her part-time job if it came to that? Maybe she had plenty of handyperson work. Maybe she'd be delighted to take the package. But even if that were true, she'd be furious with Imogen for springing it on her. *What else could I have done?* The answer was nothing.

Maybe Hazel would escape redundancy. The list wasn't final. There would be consultations with staff, voluntary packages taken, before the final decisions.

Tamika leaned against the fridge.

Imogen took a pace forward. "Good morning, everyone, and thank you for coming here so early. Of course, this meeting will be paid time. My name is Imogen Alexander, and I'm the new area manager for the central coast." She went on to talk about Good 'n Fresh's history and the need to bring the chain back to a profitable status.

She tightened her stomach muscles and took a look around the room, meeting several people's eyes as she did so. There was Nat, sitting on a coffee table near the back of the room.

And then she saw Hazel. She was sitting on the arm of one of the couches. Her prosthesis was on full display, the titanium glinting under the overhead light. Hazel wore shorts, and a Good 'n Fresh branded polo shirt. Her hair was tied back in a fat ponytail that still spilled over both shoulders. And her face… Her gaze fixed on Imogen, utter contempt radiating from her eyes.

Imogen stuttered her words and for a few seconds was unable to speak. "Excuse me." She turned to the sink and, taking what she hoped was a clean glass from the drainer, filled it from the tap and took a few mouthfuls.

She put the glass down and resumed. "Good 'n Fresh isn't closing. We're not shutting the doors, although there will be changes. The new look will better serve a changing population. Nowadays, people want more than the basic meat, potatoes, and green veg. They look for variety, and fresh, local produce. We will continue to serve our local population, and provide the excellent customer service we're known for, but we will also offer gourmet lines, a larger range of organic produce, and a well-stocked deli.

"We'll continue to trade during the change, but while the rebranding is being done, our floor space will be reduced—and this means we'll need less staff."

She continued to hold the gaze of those who would meet her eye as she talked about redundancy options and the consultation process that would be offered to eligible staff. "Tamika Carpenter from HR is here today to answer your questions about this. When the meeting concludes, you'll all receive a letter giving the number of staff to be reduced from your department, if any, and detailing your options."

Tamika stepped up and opened the room to questions.

Imogen retreated to lean against the fridge. When had she become so soft that she'd almost been derailed by Hazel's palpable disapproval? While she'd never had to instigate the sweeping changes she was doing here, she'd had to request people take on unpleasant tasks, castigate and pull people into line. She'd done it with the minimum of fuss, without allowing any arguments.

Was this what Wayne had meant about her lack of effective people management?

But those meetings had never left her with an uncomfortable feeling in her chest, a squirm of guilt, and the knowledge she had just made people's lives a lot more stressful.

And Hazel's narrow-eyed icy expression hadn't left her face.

Imogen gazed down at her shoes and willed the meeting to end soon.

Her leg ached, but it was nothing to the hollow pain in her chest. Hazel got out of the ute and slammed the door.

Her parents were in the kitchen, a jigsaw spread on the kitchen table between them. Hazel sniffed the air: lasagne. Any other day, she'd be delighted. Today, the rich, cheesy smell increased her queasiness.

"Hi, Hazel, how was your day? Was the meeting the usual bullshit? Are you all getting a pat on the back and a tiny pay rise?" Her father paused, a piece of sky-blue edging in his hand.

"Not exactly. Read this while I take Petunia off." She threw the letter from Good 'n Fresh onto the table, avoiding the jigsaw. "It's been a bitch of a day."

Her parents exchanged a glance.

"Do you need anything?" her mum asked.

"A bucket of wine," she said over her shoulder as she headed for her bedroom.

Inside the bedroom, door closed, she sat heavily on the bed, and leaned forward, her head in her hands. What a shit of a day, what a bitching, stinking, fucking turd of a day. And the worst part? It wasn't the letter, it wasn't consoling Nat and reassuring her, it wasn't the shock and anger of her workmates, who had then had to go off and work their shift as if nothing had happened. It was the slithering feeling of betrayal in her stomach that had threatened to choke her when she'd seen Imogen walk into the room. Imogen, in her crisp business suit, perfect hair and make-up. Imogen, whose new job was area fucking manager of Good 'n Fresh. Imogen, who knew she worked there, knew what was coming, and hadn't even given her a friendly heads-up.

Even Zak's girlfriend's mate had passed on a bit of forewarning.

With a long sigh, Hazel removed the covering holding Petunia in place. Her nubbin was angry red and swollen—like the rest of her. She huffed a laugh. Her nubbin had come out in sympathy. They were a workplace union of two.

She spent a few minutes massaging her leg and applying cream where the swelling had caused Petunia to chafe. Then she rose on one leg and hopped over to her kneeling crutch and scooted back to the kitchen.

What looked like half a bottle of red wine in a beer glass sat on the table by her place, and the jigsaw had been moved to one side.

"So, the employee of the month is on the redundancy list," her dad said. "It's not all bad, is it? They've offered you a place in the Cressingham store if you want it, and once Dry Creek fully reopens in"—he consulted the letter—"an anticipated four months, you'd be transferred back here. Alternatively, you can take what seems like a reasonable payout, considering you're only part time. Are they stopping deliveries completely?"

"No. But they're keeping only one driver, and of course it's Pete, who's the only full-time driver, and who also works stocking shelves."

Her parents exchanged a glance. "It could be worse," her mum said. "With all the work George is giving you, you don't need the supermarket work. Wasn't that always your goal?"

"Yes, but not yet. I'm not established enough to get the decent jobs once George's ends. But it's more than that."

Swiftly, she related Imogen's part in all of this. "She didn't tell me what her fabulous new job is. No wonder Good 'n Fresh hired her, an out-of-towner." She could hear the bitterness and contempt in her own voice, but she couldn't change it, couldn't disguise it. Her Barbie-Bright-Side facade had well and truly flown south. "They wanted someone who could do the dirty work without the local connections. They wanted someone ruthless, someone uncaring, someone without any compassion—" Her voice rose, and she dragged in a deep breath and shut her mouth.

Her mum rose and came around behind Hazel and hugged her around the shoulders. "I know it's raw right now, but try to see it from Imogen's point of view. She couldn't tell you—that would have been a huge professional breach on her part."

"She didn't even tell me who she worked for. That wouldn't have been a professional breach."

"I'm not excusing her," her mum said. "I just…" She squeezed Hazel's shoulders and straightened up.

"How's Nat?" her dad asked.

"She was crying when she read her letter. She and Djalu need her wage to get by. It's different for her, though. They need seven redundancies from the full-time cashiers. Maybe there'll be seven volunteers who want it. She could get to stay."

"What's to stop you taking the redundancy and then trying for work at one of the national chains?"

"Nothing." Hazel sighed. "Except that I don't want to. I like Good 'n Fresh. They've catered for me well—until now. I liked their small-town service—until now. I'm not sure working for one of the bigger stores would give me that. I just want everything to stay the same."

"Nothing ever stays the same," her dad said. "And it's been obvious Good 'n Fresh has been struggling for a while. This idea to reposition themselves in the gourmet market is a good one."

"Artisan sourdough and sundried tomatoes?" Hazel snorted.

"It could work. And you've done so many different things in your life, made so many changes. You've coped with the biggest change of them all"—he gestured to her missing leg—"this one seems not that terrible, for you anyway. What aren't you telling us?"

She schooled her face to immobility. "Nothing."

Her dad reached across the table and took her hand. "Really? Nothing?"

His warm hand and comforting expression undid her. "It's Imogen. We've had this roller-coaster of a time. It's been bad, it's been good, it's been awkward, and then we were friends, and then we were—" She hadn't mentioned the kiss to her parents. Indeed, why would she? She wasn't in the habit of telling them everything, not like some of her friends.

"You were what?" her mum said. "Imogen's an attractive woman. And she's obviously curious about you."

"Curious. That's the word. I'm a curiosity. The amputee friend."

"I don't think so," her mum said. "But you would know."

"Okay, we kissed. Once. But since then, it went wrong. I overstepped a line, and she didn't take it well. She's been cool ever since."

Her parents exchanged glances. "So, you were getting close, and then you weren't, and then she got this job, and then she made you and a couple of dozen others redundant, and you're taking it personally," her dad said.

"Yes!" Hazel thumped the table, and the beer glass shook. She picked it up and took a large mouthful. She looked at her parents' expressionless faces. "Okay. You obviously think I'm over-reacting. And maybe I am. But right now"—she swiped at her suddenly leaky eyes with quick, impatient moves—"I can't get past this."

"Would lasagne help? Massive carbs, tomatoey beef, and melting cheesy goodness? Because it's ready."

Her stomach churned – even the thought of lasagne wasn't helping. "Sure. Let's eat." She took another swallow of wine, hoping she'd be able to force down enough of her mum's dinner to appease her.

CHAPTER 28
THE DUST SETTLES

Ruth consulted a pad. "It's been two weeks since the meeting in Dry Creek and so far, five of the cashiers have accepted the redundancy offer, and two of the night fillers. Others have indicated they're considering it. So, it seems likely there will be no forced redundancies from those groups."

"That's good." Imogen leaned back in her chair.

"The consultation process has started for those with no option. So far, though, no one has taken up the offer to work from another store. It's quite an increase in travel time for people, and many of them have childcare to consider. These aren't highly paid positions. Add an hour's travel time, and fuel costs, and I think some will take a position with the national chains. Both Woolworths and Aldi are hiring in Dry Creek."

"What about the delivery drivers?" Imogen asked.

"Nothing from them. But one didn't show up for his shift this morning. The other affected driver said she was unable to cover at short notice." Ruth consulted her notes. "That driver is apparently disabled in some way. We need to ensure she takes advantage of our career counselling."

Imogen lined up the pens on her desk. "Why her in particular?"

"We don't want any accusations of discrimination. Our process has been impartial, but if she were to go to the tribunal with an unfair dismissal claim, it could negatively impact our image."

Imogen opened her mouth to say that Hazel wasn't like that, but closed it again. The Hazel of now was different from the Hazel of a few weeks ago. The Hazel she'd shared dinner with, flirted with. The Hazel she'd kissed. "I'm sure Tamika will ensure it's all fair."

"She will." Ruth stood and brushed her skirt. "We're genuinely trying to do the best for these people. Tamika is making sure it's all documented and that we're doing more than the legal minimum. I'll leave you to it. I'm doing a coffee run in an hour or so." She wrinkled her nose. "The coffee machine here isn't bad, but nothing compares to the freshly brewed stuff from the café next door. Do you want anything?"

"A skinny latte would be good, thank you." Imogen reached for her bag.

"I'll get this," Ruth said. "You can get the next one."

Very different from Serenity.

It seemed her people skills had improved since taking this position—with one glaring exception.

Since the meeting, it was obvious that Hazel was making sure she didn't cross paths with Imogen. She arrived at George's place after Imogen had left for work, and she was gone when Imogen arrived home. Not that the latter was difficult—sometimes Imogen didn't leave the office until seven. She bit her lip. That had to change. Much of the reason for moving to Dry Creek was to be there for George— and here she was, gone for twelve hours of each day. She'd have to start utilising her work-from-home option, at least for a few hours each day.

Imogen pushed open the front door at just gone four. Mid-afternoon, she'd told Ruth she'd finish working on the figures at home, and she'd see her tomorrow.

Hazel's ute was outside George's door. Maybe this was a chance to see if she could mend things with her.

"I'm home, George," she called up the stairs. "I'll be up in a minute."

She entered the downstairs area via the new door Hazel had installed to separate the living areas. Inside, the whine of a power tool greeted her and dust hung in the air. She walked around a sawhorse and a stack of floating timber flooring and followed the noise into the bedroom.

Hazel was sanding the window frames. Her hair was bundled into a messy bun at the nape of her neck, and she wore a baseball cap, T-shirt, and baggy shorts that hung to her knees. Petunia was covered by the sleeve—to keep the dust from the joint, she supposed. Fat earmuffs and a dust mask completed the outfit.

Imogen waited until the whine of the sander had stopped and Hazel leaned forward to inspect the timber, then she came alongside.

Hazel straightened, and turned to her, removing the earmuffs as she did so.

Was that a flash of welcome in Hazel's eyes? If so, it quickly vanished, and her face smoothed of any expression.

"Hi," Imogen said. "It looks like things are coming along." Dust tickled her throat, and she coughed.

Without a word, Hazel turned to an open toolbox and picked a dust mask from a packet. "You'll need this, if you're going to stay here. Although you might want to reconsider in those clothes."

Imogen looked down at herself. Sure enough, fine grey dust was already covering her shirt. "I'd go and change, but I have a feeling you'll leave if I do." She folded her arms and raised an eyebrow.

Hazel gave her a measured stare. "Go and change. I'll be here." She lifted the sander. "Noise coming up."

Imogen took the hint and left. Upstairs, she kissed George's cheek. "I'll be back. Just going to talk to Hazel for a few minutes."

"You're not her favourite person," George said. "You treat that girl nice."

"I'm trying." Imogen sighed and headed to her room to change. A minute later, clad in cotton shorts and an old T-shirt, she went back downstairs.

Hazel had left the bedroom and was measuring the length of wall above the counter. Silently, Imogen took the far end of the tape and held it in place, taking her cues from Hazel. When she had all the measurements she wanted, Hazel snapped the tape shut.

"I'm letting the dust settle in the bedroom. Then I'll do a quick hand-sand of the sills, before the undercoat. Is there something you want to know?"

Was there? Imogen mentally reviewed the list of stages for the conversion. Nothing jumped out at her. "Nothing in particular. I just wanted to see how it was coming along."

"You don't need me for that." Hazel picked up the pen and let it drop again. "You can come down anytime. I'm sure you have. You're not the sort of person who leaves things alone."

Imogen's stomach tensed at the barb. "It's good to hear from the person doing the work, rather than simply looking around."

"Fine. The bathroom is finished, except the plumber has to return to install the shower and laundry fittings. Once the window frames in the bedroom are stripped and repainted, I'll be installing that floating timber flooring, and George and I will go and look at window coverings for the entire apartment. The kitchen is complete, except that George now wants upper cabinets as well as lower, so they have to be added. The outside area is yet to be started, but as it's you living upstairs, the privacy between the two parts of the house is less important. There. That's it."

"Have you any idea of timeframe to completion?"

"You can't get rid of me from here as easily as from the supermarket. George has asked me to update the upstairs bathroom so that you'll be comfortable." She picked up the measuring tape and stalked toward the bedroom.

"I realise you're upset about Good 'n Fresh. Do you want to talk about it?"

Hazel stopped dead and swung around. "Of course I'm upset. I'm trying not to take this personally." She threw down the tape and jammed her hands on her hips. The strands of her hair that had worked free of the bun crackled around her head with static. "You think I'm an unmotivated, ambitionless person so I expect you think I don't care about losing my job. I've been trying, Imogen. I try to be kind and considerate to most everyone I meet. I've given my time to many things without payment or recognition, and I'm fine with that. Losing a leg, becoming disabled, teaches you many things, and you can sink or swim. You can fall into a morass of self-pity, or you can become better, stronger, happier. Not everyone is as lucky as me—I was able to choose the second path. For many people, it's not that easy."

Imogen closed her eyes as if that would block out the tirade. It didn't, of course, and she owed it to Hazel to at least listen.

"But the one thing I ask of people is that they treat me with the same kindness, the same *respect*, that I do them. And that's where you've failed. You knew I worked at Good 'n Fresh. Nat told me you came in some time ago. But you never mentioned it. Stupid, naïve me thought you actually wanted to see me, not that you were scoping the place out for the job that you took, a job that probably pays five times my pathetic wage, and has a lot more security as, after all, you're the one doing the firing. There were many times you could have told me about your new position, but you didn't. When you moved here, I asked George where your new job was, but he didn't know. So you were hiding it. That's disrespectful, and not what a *friend* does."

"Is that all?" Imogen asked quietly. Hazel's words bit deep, like a scalpel to bone. There was truth in them, but equally…

Hazel turned away and picked up the discarded measuring tape, clipping it to her tool belt. "That's enough to be going on with."

"Then it's my turn. No, I didn't tell you before I took the job because if I told you, it would only be fair to tell George. And if I didn't get it, he'd be disappointed. Also I didn't know the state of the company. How could I? No company tells someone its business model and finances before they've signed a contract. So, while I'd thought Good 'n Fresh would be better off positioning itself as a speciality chain, I didn't know if I could even suggest the idea, let alone run with it. That redundancies would be needed were inevitable. And again, what was I supposed to do? Give you the heads-up, so you could… could what? What could you possibly do except maybe warn your colleagues?"

"We were warned. Someone's girlfriend has a mate in Head Office."

"I'll pretend I haven't heard that, as that mate would have been in breach of their contract—a firing offence. But, Hazel, there's no way I could have protected your job. That would have been favouritism, and unfair to others. How would that have fitted in to your kindness and consideration model?"

"You could have talked to me. Explained. Given me a heads-up in confidence. Did you know I was made employee of the month the week before? And then I'm dumped like out-of-date sausages."

"Telling you would have been a firing offence—just as it would be for your friend's mate. I couldn't do that. Being made redundant isn't anything against you, personally. It's just business."

"Really? Because right now, it sure feels personal," Hazel snapped. "You've been avoiding me ever since. You didn't even check to see if I was okay. That's what *friends* do."

Imogen ran her hands through her hair. "I'm sorry. You're right. I should have done that. But you're the one avoiding me. You arrive later than you used to, and you're gone when I get home."

"You're gone for twelve hours. I have limits. It takes me longer to do ordinary things in my day. You can probably shower in ten minutes. It takes me thirty. Waiting around for you to arrive home isn't an option for me most of the time." Hazel sat on a painter's trestle. "We can argue until the cows come home, but it won't change anything. I'm hurt at the lack of consideration from someone I considered a friend." She stared down at her hands, resting on her thighs. "Someone who might have been more than a friend."

Her quiet words sliced into Imogen. How many kisses had they had? One. A single, solitary kiss—or kisses—under the sink that Hazel now sat in front of. When she glanced at Hazel, she, too, was staring at that same cupboard.

"We agreed we shouldn't repeat that kiss."

"You said it; I had to agree." Hazel didn't look at her.

"Because I was in Brisbane. Because we were so different. While distance isn't the issue, it seems I was right." She sighed.

"Let's just leave this." Hazel's mouth twisted. "We're not going to resolve anything. Let's just be civil—for George's sake."

"Yes." Imogen turned for the door, then hesitated. "What will you do? When you no longer work at Good 'n Fresh?"

"A bit late to wonder about that," Hazel said in a tired voice. "And the answer is, I don't know. Build my business. See if Woolworths is hiring drivers. Train as an aged-care worker. Or just sit on my arse and collect disability support payments as I could have been doing all my working life."

"You could take advantage of the counselling on offer."

"I could do lots of things. Go backpacking around Europe, do another parachute jump, go to university, have a date with a decent person, learn to ride a horse. Strangely, listening to some half-arsed career counselling is a low priority."

Imogen opened her mouth to reply it wasn't like that, but closed it again, leaving the words unsaid. Hazel was unlikely to believe her right now. "Then I'll see you around." With a stiff nod, she let herself out of the unfinished apartment and headed back upstairs to George.

CHAPTER 29
UNCOMFORTABLE TRUTHS

The last thing Hazel wanted was to go in for her final day at Good 'n Fresh. The thought of having Imogen shake her hand and pass her a cheque made her stomach turn. But she wanted to see her friends and hear their plans, and of course there was paperwork to sign, and keys, swipe cards, and other paraphernalia to return.

To her relief, it was Tamika who conducted her exit interview.

"You can still take up the offer of career counselling and financial advice for the next six months," Tamika said. "And of course, we will give you a glowing reference."

Hazel managed a stiff smile and thanked her, closing the door softly behind her rather than letting it slam. *So, that's that then.* Nearly six years of employment ended with a handshake, an admittedly generous cheque, and hugs from her friends.

She found Nat on her way out.

"I'm sorry you're going," Nat said. "But we'll still see each other."

"We will," she assured her. "And I'm so happy you got to keep your job."

Nat hugged her hard, and then Hazel walked out, down the corridor, past the Employee of the Month photos, and into the sunshine.

Onward. Now she was no longer Hazel Lee, part-time delivery driver, but Hazel Lee, handywoman and small business owner.

Her stomach lurched. She could do this.

She had to.

"Incoming!" George's triumphant cry made Hazel smile. Then the whir of the stairlift sounded.

She continued to screw on the final handle for the kitchen cabinet. Any second now…

"It's like a magic carpet." George appeared in the doorway, leaning on his stick. "Mebbe I'll go back up and come down again, just because I can."

"You could. You could also take Chip on it, although better if he takes the stairs. He might lose some weight."

Chip appeared behind George, as if summoned.

"Want to take me out to lunch?" George asked. "Seeing as how you've got your truck here."

She swung the cupboard door back and forth, checking it closed correctly. "Sure. Best offer I've had all week. Where do you want to go?"

"How about a picnic? Immie made me a sandwich before she left for work. We could have half each, and take the salad she made for dinner as well."

"Then what will you have for dinner?"

"Something that isn't rabbit food," George said.

"Sure, we can do that." If Imogen had to make a different meal, well, so be it. "We can go to the town overlook. Chip can waddle in the park."

Thirty minutes later, Hazel pulled the truck up at the overlook then carried the food across to one of the shaded tables. George sat and opened the cooler. "Tinned salmon sandwich. It's my favourite now Immie's stopped me eating salami."

Hazel divided the salad onto two plates and added half a sandwich each.

"Christine and I came here in our courting days," George said. "It wasn't like this then, of course—just a dirt track and no picnic tables. It was here I asked her to marry me. Here we decided to buy the house. And here that Christine told me her cancer had come back."

"I'm sorry," Hazel said. "I wish I'd met her."

"She'd have liked you. She was as kind in her way as you are. You know, Hazel, in a lot of ways, I think of you as the daughter Christine and I never had. If we'd had a child, I would have hoped they would turn out like you."

Emotion choked her throat, and for a moment she couldn't speak. She squeezed his hand where it lay on the table. "Thank you. That's the nicest thing anyone's said to me lately."

His filmy eyes gazed at her. "No one's said many nice things lately, have they? Certainly not my niece. Although, I think you gave as good as you got."

"How do you know?"

"I could hear you arguing through the floor. And then Immie came back upstairs with a face like sour milk. Oh, she shook it soon enough, but you upset her, Hazel."

"It takes two."

"I know. And she didn't handle the whole Good 'n Fresh thing well at all."

The bile rose again in Hazel's throat. "Guess when you're that successful, you don't have to answer to anyone."

"I don't think it's that." George took the top off his sandwich and inspected the contents. "I wish Immie wouldn't put cucumber in these." He flicked it out. "I think she didn't know how better to handle it. Her parents are the distant, hands-off sort. For all that they're academics, they don't communicate very well. No wonder Immie's the same. She just doesn't do people well."

"Guess she's in the wrong job then." The words came out with a bitterness she didn't intend. She was over Imogen. What she did, how she behaved, and who she fired was no longer her concern. Distant civility was their new normal.

"She's good at her job, from what I hear. But she's been taken advantage of in the past, because she's always put her head down, her bum up, done the work, and ignored the social niceties." George replaced the top of his sandwich and took a bite. "You have social skills. People skills. You can talk to anyone—look what you do at the *Borrow a Person* days at the library."

"I'm too soft. Maybe too gullible." She put her sandwich down. "A tougher person would have challenged Imogen at that staff meeting."

"And what good would that have done, except make her look bad? You wouldn't do that, Hazel."

"You're right," she said with a sigh. "I'm too nice."

"She's cooking dinner tonight," George said. "She doesn't know it yet, but she has to—we ate the salad. Will you stay?"

"I can't. Not tonight."

"Can't or won't?"

"Okay, won't. She doesn't want to see me, so you can stop your matchmaking."

"No matchmaking. But I would like it if two people I love would be friends."

Her heart melted. "You big old softie."

His jaw jutted. "Yup. Of course, I'd like it better if you were dating, but I know when I'm beat."

"I still can't stay tonight. I've got a massage booked. All this physical work is hard on my nubbin. It's swelling more than ever. The hot weather doesn't help, either."

George levelled his gaze at her. "And the delivery driving didn't do this?"

"No, it wasn't as tough. There wasn't as much friction on the prosthetic cup from the different movements."

"Will you get used to it?"

She sighed. "I hope so. But since I've been working nearly full time on your apartment, it hasn't improved." And that was a problem she wasn't yet ready to face. How could she run her own business if her disability was going to restrain her? She'd always prided herself on not letting it get in her way, not allowing it to hold her back. Wasn't she the first amputee ever to play on her school netball team? Okay, only the third team, only in goal defence, with less court to cover, and only for part of the match, but she'd done it.

"You could work less." George took a forkful of salad and ate it with a dismal expression.

"I know you're fine with that, but if I'm to run a business, I'll have to work long hours." She looked down at her hands. "And I don't know if I'll be able to do that. I don't know if I'm fooling myself. I've always tried not to let my lack of a leg hold me back, but now…I'm beginning to wonder."

A magpie's warbling call, and the frantic twittering of a crackle of cockatoos doing a fly-past echoed through the static in her head. Her fingers pressed the tattoo on her wrist: *I can do more*. Her mantra, one that had sustained her, kept her striving to be as good or better than other people. *But at what cost?* Her heart thundered. Why had she admitted to George something she'd never dared admit even to herself?

"Has it always been like this, if you work too hard?" he asked now, his lined face awash with concern.

"I've never worked as many hours on a renovation project before. I've been telling myself it's just the summer heat." She looked down at her hands. "But I don't think it is. I know my body pretty well. My nubbin is swollen by mid-afternoon. It's rubbing on Petunia's cup. I've been having a couple of massages a week, I've seen the physio and I have an appointment with the prosthetist, but not for another three weeks."

"You've had Petunia altered before," George said. "You said it happens quite often."

"Yes, but it's not like this. In the mornings, everything is fine. But later." She massaged her leg over the covering securing Petunia.

"Do you have to work all those hours?"

"I'm proving myself. Not just myself, but for anyone less able-bodied who is sick of being told they can't do things. Or is passed over. And now I'm failing."

"What rot," George said. "Everyone needs different things, different times and assistance to get through their life. Look at me: a few months ago, I was looking after myself. Now I need Immie to be around, and Emma to clean the skirting boards, and a stairlift to get around me own home. That's not failing. That's just me being different from others. The payout you got from the supermarket… What are you going to do with it?"

"I was going to put it into my business. Maybe get a better truck. More tools and equipment. Maybe a ride-on mower."

"Hmm. Is this your dream, Hazel? Mowing lawns and fixing my kitchen cabinets? Even doing all the work on my downstairs space. Will you still be complaining your leg hurts when you're fifty?"

She glared. "I don't complain."

"You don't," he agreed. "And mebbe you should. But mebbe, you could think if there's something else you want to do. Something that doesn't make you cry with the pain of your leg hurting. There's no shame in wanting that. And you're smart. As clever in your own way as Immie is in hers. Why don't you study? Use the money, study, work part-time doing this handy stuff if you want. Be a librarian like your mum."

"I like working for myself. That way I can pick my hours, do other things. I can't do that as a librarian."

"A designer then. One of them people who designs buildings."

"An architect?"

"Yes, that. Look how you made my new apartment work so well for me, jigging around the space to get the best use from it."

"I think that's an interior architect. Or a designer." Scenes ran through her head: measuring and calculating the best use of space in George's tiny new kitchen. Working out the most efficient way to hang the doors, angle the counter. A bench that would fold away when not in use. Was that what a designer did? Or was that another profession? She shoved the thought out of her head. Right now, she had a customer to keep happy.

She gathered up the remains of the picnic. "Is there anywhere else you want to go while we're out? Or shall we go back? You can tell me where you'd like the built-in wardrobes in the bedroom."

"Had lunch with Hazel today," George said.

"You have lunch with her most days." Imogen straightened from peering in the fridge. "By any chance did you eat the salad I'd made for dinner?"

"Might have. Definitely did. But Hazel texted her mum, and Maxie dropped off two plates of their dinner to make up. Liver and bacon."

Imogen's face stiffened. "I can't eat that."

"Only joking. Worth it to see your look of horror. It's some sort of chicken, with lots of vegetables. French, Maxie said."

That sounded a lot better. Imogen pulled out the casserole dish she'd seen before and peeled back the foil covering. Chicken thighs nestled next to button mushrooms and sliced leeks. She had to admit it looked better than the salad she'd made. "How's Hazel?" She forced herself to sound offhand as she put the chicken in the microwave to heat.

George heaved a long sigh. "I'm worried about her. She's trying to do too much, trying to get the downstairs finished. But she's hurting."

Hurting? Concern flashed through Imogen's mind. What was hurting? Her leg? Was she still stewing over her redundancy?

"Her leg isn't good. And she's worried about money now she no longer has a job." The unspoken, *"Thanks to you!"* hung in the air in glowing letters of fire.

"I'm sure she'll find something. Do you want broccoli or green beans with this chicken?"

"Broccoli. It's not easy for someone in her position. A little thing like her, she gets a lot of discrimination against her. Mebbe she's wondering why she got let go and more able-bodied people were kept on."

"Is she? Or are you putting words in her mouth?" She pulled the broccoli from the crisper and rinsed it under the tap.

"Don't know. But I wouldn't blame her if she did."

"George!" Imogen dropped the broccoli in the sink. "It's not like that. It's done on job titles, and comparing like with like. There's nothing to stop Hazel applying for any job she feels she can do. It's not personal, it's just business."

"So I keep hearing. What about you, Immie? How are you doing with the new job? Is it everything you hoped?"

"It's going well, so far."

"Firing people, making it harder for us oldies to get our groceries."

"There'll still be delivery drivers. Just with more limited hours."

"Mebbe I'll try the big Woolies supermarket." He folded his arms.

"You do that." She bit her lip. First Hazel, now George. A wriggle of doubt squirmed through her belly. Was she doing the wrong thing? But no, her job was to get Good 'n Fresh back on track, and so far, the feedback from management was positive.

It was definitely a wine night. She picked out a bottle of red from the small wine rack and poured a glass.

"I invited Hazel for dinner, but she had to get home."

"I'm sure she did." She couldn't quite keep the sarcasm out of her voice. Her stomach weighed heavy, as if she'd swallowed a rock. Strange. She didn't miss Hazel, of course she didn't. She didn't miss their growing friendship, and she certainly didn't miss the kiss they'd shared.

No. She didn't miss that at all.

CHAPTER 30
A SCHEMING OLD CODGER

"Tell me honestly," Jess said through the video link, "do you miss the city?"

Imogen stroked her chin. "Let me think about that for a sec—no. No way. Strange, but true. Coming here has been freeing in so many ways."

Except one. For a while, she'd thought Hazel and she had potential. Never more than that, they simply had too many speed bumps in the road to get past. But there had been potential. And it had been so long since Imogen had felt that.

"I'm happy for you. Maybe I need to come and visit. See this bucolic paradise for myself. I hear there are cows. And I particularly want to meet the dog. That snappy ankle-biter is what's sold it to me."

"I'll let Chip know."

"Now, tell me something that isn't about work or about George," Jess said.

"You realise that's my life in a nutshell?"

"Really? What about the annoying handywoman? You haven't mentioned her in a while."

"Hazel is still around. She's finished George's apartment, done an amazing job. It looks very professional. She thought through all the small things that will make life easier for George. No really low cupboards. An induction cooktop—no gas that he might leave on.

Large window locks, easy to manipulate with arthritic fingers. A walk-in shower. No trip hazards anywhere."

"I guess she's hyperaware of such things herself. You said she has a prosthetic limb?"

"Yes, and I'm sure you're right. It's second nature for her to ensure a safe environment."

"You could take her out to dinner to thank her." Jess wiggled her eyebrows. "A good excuse to ask her out."

"Not happening." Imogen shut her mouth with a snap. "There is no conceivable alternate universe in which that could happen."

"Why not?" Jess looked away for a second. "Last we talked, you were getting on well."

"That was then and this is now. We're too different, Jess. I'm an old thirty-four, she's a young twenty-five. And she's still hurting over the whole redundancy issue."

Jess sucked her lip. "That is a bitch for most people. Apparently, it's right up there with divorce and moving house. Probably worse than moving house, before you jump in on that. Have you apologised?"

"For a business decision? I wasn't responsible for picking names."

"But you miss her."

Imogen caught her breath at Jess's bold statement, and a wave of yearning knifed her guts. She pinned back her shoulders and pasted on a cool smile. "What makes you say that?"

"You've got your blank face on. You only wear that in business meetings or when you're hurting. And lately, the two have been combined." Her voice dropped to her soothing sympathetic-ear voice.

"I couldn't have done anything different." Imogen tutted. "It would have been a breach of contract to let her know ahead. Professional misconduct. A conflict of interest."

"But you wanted to."

Imogen studied her nails. They needed buffing. She had a small hang nail. "That's correct."

"And maybe you're feeling guilty—"

"Will you drop this, please? Hazel is—was—a friend who can't differentiate between business and friendship. And it's a bloody good thing we never took things too much beyond friendship. Imagine how this would be playing out if we'd been girlfriends."

"Don't double down, please, Imo. You've been a different person since moving to Dry Creek. Lighter, more relaxed. Happier maybe. If Hazel has been a part of that, please don't shut her out."

Her throat tightened almost painfully as if she was holding back threatening tears. But that couldn't be. She never cried. Missing Hazel? Maybe. But letting Hazel back in, and in the way Jess was intimating?

Never.

Hazel stood in the middle of George's new living area and turned a slow three-sixty. Pride pulsed in her chest. She'd done this. Her, and no one else apart from licensed tradespersons. She'd designed, priced, budgeted, and managed the project from go to whoa, and the result was amazing.

Three months, it had taken her. Three months of long days and six-day weeks, but she'd needed to get it finished so she could move on. Sure, initially, she'd be moving on to revamp George's upstairs bathroom for Imogen, but after that, she'd need other work.

She rubbed her leg where Petunia dug into the skin. The prosthetist had pursed his lips and given her a bigger cup plus various sized liners for different times of day, but her nubbin still ached with a dull pain by the afternoons. And even the liners couldn't entirely eliminate the pressure on her skin.

Still, it would all be worth it if she could secure other work like this, build her business, establish herself.

But so far, that work hadn't materialised.

The curl of worry pushed into her throat again. At this rate, if there was nothing on the horizon once the upstairs bathroom was finished, she'd have to find another part-time job.

A clatter on the stairs made her look up. Imogen, dressed in shorts and a sleeveless blouse, the kitchen waste bin in her hands, swished past the open door to the apartment and continued out the front door.

Hazel dragged her eyes away from Imogen's tight bottom in the close-fitting shorts. No point looking. The only exchanges she'd had with Imogen over the past few weeks had been polite exchanges about the apartment project.

Hell, she talked to Emma the cleaner more than she did Imogen.

She turned back to survey the room. She'd done a bloody good job, and she wouldn't let her discomfort with Imogen take that satisfaction away.

The front door closing made her turn around.

Imogen set the bin down by the door and walked into the room. "This looks great. You've done an amazing job, Hazel. George is very happy."

She nodded. "He's told me so, yes." She studied Imogen, seeing too-pale skin, dark circles under her eyes. A wave of concern washed over her. "What about you? Are you happy?" The words were out before she could second-guess them.

"Me?" Imogen seemed surprised by the question. "Sure, you've done a very professional job. You should be proud of yourself."

Hazel walked closer, her heart twisting as Imogen took a small backward step. "I didn't mean about the apartment. You look tired. Is everything okay?"

Imogen's eyes hooded. "Sure. Just working long hours. The Dry Creek store reopens in full next week with its new branding, as I'm sure you know. Nearly three weeks ahead of schedule."

"I do know. Nat tells me it's going to be good. Chocolate-covered coffee beans and a dozen types of olives. Jamon serrano imported from Spain. Thirty types of hot sauce."

"You're well informed. You'll have to come in for a look."

"I will." She didn't move. "But you don't look happy for someone about to complete a successful major project."

"Just tired. There's always a lot to do for George when I get home. I guess I didn't allow for that when I moved here." She ran a hand over her hair. "I thought just being around in the evenings would be enough for George."

"But it's not," Hazel finished. "It will be easier, though, when he moves down here. Safer for him. You won't have to worry about him tripping or leaving the stove on. I tested the new intercom, too; it works fine."

"He tells me you're spending a fair bit of time helping him. Cleaning that Emma misses, cups of tea, taking him out for lunch sometimes."

"Don't worry; I don't charge him for that. He's—"

"A friend. Yes, you've told me. Often. And that's not why I mentioned this. I wasn't having a dig at you." She looked down at her feet. "Can we talk about this? Maybe away from here?" She flicked her gaze up to the ceiling.

Hazel hesitated. "You want to talk about George? Or something else?" Tiny wings of hope unfurled in her chest. Was this going to be a mending of the distance between them?

"George mainly. We could go for coffee."

"Sure. I'm actually done here for today."

Imogen nodded. Her hair was disarranged, and there was a smudge on her otherwise immaculate blouse. "Let me change and I'll come down. I'll drive."

"How did I know you were going to say that?"

"Because you know I don't like sharing a bench seat with boxes of screws and god knows what else," Imogen shot back. She turned for the door. "Give me five minutes."

It was longer than that, as Hazel heard Imogen's voice rising and falling as she talked with George, but in not too long, they were driving up the road toward town.

"Do you want to sit in the park?" Hazel asked. "There's a coffee stand that does fantastic muffins. Not that you'll eat the muffin, of course."

"Too many carbs." Imogen nodded. "The park sounds good though."

She parked the car under a silky oak, and they walked the short distance to the coffee cart. They took their drinks to one of the shaded picnic tables.

Hazel bit into her muffin. "This is amazing. Are you sure you wouldn't like some?"

"No thanks." Imogen blew on her Earl Grey.

"It's white chocolate, raspberry, and macadamia," Hazel tempted.

"I'm sure. You're enjoying it far too much for me to take any of it away from you."

"I don't mind." Her fingers twitched. This was the first approaching normal conversation she'd had with Imogen in weeks. Before the redundancy. Before they'd realised how utterly incompatible they were. Before Hazel had cut her off. And here they were, joking and talking without that thick tension between them. She broke off a piece of muffin and held it out.

Imogen took it and popped a dainty piece into her mouth. "It is good." She ate a second piece.

"Maybe I should have bought two."

"That would be about three-quarters of a muffin too much."

Hazel waited as Imogen finished her piece of muffin, then broke off another piece and put it down on the lid of Imogen's cup.

Imogen stared at it for a second, then with a sigh, put it into her mouth.

"You wanted to talk about George," Hazel prompted, when Imogen had finished eating.

"I do." She was silent for a moment, seemingly collecting her thoughts. "This position with Good 'n Fresh is intense. I need the Dry Creek store to be successful, so I'm working the hours, doing what I have to. I need this to succeed."

Right. Hazel squashed the thought that Imogen hadn't cared about the people she'd trampled on to make it this far. But she pushed that thought aside; now wasn't the time to go there again.

"I moved up here for George, but also for my career. I thought I could have both, but it's not that easy. Every evening, I spend cooking, preparing lunch for him the next day, cleaning, walking his porky dog, gardening. I'm not sure how long I can keep doing this." Again, that tired pass of her hand over her hair.

"Did he ask you to do all of that?"

Imogen frowned. "No. But someone has to do it."

"Do they?" Hazel asked. "Because when you're not here, George often makes his own lunch—sometimes for me as well. Frank or Mavis come around. He lets Chip out. Does some light gardening.

Goes for a short walk with Chip. When you're not with him, Imogen, he manages quite well."

"But I make his lunch every day! What does he do with it?"

Oops. "Um… He has quite fixed ideas of what he likes to eat."

"He throws it away?" Imogen's shoulders slumped. "I thought he was finally getting to like salad, and chicken breast, not those greasy wings."

"It doesn't go to waste."

She could almost see the cogs turning in Imogen's mind.

"Chip! That's why he's getting so tubby."

"He loves the chicken, yes. And George gives me most of the salad."

"Then why does George let me make his lunch if he doesn't eat it? What else do I do that he doesn't like?"

"Nothing," Hazel said. "He appreciates what you do very much. But as for the lunch… I think he believes that if you don't feel you're useful, if you start thinking he doesn't need you, then you'll leave. And he doesn't want that. He loves having you here, Imogen. He tells me all the time. As for the other things you do…he appreciates those. There's nothing else he doesn't like, but…" Should she say this? She had already partly broken George's confidence.

"But what?"

"He's not as helpless as maybe he makes himself out to be. Sure, he's not too mobile, and he definitely needs to move downstairs for his own safety. But he can bend to load the dishwasher. He can't clean the skirtings, and he can't mow the lawn, or even vacuum. But he can do light housework, prepare his food, hang out his laundry…"

Imogen threw her head back, so the pale length of her throat was exposed. "The bastard. There's been evenings when all I've wanted to do is shower and go to bed, but I've cleaned the kitchen, prepared dinner, cleaned it again, vacuumed, taken Chip out…"

"He's not being deliberately lazy. He loves you, and he really thinks you want to be needed."

Hazel waited until Imogen looked over. "I thought you wanted to be needed, too. I thought that's why we had our falling out. Because I didn't need you enough. Because I wasn't grateful for a redundancy payment. Because I was angry with you, yes, but because I didn't need you enough to retain our friendship." She shook her head. "But this isn't about me. Maybe you need to talk to George. That is…if you want to stay. Maybe you're delighted you can return to Brisbane now. Because once George is settled downstairs, you could."

"I'm not going anywhere. I've got an uncle I need to talk to." She drank the last of her tea and flattened the paper cup. "What about you, Hazel? Is George also trying to keep you around in the same way? This upstairs bathroom renovation… I'm fine with the bathroom the way it is. It's quaintly appealing. If you've got other work you need to get to…"

Hazel tried to breathe quietly. And there it was. Her only other handyperson job evaporating before her eyes. She swallowed away the disappearing dollar signs.

"George said he was doing it for your benefit, so if you're happy, then there's no need." *Shit and damn.* But what else could she do? Unless another customer crawled out of the woodwork, she'd be applying to the other supermarkets before the end of the week.

"And you have other work you can bring forward?"

She raised her chin. "Of course."

"Then I'll let George know about the bathroom."

She managed a smile, even though her chest was tight with worry. She'd be finished with George's apartment in less than a week. There were bound to be some small changes once he actually moved in, but still. One week. And then a big, fat nothing.

Despite her new business cards decorating every community noticeboard in town, despite George singing her praises to his mates, despite her basic but functional new website now linked from the local chamber of commerce, despite quoting on everything from reattaching a mailbox, and lawn mowing, right up to converting a walk-in wardrobe to an ensuite, she had nothing. No new work at all. Maybe it was her lack of formal qualifications. Maybe it was because she was a woman. Maybe one of the more established services in Dry Creek was beating her quotes. Or maybe it was that people saw her prosthesis and thought she wouldn't be able to cope.

So much for George's work marking the start of a successful business.

She'd drifted off. This was something to think about later, maybe on her way home. And maybe she'd stop at Aldi and see if they were still taking applications. She rubbed her leg which ached. Again.

As usual.

Grayson leaned forward in his chair and steepled his fingers. Around them, Marilyn's was bustling with waitstaff placing plates, and pouring wine. "We're very happy with how the re-branding at Dry Creek has gone. When the store is fully open next week, it will be a major step forward. Of course, it will take a while to become profitable, but we're confident that it will."

Imogen nodded. "Thank you. I'm pleased, too. Suppliers are in place, and the new assistant manager is very proactive. More so, maybe, than Roy, the current manager."

"Roy's been there most of twenty years," Grayson said. "I'm sure he'll step up."

"Beth, the assistant manager, has got tastings lined up from some of the new gourmet suppliers," Imogen said. "The sourdough bakers, the olive farm, and the speciality sausages. That's week one. There's more to follow."

"Good. Good." Grayson nodded. "The only thing not going to plan is staffing. Tamika says staff are still leaving. Partly because Aldi is still hiring, and partly because their hours have been cut."

"We knew this would be unavoidable." Imogen folded her hands in her lap and kept her expression composed. "People want job security. Despite our best efforts, some staff felt their best option was to look elsewhere."

"Maybe we were too hasty with the redundancies. We're now in the position where we need to recruit."

"Would you be open to rehiring some of the staff previously let go?"

"Of course, although not with their previous seniority, if that applies. Are you thinking of any positions in particular?"

"We always need cashiers. Nat who now heads that team says they're down five staff if they're to open at full capacity next week. We need another experienced deli hand, and if we're to return to the delivery hours we had prior to this, we'll need another two delivery staff." Would that be enough to get Grayson on board? She didn't know, but there was no more she could do.

"Have Tamika look through those staff who might fit those positions and identify any we'd be open to rehiring." Grayson cut into his chicken breast. "This is exceptionally good. We should find out where Marilyn's source their chicken."

"Already have," Imogen said. "It's local and free range. We'll be stocking it."

Grayson took a mouthful of wine. "Excellent. Good job, Imogen. We made the right decision taking you on."

"Thank you." She toyed with her cutlery, lining up the knife and fork on her plate at a better angle.

"Now that Dry Creek is done and dusted, we can move on to the next store in line—the Gracemere store, just outside Rockhampton. There will be no need for redundancies there—staff can be moved to one of the Rockhampton stores. I'd like you to take a step back in overseeing this."

Imogen's smile froze on her face. Why? What had she done?

"We hired you as area manager; we diverted you into overseeing the Dry Creek store upgrade, but now that's complete, we'd like you to move into the original role." Grayson ate a piece of chicken. "We need you comfortable in that role if we're to consider moving you further up in the company. Queensland manager."

Already? She took a sip of water to calm her excitement before replying. "Of course, I'm delighted to have that opportunity."

"My niece is in the position now, but she wants to step back. Spend more time with her family. We're looking at a six-month timeline for her resignation. You've moved up here permanently?"

"Yes, I live with my elderly uncle in Dry Creek. The arrangement works well."

"Good. So you still see your future with Good 'n Fresh?"

Did she? What had started out as a way of getting away from Whistlestop was now something she enjoyed. Pride swelled in her chest: she was a major part of the turnaround of a failing chain of old-fashioned supermarkets.

Somehow, in the past few months, living with George and tolerating Chip had become the norm. And, since her talk with him, he'd taken on more around the house and she had more time to relax in the evenings. Their evenings on the back balcony, she with a glass of wine, George with his after-dinner port, were pleasant times filled with rambling conversation. It was a long way from her Brisbane townhouse, and the wine bars and restaurants she'd go to with friends—when she'd had the time.

She focussed on Grayson. Did she see her future here, in Dry Creek, with Good 'n Fresh? A contentment stole over her. "I do, yes."

CHAPTER 31
MIDNIGHT OIL

Hazel scrolled through the listings on one of the job-seeker sites. There was plenty of work she could do; but the question was, did she want to? Working for herself had shown her that while she could do long hours, her limb difference made some jobs more physically challenging for her. Barista—too much standing. Fruit picker—ladders. No way.

She switched over to the Disability Employment Services website. They would help her, but it seemed such a step back. She, who prided herself on her independence, accepting help.

She added a job at a plant nursery to her short list.

Her fingers paused on the mouse. Good 'n Fresh were now advertising for delivery drivers. She'd received a call from HR two days ago, offering to reemploy her. She'd considered it, but now that the change had been forced upon her, she wanted to see where she could go. What new direction she could consider. She'd politely turned down the offer.

A display ad caught her attention. Junior interior architect based in Rockhampton. There was no way she could do that job with no qualifications, but George's suggestion tugged at her. She opened the advert. The position was suitable for someone in their final year of their degree in Interior Architecture.

If only she'd taken the study option when she'd left school. Instead, she'd been so determined to be independent, to prove she was as good as an able-bodied person, she hadn't looked past the need to earn money and work for herself.

She opened the company website and read. A hollow feeling in her stomach gripped her. She would *love* to work at this company. Catley & Arnold specialised in designing houses and units for less abled people. They worked for individuals as well as government organisations, and they were a leading Australian firm in their field.

If only she had thought this through years ago. Hazel sucked in a breath. But no. That was not true. To be the person she was now, the person who had got to this point, she needed to have had the life experience she'd had. But maybe it wasn't too late. She could try to get into university. Remote learning maybe. She could work part time and instead of doing odd jobs, she could study.

A link at the top of Catley & Arnold's website caught her eye. *Work with us.* It was probably for clients, but she clicked the link anyway.

Jobs. There were jobs available in what had instantly become her dream firm. The first was the junior architect position she'd seen earlier. But the second… A part-time receptionist, working three days per week. Days were flexible, and it was suitable for a student. Preference given to someone studying architecture.

A trickle of premonition ran down her spine. Maybe this was it. Her thing. Her job. A sign, if you believed in that sort of thing. She snorted. She'd never given much credence to signs and symbolism before, but right here, right now, this website she'd stumbled across seemed to be shrieking her name.

She'd apply for the receptionist position, but first, she needed to do some research.

Imogen sat back in her office chair. Tamika had said that three cashiers and night fillers were keen to be rehired, however none of the delivery drivers were. Hazel had to have enough work as a handyperson.

She got up and stared out of the window. Orla across the road was hanging out her washing, her two yappy dachshunds darting around her feet. George had threatened to set Chip on them, but the threat was an empty one. Chip—deprived of his chicken breasts—had lost some weight, but was still too chunky to catch a dachshund.

Imogen left the room and went to find George. "What would you like for dinner? The choices are lamb chops and veg, spaghetti bolognaise, or salad."

George's eyes twinkled. "How can I pass up the salad? But I will. Spag bol would be lovely, Immie, love. Thank you."

George's preferences were changing her diet, but at least George was happy.

He sat on a stool and watched as she bustled around, slicing mushrooms, removing the ribs from capsicums, and browning the beef.

"I had a good day today." She told him about her lunch with Grayson and how things were working out well.

"So, they're hiring more delivery drivers." He snorted. "And poor Hazel lost her job."

"She was asked if she wanted to return, but she turned them down." She kept her eyes on the frying pan, turning the mince over as it browned.

"I'm not surprised. It's a bit like you, running away from where you weren't wanted."

She turned from the stove, spatula in hand. "What do you mean? I came up here to be with you."

"Did you? Oh, I know that was *a* reason, but you got this good job, too. The one you didn't tell me about. Or Hazel. You were so secretive it was like you'd been recruited by ASIO."

"They asked; I said no," Imogen said, deadpan. "As for why I didn't tell you, I thought if I didn't get it, you'd be disappointed."

"And after you got it? You changed the subject every time. I don't like being taken for an idiot, Immie. It was only when I heard you on the phone one time and you said you were from Good 'n Fresh that I realised."

She was silent. The reason she'd held the information close now seemed so pointless.

"It was because of Hazel, wasn't it? You thought it likely she'd lose her job? And somehow in that clever brain of yours, you thought it would be easier if she didn't know it was you." He tapped his head. "I have no idea what you were thinking."

"Neither have I. At least now, in hindsight. And it's made no difference. Hazel and I…well it's best that we're polite, not very close friends."

"Says who? Thought you two were getting along well."

"We were. Until Hazel lost her job. It shouldn't be that big a deal to her—she always said she wanted to build her business. Her redundancy money should help her do just that."

"Use your eyes, Immie. Yes, Hazel always wanted that. But have you seen how tired she looks lately? How often she rubs her leg? How she limps when she thinks no one is watching? She's been working too many hours here, and she's struggling. She never asks for help. Never asks for special treatment because of her limb difference. She just gets on with it. I said she could slow down on the work, but she refused. Said she needed to show she could work well and work fast. But it hasn't paid off for her. She's going to do my bathroom next, but it seems she has no other work after that."

"Oh." A chill seeped through Imogen. "About your bathroom. I said to her there was no need. That I'm happy with it the way it is. She said fine."

"Immie, you are so slow sometimes. The bathroom wasn't for you. Well, the finished thing was, but I was getting it done so Hazel had the work. She's done so much for me over the years, never charged me labour. I don't know what she'll do now."

"But if she's physically struggling…"

"I can't do anything about that, except tell her to go slow. But it seems she'll have plenty of time to slow down now, with no work."

She'd been a thoughtless idiot. Offering unwanted help was one thing, but she should have been more observant. That's what friends did—they looked out for each other.

"You need to apologise to that girl." George folded his arms. "Sit her down, tell her you've been an idiot."

"Excuse me!" She put down the spatula and folded her own arms. "It takes two."

"It does. But you're in the better position here. Hazel is a bit lost right now."

Exactly how she'd felt when she'd been overlooked by Whistlestop. She remembered the helpless feeling, the knowledge that whatever she did, it would never be right and certainly wouldn't be easy.

But would Hazel want to talk with her? Had she taken the offer of her old job as a pity gesture? Maybe that's why she turned it down.

Possibly.

Okay, probably.

She pulled a couple of tomatoes from the fridge and washed them under the tap. "When's she next coming around?"

"Don't know. She doesn't bring my groceries anymore, since she lost her job, although she'll pick up things for me. You might have to go find her."

The tomatoes were rosy-red, perfect spheres. Juice spilled out when the knife sliced in. Swiftly, she diced them and added them to the pan.

"She'll be at the library tomorrow for *Borrow a Person*," George said.

"She'll be busy being borrowed."

"You can see if she's available. Use my card and book her."

"And do what? Talk in a library? With people—probably including her mother—listening in?"

"They have those private rooms. But if you don't want to, you don't want to. You must have got my stubborn gene."

"I didn't say that." Maybe George had a point. The library was neutral ground, and the small rooms were more private than in the house with George listening in.

"I'll have a look after dinner."

George shot her a look from under his bushy brows. "She books up quickly."

"Guess I'll find out when I try to book. Now, if I make salad to go with this, will you eat some?"

"Some," George said. "Seeing as you're making it. Will you eat the pasta?"

"Some." She nudged him. "Seeing as I'm making it."

Hazel's eyes ached with tiredness. It was gone midnight, and she had to be up at seven to be at the library by nine. But the entry requirements for a Bachelor of Interior Architecture with the University of New South Wales were up on her screen. And she fitted them. Best of all, it offered remote learning.

Four years of study. Was she up for this? Was she *able* for this?

If she didn't get the job with Catley & Arnold, she could limit her chances of getting another job—it was hard to find employers willing to accommodate study timetables. But the seed that George had inadvertently planted was growing branches in her chest. Practicality and creativity. The career seemed as if it were made for her.

She pulled up Catley & Arnold's website. The closing date for applications for the receptionist position was tomorrow. She flicked to her resumé on another screen. It needed amending if she were to have any chance at this.

Hazel stood, rested on her knee crutch and went to the kitchen to make a coffee.

It was going to be a long night.

Chapter 32
Eavesdroppers

"There's no need for you to come to the library with me," Imogen said. "I can pick up your books. And if Maxie's there, she'll give me suggestions for other books you might like."

"Mebbe I just want to get out the house." George pulled his ratty old cap from the peg in the hall and jammed it on his head. "Ride in that fancy car of yours. Mebbe we could go for lunch afterwards?"

Guilt slashed through Imogen. It had been a while since she'd been anywhere with George that wasn't the back balcony. "Sure. Would you like to go to the pub by the beach?"

"That would be good. They do a nice steak pie."

She nodded. When had she stopped policing George's food choices? Some time ago was the answer. Hazel was right; he was well able to make his own decisions.

"You'll have to do your own thing at the library though. I'm going to see if Hazel is free, and if she is, I don't want you listening in."

"She'll be free." George nodded. "And I'll sit in the reading area with a magazine until you're ready."

Would he? Maybe.

The library was quiet when they walked in.

"Hello, George, Imogen." Maxie pushed a couple of books across the counter to a teenager. "Nice to see you both. George, it's war stories week. If you come with me, I'll show you the recommendations."

"That's nice, Maxie. Thank you."

"Imogen, your *Borrow a Person* with Hazel starts in five minutes. There's no one booked for the next session, so you've got forty minutes if you want."

Imogen swung around to glare at George. "I told you not to book! Hazel will have escaped out the fire exit if she's seen me on the list."

"She won't," George said.

Just as Maxie said, "The fire exit's locked."

"And that's illegal. What if there's a fire?"

"We're waiting on the locksmith. Someone tried to break into the library last night. Goodness knows why. They could have strolled in anytime they wanted during opening hours. Hazel's in the small room at the back." Maxie took George's arm, and they meandered toward the rear of the building.

Imogen blew out a breath. So Hazel already knew she was coming. So much for surprising her—she'd wanted to see the expression on Hazel's face when she entered the room. That would have told her so much…such as whether she'd smashed what they might have had. Or not.

She wiped her palms on the legs of her shorts and stared at a cover of a bare-chested man with flowing golden hair. Her lips twitched. Not a book for George. Or her, either.

She hoisted her bag higher on her shoulder and started to the back. The door of the room was open. Hazel was sitting inside, Petunia outstretched in front of her.

"Hi." Imogen hovered in the doorway. Should she just enter and sit down, or wait for Hazel's invitation?

"Hi, yourself." A small smile. "I saw George's name on the list and figured it would be you. Have you got more interesting questions this time?"

Had she? She couldn't think of a single thing to ask—about anything. And she certainly didn't want to ask predictable questions about how she cleaned Petunia after she'd been to the beach. "Probably not."

Hazel held up a typewritten list. "I have a list of common questions. Feel free to ask any of them."

She barely glanced at it. "You must know George booked this without my knowledge. You must guess he did it in an attempt for us to become…friends again. And I'm sure you realise I don't want to ask whether you have a wheelchair or if you can go rock climbing."

"No to the first, and I wouldn't do the second anyway," Hazel said. "I'm not great with heights. So why are you here?"

Out of the corner of her eye, she caught a glimpse of Maxie and George lurking on the edge of the stacks. They each had a book in their hand, but their attention was fixed on her. When they saw her looking, they both opened their books and started flipping through the pages.

"There are eavesdroppers outside. Can I close the door?"

"Sure. I think I'm safe enough. At least in a physical sense."

There was something she wasn't saying. "But mentally?" She took a pace inside and closed the door.

"You mess with my head, Imogen. You're a professional career woman caring for an aged uncle when most people would shuffle him off to a home. You're a city girl, but you've moved to a small regional town—and you want to stay. You're kind to George, but you were ruthless in your cull of Good 'n Fresh's staff. You work long hours, and while you're pleasant to people, you haven't made any friends here. The one you did make—me—you pushed aside. I don't understand you. You're one huge contradiction."

She pondered Hazel's words. True, not true, true. "Aren't we all inscrutable in our own way? You're the bubbly young thing with deep wells of caring. The positive, upbeat person who, on the surface, has less reason for cheer than most. You're obviously intelligent, but you choose to work in low-skilled jobs. You're independent, but you live with your parents."

"I'm lucky that I have the nature I have. And the last two are personal choices and not for anyone to second guess."

"I apologise," she said, stiffly. "I'm not trying to antagonise you further, Hazel. The truth is… I'm trying for the opposite. I'd love it if we could get back to what we had."

Hazel's face smoothed to a blank mask. "What exactly do you mean by that? What did we have? Because it seems to me, there are lots of things we could get back to. Mistrust, irritation, tentative friendship, or even more tentative attraction."

"Not the first two. Never those. But I miss our friendship. The day by the beach, coffee, dinners. Conversations." She lifted a shoulder. "You mentioned the jazz session at a pub. We never went. That could be a start. If you want."

"And what about the kisses part? Do you miss that as well? Or do you just want a mate to hang with sometimes?" Hazel folded her arms across her chest and met Imogen's eyes.

"I miss that, too," she said in a low voice. "It was just one kiss, but I can't forget it. You set me alight, Hazel."

"It was a good kiss. But I'm still not sure what you want. You want kisses? You want a girlfriend? Friends-with-benefits? A fuck buddy?"

"I don't know what I want." She spread her hands out. "Does anyone? Do you?"

"No, of course not. Who can chart the course of a relationship, whether it's friends or more? But you're so ordered, so methodical in all that you do, I wondered if you already had this laid out in your head."

"You upend me." She took another pace into the room and perched on the edge of the second chair. "I'm used to being in control. But since I've been here, it's all so chaotic."

"The thing about people is they like autonomy in their lives. George makes unhealthy food choices a lot of the time. But they're *his* choices. But thanks to your influence, he's eating more veggies and salad." Hazel unfolded her arms and leaned forward.

"I lost so much control when my leg was amputated. I was in hospital. I was in a wheelchair for a while, then I had to adapt to using crutches, learn to wear a prosthesis, to walk again. All that put my life in the hands of other people. I guess my choices came as a reaction from that. Work for myself so no one can tell me what to do. I live with my parents as it works for all of us. They understand. I have all the freedom I want with them. You've taught me a few lessons along the way though."

"I have?"

"In some ways, I take the easy road. It's easier to work for myself than it is to live up to the expectations of others. Delivering groceries, even though I was an employee, I still had autonomy in how I went about it. But it wasn't challenging. I've learned we all need challenges in life."

"Is that what I showed you? Challenges?"

"When I was made redundant—and yes, I realise now there was little you could do about that—it made me look harder at some things. And I realised I was fooling myself. I *am* less abled. Disabled, if you prefer. My limb difference means a lot of things are physically harder—I can do more"—she touched the tattoo on her wrist—"but that doesn't mean it's best for me. My own handyperson business was my dream. But I've had to let that go. I just can't compete physically with the demands, the long hours. My nubbin is still recovering." She touched her thigh. "It's not easy to accept that your goal of the last few years isn't possible." She stared down at her hand smoothing over the neoprene. "I feel like a failure," she whispered.

So like her own experience with Whistlestop. A focus, a drive that was ultimately wrong for her. Her hand shook, and she tucked it under her leg. "You're not a failure. But I think you realise that. You don't need me to affirm it for you."

"I do. Last night, I started the process of making major changes in my life. You inspired part of that change. You and George. So, welcome to the bold new Hazel."

Imogen waited. Was Hazel going to tell her more? And what did this mean for them?

"Would you like to go out with me, Imogen? I'm doing the asking, so if you say yes, I'll drive, and choose where we go."

Her heart seemed to have found a different rhythm. She'd always been the one doing the asking, booking the restaurant, researching interesting wine bars, or a festival that might appeal to both her and her date. But Hazel had thrown this wide open. "I'd like that."

"Tonight? I'll pick you up at five."

That was early. "Sure."

Hazel reached out and took Imogen's wrist, tugging it until her hand came out from under her thigh, then she clasped it loosely between her own. "I'm sure my parents would love to have George over for dinner. If he'd like that, they'd pick him up and drop him back. Or maybe he'd prefer an evening alone?"

"I'll ask him. What's the dress code for our date?"

Hazel looked her up and down, her heated gaze lingering on Imogen's bare thighs. "Casual. I'll be wearing shorts and a T-shirt, and runners. There's uneven ground. It's not the place to wear your shiny business heels."

"I didn't know you'd noticed them."

"I've noticed a lot of things about you." Hazel squeezed her hand, her fingers linking them together. She stood and tugged Imogen up as well. "I need to do some organising for this evening. But I want to do this." She moved closer and stretched up so she could press her lips to Imogen's cheek.

The suddenness of the simple caress made her gasp. Just Hazel's lips against her skin sent a thrill of longing down her neck to her chest. Her nipples tingled.

"I think we can do better than that." She wrapped a hand around the back of Hazel's neck and lowered her lips so they touched Hazel's. For a few moments, their lips moved together, softly pressing, then parting, only to return again for a longer taste.

"So, not just friends then," Hazel said as they broke apart. "Nice work, Ms Alexander."

"Thank you. I'm trying." Reluctantly, she released Hazel, who took a step back, her fingers touching her lips as if sealing the kiss there.

Hazel licked her lower lip with her tongue. "So, until later then."

"Until later."

Later couldn't come soon enough.

CHAPTER 33
CRIKEY!

"Are you channelling the Crocodile Hunter?" Hazel's dad asked. "Was there an explosion in a khaki factory?"

"Very funny." Hazel adjusted her broad-brimmed khaki hat so that it flattened her mop of hair more. "I'm just dressing for the conditions."

"I thought you were taking Imogen for a picnic at Wura Mountain, not going lion taming."

Hazel's lips twitched. *There might be a bit of that.* "I want her to see me, the person, not me dressed to impress or to highlight my body."

"You're definitely not doing yourself any favours dressed like that," her mum said. "But I applaud your choice. I'll give you a ten-minute head start before I go to collect George."

"No talking about us," Hazel warned.

"Don't worry. We'll wait until you're out the door first."

"You must have more interesting things to discuss like—"

"Who will win *The Voice*, what actually happened to Harold Holt, was 'orange' a fruit or a colour first, why my daughter can never load the dishwasher correctly. Big plates go at the back."

"Makes no difference," Hazel said. "I'm off." She kissed her parents' cheeks, picked up the picnic basket and headed out of the door.

A few minutes later, she stood at George's front door, listening to "Waltzing Matilda".

Imogen answered the door and her eyebrows raised as she took in how Hazel was dressed.

"If you make a Crocodile Hunter joke you can turn around and go back into the house," Hazel said. "I've already heard them all from Dad."

"Wouldn't dream of it." A beat. "Crikey, you look bonzer."

Hazel snorted. "Careful. It's not too late to take George instead of you. It's usual to compliment your date on how they look, but I'll let you off the hook this time. You, though, look lovely." The pale-blue T-shirt complimented Imogen's blonde hair and faint tan. Navy shorts showed her slim, toned legs.

Once in the ute, Imogen fastened her seatbelt and looked around. "Have you cleaned this?"

"I might have. It needed it. It's not just for you." She glanced sideways. "Okay, it's mostly for you." She pulled away from the kerb. "Get comfortable. It's about a twenty-minute drive."

The winding dirt road to the top of Wura Mountain was steep enough to make the ute's tyres spin in a couple of places. Hazel drove slowly so that Imogen could appreciate the view. The narrow road passed through eucalypt forest before bursting out of the trees at the top of the mountain. She parked at the top, where a grassy area ended at an escarpment offering a panoramic view toward the ocean.

"Wow." Imogen exited the truck and brushed away a sprinkle of dust. "I've never been here. The view is incredible."

"The road was only put in a few years ago," Hazel said. Imogen's reaction to the view warmed her. *So far, so good on the date.* She unstrapped the cooler from the back of the truck and carried it over to a table under a shade shelter, then returned for the basket. "Let's go over to the lookout proper before we eat."

They climbed the steep wooden stairs to the top of the rocky overhang.

"This view is even better," Imogen said.

Hazel pointed out Breakwater Bay and the lighthouse, and the snaking Fitzroy River with the Rockhampton suburbs spreading out on either side.

Imogen slung an arm around Hazel's waist and pulled her close. "Thank you for bringing me here."

"Not such a bad date then?"

"Not so far."

Hazel stopped as they descended the steps. "Look."

A dozen kangaroos grazed in the cleared area of the lookout.

"This is the country of the Darumbal people. Wura means kangaroo in their language. Guess the mountain was well-named," Hazel said.

The kangaroos scarcely moved as Hazel and Imogen walked back to the picnic table. Hazel opened the cooler and took out two champagne glasses and a bottle of bubbles before handing it to Imogen to open.

She pulled out a tablecloth from the basket, several small containers, and wooden boards, then arranged crackers, cold meats, and cheeses on them. A bowl of salad followed.

Imogen splashed the sparkling wine into the two glasses and handed one to Hazel. "Here's to us and a wonderful date." She clinked their glasses.

"I second that." Hazel sipped the wine, then set about opening the containers. Olives, semi-dried tomatoes, and dips appeared.

Hazel sipped slowly, content to enjoy the moment. Birds sang in a discordant chorus and the sun was low in the sky. "I haven't been up here for a few months. It seems to have escaped the tourist trail—there's seldom anyone else up here. Sometimes, I do a sneaky overnight and throw a swag on the tray of the truck. It's a lovely place to wake up."

"The only time I've ever camped was when I stayed with George as a kid," Imogen said. "We went north and stayed on a beach somewhere. It was fantastic. We put our tent right on the sand."

"Sounds like Carmila Beach. It's a rite of passage for every kid around here. Camp on the beach. Scream if you see a crocodile. Never were any, but you wouldn't know it going by the screams of the kids. Maybe we should go camping sometime. It's unAustralian not to go to the beach in the heat of summer, set up a tent, drink beer, go swimming, and then crawl into a baking tent full of sandflies because someone forgot to close the flyscreen, and try to sleep in a sleeping bag full of sand, with a sheet over your head to keep the sandflies away, and then swelter through a hot and humid night."

"You make it sound so appealing. How can I resist?"

"I love it." Hazel gave her an impish smile. "It's also the Aussie way to make it sound so terrible no one else wants to go, so you have the beach to yourself."

Imogen took a cracker and added some prosciutto and a sliver of brie. "Maybe I'll get brave and give it a go sometime. Are you suggesting we go together?"

Was that a step or three too far? Was Imogen thinking—as she now was—about sharing a tent, about sandy, sun-bloomed bodies, making love to the sound of the waves? Sand everywhere. Not so good that last one. "I was, yes. Friends go camping all the time. If we're more than friends, then girlfriends can do too. I'm not pushing you. There's no schedule for this." She shot her a sideways look. "No list of steps to tick off."

"Nowadays, my preferred camping is an air-conditioned room with a balcony overlooking the beach."

"We can do that, too." Although whether she'd have the money for such luxuries was another thing. They'd been no acknowledgements to her e-mails so far—but then it was the weekend. Not business hours, either for architects or for college admissions. Her mind fizzed white at the implications of what she was setting in motion.

"Where did you last go on holiday?" she asked Imogen.

"The Whitsundays. My friend Jess and I stayed at a resort there. We had that air-conditioned room and an amazing balcony with a view over the water."

"Is Jess a good mate?"

"The best. I don't have a wide circle of friends, but we've known each other since university. We were roommates for a while."

University. That word again. She looked across at Imogen. She was eating lightly but seemed to be enjoying it. "Are you glad you went to uni?"

Imogen's eyebrows arched. "Of course. I wouldn't have the career I have now without it. That's not to say it's for everyone. Trades follow a different path, just as difficult, just as worthwhile. Like you."

Brownie points to Imogen for that acknowledgement.

"My parents are academics," Imogen continued. "Professors at Melbourne Uni. They're exactly what you imagine professors to be like. Rather highbrow, extensive vocabulary, plummy accents—even though they're both Australian, you'd think they were from the Home Counties in England."

Oh. That sounded…intimidating. She imagined herself in a lecture hall, or over a video link struggling to comprehend some wordy professor talking about…whatever architecture professors talked about. She knew so little.

Her stomach turned over as doubts churned. "Did they want you to follow them into the academic world?"

"I don't think they cared. They're very much a self-contained couple, and academia is their world. Their friends and social life all revolve around the uni. They're both past retirement age now, but it's hard for them to give it up. My father, Bill, is a law professor. He suggested I go into law, but I prefer numbers to words. And law has a *lot* of words. I did an accountancy and business degree instead."

Imogen's parents sounded so distant, almost uncaring. Her own had never pushed her in any direction. They silently supported her, letting her work through her choices, trusting her to make the right decision, even if it was the right decision for now, and not the long term. "I've applied to uni," she said in a rush. "The University of New South Wales. Distance learning. A degree in interior architecture. And I've applied for a receptionist position at a firm of architects in Rockhampton. They encourage students to apply. I only did that yesterday, and now I'm thinking I can't handle it. That I'm not cut out for study. That…and well, many self-doubting reasons."

Imogen's hand paused in the motion of moving an olive to her mouth. "Don't doubt yourself, Hazel. If that's what you want to do, well, that's what you will do. Haven't you succeeded in everything you set out to do, despite your disadvantage?"

Her lips thinned. "Not a disadvantage. Just different. And no, I haven't succeeded."

"I'm sorry—I often choose the wrong words. I'd be a lousy lawyer. You *have* succeeded. Look at George's apartment. That's a massive achievement. But the main thing stands—you can make this change. Do you have the scores for the course or are you going on life experience?"

"I'm just below the cut-off score, but I have relevant life experience, and yes, equal opportunity"—she gestured to Petunia—"should be enough to guarantee me a place when the year starts in February. It's a four-year degree. And of course, I'm worrying how I'll manage if I don't get the job with Catley & Arnold."

A magpie swooped down to sit on the edge of the picnic table. It eyed the food with a beady eye. Imogen waved it away, but it didn't budge.

"Your handyperson business—"

"Is a failure. Oh, George's apartment conversion went really well, but I struggle—have always struggled—to get work. The only thing I had lined up after that was his upstairs bathroom, and now that's not happening."

Imogen flushed. "I'm sorry. I didn't realise—"

"No! I don't want pity work. I'm sure I'll pick up a few minor jobs if I work at it. If necessary, I'll apply to the other supermarkets."

"I heard you turned down Good 'n Fresh's offer to return."

"I considered it, but I thought a new start could be better." Hazel chewed her lip. "And I don't want charity. Did you put them up to that?" She fixed her gaze on Imogen.

"No." She hesitated. "I don't have input into HR, Hazel. Please believe me. I didn't put you on the redundancy list; I couldn't have taken you off it. And I couldn't have put you on the rehire list without greatly overstepping my position."

Hazel's heart pounded. "What I do, I do on merit. Or not." She chewed her lip.

The magpie shuffled closer, then in a swoop made off with a cracker.

"Pesky bird," Hazel said. "But they sing so beautifully, all is forgiven." She moved the food closer to Imogen. "Delivering groceries again seems like a backward step. You moved on from a position to a better one. Maybe I should be brave as well."

Imogen finished her glass of sparkling wine. "Another?"

"Not for me. I'm driving."

Imogen poured another glass, then she gazed out over the view to the coast. "Did George tell you why I moved on from Whistlestop?"

"He said very little—he barely seems to know what you do."

"He said I was holding out on him—not telling him about my work. I'm just not as good at sharing my failures."

Hazel's fingers froze on her own glass. Failures? Surely not. Cool, confident Imogen had probably never failed at anything since primary school sports day. Although weren't all the kids winners at that? She waited. If Imogen wanted her to know, she'd share.

"I was overlooked for promotion at Whistlestop. I worked there for nine years, doing more than my job description, taking on extra work. My goal was national manager before I turned forty and the next step was Queensland manager. When the current one retired, I asked to be considered for his job but was told my skills weren't a fit. It went to someone who didn't do the hours or the work that I did, but was good at schmoozing, and getting the best out of people."

Hazel touched Imogen's hand. "And they didn't offer you any upskilling in nine years?"

"None. But the job at Good 'n Fresh came up. And there was George, who was a huge part of the decision."

"I'm glad you moved up here. I'm glad you want to stay. Whatever happens with us, I'm happy."

"It's working out with Good 'n Fresh. I tried to learn my lesson from Whistlestop. I believe I'm more approachable now. The redundancies…they were inevitable, Hazel. Good 'n Fresh was bleeding money. But now they're in a position to build back up."

"Nat's very happy. Delighted with her promotion."

"That's good. I'm learning that management is more expendable than the workers in many ways. I didn't think that before."

"Workers can make or break a business."

"Truth. I'm happy here. The new job, living with George. You."

"You just need your piano."

"That's a difficult one. I'll have to talk to George. I could get a smaller one that would fit. But whether he'll want to hear ragtime… well, that's another matter."

"I'd listen." Her hand still rested on Imogen's. Her skin was warm, soft, and the simple touch started curls of heat in Hazel's body. Around and around they spiralled.

"One jazz fan here at least." She lifted her glass. "I'm enjoying this. You, me, this place, this food. The wine. It's relaxing. Great company."

"I'm glad." Hazel plucked at the neck of her khaki shirt. "Next time, I'll wear something more appealing." She tilted her head. "I'm assuming there'll be a next time."

"That depends on whether you brought mossie spray." She slapped at a mosquito on her arm.

"It's in the ute. I'll get it."

At the truck, Hazel put her hands against her heated cheeks. Imogen was different today. She was more relaxed, opening up, admitting failure. She was also damn hot in those shorts and the T-shirt that highlighted her small breasts. This new, softer Imogen made her think of romance.

And sex.

But before she could put that on the table, there was another big step to take. She grabbed the Aerogard, sprayed her exposed skin, then returned to Imogen.

"Thanks." Imogen took the spray, walked a short distance from the food and applied it.

Hazel shifted so her back was against a pole and rested Petunia along the bench. Her heart thumped. If she and Imogen were to consider more, then they needed to get past this.

"I want to show you something," she said, when Imogen returned. "Sit there." She gestured to the far end of the bench. "I told you about my date with Angus. How he assumed I was so desperate as an amputee that I'd go straight to sex without any intermediate steps?"

She waited for Imogen's nod, before continuing. "I'm not saying we're going to have sex. I'm not saying we're going to be romantic partners. We're still feeling our way around that. But even as friends, there's something we both need to be comfortable with." She touched the sleeve at the top of her prosthesis. "Petunia works on suction. My nubbin sits in a liner in the cup and is secured by the neoprene." She glanced at Imogen. If she looked uncomfortable in any way, then she could still abort. But her gaze was steady on Hazel's leg.

"I have different sized liners for different times of day. If I'm on my feet a lot, my nubbin swells. That was the problem doing George's work. It swelled, it rubbed, it gave me a lot of pain, and some skin damage. So, in the day, I try to sit often, I vary my movement. And when I get home, I take Petunia off and use a knee crutch to get around that house. At night, I let my nubbin breathe. It's impossible to sleep in a prosthesis. Previous partners have been okay with that. But I need to feel I can do this around you. And I need to know you're okay with it."

Imogen reached out and rested a hand on Hazel's thigh. "You can take Petunia off."

"It's not pretty," Hazel warned. "It's a weird shrunken shape—not like a normal leg that just stops. Sometimes it's swollen. There are scars." She swallowed away excess saliva as nerves made her stomach churn. This wasn't something she did often. Indeed, many friends had never seen her bare nubbin. Doing this made her feel more naked, more exposed than if she were to strip and walk down the main street waving pom-poms. If Imogen baulked at this, if she were to be revolted… She pushed aside the memory of one potential sexual partner who'd been unable to handle it. She lifted her chin and stared Imogen in the eyes.

Imogen moved her hand to the sleeve. "Can I? Tell me how to take it off."

Hazel swallowed. No one had asked to do that before. The intimacy of the gesture, the caring, made her throat ache. "Turn down the sleeve until the cup is exposed, then ease Petunia away from my leg. Slowly, to allow air into the seal."

Imogen's hands made caressing sweeps up Hazel's thigh.

Despite the tenseness of the situation, the slow glide of hands over her thigh reignited the coil of heat in her belly.

Then, Imogen slipped her fingers under the neoprene and rolled the sleeve down, below Hazel's knee until the cup was revealed. She gripped Petunia's cup and applied gentle pressure. With a slight pop, the suction broke, and the cup came free.

Imogen lifted Petunia. "It's lighter than I expected."

"About four kilograms. Your leg probably weighs more." Was that her own voice, hoarse as if her throat scratched, tight with tension?

Her nubbin was exposed to the warm air. Hazel looked at it, trying to see it through Imogen's eyes. Pale skin, a weird squishy sausage shape, like a tube of flesh. Nothing like a leg. She glanced up at Imogen.

She stared down at her nubbin, her hand still resting on Hazel's thigh.

Hazel searched Imogen's face. Horror, shock, revulsion—she'd seen it all, but Imogen's gaze was steady, her eyes moving from the end of her nubbin to her thigh and back again.

"It's not what I expected." She traced a finger down, hesitated, then circled around the nubbin and back up to Hazel's thigh. "Does anything hurt right now?"

She shook her head.

Imogen's finger descended again, and this time traced the scar, like a wide H that curved around the base of her nubbin.

"It must feel good to let it breathe."

"It does. Cooler, too, at this time of year." She swatted away a mosquito.

"You have incredible thigh muscles." Imogen's hands moved up again, to curve around the bulky muscle on Hazel's inner thigh…then lower once more, until she cupped Hazel's nubbin, her fingers first exploring, then gently massaging in a way that was almost a caress. "Is this okay?"

Hazel could only nod. Never had she had this initial reaction to her nubbin. Not this concern, consideration, and acceptance. Her eyes filled with tears.

Kisses and sex…well, they came second on the scale of trust and intimacy compared to exposing her nubbin.

Imogen shuffled forward and turned so she straddled the bench, Hazel's leg between them. She leaned forward and twisted a curl of hair away from Hazel's face. "You're beautiful. All of you."

Longing slid down Hazel's spine like melted chocolate. All she wanted was to feel Imogen's perfectly shaped lips on her own, taste the dry wine on her tongue, smell the fresh spiciness of her skin. She met Imogen halfway and pressed their lips together.

Explosions of longing went off like sparklers. With the deepest thing she could share revealed, she held nothing back in the kiss. Her lips opened, and she traced Imogen's lips with her tongue, urging them apart.

When they did part, she swept her tongue inside Imogen's mouth, and yes, she tasted of champagne, and yes, she was as hot and silky soft as she remembered.

Imogen's grip tightened in Hazel's hair, and the breeze blew further strands of it across her face. She brushed them back with an impatient motion then placed her palms on either side of Imogen's face so she could deepen the kiss.

When had this difficult woman become so important to her? So special? Imogen had a depth to her underneath the brittle facade she showed to the world. She had let Hazel in, trusting her with her inner self.

For long moments, they kissed, their lips moving together. When Imogen released Hazel's hair, she ran her hand down Hazel's neck, passing softly over her breast.

Hazel's nipple peaked into instant hardness that remained as Imogen's hand travelled on. Lower, across her belly, and then, when she thought it would go lower still, between her thighs, it changed direction and meandered across her left hip.

It was as if her fingers trailed fire. Her skin tingled where they had passed. They moved lower, travelling over the material of her shorts. One finger stroked over skin at the hemline, before moving on down, over the hard thigh muscle to her nubbin. She cupped it in her palm, her thumb stroking small circles over the tender skin.

For long moments they stayed like that, until, with a flutter of wings and a squawk, the magpie landed in the middle of the table and made off with the container of crackers.

"Guess it's telling us if we've finished eating, our food is fair game," Hazel said. Her mind meandered through a mist of arousal, the words awkward on her tongue.

After a last caress of Hazel's nubbin, Imogen stood. "I'll pack away."

"We'll both do it." Hazel stood on one leg and rested her nubbin on the bench as she packed the basket.

The sun was nearly set with only the barest glimmer of red on the horizon. They packed everything away in silence, stoppering the unfinished sparkling wine, and then Hazel reattached Petunia for the short walk to the ute.

Hazel slid into the driver's seat. "It's still early. The lack of daylight saving makes for early nights. Would you like to go somewhere for a drink?"

Imogen reached for her hand. "I'd suggest George's place, but I don't think he'll stay out late." She grimaced. "I feel like a teenager sneaking around."

"Are you inviting me back?" Hazel stroked each of Imogen's fingers in turn. Up and down in a lazy way.

Imogen shuddered. "If you keep doing that, then yes, I am. But that's not what we agreed."

Hazel continued stroking. "Tell me again what we agreed. Because I thought we'd just agreed to see what happened. No plan, no timetable. No lists to tick off."

"You're right," Imogen said with a sigh. "But George will be home, talking about what Maxie gave him for dinner. Do you want that?"

"Not really. But next week, when he's ready, George can move downstairs. You'll have your own private apartment then."

"With a stairlift for my nosy uncle."

"You'll just have to teach him boundaries. Him *and* Chip."

"I'll talk to him. Set a moving date. Agree on how much rent to pay."

"Teach Chip to use the doggy door I put in. That's important if you don't want accidents."

"That bloody dog," Imogen grumbled. "He still doesn't like me."

"That makes two of us." Hazel leaned in, and her hair fell across Imogen's face.

She pushed it back with both hands, and Hazel completed the move, kissing Imogen once more. Then she pulled away. "I better take you home."

They didn't talk much on the way. Hazel concentrated on driving, watching for kangaroos by the side of the road, and Imogen seemed content with that.

George's house was in darkness when they arrived. Hazel left the engine idling. "Thank you for coming out, Imogen. I really enjoyed your company." An image of Imogen cradling her nubbin so tenderly, so carefully, rose in her mind.

"Thank you for trusting me." Imogen's face was half in shadow from the streetlight. "Will you come out with me again? My turn to arrange the date."

"I'd love that."

"You know, this was a first for me. Not the picnic, not just your leg, but letting someone take control like that."

"I hope it wasn't awful."

"No. It was rather freeing. I just had to sit back and enjoy and try not to be a backseat driver."

"You managed that perfectly. Although I like to think I'm a good driver."

"You are." Imogen leaned across, and once more her lips touched down, but this time on Hazel's cheek. "I'll see you soon."

Hazel watched as she walked to the door, turning to give a wave before letting herself in.

Her mind and skin hummed in tandem with the memory of Imogen's kisses. Hopefully, it wouldn't be too long before she sampled them again.

CHAPTER 34
MOVING IN

"How about I move this weekend?" George said. "Have you got time to help, Immie, love? Mebbe we can ask Hazel too?" A sideways glance. "I think you'd like that."

"I would." She knew her smile was too wide, too intense, too joyful, compared to her usual restrained one, but the pleasure of her date with Hazel still hummed in her blood. "You don't have to take everything immediately. I'll need a few basics until my furniture arrives from Brisbane. What would you think if I bought an upright piano? Would it annoy you?"

"No, I like a soothing bit of piano music. Might help me sleep."

She didn't think ragtime would count as "soothing", but she'd play some Brahms for George if that was what it took to get a piano.

"We'll leave the dining table here until my furniture comes. After all, you'll be eating dinner here every night."

"I will, won't I? What's for dinner tonight?"

"Salad." It was now a running joke. "Or roast chicken. Your choice."

"Take that chook out of the freezer and make sure you do plenty of roasties. Nice and crispy."

"Of course."

She left George on the balcony and went to get ready for work. She was working from home so she could drop George off at the Men's

Shed. So far, he'd made a dozen drink coasters out of slices of banksia wood. He also seemed to have found a mate to play cribbage with.

When she logged in, she found a message from Ruth.

Check your e-mail. There's an interim Profit & Loss for the Dry Creek store. Looking good!

She opened her e-mail and found the P&L file. The figures for Dry Creek for the past six months were a long streak of red. Except for, in the final column representing the first month since reopening, the figures turned to black. Not a huge profit, but profit none the less.

The next e-mail was a congratulatory message from Grayson thanking her for spearheading the change. Satisfaction glowed warm. What a difference from Whistlestop.

In Brisbane, there'd been no one except Jess to share her small wins with. But here, why she had George to tell, even Chip, but her biggest urge was to pick up the phone and share it with Hazel. Were they at that stage yet? Maybe not. Maybe Hazel would think it boastful, especially when she was hoping to hear back on a more low-key job and a university course.

Hazel. She had a date to plan, too. Something different, something to surprise Hazel. Something that wasn't just dinner and drinks.

Hazel pulled up outside George's house and unloaded the stair dolly and some old carpet and towels. They would act as padding to move George's larger items.

She looked up at the house. Funny, how a house could mean so much. It was just bricks and mortar and empty space. Just glass and timber, and a large garden. It was her biggest project, sure, but mainly it was because of George. And now, it was where Imogen lived. Would she mean as much in time?

Nerves jumped in her stomach. Maybe. She hoped so.

The front door was open, and Chip sniffed around the porch. She wheeled the dolly in, ignoring Chip's snarl and half-hearted snap.

She found Imogen and George in the new apartment. Imogen spun around as she entered and came across.

Imogen gave her a hug. "Can I kiss you?" she whispered. "In front of George?"

"Nothing X-rated."

Imogen's kiss was brief, but intense, and Hazel melted, her nipples instantly hardening.

"It's so nice to see the young people in love."

They broke apart to see George staring at them, a twinkle in his eye. "Mebbe you should move in upstairs, too, Hazel."

"One step at a time." Hazel pressed her palms to her flushed cheeks.

"We were just talking about where to put everything," George said. "You've done such a great job here."

Hazel looked around, trying to see it as if for the first time. It *was* good, it was better than good. And she'd done it within budget and within the time frame. Her nubbin twinged. That last one had come at some personal cost though. *How long until I hear back from the uni? And when will Imogen kiss me again?* It seemed life was one long waiting for things to happen.

Imogen waved a hand in front of her face. "So, Ms Spacey, we're thinking of putting the bed below the window so George can see outside from bed. The TV mounted on the wall between the entrance and the sliding doors. Couch and recliner there. That's the main things. The rest will just fall into place. A small fridge is being delivered on Monday; the large fridge/freezer is staying upstairs."

"Got it." Hazel snapped back to the present and away from the taste of Imogen's kisses.

It was surprisingly quick to move George's furniture downstairs, with the biggest debate being where to put Chip's basket. George won, and Chip got to stay in the bedroom.

"Don't worry," Hazel whispered to Imogen, "the floor is water resistant, and shouldn't stain."

"Stay for dinner," George said. "Immie's cooking. It's salad of course."

"I'd love to." She caught Imogen around the waist. "This doesn't let you off the hook for planning the perfect second date."

Dinner was salad alongside a shepherd's pie. After dinner, George rode his stairlift downstairs, saying he wanted to sort a few things before bed.

Hazel started loading the dishwasher as Imogen handed her the plates. Little pops of tension fizzed in her blood. What would happen now?

"A glass of wine on the balcony?" Imogen asked.

Hazel nodded, and they took their glasses outside and sat side-by-side on the old couch.

Hazel sighed. "This is so nice. And I'm so tired if I fall asleep, I have this lovely long couch to sleep on. You can just cover me with a sheet and leave me be."

"I wouldn't do that. I'd carry you to bed, so you'd be comfortable."

The pops of tension now were a constant stream, like bubbles in a flute of champagne. "Would you? And then what would you do?"

Imogen's eyes hooded. "Whatever you wanted. Kiss you. Make love to you. Play scrabble."

"That's okay. Cribbage would have been a deal breaker." She picked up Imogen's hand and played with her fingers. Her eyes followed the line of stars, and rested on the bright glow that was Jupiter, low on the horizon. A willy wagtail chirped its nighttime song.

"If you get into the architecture course, will you have to study in Sydney?" Imogen asked.

"It's mostly online. Some industry placements. Only a couple of weeks each year in Sydney. That's doable. I really don't want to leave Dry Creek." She lifted Imogen's hand to her lips. "Especially now. Am I being foolish?"

"No, I don't think so." Imogen tugged until their shoulders touched, then wrapped an arm around her.

Hazel nestled into the touch. Her body tingled where it rested against Imogen's, and her hand stroking up and down her bare upper arm made it difficult to think clearly. Giving into temptation, she rested her head on Imogen's shoulder.

"Your hair tickles. It's like the multiverse—everywhere all at once."

"I've tried having it short. It really doesn't work. Big '80s hair has nothing on me."

"We'll get you some aerobic tights and leg-warmers—" Imogen stopped. "Uh, leg-warmer."

She lifted her head from Imogen's shoulder so she could look her in the face. "It's okay. That's not upsetting. And I could wear two leg-warmers if I had my sleeve on that covers the metal part."

"You don't wear it much."

"No. It's just another thing to put on in the mornings. If I'm lucky enough to get an interview with Catley & Arnold, I'll wear it. Not to hide my disability—I mentioned that in my resumé—but so they know I can dress discreetly and professionally." She waved a hand over her T-shirt, grubby from moving furniture, and cotton shorts. "Not like this."

"I like you like this, but dressed up is good too. Like when we went to Marilyn's."

"You mean forever ago. Will I need to buy fancy clothes for our next date? You're not usually the picnic sort."

"Which is why you took me on one?"

"Of course." Maybe Imogen would take her somewhere in Rockhampton. That was about as fancy as things got around here, without leaving the postcode.

"You'll have to wait and see."

"Not too long, I hope." The steady glow in her lower body drove her to add, "Now that you have your own place, so to speak, we have more freedom."

"We do. We have freedom tonight, if we want it."

Oh! So much for Imogen taking it slow. The glow increased to a burn then faded as reality kicked in. "I can't, not just like that. I wish I could, but I have to allow for showering, and care of my nubbin. Spontaneous sleepovers are difficult for me."

"I'll remember that."

Hazel relaxed. Imogen's shoulder made a comfortable pillow, and she curled into her body, her hand resting across her belly.

Imogen stroked down from Hazel's shoulder to her elbow and back up again. "Would you be more comfortable if you took Petunia off?"

"I would, yes, but I won't. I'll fall asleep if I'm any more comfortable, and I should get home. In fact, I will go home." For a moment she stayed where she was, luxuriating in the comfort of a warm, sexy body next to hers. Very close to hers, and the buzz between her legs was telling her how near she was to blowing all the reasons she needed to go home out of the window.

With a sigh, she sat up and swung her legs to the floor. "Walk me to my car?"

Hand in hand, they descended the front stairs. "Bye George," Hazel called. "See you soon."

George came out and took in their linked hands. "Very soon, it seems. Bye, love." He kissed her cheek.

Hazel rested against the truck and welcomed the slight press of Imogen's body as she leaned in to kiss her goodnight.

"You're a comfortable person to be around," Imogen said.

"I hope that means you want me around more."

"I do."

The quiet words sent a thrill of delight through Hazel's body. "Me too," she whispered. "Me too."

CHAPTER 35
RED WINE AND MUSIC

"Our date," Imogen said over the phone. "Are you free this Friday?"

Most of a week away. Hazel bit her lip. That didn't seem like an eager can't-wait girlfriend.

"I am, yes. I'm also free Wednesday and Thursday." Too keen? Would she put Imogen off?

"I wish I was. But I have a work function on Wednesday evening. And honestly, I'd rather our date was on Friday if it suited you, so I don't have work the next day."

Did that mean what she thought it meant? "Shall I bring my shower kit and everything?"

A pause. Her stomach plummeted. Maybe Imogen was one of those people who didn't like people in her personal living space. "On the other hand, it would be a lot of effort just for a shower."

"It's not that. I'm just admiring your directness. People I've dated in the past have seldom just asked for what they want. It was always a guessing game and non-verbal signals. Please bring your shower kit, Hazel. And, just so you know, I have nothing planned for the weekend, except a Friday night with you and whatever we want to do afterward."

Oh! Thank god Imogen wasn't there to see the flush creeping up her neck. "I'll bring a change of clothes, too. Is this going to be a very long date?"

"It might be. I'm learning from you how to wing it."

"And I'm learning from you how to plan ahead. I'm looking forward to Friday, Imogen."

"Me too." The answer came in her husky voice. "Me too."

Imogen wandered around her part of the house, resisting the urge to stare out of the window and watch for Hazel's arrival.

The doorbell rang promptly at six, and her heart leaped in anticipation. She was only halfway down the stairs when the front door swung open.

"Come in, Hazel," George said. "Immie won't be long. At least I don't think so."

"It's nice to see you looking so well," Hazel said.

Imogen hurried down the rest of the stairs to join Hazel and George. *Wow*! Her footsteps slowed as she took in Hazel's appearance. Her wild hair had been forced into the crinkliest, thickest plait she'd ever seen. She wore a dark-grey jacket over a white shirt, open at the neck. Narrow-leg pants matched the jacket, and she'd topped the ensemble with a dark fedora. The effect was so delightfully androgynous that Imogen's breath caught in her throat. Who'd have thought Hazel would wear the look so well.

And it was unexpectedly perfect for where they were going.

"Am I dressed okay?" Hazel tugged at the jacket. "I can change."

She must have been staring. "No, it's perfect. You're perfect." She struggled to find the words.

"She is," George rumbled. "You both are. Now get out of here. Frank's on his way. We're going to the RSL."

"My bag and crutches are in the truck," Hazel said. "If you haven't changed your mind, of course."

"I haven't. You talk to George, I'll get them."

It took a minute for Imogen to secrete the bag and crutches where she wanted them.

They both said good-bye to George, then went out to Imogen's car.

"Do I ask where we're going?" Hazel settled into the passenger seat of the Tesla. "And, I love this car. Makes my truck look like a go-cart."

"It is a go-cart," Imogen said, straight-faced. "Goes about as fast as one, too. And we're going to Rockhampton. Past that, you'll have to wait and see."

"Exciting." Hazel rested her arm on the windowsill. "I get to relax in your luxury car for longer."

"Don't go to sleep. You'll need your energy." She stole a glance at Hazel's feet. "Lucky you're wearing flat shoes."

"I always wear flat shoes. Anything else isn't possible with Petunia."

"Of course." Imogen mentally berated herself. *On a scale of one to idiot, that was about a seven.*

"Don't stress." Hazel reached out a hand and gripped Imogen's knee. "I'm not." She jiggled in her seat. "I'm just happy to be going places with you. If I had to guess, I'd say we're going for dinner. Somewhere with mood lighting, discreet waitstaff, and white linen."

"One out of three isn't bad." So not what she'd arranged.

"So…the waitstaff are exuberant, and the linen is actually bare table. Or butcher's paper. Are we going to a paint and sip place to sketch terrible landscapes as we guzzle fine wine?"

"You're getting warmer. There will be fine wine and mood lighting. Don't try to guess." She smiled as she swung the car onto the highway to Rockhampton. Hazel was so cute when she was excited.

Her hands gripped the steering wheel tighter. When had "cute" been what she looked for in a partner? Cute, warm, genuine. They all described Hazel, but previous girlfriends, not so much. Reserved, professional, or highbrow were the descriptors for them. But Hazel's positivity had wormed its way in like sunshine on a winter's day.

By the time she stopped the car outside an ordinary looking Queenslander house in Rockhampton, Hazel was sitting bolt upright in her seat. "You have friends here?"

"No." Cars lined the street on either side, and a couple walked up the concrete driveway and disappeared around the side of the house. "I have no idea who lives here."

"We're crashing someone's party?"

"No. We're invited." She'd memorised the instructions, and she led Hazel up the driveway and around the side of the house.

A black-suited bouncer stood by the nondescript door that seemed to lead into the space underneath the high-set house. He scanned the tickets on Imogen's phone and opened the door for them.

Hazel gasped.

What was could have been an ordinary TV den in the daytime took up the entire area under the house and had been transformed into a dark and intimate jazz club. A tiny, raised stage took up one end of the room and cosy tables for two dotted around the remaining space. Red lighting gave a moody feel. Waitstaff in black and white circulated with trays of champagne.

Imogen took two and handed one to Hazel.

"This is surreal." Hazel took a sip. "It's like a speakeasy. Is it actually"—her voice lowered—"legal?"

"Absolutely. It's a club that does pop-up events in unexpected places—warehouses, barns, parks, private houses. Membership is limited. Jess and I go often when it's in Brisbane. We got lucky with this though—they don't often do regional events."

"I love it. And I'm guessing the band isn't Aussie classics or punk rock."

"Jazz." She watched Hazel light up. "They always have top-rate performers."

"I must have known on some level." Hazel glanced down at her sharp suit.

"It couldn't be more perfect."

They found a table off to one side where they could see the stage. The silent waitstaff brought out plates of tapas and set one down on each table.

"This is awesome, and to think I dressed as the Crocodile Hunter and took you on a picnic. I'll have to up my game."

"You don't need to change a thing." She pushed the plate of tapas toward Hazel who selected some marinated octopus.

"Do you know who's playing?"

"No, that's part of the whole experience. The musicians come out and that's the first you know. It will be jazz, but beyond that—no idea. I've seen Dixieland, free jazz, swing, ragtime—"

"You must have loved that one."

"I did. Possibly my favourite."

"I wonder what we'll have tonight."

Imogen nodded to where musicians in bright shirts were coming out from behind the backing curtain. "Guess we're about to find out."

A few minutes later, without fanfare or introduction, the music started.

Hazel was soon tapping her fingers on the table. "This is fantastic. What sort of jazz is it?"

"Afro-Cuban." The rhythms were heavy on trumpets and drums, and the musicians played with an infectious joy that transmitted itself to the audience. Imogen requested a bottle of red wine from the server and poured them glasses.

"I hope the neighbours are here," Hazel said. "There's no way they'll get any sleep otherwise."

Imogen looked across at Hazel, at her animated face under the jaunty fedora. She'd discarded the jacket, and the curve of her breasts pushed out the white shirt in a way that pulsed heat low into Imogen's core. Her face flushed warm as a sudden shaft of longing gripped her, and she tried to distract herself with a sip of wine and some tapas.

A few people got up to dance a fast-moving mix of jazz and salsa steps to the catchy beat.

"Would you like to dance?" Imogen asked.

"I can't. Not like that. Petunia doesn't have the flexibility to allow it." She turned luminous eyes on Imogen. "If there's such a thing as a slow dance though…well, I'd love to dance with you."

The trickle of heat was now an inferno. "We'll do that."

For the next couple of hours, they talked and laughed or listened silently to the music. The room grew hotter, the music more vibrant, and the bottle of wine emptied.

The musicians came on for what they said was their final set. After a couple of faster numbers, the sultry sound of the saxophone led them into a slower tune. Couples came together on the dance floor in loose embraces or slower twirling steps.

"Shall we?" Imogen held out her hand.

Hazel grasped it, and they took the few paces to the tiny dance floor.

Imogen tugged her closer, sliding her hands down Hazel's sides to rest on her waist, her supple body gliding under her hands.

Hazel mirrored the gesture. For a few steps, they swayed together, their shuffling feet bringing them closer, centimetre by centimetre until their bodies brushed.

Hazel slid her arms around Imogen's waist and rested her head on her shoulder.

With a sigh, Imogen held Hazel in her embrace, urging her closer still. The music wove a cocoon around them, liquid silver notes that sent shivers down her spine to blend with the trickle of anticipation in her stomach.

She thought of the overnight bag Hazel had brought and a frisson of joy rippled in time with the music.

She fingered the strands of hair that had worked loose from Hazel's plait. They had a life of their own, an electricity about them. Just like Hazel.

Hazel slid her hands up Imogen's back to smooth over her nape and into her hair. She urged her head down as she reached up and then they were kissing.

Imogen fell into the moment, into the kiss that engulfed her in a silken web of longing. The dark room fell away, and it was as if they were floating in space on a carpet of liquid notes. Hazel tasted of the wine they'd been drinking, her hair tickled Imogen's cheeks, and her body was a sweet press against her own.

The dance was everything she'd wished for, but suddenly, she couldn't wait for it to end. For once it ended, the rest of their night would begin. They would leave the jazz club, they would go out into the night and make it their own.

Maybe it would be their beginning.

The music ended, and the musicians stepped forward to receive the applause.

With a final touch of lips, Imogen moved apart from Hazel so she could add her applause.

The lights came up. Imogen glanced at her watch—midnight. The taxi she'd prearranged should be a few minutes away.

"We should go before the rush to leave," Hazel said.

Hand in hand, they walked the few metres to Imogen's car.

"Are you okay to drive?" Hazel's forehead creased. "You had rather a lot of wine."

"I've ordered a taxi. We're staying here tonight. Your bag and crutches are in the boot of my car. We'll collect them, and the taxi will take us to the hotel I booked."

Hazel licked her lips. "A hotel? I didn't expect that."

"Is that a problem? I can sleep elsewhere. I'm not presuming, Hazel. If this is no longer what you want, then that's fine." She waited with a thundering heart.

"It's what I want."

Sweet relief made her limp. "Me too. So very much."

They retrieved Hazel's things and returned just as the taxi pulled to a halt.

It dropped them outside an ornate two-storey Queenslander. From the immaculate white paint and intricate lacework on the verandas, to the formal Victorian-style garden, the large building screamed understated opulence.

"Wow," Hazel said quietly. "I know of this place, of course, but I've never been inside. How will we check in? It doesn't look like a twenty-four-hour place."

"I checked us in when I finished work." Imogen produced keys from her bag. She handed them to Hazel, curious to see her reaction.

Hazel opened the door into the lobby. The dark-blue carpet yielded underfoot as Imogen followed her across the room. Hazel touched the walnut reception desk and turned a slow circle.

"I hope they don't have security cameras in this lobby. They'll be laughing at my naïve wonder."

"If they do, I'm sure they'll be delighted to see your appreciation." Imogen didn't point out the security camera above the reception desk. "We're on the first floor, and there's a lift if you don't want to take the stairs."

"The stairs are fine. They're so grand." She held out an arm to Imogen with a small bow, and arm-in-arm they ascended the wide staircase.

Imogen led the way to their room and opened the door before picking up Hazel's bag and crutches and placing them on the rack by the door next to her things, which she'd left earlier.

Hazel's lips parted in a soundless "Oh" as she took in the room.

Imogen knew how she felt. She'd seen many luxury hotel rooms in her life, but the rooms at the Charlestown Boutique Hotel were next level. Furnished in keeping with their heritage listing, they were nevertheless updated with modern comforts. Best of all, the king-sized four-poster bed had an incredible mattress.

"This is a disability suite," Imogen said. "So, there's a walk-in shower, rails, and a shower chair."

Hazel came back and pulled Imogen's head down for a heated kiss. "Thank you. This is unbelievably perfect."

Imogen held out a hand. "Would you like a glass of wine on the balcony? Or…?"

Hazel bit her lip and glanced away. Her shoulders hunched. "Imogen, I would love nothing more than to sit with you in the moonlight, before maybe showering together, and then drifting to that sinfully large bed to make long, exploratory love. That's the romantic dream this room conjures. The reality is quite different."

Imogen's face froze into immobility. After all their talk, trying to ensure they both wanted the same thing, had Hazel changed her mind, or had she just read the situation wrong?"

CHAPTER 36
NOT A ROMANCE NOVEL

The room was amazing. Opulent, with old-fashioned charm; grand and beautiful enough for a princess. One part of Hazel melted in the knowledge that Imogen had gone to so much trouble to make their first night perfect—the embodiment of a romantic fairytale.

But the reality had always been different for her.

"I love this, the effort you've gone to. It makes me feel…cherished. As if I'm someone special to you."

"You are," Imogen said. "I wanted this to be perfect for us. If you've changed your mind, even now, Hazel, that's okay. This is for both of us. If you're not comfortable, then we just spend the night here as friends. You can have the bed, and I'll—"

"No." Hazel stopped her talk with a finger against her lips. "It's not that. It's just…" She licked her lips. "There's no other way to say it. You're probably thinking of long slow kisses that end up in bed, and even longer, slower lovemaking. And I want that. But for me—for most amputees—I can't just go to bed. I have to remove Petunia, then wash my nubbin. I have to rub cream in to keep the skin healthy. Sometimes I have to massage it to get comfortable. Other times, I have to sleep with a pressure sock to keep the swelling down. And I have to manage all of this using crutches. It's not a problem, but it's slow. Everything is slow. It will take me twenty or thirty minutes to get ready for bed. It's not a sexy striptease, or a graceful disrobing. I'm ungainly and it's medical and practical and certainly not stimulating in any way." Her heart thumped with nerves.

"Sure, I could do a lot of it after lovemaking, but I'm not comfortable with that. I wouldn't be able to relax, be intimate with you, knowing I had all that to do before I could sleep. I want to focus on you, not my nubbin." What if, after all this, Imogen was impatient? Annoyed that her carefully planned evening was not going to be perfect?

"Stop." It was Imogen's turn to halt Hazel's words. "Maybe I didn't know the specifics, but I knew there'd be things you'd have to do. If it makes you more comfortable, I can sit out on the balcony until you're ready. Or leave the room and go elsewhere for thirty minutes. But I don't need to do that. It's you I want to spend the night with, and your self-care won't change that. Is there anything I can do to help?"

"Really? It's not glamorous. It's weird skin and body parts, and probably stinky neoprene liners. They have to be washed out, too, and left to dry overnight." She turned her face away. "I'm not making this seem any more appealing, am I?"

"It's real. Maybe this scenario will never make it into a romance novel, but that doesn't make it any less for us. Would you like privacy to deal with your nubbin?"

The hard knot of tension in her chest eased somewhat. It would be okay. Imogen was looking at her with such concern and care in her eyes…but there was still that something else. Something soft and sensual. An expression that said Imogen saw her as a desirable woman, as a person, not a disability, as someone she wanted to be with tonight.

"No, stay there. Relax on the bed, have a glass of wine."

She walked into the bathroom and set the stool in the walk-in shower where she wanted it, along with the towel and toiletries within reach. Returning to the bedroom, she opened her case and removed her lotions and the special wash for her sleeve.

She eyed her pyjamas. Nothing special, just lightweight cotton jammies for warm nights. Should she put them on or just return to the bed naked? She compromised with the top and a fresh pair of undies, carrying them into the bathroom. Then she took the crutches and propped them by the wall near the shower.

Imogen hovered in the doorway as she sat on the stool and rolled the sleeve down her leg. The suction released with a slight pop, and she was able to remove Petunia and the sleeve together.

Imogen walked over and bent to wrap her arms around Hazel's shoulders.

Hazel melted into the comfort of the touch, letting the tension unwind.

Imogen pressed a kiss to her forehead. "I'll be waiting for you for as long as it takes." She left, closing the door behind her.

Hazel blew out a breath and set about undressing and showering. Twenty minutes later, clad in her pyjama top and undies, she used the crutches to return to the main room. She sat on the bed, leaving the crutches nearby, and picked up her cream.

With a small smile, Imogen went into the bathroom with her own toiletries.

Hazel inspected her nubbin. All things considered, it wasn't too swollen. She shouldn't need the compression sock.

The shower had started and stopped by the time she'd finished the nighttime routine for her nubbin. She pulled back the quilt and lay on the bed. It was as if a cloud overlaid the firmest of mattresses. Hazel wiggled. If only her bed at home was like this. She propped herself up on the pillows and closed her eyes, summoning the earlier yearning.

Then the bathroom door opened, and Imogen came out. Her short blonde hair fluffed around her face, but Hazel couldn't help but look lower. Imogen wore a silky cream camisole with loose spaghetti straps. Her collarbones arched delicately to her finely muscled arms, and the silk skimmed the slight curves of her breasts. A pair of silky boxers clung to her hips and revealed more of her slender thighs than Hazel had ever seen.

"You're beautiful." Her voice lowered, husky with desire. "I can't believe I get to sleep with you tonight."

"Me neither." Imogen lowered herself to the bed and rolled onto her side, facing Hazel.

"You can't believe you get to sleep with you either?"

Imogen chuckled. "Believe me, I'm nothing special."

"To me you are." She gave into temptation and traced the lines of Imogen's collarbones with a finger, then slid her finger down to repeat the swoop along the edge of the camisole.

Meeting Imogen's steady gaze, she palmed first one breast then the other over the silk. Imogen's nipples peaked against her palm. They would be soft pink, a delicate shade against her pale skin. Hazel's body thrummed, and the wanting that had tamped to a slow burn flared anew.

Simultaneously, they leaned in, and their lips met in a kiss that grew from sweetly sensual to fiery hot in seconds. Imogen's tongue swooped around Hazel's mouth, and her fingers gripped her waist, hot through her cotton top. And then one of her hands slid underneath the material and stroked its way around to her belly.

It would have been a soothing, sensual movement, but the second Imogen's hand touched Hazel's skin, in a place not normally seen, her senses ignited. The quiet room, lit only by a dim lamp. The luxurious bed with its opulent canopy. And Imogen's skin touching her own. Her senses pinpointed the sweet touch. Each finger pad, the slow glide of her palm. The back-and-forth movement, so slow, so deliberate.

Imogen broke the kiss. "Is this okay?" Her hand made another sweep, fingers drifting lower to tease the band of Hazel's undies.

"More than okay." She eased back to give Imogen's hand more room. Her own fingers plucked the strap of Imogen's camisole, lowering it from her shoulder, then replacing it, only to lower it again. Each movement eased the material down until the tops of Imogen's breasts were revealed.

Hazel's nipples tingled and hardened. The cotton top was suddenly too hot, too constricting. She shifted restlessly. And then heat was forgotten as Imogen's hand reversed direction and moved up, a slow, steady glide over her stomach, up to her breasts. For a second, the movement stopped, before continuing on to circle a breast, moving closer to the nipple.

She caught it between two fingers. "Can I take your top off?"

Hazel sat up, stretching her whole leg out and curling her nubbin up for balance. "Do your worst."

Imogen sat up, too, and pushed Hazel's hair from her shoulders. She opened one button, then another and another until the top hung loose. Then she pushed it from Hazel's shoulders. Her gaze roamed Hazel's body, lingering on her breasts, on her nipples taut in the air-conditioned room. With a gentle hand, she urged Hazel to lie back.

Hazel's heart beat an erratic tattoo. Imogen's gaze raked over her from her face down to her legs. Was she okay with what she was seeing?

A gentle hand pushed on her shoulder. "Relax." And then Imogen was kissing her again, before her mouth travelled down to her right nipple, to take it in her mouth.

Exquisite sensation exploded in her mind. Imogen's tongue swirled patterns across the tip, around the areola, back to the sensitive top once more, before moving to the other breast.

Hazel's mind swirled in unison with Imogen's tongue. Such complex sensations from such a simple touch. But one part of her mind shuddered with the knowledge that it was *Imogen* touching her this way, *Imogen* lavishing such care on her.

Imogen making love with her.

Emotion flooded her mind. When had she come to care for this complex and infuriating woman? When had she come to mean so much to her?

Her lips parted in a soundless gasp as Imogen sat up, and her nipples instantly chilled in the cool air.

Imogen placed her hands on Hazel's body and started a slow caress. Circles over her flesh, covering every centimetre in a steady sweep. Her fingers brushed the top of the undies, and Hazel clenched her core, waiting to lift her hips so Imogen could remove them, but she passed on, over Hazel's mound, and down her thighs.

Her hands paused, one on each leg, just above her knees.

Hazel swallowed. Imogen had already shown she was comfortable with her nubbin, but in this context, things could be different. Past partners had hesitated at this point, as if naked, exposed, and vulnerable, the difference between them was magnified.

Imogen gave her a soft smile. "You're beautiful. All of you. Inside and out." And her hands travelled further, one down her right shin to curve around to her calf, the other cradled her nubbin, her thumb stroking the soft flesh, avoiding the areas where Petunia had rubbed.

"This is you, Hazel," Imogen said. "A part of you, and no less desirable. Everyone is different. Everyone has a different appeal. But to me, it's about the person inside the body as much as the outside."

Her hands mapped a slow path upward once more, curving around her inner thighs until her thumbs brushed the undies. Imogen raised one eyebrow in question.

"Yes. But first, it's my turn."

Hazel surged up, encouraging Imogen to come closer. She plucked at the camisole strap, and then bunched up the hem until her breasts were uncovered.

She flicked a glance at Imogen's face. She was watching Hazel's hand, an intent look in her eyes. Then she met Hazel's glance and the smouldering heat in her gaze made Hazel's breath catch.

She'd imagined Imogen's breasts, but the reality was so much more. Small, perfectly formed, and yes, her nipples were the palest pearl pink.

Impatiently, Imogen took over, pulling the camisole over her head, leaving her dressed in only the silky boxers. "Now we're equal."

Another kiss, deep and desirous, had Hazel's head spinning. When the kiss ended, her pulse pounded a deep beat that seemed to echo throughout her whole body. *Desire. Want. Need.* Each beat seemed to thunder a word.

She kissed Imogen's shell-pink nipples, taking each into her mouth in turn.

Imogen's hands wound into her hair, and her grip teetered on the edge of pain.

"Hazel, please." Imogen's voice tightened, the tension threading through those two words, sending an answering tug in Hazel's belly.

She moved down Imogen's body. A kiss on her belly button. Another at the top of those boxers. Hooking her fingers in the sides, she dragged them down.

Imogen lifted her hips, and the boxers slid down in one smooth movement, and she kicked them away, down to the end of the bed.

Hazel's mouth went dry. Imogen's curls were pale to the point of invisibility, but damp with her arousal. She palmed between her legs, covering her with a hand. "What do you want?"

"I want you. Us, together."

How…?

"Take off your undies."

Hazel complied. Imogen's spicy scent clung to her hand. She threw the undies to the end of the bed where they rested on Imogen's.

"Sit up and face me, legs apart."

Did she mean for them to bring themselves off? Her mind was a blur, and her stomach clenched in anticipation.

"Put your left leg over mine."

Imogen mirrored her posture, and they sat, facing each other legs apart, Hazel's legs resting on Imogen's thighs, Imogen's slender back curved as she leaned forward and extended a hand, palm up. Her fingertips grazed Hazel's lower lips, and stroked, softly, before one fingertip pushed further.

"Is this okay?"

"Yes." Her voice grated in her throat. "Oh yes."

She copied Imogen's movement, her own palm up as her fingers first touched and stroked, then inched their way inside.

"You're so wet." Imogen's husky voice fell quietly in the silent room.

"All for you." Hazel withdrew and stroked along the side of Imogen's clit. "You like this?"

"Mm." Imogen's head fell forward, baring the nape of her neck, the prominences of her spine. "Don't stop."

"I won't." *Not ever.* The thought chimed in her mind and for a moment, her fingers stilled. But then Imogen pushed forward, a tiny movement, and "not ever" became "forever" in her head with a clarity that made her gasp.

She stroked and circled, using Imogen's hums and cries as her guide. When her leg pressed up on Hazel's, and the fingers that rested between Hazel's legs stilled, she pushed a finger inside the slick channel, and stroked with her thumb, a steady rhythm that increased until with a high keening cry, Imogen's thighs jerked and she clenched around her finger.

When she raised her head, her fine hair was damp on her forehead. Hazel removed her fingers and bent forward to kiss her lips.

"You…are incredible." Imogen's smile trembled, and her eyes were damp and pink. "So very lovely."

Hazel exhaled and tried to ease her leg from on top of Imogen's.

"We're not finished." With a swift movement, Imogen stopped her movement with a hand on her shoulder. She leaned forward and stroked up Hazel's legs, from the base of her nubbin and mid-calf to the juncture of her thighs. Her thumbs ran lightly up each side of her lower lips, then her fingers trickled down the centre, passing over Hazel's clit with the lightest of strokes.

She shuddered as sparks exploded out from her centre.

Imogen repeated the movement once more, then settled into a slow rhythm, alternating pressure on the side of her clit with a finger slipping inside. "Which do you prefer?"

"My clit. I can't come from penetration alone."

Imogen's lips curved upward. "You're going to come, Hazel." Her fingers stroked untiringly, hard and soft, up and down.

Hazel closed her eyes and concentrated on the sensations spiralling out from her centre. But as the pleasure built, as the sensations grew more intense, she opened them again. This was not a solitary orgasm, alone with her own fingers, this was with Imogen, and to shut her out seemed wrong.

And then with a final press, and a circle, Hazel exploded into a climax, her hips jerking forward, tight with need until her entire body went limp.

Imogen continued stroking, slowing her strokes, coaxing a second smaller orgasm from Hazel, until it all grew too much, and she stilled her hand.

Her hips were stiff from the position, and she wanted nothing more than to lie down next to Imogen. Her lover.

What else they were to each other was open, but right then, Hazel's heart was full, overflowing with the joy of the moment.

Imogen shifted, and they both lay down facing each other. Imogen reached out a hand, and Hazel matched her, palm to palm. They entwined their fingers together. Sticky fingers, their essences blending.

Then Imogen squirmed the sheet free and pulled it over them. "That was incredible, Hazel. You're incredible."

"Not as much as you."

Her nubbin ached, but it was a tiny ache, one she could ignore.

As if sensing that, Imogen asked, "Is there anything you need to do for your nubbin before we sleep?"

"No. It's all done."

Her eyes drooped shut. The date, the music, the wine, the lovemaking all combined to one huge overwhelming moment. She shifted closer, rested her head on Imogen's shoulder. Her arms closed around her and there was a gentle press on her hair that had to be her lips.

The evening, Hazel thought hazily, was pretty much perfect.

CHAPTER 37
CHILL

The sun shining through the open window woke Imogen. For a few minutes, she lay there, luxuriating in the comfortable bed, amazed at the woman in her arms.

Hazel.

The night had been everything she'd hoped—and more. From the moment they'd left George's house, everything had contributed to the perfect date.

With the perfect woman.

And it wasn't over yet.

She slipped from the bed and went to pee and brush her teeth. On the way back, she paused to look at Hazel. She was curled on her side, facing the middle of the bed, her hair a snarled mess on the pillow. Guiltily, Imogen remembered fisting her hands in that glorious mass, no doubt contributing to its tangled state. The sheet was around Hazel's waist, and her muscled arms and sturdy shoulders drew Imogen's gaze.

A wave of tenderness engulfed her. When had this incredible woman wormed her way into her heart? But she was there now, and Imogen didn't want her to leave.

Maybe not ever.

She caught her breath at that. It was simply too early for that thought. Not seven-in-the-morning early, but too early in their relationship. Hazel was working through the uncertainty of a new career or study, or both. And Imogen was still finding her place in Good 'n Fresh, although that place seemed more assured every day.

And there was George. She'd moved here for him. She wouldn't just abandon him because she'd found love.

Love.

Wait.

What?

When had that even been a factor in any decision she'd ever made? She loved her parents, in an abstracted sort of way, because one was supposed to love one's parents. She loved Jess and how they had each other's backs. She loved George, in a way that was deep and more heartfelt than how she loved her parents.

Where did Hazel fit into this?

That was one for later.

Right now, Hazel was turning over in bed, stretching, and any moment now she'd open her eyes, and Imogen wanted to see that first reaction. To make sure she wasn't alone on this journey. To make sure everything they'd done last night was still what they both wanted.

Hazel's eyes opened and widened. She sat up and focussed on Imogen. "Hey."

"Hey yourself." Her heart stuttered and beat wildly in panic. Was Hazel about to hop out of bed and say she had to go?

Hazel reached out a hand and took Imogen's. "What an amazing night. What an amazing person you are." She squeezed Imogen's hand, and Imogen's heart resumed its normal rhythm.

"Everything you just said, back at you twofold." She sat on the bed and leaned over to kiss Hazel.

Their lips moved sweetly together, then Hazel rested a hand on Imogen's chest. "I need to pee. And brush my teeth. Then I'll come back and kiss you again."

She swung her legs out of bed and stood, balancing on one leg while she reached for her crutches before heading to the bathroom.

Imogen sat on the bed. Hazel's trim waist and firm bottom drew her gaze until Hazel closed the bathroom door. A slow burn started in her body.

The bathroom door opened, and Hazel returned to the bed. She fell backward onto it. "I wish I could take this bed home."

Imogen ran a hand from her nubbin to her neck. "I wish I could too. But it's ours for the next six hours—I requested a late checkout."

"Oh?" Hazel's smile lit up the room. "And how do you suggest we spend that time?"

Later, much later, they sat on the balcony to their room. Croissants, home-made jam, fresh tropical fruit, and strong coffee made the perfect breakfast.

"This has been a magical night." Hazel took a bite of her croissant as she stared out over the formal garden to the street, and on to where the Fitzroy river wound its sluggish way through the town. "A bubble out of my normal life."

"We can do this again." Imogen reached out and wiped a smear of raspberry jam from Hazel's chin.

"Occasionally," Hazel said.

A chill seeped into Imogen's chest. Was Hazel putting limits on their relationship? Was this a onetime thing for her?

Hazel's brow wrinkled. "No! It's not that I don't want this with you. I want nothing more—I thought I made that clear last night. But this"—she waved her hand around the balcony, the room, the hotel—"is not something I can afford often. Especially right now, when I don't have a job. I can pay my half of this, but it's not—"

"Shh. I organised this; it's my choice, so I pay. You paid for our picnic date. We can keep that arrangement—whoever organises, pays. If you want, that is. The picnic was just as magical to me as this is to you. Please, believe me."

"I've never been a bludger. I always pay my own way." Hazel's jaw set.

"And you do. For dates you organise." She picked up Hazel's free hand. "Please, I'm not patronising you, and I don't expect anything more just because I have a higher income than you. If we do this, we're in it together. Equal partners."

"Is that what we're doing?" Hazel asked. "A relationship?"

"Is that what you want?" She drew a deep breath, heart pounding. "It's what I'd like." *What if Hazel says no? Where will that leave us when we're just getting started?*

She worried her lower lip. "It's easy to say yes, and I'd like that. But I don't know my future here. What if I don't get into the University of New South Wales and have to go away to study?"

"We'll meet that if it happens."

For a moment, Hazel chewed her lip. Then she relaxed and her usual smile spread across her face. "We will. And in the meantime, I'll just chill and enjoy this amazing place."

Chapter 38
Trivia

Hazel stretched shade cloth over the last section of George's patio. "When this is done, you'll have shade from the summer sun, but still keep your view over the valley," she told him.

He sat in his favourite old canvas chair watching her. "Mebbe we could put in a passionfruit vine. I do like them for breakfast."

"We could," Hazel agreed. She flicked a glance at the first floor of the house.

Imogen was working from home and her voice drifted down through the open window. Too far away to make out the words, but the rise and fall of her voice sounded light and relaxed.

Her furniture had arrived from Brisbane, modern, pastel-coloured furniture that at first had seemed out of place in George's older style house. But they'd shifted the rest of George's furniture downstairs to his apartment, and Hazel had helped arrange Imogen's. With pops of colour, some purchases of smaller items, the upstairs of the house had taken on a new look. More modern, brighter, and all together more appealing than George's dated decor.

In turn, George was as happy as a pig in shit to have his beloved furniture back.

They had another date tonight—Hazel's choice—and they were going to trivia night at the pub with Nat and Djalu.

In the two weeks since their stay in Rockhampton, things had been good. They were relaxing more in each other's company, starting to build the small things that were forged at the start of any relationship. Imogen knew Hazel didn't add salt and pepper to any of her food. Hazel knew Imogen never wore green, feeling the colour made her look sickly.

Her phone rang, and she fished it out of her pocket. The screen showed an unfamiliar number. "Hello, Hazel speaking."

"Is that Hazel Lee?" a deep voice asked.

"Yes, that's me."

"This is Nick Catley from Catley & Arnold in Rockhampton. We have your application for the receptionist position, and if you're still interested, we'd love to bring you in for an interview."

Wow. She gripped the phone tighter as excitement pounded in her blood. "Yes, I'm definitely interested, and I'd be very excited at the chance to interview with your firm."

"Good. I apologise for the delay in responding to you. We had more applicants than anticipated, and it took some time to select the best candidates for interview."

So, she was one of the best. *Wow.* "I'm happy to be given the chance to show you why I'm the best fit for the position."

"That's good, Hazel. Now, I know it's short notice, but can you do Thursday at three?"

"I can do that."

"Thank you. One question: do you hold a driver's licence or need a modified vehicle? Your resumé didn't mention that."

"I can drive any automatic vehicle, including light trucks." Hopefully, Nick wouldn't say all their cars had manual transmissions.

"That's fine. The successful applicant will occasionally need to drive to worksites."

"I'd welcome that."

"Then I look forward to meeting with you on Thursday."

"Thank you. I'll see you then."

She ended the call, and turned to George with wide eyes. "That was—"

"I know, love, I heard. I'm not surprised. They'd be fools not to hire you. Now make sure you talk to Immie—she could help you with a practice interview."

The bubble of excitement in her chest expanded until she could hardly breathe. "I'll do that." She took George's hands and did a little shimmy. "I got an interview! Maybe I'll even get the job!"

"I have a good feeling about this. You'll get it. Especially if you put my lucky rabbit's foot in your pocket. It never fails."

She was so euphoric, she'd have agreed if he'd said it was his lucky cow's leg. "I'll take it."

The pub was buzzing when they arrived for dinner before trivia, but Hazel found them a table out on the deck. Fairy lights twinkled on the railings, and cicadas shrilled in the trees above them.

"Nat and Djalu are joining us later," Hazel said. "Their babysitter couldn't come any earlier."

Imogen squeezed Hazel's waist. "More time for ourselves."

They joined the queue to place their food order, then Hazel went to the bar for drinks. When she returned with a red wine for Imogen and a soda, lime, and bitters for herself, she touched her glass to Imogen's. "Here's to us."

"Always." Imogen clinked back. "You're looking particularly gorgeous tonight."

Hazel looked down at her pale-yellow T-shirt and cut-off denim shorts. "Thanks. Mum found this T-shirt for me in the op shop." She leaned forward. "To be honest, it's where most of my clothes come from."

"The colour looks good on you. Very vibrant."

"Thanks. I'm feeling particularly vibrant tonight. And you're not so shabby yourself, Ms Alexander."

Imogen wore a simple ash-pink shift dress. It clung and flowed in all the right places and highlighted her delicate colouring.

"When does trivia start?"

"Not for an hour." Hazel pulled her bag onto her lap and fossicked around until she found what she was looking for. "But I thought we'd have a quick practice round first. After all, you said you've not played for years."

"Okay." Imogen raised her eyebrows. "I don't think I'm that bad, but if you think it's necessary, then let's go for it."

Hazel slid two cards across, facedown. "Look at the first and tell me the answer."

Imogen flipped it over and read, "*What is the capital of Peru?* That's easy; it's Lima. Any fan of Paddington Bear knows that."

"Correct." No need to tell Imogen that Paddington was exactly where she'd found that question. "Now the next one." She suppressed a smile, longing to see Imogen's reaction.

Imogen turned over the second card. "*Who has an interview with Catley & Arnold on Thursday?* Oh! You?" She reached out and gripped Hazel's hands, thumbs stroking the backs.

Hazel nodded, and let loose her smile. "Yes! Me! I'd more or less given up on them calling me." She recapped the conversation with Nick Catley.

"That's fantastic. I think you'll be in with a good chance."

"I really hope so. George suggested I ask you for tips. Maybe do a mock interview with you."

"We can do that. Not tonight though. Maybe tomorrow morning?"

"I'd like that—if you've got time. I can come around at—"

Imogen gripped her hand. "I can make time. You could stay over, if you want. We could go past your place so you can pick up what you need."

"Will George mind?"

"It's not his decision. But in any case, he'd probably be delighted for us."

"In that case, I'd like that very much." It seemed like a huge step forward for them—expanding their couple space to include Imogen's home. Maybe one night, Imogen would stay over with her.

Their food order was called, and Imogen went to collect their plates. She set down their food, plus cutlery. "I got extra tartare sauce for your fish and chips."

"Thanks." Hazel's mouth watered. The chips were crispy-hot, the fish freshly cooked, and there was enough salad to let her think she was eating healthily. Although Imogen's plate of veggie fritters and quinoa salad told her she was fooling herself.

"So, do I really need to brush up on my trivia?" Imogen asked.

"Nah. I'm sure you're better than the rest of us. We're all hopeless. We don't play very often, but when we do, we're never even top three."

"We'll see what we can do then."

Hazel nodded, then put down her cutlery. "If I get this job, it will be amazing. It's the harder thing to do though. The university should take me. But this…it would mean so much to me. A new path in life, one that's better suited to me." She looked down at her plate. "I'm scared I'll blow the interview—be too breezy, too casual. Or that they'll see Petunia and decide they can't accommodate me. It's one thing to see my disability on paper; another to see it in actuality."

Imogen stopped eating as well. "They said they're eager to interview you. They obviously rank you highly. And your bright, bubbly personality is perfect for a receptionist. You've got a great chance."

"I hope so. I really do."

Later, as they lay in bed after lovemaking, Hazel returned to that conversation. Imogen believed in her. Warmth spread through her like melted butter. Imogen's quiet certainty that she could do this was bedrock to her confidence. She just had to take that with her into the interview.

She turned on her side and faced Imogen. "I'm glad you brought your bed from Brisbane. This is nearly as good as the one at the Charlestown Boutique Hotel."

"I thought it was better." Imogen looked offended, but her lips twitched into a smile.

"You know it's not. I love, too, that we can see out the window from the bed. Mainly, I love being here with you." Hazel slammed her mouth shut. The words had come unbidden, and her heart pounded a painful beat. Too much? She hadn't said I love you, at least there was that. But was it too early to show how much she loved being with Imogen?

"I need a glass of water," she said, when the silence had stretched too long. She got out of bed and found the crutches she'd left against the wall and used them to get to the kitchen. She stood at the sink, draining a large glass of water, staring out at the starlit valley. Lights twinkled on the opposite hillside, and a car with its full beam lights on drove slowly along a road on the far side of the rail line. Those people probably had lives and jobs and families. They probably had never accidentally told someone they loved them.

Like she'd nearly told Imogen.

She drained the glass, rinsed it and left it on the rack to dry, then headed back to bed.

Moonlight streamed in the window, outlining Imogen's body with silver. Hazel left the crutches against the wall and got back into bed.

Imogen rolled onto her side and kissed her gently. "I love being here with you, too."

And just like that, Hazel's heart burst wide open. It wasn't love—not yet—but it was a tentative step in that direction.

Hazel ended the call and threw the phone down on the couch. Flinging her arms in the air, she let out a whoop that nearly rattled the windows.

Her mum burst into the room. "What's the matter? Did you hurt yourself?"

"No." Hazel bounced across the room and flung her arms around her mum. "I got the job! They loved me. They loved that I want to be an interior architect—they said I'm certain to get in as I'm so close to the required score and have relevant life experience. I can shadow one of the architects some of the time, even when I'm a receptionist. The money isn't great, but it's better than being a delivery driver. And I'm to start on Monday!"

"That's amazing." Her mum hugged her back hard. "I'm so proud of you. I'm not surprised you got the job—"

"You are!"

"I'm not surprised because you're plenty good enough, and you're *you*, but I'm quietly delighted they didn't find some excuse not to hire you rather than make ergonomic changes to cater for you."

"Mum…you're the best. I love you." Hazel kissed her mum's cheek and beamed a cheesy grin at her.

"Get on with you." Her mum aimed a swat at her bottom as if she were five, not twenty-five. "Now go and tell your girlfriend the good news."

"I will." Hazel grabbed her truck keys from the dresser. "Don't tell Dad. I'll be home for dinner—I want to tell him."

"Bring Imogen and George with you. We can celebrate!"

"I'll ask them. Love you, Mum."

If Hazel could have skipped and jumped, she would have. As it was, she floated her way out to the truck. It was lucky the only Dry Creek traffic cop wasn't in his usual position tucked off the road on the far side of the bridge, as Hazel was surely speeding. She reached Imogen and George's house in record time.

George answered the front door. He looked her up and down. "I'm guessing someone has something good to tell us."

"I do." Hazel shimmied her shoulders as the bubbling excitement demanded release. "Is Imogen around?"

"She's making tea, and we're going to have it on my back patio."

He pressed the new intercom inside the door to his living room. "Immie, love, Hazel's here. Can you make a third mug?"

"Sure," Imogen's voice said. "Be two minutes."

She appeared with a tray, three mugs, and a plate of Tim Tams. "Caramel ones," she said to George. She arched an eyebrow at Hazel.

"Good girl." He beamed at her and accepted the mug she handed him.

When they were all seated, he said, "So, Hazel, what's got you as jumpy as a 'roo in a pen?"

She set her mug down so she wouldn't spill it. "I got the job with Catley & Arnold!"

Imogen stood and held out her arms. "You brilliant, clever person. This is the first step to something big."

"They're lucky to get you," George said gruffly. "But I'll miss seeing you around."

"Who said I'm going anywhere? I'll still be here. I'll still fix your leaky taps and take Chip for walks. We'll still play cribbage and go to the RSL."

"And you'll still be here with me many nights," Imogen said. "I'm so proud of you."

"I credit the wardrobe and interview advice you gave me."

"No, that was just the icing. You got this job all by yourself."

"Apparently, the uni normally responds in two to four weeks. Maybe I won't have to wait much longer."

"You'll get in." Imogen kissed her forehead.

"That's what Nick Catley said. Imagine, me, a uni student."

Imogen leaned in and pressed a kiss to her cheek. "I'm imagining being in bed with you later," she said quietly in her ear. "You, me, that firm bed. Maybe a bottle of champagne to toast your success."

"I could absolutely do that," Hazel said. "Today, it's not just that I can do more." She gripped her wrist where the tattooed words blazed. "Today, I can do absolutely anything."

EPILOGUE
SIX MONTHS LATER

Imogen's mobile rang as Ruth left her office, closing the door behind her. She looked at the screen and her eyebrows raised. Richard from Whistlestop. *What the hell does he want?* She debated letting the call go to voicemail—she had nothing to say to Richard, after all—but curiosity made her answer.

"Hi, Imogen, it's Richard here, Queensland Manager for Whistlestop."

She rolled her eyes. He knew that she knew that. He was just rubbing in his promotion again. She thought about a petty, "I'm sorry, who is this?" response, but quashed that. That was beneath her, and in light of what she'd just learned from Grayson, she didn't care. "Hello, Richard. How are things with you?"

"Good. Great. I have a few minutes before the state managers' meeting, so I thought I'd give you a call. Catch up with things. I hear you're working at a regional chain now."

"That's right. Good 'n Fresh. It's going extremely well."

"Bit of a step down for you, isn't it? Small town, struggling supermarket."

"On the contrary," she said evenly, and suppressed a snigger at his astonished silence.

"Things are good here. Extremely busy, of course, with three new stores in the Brisbane area opening soon."

She waited. It didn't seem as if Richard needed a response.

"Your replacement is a bit of a crock, to be honest. Internal transfer, so you'd think he'd know what he was doing, but he keeps asking me obvious questions that I really don't have time to answer. He should be doing the grunt work for the store openings, but he's not capable."

"I'm sure you can help him with that," Imogen said.

Another pause. Imogen glanced at the time. She needed to leave in ten minutes to take George to the podiatrist.

"Of course," Richard said, "but I have a lot on my plate at the moment. I don't know how you got through all you did—Wayne told me before he left that you handled a lot of the Queensland figures for the national reports. I'll come back to you on that, when it's the end of the financial year. I'm sure you'll be able to give me some pointers."

In your dreams, Richard. She knew for a fact his previous assistant, Vera, had handled all the reporting figures for him. She remained silent. Her spidey sense was tingling, telling her there was more to come in this conversation.

"Actually, I was wondering if you could do me a favour," Richard continued.

Here it comes. Imogen settled back in her desk chair.

"We need to set up a video call with your replacement for you to go through the timeline of work needed to get the new stores happening. After all, you handled it when you were here, and you should have trained him."

Ka-boom! "I'm sure you remember that I didn't train my replacement as it was felt there were sufficient middle managers—like yourself—to handle that. Those timelines were as much your responsibility as mine."

"Wayne always felt you were better suited to routine tasks like that," Richard said. "I seldom did the grunt work so I'm less familiar with the process."

Make that completely unfamiliar. Imogen gripped her mobile. Did Richard really expect her to give him her time now, when she was no longer an employee, simply because he obviously had no idea what he was doing? *Why yes, yes, he did.*

"Richard, I'm so busy here, I simply don't have time," she said in a syrupy voice.

"I'm sure you can make time. I'll get Serenity to set up a Zoom call directly with—"

Enough. She straightened in her chair. "Richard, I don't have time now or ever. I am no longer employed by Whistlestop. The responsibility is yours—and was yours when you were a regional manager. I don't think you can slide out of this now as you did then. It seems that you, and not my replacement, are the one lacking in the knowledge and skills for your position. Please don't call again."

"But, Imogen, you must—"

She clicked off the call, rested back in her chair and laughed, deep belly laughs that started low and didn't stop. It was only when Ruth came into her office to ask if everything was all right that she ceased.

"Everything is perfectly all right," she said between snorts of laughter. "In fact, it has never been better."

Two days later, Imogen looked around the dining room. In the preceding six months, she and Hazel had transformed the tired paintwork and fittings to a more modern style that fitted Imogen's furnishings. The house glowed with light—and with love.

Her dining table was set for two. Candles were ready in holders, and a pork fillet was marinating ready for the oven. Hazel would be here in twenty minutes, and Imogen wanted everything to be perfect.

"Are you ready?" George's voice came over the intercom. "Can I come up now?"

"Give me ten more minutes."

"Roger that, copy, ten-four good buddy, over and out."

Imogen licked her lips. The last six months had been some of the happiest of her life—and it was mainly due to Hazel.

How could I have ever thought her immature and annoying? She smiled at the memory. Hazel's positivity still rubbed on her more sombre personality at times, but with consideration and kindness they got past that.

Hazel had been accepted into the University of New South Wales and had started her degree in interior architecture. Initially, she'd struggled with the unfamiliar study and coursework, but with her customary perseverance and strength she was now doing well.

She'd made friends with other students and had a great rapport with her mentor.

Imogen twitched the napkins into place and made sure the all-important envelope was ready by Hazel's plate.

The intercom buzzed again. "How about now?" George asked.

"It's been five minutes. I said ten."

"Okay, okay," he grumbled. "Roger that, copy, ten-four good buddy, over and out."

Sometimes, she regretted installing that intercom, but it was perfect for George, giving him companionship and security. The new living arrangement suited them very well. George loved the freedom of downstairs living and being able to easily go out whenever he wanted. Frank and Mavis came around, and new friends from the Men's Shed. There were rumours of poker tournaments some nights. Imogen stayed away then. And, of course, George came up most evenings for dinner, and she usually saw him in the day. Either she or Hazel took him to any appointments.

She'd been procrastinating. The doorbell rang.

"I'll get it!" George yelled.

This was not part of her plan, but she ran with it.

Hazel's voice sounded from the downstairs hallway. "You look smart, George. Are you going out with Mavis?"

"May I take your coat, ma'am?" he said in stiff tones.

A slight silence, then Hazel said, "Thank you, Mr Butler. Then maybe you'd be so kind as to escort me to the lady of the house."

"I'll do that, love."

Not so in character then.

The whine of the stairlift, along with Hazel's footsteps sounded, and then they appeared at the top of the stairs.

Hazel came over and wrapped her arms around Imogen where she stood at the dining table. "Hi." She lifted her face for Imogen's kiss.

She kissed her long and slow, not heeding George's cough.

The kiss ended, and Hazel touched the white tablecloth covering the modern table. "You're very fancy today. Is there something to celebrate?"

"Maybe," Imogen said. She hoped that was true. Maybe she'd got it all wrong.

"I'm the waiter," George announced. "Although I prefer your Mr Butler term. Would you like a glass of champagne, madam? Although it's not the posh French stuff, it's Aussie sparkling. But it's still good."

"I'm sure it is," Hazel said. "I'd love one." She squeezed Imogen's hand. "We must be celebrating something."

Maybe two somethings. The nerves twined anew around her middle.

Imogen watched as George opened the fridge, took out the bottle, and poured three glasses. Her heart overflowed with love for this kind man. While she'd come to take care of him, he had opened his heart and house to her so many years ago, and that had never changed.

They clinked glasses.

"Are you going to keep me waiting?" Hazel asked. "This isn't our normal weekday dinner. I don't smell sausages." She winked at George.

"Nothing wrong with sausages for dinner every night," George said.

"Your cardiac specialist would disagree," Imogen said. "No sausages tonight." She fizzed inside as much as the sparkling wine in her glass. "I have news. First, I got a call from Whistlestop the other day." She related the conversation with Richard and how she'd ended the call.

"That's brilliant, Immie, love." George chortled. "He deserved it."

"Imagine his spluttering face," Hazel added. "And think of him trying to bluster his way through the new store openings. Whistlestop should have promoted you—but I'm so glad they didn't, or you wouldn't be here." She kissed Imogen's cheek.

She touched her fingers to her cheek. "There's more though. I got my promotion. I'm now Good 'n Fresh's State Manager for Queensland!"

Hazel set down her glass and flung her arms around Imogen. "You did it! Next stop, national manager before you're forty. I'm so proud of you."

She hugged her hard enough that Imogen couldn't catch her breath.

George beamed. "I'm so proud of you, Immie, love. I knew you'd get this. I'm so lucky to have you as my niece."

"There'll be some travel." Imogen looked at both in turn. "Some overnights. But not too much. Zoom meetings are preferred over face-to-face. George—"

"I'll be fine. Won't it be like when you and Hazel go away for a few days? I have Frank and Mavis, and Maxie and Simon, and I can get help from the nursing organisation the Men's Shed put me on to as well."

"You have me, too, George," Hazel said. "Always. I'll come and stay whenever you want, even if Imogen's not here."

"Thank you, love. And tomorrow, you're taking me to my doctor's appointment and then we're having lunch at the new café by the river, aren't we?"

"We are." Hazel squeezed his hand.

Hazel's job with Catley & Arnold was working out superbly well. They were generous with their paid time off, and accommodated Hazel's carer duties with George. It wasn't all one-way though. Hazel repaid them by taking on extra work in the firm. In addition, as well as receptionist duties, she sat in on many client meetings, and the weekly architects' meeting that normally a receptionist wouldn't attend.

"I can't wait to see what amazing dinner we're having to celebrate your news," Hazel said.

This was it. Imogen's nerves spiked more than the national grid in a heatwave. "Before dinner, there's something else to talk about." She picked up the envelope from the table and handed it to Hazel.

She turned it over in her hands. "Should I be worried?"

"No, love," George said. "Not at all."

Imogen swallowed. Oh, how she hoped this would be welcomed. But in the last six months, she and Hazel had solidified their relationship, even if they had yet to say the words. This seemed the next step, and one she wanted very much. When she'd asked George, he was whole-hearted in his approval.

Hazel carefully untucked the flap of the envelope and pulled out three plain white cards with Imogen's bold writing on each.

Imogen went to sit on the couch next to George. Her hand shook as she set her glass on the table. If Hazel refused, well, they would still have the relationship they already had, but oh, how she hoped she would agree.

"*Question 1: Whose turn is it to let Chip out?*" Hazel looked across at George. "I can take a hint. I'll make his doggy-door wider so he fits through it. But in the meantime, it's Imogen's turn."

Imogen forced a smile over her jangling nerves.

"*Question 2: Who backed their ute into a lamppost the other day?*" Hazel's mouth turned down. "That would be me. I'll have to fix it soon; the brake light doesn't work."

"Now read the third one." Imogen's hand shook and she clenched it on her knee. This was new to her. Thirty-five years, and she'd never asked the question before.

Hazel moved the third card to the top. "*Question 3: Will you move in with me?*" Her wide-eyed gaze flew to Imogen's face. "You want to live with me? Here?"

Imogen nodded, and the champagne she'd drunk was sour in her stomach. *What if she says no?*

Hazel's lip trembled. "I'm not easy to live with. I take up a lot of bathroom area. I need space to manoeuvre my knee crutch. I leave stinky neoprene draped over towel rails. I have—"

Imogen pressed a finger to Hazel's lips. "I already know all that."

"And as Imogen's landlord, I'm going to get the bathroom redone so it works better for you," George said. "While I'd love for you to do it, you don't have time, being an interior-architect-in-training. So, I'll get quotes."

"George, you don't have to pay for—"

"We're splitting it," Imogen said. "But it's okay, Hazel. If you don't want to move in, that's okay. We can go on as we are." The words seemed to have grown claws that clung to her throat so they couldn't be spoken, but she forced them out anyway. It had to be Hazel's decision with no pressure.

"I want this. More than anything. I love you, Imogen."

And that was it; she was undone. Her throat worked, tears sprang to her eyes, and the warmth and love in her heart overflowed. "I love you, too. I have for a while, but didn't know how to say it."

"You business types," Hazel teased. "I would have thought you'd have the words."

"Not those words," Imogen said. "Those words are only for you." She stroked Hazel's hair back from her face and kissed her, slowly, then with growing passion.

"I'm still here," George grumbled. "And I hope there's a little love left over for me."

They broke apart, smiling stupidly.

"I love you too, George," Imogen said. "Aren't you the best family anyone could have?"

"You and Hazel are," George said gruffly.

Hazel hugged his shoulders and pressed a kiss to his wrinkled cheek. "We're family. And our family is full of love."

OTHER BOOKS FROM YLVA PUBLISHING

www.ylva-publishing.com

FOR THE LONG RUN
Cheyenne Blue

ISBN: 978-3-96324-728-6
Length: 289 pages (90,000 words)

Runner Shan is tripped by a "koala", blowing her knee, and ruining her national team dreams. Life post-surgery will be hell as she lives on the fourth floor. Lizzie, the dream-wrecking koala, offers Shan her spare room. Their clashing lives and Shan's aloof training partner aren't ideal, but they'll figure it out. Right?

An enemies-to-lovers lesbian sports romance about making it to the finish line.

THE LOUDEST SILENCE
Olivia Janae

ISBN: 978-3-96324-699-9
Length: 281 pages (89,000 words)

Rising star cellist Kate is new to Chicago and the Windy City Chamber Ensemble. Its president Vivian is a complete surprise. Not only does the intriguing woman come with a formidable, icy reputation, but she's also Deaf.

A beautiful, opposites attract lesbian romance about hearing the music in your heart.

THE ROOMMATE ARRANGEMENT
Jae

ISBN: 978-3-96324-279-3
Length: 333 pages (119,000 words)

Comedian Steph hopes to finally get her big break in LA. But to afford the rent, she needs a roommate. Enter Rae, a former cop guarding her wounded soul behind a tough exterior. At first, they clash horribly, but bit by bit, Steph breaks through the walls Rae has built around her. Falling in love is no laughing matter in this opposites-attract lesbian romance with a bit of fake relationship.

THE MUSIC AND THE MIRROR
Lola Keeley

ISBN: 978-3-96324-014-0
Length: 311 pages (120,000 words)

Anna is the newest member of an elite ballet company. Her first class almost ruins her career before it begins. She must face down jealousy, sabotage, and injury to pour everything into opening night and prove she has what it takes. In the process, Anna discovers that she and the daring, beautiful Victoria have a lot more than ballet in common.

ABOUT CHEYENNE BLUE

Cheyenne Blue has been hanging around the lesbian erotica world since 1999 writing short lesbian erotica which has appeared in over 90 anthologies. Her stories got longer and longer and more and more romantic, so she went with the flow and switched to writing romance novels. As well as her romance novels available from Ylva Publishing, she's the editor of *Forbidden Fruit: stories of unwise lesbian desire*, a 2015 finalist for both the Lambda Literary Award and Golden Crown Literary Award, and of *First: Sensual Lesbian Stories of New Beginnings*.

Cheyenne loves writing big-hearted romance often set in rural Australia because that's where she lives. She has a small house on a hill with a big deck and bigger view—perfect for morning coffee, evening wine, and anytime writing.

CONNECT WITH CHEYENNE

Website: www.cheyenneblue.com
Facebook: www.facebook.com/CheyenneBlueAuthor
Instagram: www.instagram.com/cheyenneblueauthor
Twitter: twitter.com/iamcheyenneblue

A Heart Full of Hope
© 2024 by Cheyenne Blue

ISBN: 978-3-96324-955-6

Available in paperback and e-book formats.

Published by Ylva Publishing, legal entity of Ylva Verlag, e.Kfr.

Ylva Verlag, e.Kfr.
Owner: Astrid Ohletz
Am Kirschgarten 2
65830 Kriftel
Germany

www.ylva-publishing.com

First edition: 2024

No part of this book may be reproduced, scanned, or distributed in any printed or electronic form without permission. Please do not participate in or encourage piracy of copyrighted materials in violation of the author's rights. Thank you for respecting the hard work of this author.

This is a work of fiction. Names, characters, places, and incidents either are a product of the author's imagination or are used fictitiously, and any resemblance to locales, events, business establishments, or actual persons—living or dead—is entirely coincidental.

Credits
Edited by Sarah Smeaton and Sheena Billet
Cover Design by Ronja Forleo
Print Layout by Streetlight Graphics

Printed in Great Britain
by Amazon